Praise for
WITHIN THE BOUNDS . . .

"LAWYERS AND A SERIAL KILLER . . . spark the action in this fast-moving thriller . . . a likable, honest first-person narration; his legal anecdotes and procedural descriptions are pointed and concise."

—*Publishers Weekly*

"JUST WHEN CRIME FICTION FANS are groggy from blockbuster legal thrillers and suffering from a surfeit of fictional serial killers, first-time author Marc Lodge uses both themes to explosive advantage in *Within the Bounds*."

—*The Toronto Star*

"THIS WELL-PACED SUSPENSE THRILLER about attorneys and a serial killer has good character development, clever plot development and surprise twists integral to the intrigue."

—*The Reader's Review*

WITHIN THE THE BOUNDS

MARC LODGE

BERKLEY BOOKS, NEW YORK

This is a work of fiction. The events and characters portrayed are imaginary. Their resemblance, if any, to real-life counterparts is entirely coincidental.

WITHIN THE BOUNDS

A Berkley Book / published by arrangement with the author

PRINTING HISTORY
G.P. Putnam's Sons edition / October 1993
Berkley edition / November 1994

ISBN: 0-425-14457-7

BERKLEY®
Berkley Books are published by The Berkley Publishing Group, 200 Madison Avenue, New York, New York 10016.
BERKLEY and the "B" design are trademarks belonging to Berkley Publishing Corporation.

PRINTED IN THE UNITED STATES OF AMERICA

10 9 8 7 6 5 4 3 2 1

For Suzanne, with love and gratitude

"A Lawyer Should Represent a Client Zealously Within the Bounds of the Law."

—*Canon 7, American Bar Association Model Code of Professional Responsibility*

PROLOGUE

He watched Maria Perez and the other girl stop next to the bar, thirty feet away from his table. Behind them, spotlights swept the dance floor as the band repeated chorus after chorus, fusing the crowd into a mass of waving arms and sweating faces. It was billed as the loudest band on the Monterey Peninsula.

The other girl had to put her mouth to Maria's ear to be heard. Maria held her hair back with one hand and bent down slightly, concentrating, a broad smile on her face. He saw her gold earrings flash as the spotlight swept past. Double loops. Maybe he should leave the earrings. That would be a nice touch.

He sat in a dark, quiet corner of the club. In the Taproot's main section, where the band played, the waitresses struggled to carry drinks to the overcrowded tables, screaming the amount due over the din. He had found Maria there, but before long they moved to this side, where couples huddled and talked intently at booths lit only by dim candles. The waitresses rarely made it back here. The Caliano locals called it the Mating Pit.

The other girl gestured to the dance floor, then to the door. Maria's smile grew even wider. She said something in the other girl's ear and pointed to him. They both looked his way. He waved his Budweiser bottle high as a toast. The other girl waved back; Maria winked.

The other girl's face grew serious as she spoke into Maria's ear. California girls were supposed to be big and blond and athletic, but this one was short and skinny, with mousy brown hair and dull eyes. Maria was another kind of California girl, with bright eyes, shining black hair, and a quick grin that flashed white against olive skin. Gold was her color: the shimmering tunic bloused over white shorts, the link belt around her waist, the looped chains holding the cross between her breasts, and those earrings. Exotic, he thought. If she has money, she'll be perfect.

Finally, the other girl pulled back and looked at Maria with a worried, hopeful expression. Maria nodded, said something, and hugged her. The other girl took a deep breath and reached into her purse; she pulled out what looked like car keys and handed them to Maria. A final hug, and the two separated. The other girl disappeared into the Taproot crowd. He decided not to worry about her. It was dark, he had only spoken a few words, and Maria had great potential. You had to take some chances in life.

Maria wound her way through the Mating Pit and sat next to him. "Melissa found a guy," she said, dropping her eyes to look at her Bud Light. She smiled and bounced her shoulders slightly to the music. "She doesn't usually do that."

"What does she usually do?" he said.

"Usually she works. Or goes to church. But, hey . . . " she looked into his eyes and smiled. "This is vacation. Once in a while you have to let loose."

He nodded and drew his finger along her arm, letting his hand come to rest over hers. They watched Melissa emerge near the distant exit, where a man waited for her. The two embraced and left.

He turned back to Maria. "So, Maria Theresa Perez." He pronounced her name with a heavy Spanish inflection, even though she had no trace of an accent. He enjoyed the feel of it rolling off his tongue. "What do you usually do?"

She rolled her eyes. "Well, I'll tell you, John." She mimicked his accent with an exaggerated Southern drawl. "I do what you do when your daddy's a judge and you don't want to be a lawyer. I'm a legal assistant at a big L.A. firm." She pointed to the tattoo on his left biceps. "Where did you get that?"

"The service," he said. "What's a legal assistant?" His instincts had been right again. Judges live in big houses and belong to the country club.

Maria shrugged. "Same as a paralegal. A glorified file clerk. I do whatever crummy job the lawyers don't want to do." She squeezed his hand and grinned. "That's at work. On vacation, I play." She glanced around her at the couples huddled in the darkness. "Especially when I don't have a roommate to worry about," she said in a low voice.

He sensed a trace of nervousness: she was trying too hard. Cute. He put his arm around her shoulder, nuzzled her neck, and moved his lips to her ear. She leaned into him, enjoying the feeling. Then she suddenly straightened and stared at him, serious now. "John," she said quietly. "I usually don't do this either. I work hard, I go to church. I was just talking tough. I don't go around picking up men. Really." She searched his eyes for disappointment.

He smiled to reassure her and squeezed her hand softly while he pulled her close to him and pressed his lips to the back of her neck. Her body relaxed, and her head rolled

*slowly as she pushed against him. Perfect, he thought.
She put her hand on his neck, brushing aside his long
brown hair, then turned to kiss him. The pressure made
his mustache tickle.*

Ten minutes later, she pushed him back and took a deep
breath. "Let me go to the little girl's room first," she said.
She rose, smiled at him, and walked around the rear of the
bar, picking up speed as she went.

He watched her with satisfaction, then nodded. "Rich
bitch," he muttered.

Maria Theresa Perez arched her back and moaned. The
sound echoed through the clearing. He had considered the
beach but decided it was too risky. Someone might come
along and interrupt them. These woods were high above
the rocky coast, but close enough that he could hear the
surf crash in the distance. Not a long drive either: only
ten miles from Caliano. The moon provided light through
the trees. A perfect site. A perfect girl. A perfect night.

He felt the sweat on her body as she writhed beneath
his hands. Maria's breath came in short gasps; the tip of
her tongue showed between her teeth. She was naked, both
of them were, except for her earrings. They made a small
tinkling sound as she flung her head from side to side. One
of her hands clutched her own breast. The other dug into
his shoulder. She was ready. So was he.

He rose to his knees. She lifted her head in surprise and
groaned as he pulled away, then fell back as his left hand
entered her. With his right, he opened the gym bag at the
edge of the blanket and rummaged inside. He found what
he wanted and straddled her. She looked at him through
half-closed eyes.

He handed Maria the condom. "Put it on me," he said
softly.

He stroked her as she fumbled with the package, moaning in excitement. She looked up with a shy smile, then frowned in concentration as she unrolled it on him. She smoothed it and guided him into her as she fell back.

He varied his tempo, bringing her to the brink and back. She groaned each time he slowed. Finally he felt himself grow ready. He brought her up to the edge, his own breathing harsh. "Now," he gasped. She pulled him deeper.

He straightened his arms and lifted his upper body, thrusting hard, resting on his hands. As his explosion neared, he moved his hands to her neck and found the pressure points. He applied his full weight.

Her eyes widened and her movements became frantic, desperate. She clawed at his arms. He thrust harder. It was perfect. He came just before she slowed.

He held the pressure until she was completely still, then pulled out and studied her. "Was it good for you too?" he asked her quietly. Then he chuckled. She was unconscious, limp, eyes rolled back under the lids. He heard her shallow breath. A sharp blow to the larynx with the edge of his hand stopped that.

He brought his gym bag over to the blanket and found the clothesline, the box of Ziploc plastic bags, and the moistened towelettes. With one of the towelettes, he wiped his arm where Maria had scratched him. The wipe and the used condom went in one of the bags. Then he pulled out a long-neck Bud from the cooler, popping the top with the opener on his Swiss Army knife. He would have preferred to enjoy the beer before beginning to work, but he settled for a couple of swigs, then slipped on the surgeon's gloves.

He turned the body facedown and tied the elbows together in the back with several turns of the clothesline. When they were secure, he looped the line around the neck and pulled the arms as high as they would go without breaking. A turn back through the elbow knot held them in place. The awkward part was bending the legs at the knee and wrestling the body to a squatting position so it rested on the shins and the butt. He held her steady with one hand and ran the clothesline back and forth between the knees and neck and ankles, as if erecting a tent pole. A little adjustment of the tension, and Maria Theresa Perez knelt upright, with no additional support required. It wasn't quite the technique he had been taught, but then again, she was already dead.

Now he took his beer break. He sat on the blanket and enjoyed the slight breeze on his naked body while he studied Maria. This one might have been in the top two or three. No, it was definitely in the top two or three. He wasn't sure if she was rich; that was the only possible flaw. Other than that, it was great. And summer was much better than winter. In winter, with all the snow, you had to coax them into a sleeping bag or use the backseat of the car. And you couldn't sit naked in the snow and drink a beer afterward. Too damn cold.

He lifted his Bud in salute to Maria.

The game came next. He had chosen the beach this time. No trees—sometimes he liked to hang them from a tree for hikers to find—but he could leave a real surprise for tomorrow's sunbathers.

It was four A.M. when he drove past the Taproot on his way to a beach between the Caliano business district and the planned communities to the west. The sea lions on the off-shore rocks had attracted a large crowd there yesterday.

He pulled into a scenic overlook and parked the car behind a dumpster to hide it from the road. The gym bag and the body were in the trunk; he hoisted both over his shoulder, using the clothesline knot at the elbows as a handle. She was heavy, but not as bad as some.

The sandy part of the beach lay below and to the left of the overlook, surrounded by huge black rocks in craggy formations jutting out into the water. He climbed down carefully and located an indentation in the beach that was partially shielded from the water, not visible from the overlook, and well past the high tide line. Any casual beach walkers in the morning probably would miss her, but an explorer or a trysting couple would find her later. At worst, someone would investigate the birds she would attract.

After his eyes adjusted to the darkness, he pulled out the shielded flashlight. I should buy myself a night-vision device for Christmas, he thought as he slowly surveyed the area.

One of the rocks had a flat top that made a fine platform. He set her up so she looked out toward the sea and secured her by wrapping the free end of the clothesline around another boulder. The perfection of the night held true: the line was just long enough to reach.

He slipped on another pair of surgical gloves and wrapped his feet with plastic bags to avoid footprints and blood stains on his shoes, then studied the body. He had cleaned her up back in the woods, but he double-checked for leaves and twigs or anything else that might lead a searcher to their forest hideaway. Her face was relatively peaceful. Ready to go.

He took the six-inch, double-edged knife and inserted it just below the sternum, then brought it down in a single stroke to the pubis. He spent some time with the rich bitch cunt, carefully cutting it out, slicing it open, and placing it at the bend of her right hip and thigh.

The heart went on the other hip.

He hummed tunelessly as he worked, fast but thorough. Every few minutes, he paused for a quick recon sweep, but he knew he was alone. His senses were so heightened that he would hear or see or feel any potential source of danger. That was a main reason he played the game: the sensation.

Part of his work involved eliminating evidence. The neck took some time, because of the rope, but he liked to obliterate the esophagus and excise any bruises near the pressure points. He severed the fingertips at the first joint and put them in one of his plastic bags for disposal with the other leftovers: the condom, the wipes, the blanket from the woods, her clothes. The cops probably thought it was an effort to remove fingerprints, but he did it to avoid any traces of skin under the fingernails. The girls often scratched him during lovemaking. This one had.

He ended, as always, with the breasts. They were his artist's canvas, his most original accomplishment.

When he finished, he stepped back to study the effect. Good. He reached over to tuck her hair behind her ears so the earrings showed. Perfect.

The final touch was to sign his work. He bent over to carve his trademark, the little elephant outline, in what remained of the right breast. He was no artist, but he thought it was not a bad replica under the circumstances. The papers had never mentioned this, so either the cops hadn't recognized it yet or they were holding it back.

Satisfied, he stowed his gear, policed the area, and carefully wiped away his tracks in the sand. A final inspection, and he was ready to call it a night. A perfect night.

Back at the car, he took a minute to make it official. He pulled the notebook from the other bag in his trunk and printed carefully:

"#8. Maria Theresa Perez. Caliano, California. Gold earrings."

CHAPTER

1

The reporter tossed the newspaper on my hotel room table. "Have you read that, counselor?" he asked.

I glanced down at this morning's edition of the *Queenston Star*. "RESORT RIPPER SUSPECT CAPTURED," the headline read. "Four-Year Reign of Terror May Be Ended by Arrest in Johnston Beach," was the subhead. A chart in the lower right of the front page listed all thirteen victims, with pictures of three: Brenda Petrillo, victim number one, nearly five years ago; Maria Theresa Perez, victim number eight, two years ago; and Allison Bolder, the latest victim at Mount Passarell last February, around four months back.

I looked back up at Tim Stevens. "I read it in the Queenston airport," I said.

Stevens reached over and tapped the list of victims with his forefinger. He glanced at Edgar Browning, then frowned at me. "Let me tell you something, Cliff," he said. "If your client really is the bastard who's been chopping up these women, I hope he fries in hell forever."

I sighed and stretched my legs under the table. "I told you, Tim. I don't know if he's our client or not." I tried to hide my impatience. I was operating on virtually no sleep, and my knee throbbed, courtesy of an old injury from the Queenston lawyers' intramural basketball league. These hotel chairs were not built for someone over six feet, even with good knees. Next to me, Edgar sat silently, looking more like a kindly uncle than a retired FBI agent.

"Let's see now." Stevens put his hand to his chin, pretending to analyze the situation. "One day, they arrest the Resort Ripper in the little Southern town of Johnston Beach. The next day, America's hottest criminal lawyer sends his top assistant and number-one investigator to Johnston Beach all the way from Queenston. Then you start pumping me for information about the Ripper." He paused for effect, then shook his head. "Naw. No reason to think those facts are connected. Lewis Sherwood probably just thinks you two need a tan."

I shrugged and tried to get him back on the subject. "Will you tell us about the Ripper?"

Stevens rose and looked out at the Atlantic Ocean. The sun streaming through the balcony door revealed the deep lines in his face. A stocky little man with hunched shoulders, sagging jowls, and drooping eyes, he reminded me of UGA, the bulldog mascot for the University of Georgia.

He fished in the pocket of his red-checked sportcoat for the business card I had given him when we met on the flight to Johnston Beach. "Clifford W. Nielson," he read. "How come there's no 'Esquire' after it? Aren't all you lawyers 'Esquires'?"

"In parts of the South, it's considered tacky," I said.

Stevens grunted. " 'Ramwell and Bosely, Attorneys at Law.' How many lawyers in that firm?"

"About three hundred."

"Most prestigious law firm in the South, isn't it?"

"We like to think so."

Stevens put the card back in his pocket. "The best and the brightest. I know that firm. I know Lewis Sherwood. In fact, I saw you before, in that range war case you people had in Montana. I had the impression you were the guy who really ran that case—Sherwood just took all the glory."

"Don't make that mistake," I said. "Lew runs his cases. Junior partners like me may handle the day-to-day details, but Lew calls the shots."

Edgar tapped his pen against the little policeman's notebook he always carried. For him, that was a display of irritation. We wanted some background information; if Stevens wouldn't help, we had to find other sources.

"You know," Stevens finally started in a distracted voice, "I'm the one that came up with that name: The Resort Ripper. Used it in my story on the Fort Lauderdale murder. The one that made the cops finally admit they had a serial killer on their hands. Then the damn tabloids picked it up. It's their kind of story. Blood, gore, sex."

He turned and faced us. "My editors like to think we're above that at the *Miami Observer;* that we deal in serious news, not sensationalism." He shrugged. "Course, every few months, when another victim turns up, they send me out and we sell a lot of newspapers."

I glanced at the newspaper on the table. Fort Lauderdale was victim number six on the list. I remembered Stevens' story: a copy of it lay in the pile of papers on my bed. When Sherwood's message came in the middle of the night, I had logged on to one of the computer services and pulled up a few background stories on the Resort Ripper. Stevens had won a Pulitzer for that story, according to my brief research.

Edgar spoke in a quiet voice. "Tell us about him," he said.

"What do you know about him?" Stevens countered.

Edgar's pen tapping grew louder.

I gave it one more shot. "Not much more than this." I gestured at the newspaper. "He's killed thirteen women in the past four years or so, all at resorts. Tourists, mainly. The bodies are found mutilated somehow. That's about it."

Stevens looked through me. "That's about it," he muttered to himself with a look somewhere between disgust and resignation. "You see the name LouAnne Robinson on that list, Cliff?"

I glanced at the newspaper. She was victim number ten. At a place called Tandy.

"I wrote a story about LouAnne. She was a fourth-grade teacher in Marion, Ohio: a really sweet girl. Twenty-six. Pretty. Collected teddy bears, did volunteer work at a homeless shelter, loved Ohio State football. Visited her grandmother in the nursing home every Sunday. A nice kid." He walked slowly to the chair where he had left his soft-sided briefcase.

"About a year and a half ago," he said as he picked up the briefcase, "LouAnne went skiing over Christmas break with some friends. Third night there, she went down to the lounge to have a drink and listen to the music."

Stevens pulled a manila envelope from his briefcase. "They found her a couple of days later. You want to know about the Ripper? Here. Look at LouAnne."

He tossed the envelope on the coffee table. Edgar opened it and slid out an 8x10 color photograph. He paled, pushed it back in, and looked to one side. I kept my eyes on Stevens. Through the open balcony door, we heard the children in the hotel pool, playing Marco Polo.

Stevens' voice was soft. "That's what was left of LouAnne. One of her friends made the identification. She hasn't been able to sleep without drugs since." His voice became almost inaudible. "I interviewed LouAnne's parents. Her mother, actually; the father spends most of his time just sitting in her old room, staring at the teddy bears. They still haven't told the grandmother."

Edgar leaned his elbow on the table and rubbed his forehead, looking at the manila envelope. He made no move to touch it. Stevens walked over to the table and pointed. "I have ten other pictures just like that one," he said, "and each of them has a story just like LouAnne. You know the worst part? He doesn't mess with their faces."

He puffed a deep breath through his lips. "My daughter's twenty-five. She's very pretty, takes after her mother, thank God. Works for an ad agency in Chicago. Likes to ski in the winter and go to the beach in the summer. Sometimes at night I see a pile of meat, just like that. With my daughter's face on top."

He was back at the window, searching the sky now. His hands were in his pockets, his shoulders slumped. "Hard-bitten crime reporter, right?"

Edgar took a sip of coffee. His hands shook slightly. Stevens straightened, walked back to his chair, and sat down. He looked me directly in the eye.

"You got a deal. I'll help you, you feed me background. But understand me. I don't need you to get the story. I'm very good: I'll get it anyway. I'll help you because I have to know."

"Know what?" I said.

Stevens leaned over, intent. "Lewis Sherwood's the best criminal lawyer in the country. But if this guy Travis Jeffrey Keith really is the Ripper, and I think he probably is, even Sherwood can't get him off. The most you can do is keep him out of the chair somehow, but that's okay, as long as he's locked up tight." He might be underestimating Sherwood, I thought, but I kept it to myself.

Stevens went on. "If Keith is the Ripper, I don't have to worry about my daughter anymore. But if he's not . . . " He turned to focus on Edgar. "You know it, Edgar. Cops are human. They hear about Keith's arrest here, they'll quit looking. And if Keith is the wrong guy, then one of these days somebody else's daughter, maybe mine, will end up in a picture like that. That's why I have to know. If the Ripper is still out there, I need to keep the heat on the cops."

"I won't promise we'll tell you that," I said. "We can't give you privileged information."

He smiled at that. "I'll know. See, most of these media jokers cover a story by showing up at a press conference. Sherwood will give 'em the country lawyer act, and they'll just write what he tells them."

He tapped his chest with his forefinger. "Not me," he said. "I've covered the Ripper for four years now. And I've covered Sherwood before." The finger turned to us. "I know what you have to do."

He sounded certain, which put him at a substantial advantage over me. "What do we have to do?" I asked.

Stevens shrugged as if the answer were obvious. "Word is they flat-out caught Keith in the act. He had the girl tied up and was ready to kill her. Plenty of links to the Ripper cases, they say. So, unless he's a drooling wild man, which I hear he's not, then you'll have to try to prove he isn't the Ripper. That means you need to investigate each and every one of these cases."

He pulled my business card back out and waved it at us. "People like you, working for a guy like Sherwood, at a firm like this," he said, "do it right. Now you may or may not find something the cops haven't seen, but either way, once you're done, you'll know down deep whether or not Keith's the Ripper. And so will I. You may not tell me straight out, but I'll know. And that's what I want."

He set his jaw and gave me a defiant stare. I think he was a little embarrassed to reveal human emotions.

Our damn beepers went off simultaneously, startling Stevens. It was a Special Priority message, which meant it was from Sherwood. Edgar plugged his laptop computer in the hotel phone jack and went first.

"The lawyers in your firm wear beepers?" Stevens asked in disbelief.

"Just Sherwood's team," I said. "We have the kind of practice where things come up all of a sudden, at all hours. Lew needs to be able to reach us when that happens. He sends a message with a certain priority on the firm's computer system, and we get a beep telling us to check the mail."

The beepers, universally known in the firm as "the damn beepers," actually were my fault. Sherwood once ordered everyone to leave phone numbers wherever we went, but that stirred up a palace revolt: the wives went bonkers and the single lawyers said no way. Someone nominated me to negotiate a resolution, presumably because I could empathize with all interests. By that time, my divorce had been final for a couple of years, and Anita had taken my son Preston back to Kansas, but the married lawyers trusted me to recall the demands of family life. The single lawyers thought I was one of them. The theory on all sides was that Sherwood might listen to me because I was already known as one of his favorites.

I should have rejected the honor. My peers never forgave me for suggesting the damn beepers. Sherwood liked them, though. And he eventually made me Red Team Leader, so maybe it helped from a career perspective.

"Lewis is coming," Edgar said as he returned to the table. I used his laptop to sign on for my own messages. As usual,

Sherwood's was short and full of action items. We had been engaged to "assist" a Johnston Beach lawyer named Peter Bannister, who represented Travis Keith. The scope of our involvement would be determined later. Sherwood would arrive in about an hour. I was to meet him at Bannister's office and brief them on what Edgar and I had learned. Two other team members would arrive later on a commercial flight from Queenston. When they reported to Bannister's office, we all would go meet with Keith.

That much firepower sounded like more than simple assistance. Sherwood probably intended to take the case but wanted to meet the client before committing. I wondered if this fellow Bannister had the same plan in mind.

"Congratulations," Stevens said when I came back to the table. "Welcome to the party."

Bannister's secretary sounded very pleasant and very harassed when she gave me directions over the phone. It would take about twenty minutes to get there, she said. That only left me a half hour. It was already ten hours since Sherwood's first message to Edgar and me. He would expect us to have the case solved by this time. "Tell me what you can, please," I begged Stevens. "Quickly."

He leaned back and thought, while Edgar poised to take notes in his book. "Okay," he said. "First. The official list says thirteen murders, but everyone involved knows that two of them are copycats."

"What do you mean copycats?" I asked. I was taking my own notes to brief Sherwood.

"The killers tried to match what the papers have said about the Ripper, but they didn't know everything. Those two are Stowe and Santa Catalina." Edgar made a careful notation in his book.

"What is this official list?" Edgar asked.

"The FBI helped put together an informal task force of detectives or investigators from the various jurisdictions. They share information. The FBI provides a liaison man. You haven't talked to the FBI, Edgar?"

Edgar shot me a dirty look. "We're on the Bureau's shit list right now."

Stevens raised an eyebrow but didn't ask. "Anyway," he said, "part of the problem is this guy operates in resorts all over the country, so you have a bunch of local cops working the cases. That's why it took so long to realize they had a serial killer."

"Any pattern at all?" Edgar asked.

"Just that they occur in resorts at the height of the season. Ski places, beach places, whatever. Other than that, no pattern of geography that anyone can find. And no timing pattern either. They've been as far apart as six months and as close together as two months."

"It just started all of a sudden?" I asked.

Stevens nodded. "About four years ago. The first one was at a place called Lake Wachita, in upstate New York. After that, they kept coming."

He paused and thought for a moment. "The victims definitely fall into a pattern. He targets girls like LouAnne: attractive young single woman, generally a tourist or at a business convention of some sort. The ages have ranged from nineteen to thirty-three, but they all look to be in their mid-twenties. I said single. Two of them were married, but their husbands weren't along on the trip."

Edgar took off his glasses and rubbed his eyes. He glanced at the manila envelope. "Any theories on how he gets to them?" he said. "Abduction?"

Stevens shook his head. "The working assumption is he picks them up in a bar or some other social setting when they're unaccompanied. No evidence of any forcible abduction that I know of. They just disappear. Then they turn up like that." He pointed to the envelope.

As he talked, potential defenses popped into my head, even though I had no facts and had not met my client. It was a habit. "How do they know there were only two copycats?" I asked. "Or for that matter, how do they know there's a single Ripper?"

Stevens looked at me. "The other eleven all were done by the same man." He had no doubt in his voice. "A man who gets his rocks off on the publicity."

"How do you know that?"

"Look at the pictures," he said. Edgar rubbed his eyes again, then stared at the landscape hanging on the wall. I watched him out of the corner of my eye while Stevens retrieved his briefcase from the chair. With his round face and balding head, Edgar resembled a 1950s corner grocery proprietor from a Norman Rockwell painting, but he had a law degree, a beautiful young wife, and a son whose soccer team he had coached to back-to-back undefeated seasons. He also had thirty years of criminal investigation experience. If that picture disturbed him, it must be something extraordinary.

Stevens pulled out ten more envelopes and spread the photographs out on the conference table. I prepared to look. After all, I had observed autopsies, even an exhumation. I had been at crime scenes and reviewed police pictures of some pretty gruesome murders. How bad could these be?

It took me a few minutes out on the balcony, gulping fresh air, before my stomach stopped churning. I could see the kids playing Marco Polo in the pool below; their parents were scattered around on lounge chairs. On the beach beyond the dunes, a bunch of teenagers played Frisbee. I took a final deep breath, tried not to think about LouAnne Robinson, and went back inside.

Edgar and Stevens were studying the photographs in silence. Neither of them made any comment about my sudden absence when I returned.

Anyone could see that the same person had done each of these. The remains were all cut, bundled, and positioned in exactly the same way. Some were propped up on the ground, others hung from trees. I tried not to look at the faces.

Stevens swept his hand over several of the photographs. "See what I mean? He poses them, for Christ's sake. Hell, I think he wants to see these pictures in print. But no one would publish something like that. Not even the damn tabloids. And the cops don't pass them around. Don't ask where I got these."

After a minute, Edgar looked up at Stevens. "All right. What else?" he said.

"The main thing you won't see in there"—Stevens waved at the pile of articles on my bed—"is a military connection. You ever in the service?"

Edgar shook his head. "I was in Navy JAG," I said. "Mostly on carriers."

"I spent a couple of years in Nam as a war correspondent." Stevens pushed his chair back from the table. "Show your war-hero boss these pictures; I bet he'll recognize something. The grunts used to talk about it.

"The Vietcong started it, and now it's standard operating procedure for guerrillas all over the world. You take a prisoner and chop him all up, then pose the body as a 'warning.' If you're real clever about where you put them, the opposing troops walk along and turn a corner and suddenly they bump into something like this. It's hell on morale. The Bureau thinks that's what the Ripper wants to do. And that tipped them to your client."

"What do you mean?" I asked.

Stevens grinned at Edgar. "I guess my Bureau sources are better than yours. When Keith was arrested, they ran him through the computer. Turns out he was in one of those Army special operations outfits. Even won himself a dishonorable discharge. That matches the profile they've been looking for."

I checked my watch. Time to leave. "What else do you know about Keith?" I asked.

Stevens shrugged. "Not much yet. I guess they found a clothesline, a knife, some other stuff. And he's a seasonal resort worker. They seem pretty sure he's the one."

I slipped on my blue blazer, hoisted my laptop and briefcase, and walked out to the elevator. Those pictures kept flashing in my mind. I had no desire to meet the man responsible for them. I for sure had no desire to defend the man responsible for them. Most of all, I had no desire to help the man responsible for them go back on the streets.

Of course, it wasn't up to me. It was up to Sherwood. And he could work magic on juries, when he chose to. My only comfort was that I felt certain Lewis Sherwood also would have no desire to help the Resort Ripper go back on the streets. Stevens was right. We would have to find out if Keith was the guy.

CHAPTER
2

Johnston Beach owed its existence to a barrier island—a big sandbar, really—that sat in uneasy equilibrium between the Atlantic on the east and a sound on the west, a little closer to the North Carolina Outer Banks than to Hilton Head. The sound marked the line of demarcation between two worlds. Our hotel was on the island, a resort community of condominiums, hotels, and gray-weathered shops offering T-shirts, surfing gear, and seashell collectibles to sunburned beach-goers. Across the bridge, on the mainland, was a typical small Southern town with two-story brick buildings at the courthouse center gradually giving way to strip malls, fast-food emporia, and mobile home communities.

The courthouse was one of those picturesque turn-of-the-century brick classics, complete with clock spire. We hated to try cases in a building like that: the air conditioning never worked right, the floors creaked, and they never had enough electrical outlets to handle the kind of automation that we typically set up in a side room so Sherwood could have every fact in an instant. We preferred a boring, high-tech, modern courtroom.

A small traffic jam had developed as assorted television

broadcast trucks battled for parking places around the town square. One area of the courthouse lawn was already roped off for the press, and cables snaked up the courthouse steps to a mound of microphones being readied for a press conference. Across the street, several grim-faced deputies guarded the entrance to a modern two-story brick building with sheriff's vehicles parked in front. It was the jail, now occupied by our new client, Travis Keith.

Pete Bannister's office near the town square began life as a residence, and his secretary sat in what used to be the front parlor. She gave me an exasperated smile as she hit button after button on the phone, alternating "Mr. Bannister's office, can you hold?" with "Mr. Bannister has no comment." Before she could greet me, a tall, distinguished gentleman with a mane of gray hair wandered past, a legal folder tucked under one arm. "She's kind of tied up," he said. "Can I help you?"

Pete Bannister was a very pleasant surprise. I was worried on first impression, because he looked like a politician. But as soon as we went back to his office in the former dining room, I discovered that Pete was one of those rare lawyers who actually thought before he spoke: his words came out slowly and carefully, in a folksy drawl that must have sat well with the local clientele. I immediately felt comfortable with him, and apparently it was mutual. The first meeting between local and out-of-town counsel often is like the first meeting between two dogs: each sniffs suspiciously at the other, trying to decide whether to play or fight. We skipped that process.

"I am awfully glad to see you folks," Pete said. "How'd you get here from Queenston this fast?"

"Had some good connections," I said noncommittally, not knowing what Sherwood had told him. "I saw a crowd at the courthouse."

"This thing is totally out of hand. Poor Cecilia"—he gestured toward the secretary—"has had that phone glued to her ear since she came in this morning. Newspeople from everywhere, wanting interviews." Pete rolled his eyes and sighed. "When Travis' boss called me, I thought it was just an A&B. I didn't know the whole Western world would descend on us."

"What exactly is Keith's status now?" I asked.

"Bond hearing is tomorrow. The specific charge is aggravated battery, but I'm sure they'll add more. The claim is he attacked a woman named Dorothy Catterman night before last."

"Has she said anything?" I said.

Pete picked up a seashell from his desk and played with it as he talked. "No. She's in the hospital, in pretty bad shape, but she'll live, they say."

I had pulled out a legal pad to make some notes. "I understand there are witnesses? Locals?"

Pete nodded. "Two brothers named Swilton say they heard screams coming from the woods down at the south end of the island and ran to see what was going on. They claim Travis had tied up the Catterman woman and was beating her. They knocked him out, hog-tied him with the same rope, then found a deputy. I've talked to the deputy, Bo Everson. Haven't talked to the Swiltons yet."

"What have you done with Keith so far?"

"Mainly just calmed him down some and had him keep his mouth shut. He's a little beat up himself. They brought him before a magistrate a couple of hours after the arrest— that's the procedure down here—and I declined to enter a plea. Told him to get a good night's sleep and not talk to anybody about anything. Saw him a couple of times yesterday and told him the same thing."

Pete looked at me closely. "Now normally," he said,

"with an ordinary A&B, I would have him out on bail by now. But the word came out about this Ripper thing, and I couldn't see Judge Whoten letting him walk out of jail under any circumstances, so I decided to let him sit there another day or two. Haven't asked him about the incident; thought that could wait too."

I detected some slight anxiety in Pete's voice. I was about to reassure him that he had taken exactly the right actions when Cecilia appeared in the doorway. "Mr. Sherwood is here," she said with a note of awe in her voice.

Pete leapt to his feet. I sat back to watch Sherwood, curious to see who he would be today.

I had worked for Lewis Sherwood for five years now. I wanted to be a great trial lawyer, and he was the greatest, and sometimes late at night on airplanes when I was too tired to work, I tried to analyze what made him so good. Two things, I had decided.

First, no matter where he was, no matter what the setting, Sherwood dominated the scene as if a spotlight shone on him. It wasn't his physical appearance. Certainly, he was conventionally handsome—the shock of black hair that hung over his right eyebrow, the piercing blue eyes that interviewers always mentioned, the athletic build—but nothing that would stand out in a crowd. Nor was he tall: I was six-two and Sherwood was a good four inches shorter. But he entered a room as if he were a monarch so accustomed to homage that he no longer noticed it. In a courtroom, everyone else—judge, prosecutor, defendant—was simply a member of Sherwood's supporting cast, and the jury knew it.

His other talent was the ability to come across as a peer to anyone. In front of a jury or in a press conference, he was the ole country lawyer, slouched slightly, hands in pockets, just talking to the folks with a down-home Southern drawl.

But when he was with a Wall Street client, or in front of a judge smart enough to realize that hicks don't head departments at major law firms, he was ramrod straight, a sophisticated attorney comfortable at the highest levels of society.

In moments of deepest honesty, I admitted to myself that I did not have either of those traits. But I took some comfort in realizing that neither did anyone else, at least not to the same degree. Sherwood was one of a kind.

Today, with Pete, he was mid-range: a prominent small-town lawyer, with just a hint more drawl than he customarily used at the firm. He and Pete were brothers at the bar. You'd have thought they grew up in the same town.

"When do we see Keith?" Sherwood asked after the pleasantries were completed.

Pete glanced at his watch and said, apologetically, "I have a long-standing commitment from noon to about two. A speech. I'd cancel it, but I'm afraid I'm sort of the star attraction . . . "

Sherwood raised his hand to stop him. "Clifford and I need to talk, so you leave when you have to. The others should be here when you get back."

Pete cocked an eyebrow. "Who all's coming?"

Sherwood leaned back in his chair and elevated his accent to the big-time Southern lawyer. "I've put our Red Team on it. Clifford here"—he pointed to me—"is the Team Leader. The Red Team gets the toughest cases because they're the best talent we have. And the Red Team leader's the best lawyer we have." Pete studied me more carefully. I probably should have blushed, but it was true. We had two other teams: the Blue Team, which took cases we did not have time to handle, and the White Team, which got the dregs.

Sherwood chuckled. "Don't let that go to your head, Clifford," he said. "Anyway, Ted Brookstone will be the handholder, I assume." He looked at me for verification. The Team Leader technically was in charge of assignments. I nodded. "Ted's another junior partner, sharp young man, second-in-command to Cliff."

Pete looked confused. "Handholder?"

"We assign one lawyer to stay in town as the primary contact with the client and local counsel." Sherwood paused and thought. "Who else? Kara Phillips, the lead paralegal, is flying down with Ted. Best paralegal I've ever had. Then we have Edgar Browning, our investigator. Where's Edgar?" he asked me.

"At the hotel," I said. "Interviewing a source."

"Edgar is retired FBI, solid experience both in the field and at headquarters. I lured him to the firm about four years ago, and he's put together a network of freelance investigators for us. Then we have associates and other paralegals back at the firm who may be coming and going too."

Sherwood didn't usually lay it on so thick, particularly for local counsel. Of course, most of the time the local counsel had nothing to say about our presence: the clients had selected us. Here, as far as I knew, it was still Pete's case.

Pete whistled softly. "That's a regular army for these parts. Around here, two lawyers on the same side is a major piece of litigation."

Sherwood smiled. "Well, I know it sounds like a lot, but I'd rather know too much than too little, and we can always cut back. We'll keep as low a profile as possible, though."

"What do you mean?"

Sherwood rose and began to pace behind his chair. I recognized the onset of a lecture on trial tactics. "I have what I call 'Sherwood's Rules' about how to try cases. One is that everyone in town is a potential juror, and jurors don't like the idea of a bunch of high-priced lawyers trying to get criminals off with slick legal tricks. So in small towns, especially, we try to be inconspicuous. No fancy suits, no parades of lawyers and paralegals in and out of the courthouse."

Sherwood wore thousand-dollar suits, flew his own plane, and appeared regularly on national television. I thought I should explain. "That doesn't apply to Lew," I said. "He's so famous that people expect him to be visible, so he does all the press conferences and interviews while the rest of us lay low."

"Of course," Sherwood went on, "the other visible person is the local counsel. We need that expertise dealing with the judges and prosecutors and others."

Pete ignored the bait. He shifted his position a little uncomfortably. "That's still a lot of talent for one case. You know, I really don't know anything about Keith's finances. He gave me a small retainer, so I reckon he's not indigent, and he had me call his sister in Iowa to let her know what was going on. She volunteered to help out on fees. Lew, I know you said you'd work against a flat fee of $5,000 for now until you decide for sure to get involved. I don't know if they can afford that kind of group."

At our usual rates, the $5,000 would be gone well before tomorrow's hearing. I had known Sherwood to take a case now and then on a special basis, and the younger lawyers did some pro bono work for experience, but this would involve some major expenditures.

Sherwood surprised me by waving his hand at Pete. "Don't worry about the money." He sat back down and nodded as if he had made a decision. "Pete, you still want us to handle this case?"

Pete rolled his eyes. "Absolutely. An A&B is one thing, but all this business about the Resort Ripper . . . I don't have the resources. I need someone else involved. If you'll take it, well, that means Travis has the best."

"We'd have to call the shots."

"I understand that, Lew. I'll give you whatever help you want. If you don't want any, then that's fine too."

Sherwood studied him for another long moment. "What does Keith say?"

"Lew, he's holding his breath and praying you'll take it. His only question was whether he could pay you over time."

Sherwood made a steeple with his hands and tapped his forefingers against his lips, his brow wrinkled in thought. It was a dramatic pause for effect. He had his mind made up before he walked in the door. "Okay," he finally said. "We'll take it on."

Pete's shoulders relaxed as if a huge weight had been lifted. "Oh, man," he sighed. "You have no idea what a relief that is. Thank you."

Sherwood just grinned and moved on, accepting the praise as his due. "Do you know anything about these Ripper charges?" he asked.

Pete shook his head. "Not a thing. I tried to talk to our prosecutor, Ernie Ledbetter, about it, but he's being really closemouthed. The sheriff, an old boy named Al Sanderson, won't say anything either."

I filled them in a bit on what Stevens had told us. Sherwood tilted his head back and listened without a comment, his eyes fixed on the ceiling. That was his absorption mode; the wheels were turning inside as he mentally sketched out a defense. Pete just shook his head in disbelief.

Pete left for his appointment. Cecilia brought us coffee and took our sandwich orders. When she pulled the door shut behind her, Sherwood began to prowl around the bookcases and other furnishings in the converted dining room. "This reminds me of my first office in Andis, Alabama," he said. "Wasn't as nice as this. Kind of a dump, really. But it was a converted old house, with a secretary in the parlor, just like here." He chuckled. "Of course, I couldn't afford a secretary until after the Badgers case."

That case was part of the Lewis Sherwood legend. He'd hung out his shingle in his home town after the Navy and college and law school; Thomas Badgers was his first client. Badgers was a black man accused of raping a white debutante, the daughter of Andis' most prominent banker. The dying vestiges of the old South still lingered in Andis back then, and racial tension was high. Rumors of lynch mobs swept the town. The only question was whether the State would execute Badgers before the local citizenry did. In that atmosphere, Sherwood somehow persuaded a predominantly white jury to acquit Badgers.

The Badgers case brought Sherwood to the attention of the Southern Legal Defense Fund, which engaged him to defend serious criminal cases where racial factors may have played a role. In just a few years, he was generally regarded as the leading murder trial lawyer in the country.

Sherwood studied Pete's diplomas and court admissions, all neatly framed on the walls. "How did you know Pete?" I asked.

Sherwood sat in Pete's desk chair and leaned back, resting his foot on the corner of the desk. "Didn't. I heard about the arrest, and they mentioned Pete's name. Out of curiosity, I looked him up and found out he was a solo practitioner. That got me thinking about Andis, and how it was being a solo. It can be pretty damn lonesome, sometimes. So I gave him a call, just for moral support, to wish him good luck."

I sat back and listened, enjoying the rare opportunity for one-on-one time with Sherwood. He was too busy to do it often.

"Anyway," he went on, "we talked some. He asked if I knew anyone who might take the case without any particular guarantee on fees. I gave him a few names. Then out of the blue he asked me if we were interested."

"What did you say?" I asked.

"Told him I'd think about it. That's when I sent you and Edgar down. But I wanted to meet Pete before committing, and I had to clear it with the Senator." The Senator was the firm's managing partner, William G. Braxton.

Sherwood stretched and rose to his feet again. I wanted to keep him talking. "Why do you want this case?" I asked. "It sounds like the client can't pay."

He settled into the chair next to me and drummed his fingers lightly on the arm as he studied the ceiling. "That's what the Senator said too. He doesn't understand. But you should."

I shrugged. "I guess I don't."

"Any case with this much publicity will generate more business than it costs. No matter how much it costs." He chuckled again. "That's what I told the Senator. He has a budget to meet, so you use that kind of argument with him. I also mentioned our moral and ethical obligation to represent those who cannot afford us. You know how strongly he feels about that. Those are good and true reasons to take a case like this once in a while."

"But they're not the only ones?" We had worked together so long now that I knew when he had more to say.

He rolled his head in my direction but looked past me to a framed seascape on the wall. "Most of what we do, Clifford, the white collar crime and the drug dealers—they pay the bills. But a case like the Resort Ripper is what it's really all about. A high-profile case, a crime of the century, life and death . . . that matters. Nothing more exciting than being defense counsel in a case like this."

Sherwood looked at me and grinned. "Hell, you and I ought to pay Keith for letting us have this much fun."

CHAPTER
3

Well, he sure didn't look like a serial killer to me. What Travis Keith looked like was what he apparently was, one of those pretty people of indeterminate age who run the surfboard concession at the beach or rent equipment at the ski resort. Of course he was a little beat up now, but I thought when we let his bruises heal, gave him a neat, short haircut, and disposed of the drooping mustache, he would be quite presentable to a jury. Perhaps some older women would think of him like a son. The young ones might think him attractive. Kara could give us insight on that.

He was physically nondescript, too, which was good. I had expected a Muscle Beach–type that a jury of honest working people would instantly distrust, but Keith was about five-ten or so, and slender, in good shape but not bulging. His dirty light brown hair hung almost shoulder length in the back, with sunstreaks that may or may not have been natural. They would fade. Good tan, which would fade too. He had a tattoo on his left arm. A jury would not see that when we dressed him up in a suit and tie, but it could be a potential problem if any identification witnesses were out there somewhere. I made a note to check on scars.

Keith did not act like a killer either. At the moment, he was pale under that tan and shaking slightly. He was more scared and confused than dangerous.

According to Pete, he was about my age, thirty-five, but the long hair and mustache made him look younger until you noticed the lines in his face. That's what I told myself, anyway. Of course Sherwood, who was in his mid-forties, also looked about my age. I didn't have a rationalization for that. Maybe it was his jet-set lifestyle.

Sherwood moved to the door to meet our client, simultaneously shaking hands and patting him tenderly on the shoulder. It was the reassuring father persona. "Travis, I'm Lew Sherwood, and we're here to take care of this situation for you," he said, steering Keith into the room while Ted Brookstone shut the door. "Pete's done a fine job so far, and he's briefed us on what's gone on, and we're gonna take it from here. Don't you worry about a thing; just sit on down over there and we'll talk for a bit. First, do you feel okay and are you having any problems with the guards?"

"No, sir, they've been all right." Keith glanced at the rest of us, then sat tensely in one of the straight-backed chairs around the table. "I want to thank you for coming. I couldn't believe it when Pete said you'd take my case." He spoke so softly that I had to strain to hear him. His accent was from the hills somewhere, but not thick. Pete had told us Keith was originally from Tennessee.

"Let me introduce these folks to you," Sherwood said, moving toward where we were lined up on the far side of the wooden conference table. "This Mutt and Jeff act over here are my partners, Cliff Nielson and Ted Brookstone. They're two of the finest lawyers you'll ever meet." Ted and I smiled modestly; we had been through this routine before. "And this lady is my legal assistant, Kara Phillips." A brief look of surprise flashed across Keith's face when he focused on Kara: a typical male reaction. "You know Pete, of course, and there's a whole bunch of other folks back at our offices working on your case too, but we'll be the ones you'll see. Now let's get to work, because we have a lot to go over. I assume we can talk freely in here without any unwanted listeners?" He looked for confirmation at Pete, who nodded. That was for Keith's benefit, since Sherwood had grilled Pete about it earlier.

Keith relaxed slightly. Pete took a chair in the far corner, deferring to the big city lawyers. The rest of us sat down behind our legal pads, picked up our pens, and prepared to take notes in an efficient, lawyerly fashion.

Sherwood patted Keith on the shoulder again, then strode to center stage, a few feet away from the head of the table. He took off the glasses he only wore in front of juries and the press and assumed a thoughtful pose, one of the earpieces resting lightly on his lower lip. The plain-lensed glasses were a stage prop; he thought they made him look more trustworthy to jurors. To see, he wore contacts.

After posing a moment, he began his lecture: "Now here's what will happen. As you know, you are accused of attacking a young woman named Dorothy Catterman. When you were arrested, you were taken before a judge who inquired into the reasonableness of the arrest. Pete quite properly had you remain silent at that point. Tomorrow morning is another hearing, at which you will be officially informed of the charges that the State is making against you, and during which the State—that means the prosecuting attorney—will be required to outline enough evidence to show that it has probable cause to charge you with the crime. We, of course, will go with you to that hearing."

As the professor lectured on criminal procedure, I studied what appeared to be a water stain on one of the walls of the little interview room; with some imagination, it looked like an outline of the United States. The room itself was decorated with the usual jailhouse flair: a small barred window high on the wall, a single table, and the institutional green color found only in government facilities.

I turned my attention to my colleagues. Pete listened with interest; he had not seen Sherwood work with a client before. Kara and Ted alertly drew little circles and squares on their legal pads. The light flashed on Kara's rings as she drew. Sherwood's Rule about not attracting attention was a good theory, but we never had figured out a way to make Kara inconspicuous. She was taller than average, so her honey-blond hair and exquisite features drew the first looks, then most men (and many women) did a double take and stared hard, vaguely certain they had seen her somewhere, perhaps on the cover of the *Sports Illustrated* swimsuit issue.

At least when we had Kara with us, no one noticed Ted or me. Ted was a little man with a perpetual look of concern, one year behind me in firm seniority, but several years younger since I had that time in the Navy. His dark-rimmed glasses were real, unlike Sherwood's, and his hair had thinned rapidly in the last few years. I worried about Ted. He had been a wrestler in college and still worked out religiously, but even by the firm's standards, he worked too hard. Today, he looked exhausted.

Sherwood went on in great detail about the legal process. He explained about bail, and why the judge would deny it or set the amount so high that Keith could not post it. He discussed the concept of the elements of a crime, and how the State had to prove each and every one beyond a reasonable doubt. He ordered Keith not to speak to anyone except his lawyers about the case, not even another inmate.

Keith just sat. From time to time, he seemed to drift off, but Sherwood brought him back with a question or sharp comment. The muscles in Keith's shoulders and arms flexed with tension; his fists clenched and released constantly. A habit we would have to break.

Finally, Sherwood paused and shot me the "Forget anything?" look. I rubbed my cheek.

"Oh, yes," Sherwood said, as if he had just thought of it. "Get cleaned up for this hearing; there will be some photographers there. Nice close shave, but leave that mustache on for now. Comb your hair. Wear a clean uniform. Your attitude is you've done nothing wrong, but you want to cooperate to correct this terrible mistake. Look the judge in the eye. Don't duck your head from any photographers. Got that?"

"Yes, sir."

The glasses went back on, and kindly Uncle Lew reemerged. "Now remember, Travis, you're the boss, so if you have any problems at all, you let us know." He patted Keith on the shoulder again while gently guiding him to the door. "The best thing you can do is relax as much as you can, get a good night's sleep, and let us do the worrying. We'll see you to the courtroom in the morning." He stopped before summoning the guard. "Any questions?"

Keith seemed much less tense now, but he still looked dazed by the whole thing. The fists kept clenching and releasing. He gave Sherwood a quizzical look. "Just one, Mr. Sherwood. You didn't ask me if I did it or not. I didn't."

We probably never would ask Keith if he did it. Nothing good could come of an answer. Presumably, he would claim innocence, but it wasn't worth the risk. If he were to blurt out something damaging, or God forbid admit the crime, then we could be hamstrung by the ethics rules. A lawyer cannot ethically assist a client to lie or promote deceptions on the court. The easiest way to deal with that prospect is to avoid the situation.

At some point we would ask for his version of the events of the night in question, but first one of us would explain exactly what the State had to prove to convict him, then give him plenty of time to think about it. It was a Sherwood's Rule. If your client needs to make up a story, he at least should know what it has to cover. For tomorrow's hearing, though, it didn't matter whether Keith did it or not, or even what his story was. The prosecution would put on a pro forma case, and the judge would bind him over for trial and deny bail.

Sherwood, of course, did not explain any of that. Instead, he gave Keith his best big warm smile. "Forget that Mr. Sherwood stuff, Travis," he said. "You call me Lew." And he called for the guard.

As soon as the door swung shut, kindly Uncle Lew laid his glasses on the table, brushed the shock of black hair off his forehead, and turned into General Patton. The slightly rounded shoulders pulled back, the gentle lines in his face hardened, and his drawl went back upscale. This was the Lewis Sherwood that we saw most often at the firm.

Sherwood looked around the table. "Okay, people, what do you think?"

I led. "He looks pretty good to me, Lew. Polite. He'll be very presentable when we get him cleaned up."

Sherwood nodded in agreement. "Good work on that shaving reminder, Clifford. Kara, what's your reaction?"

When Kara talked, you could almost smell the magnolias. Her lineage was strictly FFV—First Families of Virginia—but somewhere along the way she had laid some Mississippi drawl over the Richmond accent. Probably from beauty pageants: the judges were suckers for that kind of thing. Part of her job here was to furnish the female perspective. "He seems real nice, Lewis, and if you have any younger women on the jury, they'll like his looks. But I don't think I'd take him home to meet my mamma. He's more like the kind of guy you party with, not the kind you take to the Club. And he kept squeezing his fists." She had noticed it too. "That could make him look a little scary if he does it at the trial."

Ted offered his usual precise, clipped analysis: "I believe we will have to be very careful about the image we project when we tell our story. At Keith's age, people will wonder about him still being a beach boy." Ted was thirty, looked thirty-five, and acted forty. He knew about respectability.

A knock sounded on the door, and a young deputy stuck his head in. "Excuse me, Mr. Bannister. Sheriff Sanderson wonders if he might speak to you and Mr. Sherwood? I can take you to his office."

Pete rose to his feet, but Sherwood stopped him with a gesture and fixed the officer with a withering stare. "Tell the sheriff we will be here for a few more minutes. He can come over if he wants to."

"Yes, sir." The man took care to shut the door without a sound. Sherwood caught my eye and winked.

Two minutes later, we heard a louder knock and the door flew open before we could respond. A huge white-haired man, wearing a khaki uniform that struggled to contain its contents, stood at the door and glared at Pete Bannister. Put a beard and a red suit on him, I thought, and you have Santa Claus. But he did not seem very jolly at the moment. He looked geared up for a fight.

"Pete," he rumbled in a deep voice that matched his bulk. "I need to talk to you."

"Hey, Al," Pete said.

Sherwood dropped back to his old country lawyer routine. "You must be Sheriff Sanderson," he said, shaking the man's hand. "Appreciate you coming over, Sheriff. I thought you'd rather we didn't march this crew through your building—don't want to be disruptive."

Sanderson frowned as Sherwood made quick introductions, led him to a chair, and sat next to him. "Hope we haven't caused you any problems," Sherwood drawled with an ingenuous smile. "Trying to keep it as low-key as possible here. What can we do for you?"

Sanderson shook his head and rolled his eyes, then took several deep breaths. "Mr. Sherwood," he said slowly, "I got more reporters out there than fleas on a hound's butt. They got their damn trucks and cameras all over the town square and they're standing in the middle of the damn road and I got a three-mile traffic jam building. I had to call in half my off-duty men for crowd control and that's gonna put me over my damn budget and the damn County Commissioners will scream to high heaven about it."

Sherwood gave him a sympathetic look. "How can we help?"

The sheriff looked at him carefully. "Would you please go out and talk to those people?"

Sherwood looked surprised. "Oh," he said. "We just planned to slip out a side door. I don't believe in trying cases in the media." I watched Kara bite her lip to keep a straight face.

"Well, that's fine," Sanderson said. "But I wish you'd go over on the courthouse steps where they got their microphones set up and tell them that or whatever you got to say to them so I can get them out of my jail lobby and off my street."

Sherwood looked at his watch. "If you're sure that's what you want . . . "

"It is," the sheriff said. "I can walk you over there so they won't bother you on the way." Now Sanderson and

Sherwood were buddies, trying to solve a mutual problem.

"How about fifteen minutes? That work for you?"

"That'd be fine." Sanderson rose to leave.

Sherwood walked him to the door. They were not quite arm in arm, but they could have been. "We need to talk to your man about the incident the other night," Sherwood said. "You too. Can you schedule that for us?"

"Sure. Just let me know when."

"Pete will call you. And one other thing. Travis says you all are being real nice to him. Thank you for that. You think maybe we could get him a clean uniform for the hearing tomorrow? And a good hot shower? I want him to look good, and we want those press people to see how well you treat your prisoners."

"I'll take care of it," Sanderson said. They shook hands, and the sheriff left. Sherwood turned back to us.

Pete laughed. "I think I just saw two con men trying to outcon each other. Al's been around a long time, Lew. He's a sharp ole boy. He'll tell you what he wants to and not a word more."

Sherwood grinned and shrugged. "Might as well start out friendly. We can always go to war later." He began to pack up his briefcase. "Okay, people. Good work, as always. Clifford, you know what we have to do. Let me know about the arrangements, Kara." He slipped on his glasses, said, "Give me about fifteen minutes to deal with our press friends," and left.

That meant for us to stay put while he appeared on the courthouse steps before the assembled multitude. He wanted to look like the Lone Ranger rather than like General Grant. Sherwood's Rule again. Once he had the crowd's attention, we could skulk out the back door unnoticed and set out on our mission in the cause of truth and justice and our client.

CHAPTER
4

We did not arrive at the hotel until after five, but the June sun was still high in the sky and the customary afternoon thunderstorm had not made an appearance. As the senior lawyer present, I led us through the lobby to the front desk, where the receptionist handed me a sheaf of messages, shot Kara a look of mixed envy and disapproval, and announced that she could not possibly accommodate our request for additional rooms. She was very sorry, but this was the height of the season.

Kara politely listened to my feeble efforts to persuade the clerk to help us out, then tugged at my sleeve. We moved off to one side. "Maybe you and Ted would rather go wait somewhere."

Ted and I wandered off past the gift shop and found an empty table by the little bar next to the pool. Kids yelled and splashed in the pool, getting in their last swims before dinner. The Marco Polo game was still on.

We both were too tired to do anything serious, so we sipped iced tea and talked idly about logistics while we watched the swimmers. Ted was in a foul mood. "What's your problem?" I asked him.

"My youngest daughter has the flu and spent the night throwing up. I had just fallen asleep when the damn beeper went off."

At least you didn't have to get up and catch a plane before dawn, I thought, but I tried to look sympathetic as his litany of woe continued: "Tomorrow's my other daughter's birthday. She's having a clown and twenty second-graders. Martha planned a big dinner party for Friday. Our minister and the deacons. Now I'll be here in Johnston Beach, and Martha will have to do the parties without me and she's going to kill me. Why can't Lew make an associate the handholder?"

"Maybe he will later." I knew he wouldn't. Sherwood would never trust an associate with that assignment in a case with this much publicity.

Ted continued to moan into his iced tea. I liked Ted, but when he whined about how tough his life was, I had trouble working up much sympathy for him. Ted came from a wealthy Alabama family that sent him to an exclusive boarding school in Chattanooga, then paid his way through college and law school—expensive Ivy League institutions. I had scrambled to find a small college in Virginia that would give a basketball scholarship to a slow guard without a perimeter jump shot, and Anita and I both worked during law school until the Navy picked up the tab in exchange for a few years of service. Ted didn't have it so bad. Martha was his prep school sweetheart, and his two children attended the most exclusive private school in Queenston. At least he still had a family.

"Sorry," was all I said. Someday I would have a heart-to-heart with him about the benefits of having a wife and children to go home to. But I was too tired myself right now.

Kara showed up with a fistful of keys. "Hey, you all. I talked to the hotel manager. He's the nicest little man.

He'll give us winter rates on a set of ocean-front rooms, with a suite for a war room. There's enough power for our computers, and the manager will put in a dedicated phone line."

She tossed keys at us. "These are for your rooms and the suite; your luggage is already up there, Ted. Cliff, you and Edgar can move your stuff tonight or tomorrow, then drop the old keys off at the desk. Breakfast is included, and the suite has a kitchenette." She gave a cocky grin. "Anything else? I want to catch some rays at the pool."

We both stared at her, even though we had seen her work that kind of magic before.

Ted said, "I never cease to be amazed." Kara just winked at him.

Edgar was still in my room, summarizing on his laptop computer the information that Stevens had given him. Papers lay strewn across my bed; the manila envelopes with the victims' pictures were on the desk in the corner. He looked depressed.

Edgar briefed me on some of the details. The physical evidence, as far as Stevens knew, was very skimpy. The victims were nude; no clothes had ever been found from any of them. The police had a few hairs and fibers that might or might not have come from the killer. The rope used to tie up the victims was ordinary clothesline. The killer expertly covered his tracks: another tie-in to the military experience. No fluids: all the blood apparently came from the victims. Indications of recent vaginal intercourse, presumably rape. No sperm. Stevens guessed he used a condom. Maybe he was worried about AIDS, I thought.

"What's the precise cause of death?" I asked.

"They're not quite sure," Edgar told me. "The victims are sliced up so badly that the pathologists have a real problem deciding what happened when. Some of them think they see signs of oxygen deprivation, but the faces don't have the usual look of strangulation, so the leading theory is the killer uses one of those commando death grips. Tim said that's another tie to our client. How was he?"

I gave him my impressions of Keith, such as they were. "He doesn't seem like the kind of person who could do this," I said.

Edgar grunted. "You never can tell. Did you ask him about the attack here?"

"No. Lew likes to wait. Probably get into it tomorrow or the next day."

Edgar printed as much of the memo as he had finished, and I reviewed it while he worked on the remainder. Attaching names and backgrounds to those pictures made the whole thing worse. Fortunately, he used flat, technical language for most of the details, which took some of the reality away and made it more of an intellectual problem. At least that's what I told myself.

After Edgar left, I shifted my belongings to the new room, which was larger, with a better view, and slipped into some gym shorts to go lie down on the balcony lounge chair.

As I started out, the phone rang.

"You alone, Shug?" the voice on the other end asked.

"Yeah."

The phone clicked, and the door to the adjoining room opened. "I thought we might want to leave this unlocked," Kara said with a sly grin. She put her left arm around my back and slid her right hand down the front of my gym shorts. "Now," she whispered. "Where were we last night when the damn beeper went off?"

• • •

I had started to drift off for good when Kara poked me in the ribs. "I'm hungry," she announced. She had burned up a lot of calories in the last couple of hours. I wanted to sleep until morning, but duty and chivalry called.

"Okay," I sighed. "Let's get back to work." Kara padded off into her room to shower while I put on my official lawyer-at-the-beach costume: khaki pants, Polo shirt, and Topsiders. When she reappeared in wonderfully tight shorts and a halter top, I studied us in the hotel room mirror. We made a lovely couple. Or, more accurately, she was lovely, and I was presentable. Stomach still flat, still only one chin, hair mostly still there with only a few strands of gray beginning to show among the brown. The soon-to-be-aging yuppie and his young companion, ready to hit the hot spots.

We took the Honda that Kara had rented at the airport and headed south on the beach highway. The north end of the island, where the bridge connected the mainland, was primarily houses, condominiums, and a few family-oriented hotels like ours. The south end was wooded marshlands, but a few years back, some developers talked the local authorities into significant drainage in order to build a five-star resort. When the money ran out, they began selling off small pieces of land, which led to the emergence of a honky-tonk, low-rent section known as the Strip. The banks finally took over, and the remaining parcel ended up as a self-contained singles resort called Clippers. Between Clippers and the Strip, Johnston Beach had developed a reputation as a place where anything goes for the fun-and-sun crowd.

Travis Keith worked at the Mariner, a Strip hotel adjoining the Clippers property. Dorothy Catterman had been on vacation at Clippers; the police believed Keith had picked her up at the Mariner's nightclub.

The late dinner hour traffic overwhelmed the two-lane "highway." A half mile from our hotel, we sat behind two cars from New Jersey who were determined to make a U-turn against the endless stream of north-bound vehicles.

"Did you call Preston?" Kara asked.

"No, I forgot." My son had a soccer game today. I usually called for a report after his games. "I'll try tomorrow."

"I'll remind you." Like many of the best paralegals, Kara worked hard to keep "her" lawyers on track. It was a challenge. Lawyers as a group tend to drift off course throughout the day. In my case, Kara also viewed my personal life as part of her domain. I was agreeable and willing to follow orders. Our only problem was keeping our relationship a secret. The firm strictly forbade fraternization, and neither of us wanted to become a test case for the Executive Committee.

"What more did Edgar find out about the Resort Ripper?" she asked.

"He got quite a bit from the reporter, Tim Stevens," I said. She would read Edgar's memo and see those pictures soon enough. Too soon.

She turned to look at me closely. "It's pretty bad, isn't it?"

"Yeah."

"Could Keith be the Ripper?"

I shrugged. "Don't have enough yet to say. Stevens thinks he probably is . . . Jeez, finally." The New Jersey plates triumphantly made their U-turns.

The Mariner was an unimpressive building, separated from the Clippers property by a dense forest of wind-blown stunted pines. The hotel lobby entrance was in the center of the building; to the right, on the Clippers side, a separate door led to the Seaside Lounge and Shag Shack, featuring Beach Music by the Fabulous Bombardiers.

Within thirty seconds, I realized that I had passed the point in the aging process where my body could tolerate places like the Shag Shack. Between the Fabulous Bombardiers and the mass of humanity screaming to be heard over the music, it sounded like the interior of a vacuum cleaner. Kara, on the other hand, snapped her fingers and swayed with the beat.

I tapped her on the shoulder and pointed to the bar, which sat on an elevated platform about as far as we could get from the bandstand. We began to push through the crowd; finally I let Kara lead. People moved to let her pass, although she was rubbed a lot and invited to dance about twenty times. At least I think that's what they invited her to do.

Past the bar, we found a door labeled Lounge. It was an escape hatch to the Seaside Lounge: a grill with its own bar and a glassed dining area overlooking the ocean. Even better, when I pushed the door shut behind us, I could actually hear, although the Bombardiers' bass vibrated through the floor and up into my stomach.

The Lounge was dark and quiet. Near the entrance, an aquarium separated the tables from the bar area, creating a secluded section for even more private dining. Only a few couples were having dinner; Clippers' resort package included meals there. The bartender and a waitress watched TV at the far end of the bar.

I sighed with relief as we sat at the bar and asked for beers and menus. The waitress gave Kara a dirty look and moved off to check her customers. The bartender looked at me sympathetically. "Can you hear yet?" he said. He could tell I was not a Shag Shack regular.

"How do you rate working in here?" I asked.

He shrugged. "We rotate. The money's a lot better in the

Shack, but two nights in a row is about all your ears can handle. You should hear it on Fridays."

The TV over the bar was tuned to a local station that had an evening newscast. FiveAlive News, with Ed Bernsten. The Resort Ripper was the lead story.

Sherwood's performance on the courthouse steps highlighted the coverage. Slouching slightly, hands in his pockets, he patiently stood in the bright sun and fielded shouted questions from the press as if he were chatting over the back fence. The ole country lawyer told the world that Travis Keith professed his innocence and his eagerness to work with the prosecution and clear up the confusion. Resort Ripper? Sherwood did not know anything about that nonsense. His client had not been charged with any other crimes and there was no reason to think he would be. Justice would prevail. God Bless America. Thank you all for coming.

I leaned over to Kara. "We need a VCR to record these newscasts," I said in a low tone.

"It'll be here tomorrow morning," she said, without taking her eyes off the TV. Prosecutor Ernie Ledbetter was on now. He came in a poor second to Sherwood, in my unbiased opinion. Visibly nervous, he wore sunglasses, which (according to one of Sherwood's Rules) made him appear to be hiding something. Worse, while Sherwood had appeared alone, Ernie was backed by a dozen grim government officials, all wearing sunglasses. Sherwood would be pleased with the contrast: the massive power of the State arrayed against the outmanned Lew Sherwood.

"That Keith worked here, didn't he?" I asked the bartender. "You know him?"

"Yeah, I can't believe it. He's only been here since the start of the season, but he seemed like a good guy. Ran the beach umbrella concession. My buddy told me he got his job through a friend of the manager." The bartender talked to me, but he watched Kara.

I glanced at her too, and almost laughed at her blank expression and wide eyes. That was her typical investigator role: the blond airhead. People tended to think that anyone that good-looking could not possibly have a brain, so they talked freely in front of her. That was why I wanted her to attend witness interviews like this one. She would write a memo later reproducing everything word for word, complete with astute observations about the witness's credibility and motivation.

"I don't know Travis except to say 'Hey,' " the bartender continued. "Nobody really knows him. Kind of sticks to himself. You know, he's a little older than most of us, and a lot of us have worked here before; we have our own group. Don't get that much mixing between the night shift and the day shift anyway. We go party after work and sleep late. The beach guys have to be out early." He wiped the bar with his towel, trying to impress Kara with his efficiency. "He showed up in the Shack every few nights, real successful with the ladies. They go for that type. In fact, I saw him there that night."

"Did you see the woman?"

"She looks familiar, but you saw how it is out there."—he pointed to the Shack—"and Clippers gets a whole new set of people every week. She could have been there that night. They say that's where he picked her up. I remember Travis talking to a pretty brown-haired girl, but it's hard to tell from the picture on the news whether it was her or not. The picture the cops had wasn't any better."

"Oh, they've been around?"

"Man, they've covered this place like a blanket. Talked to everyone. Wanted to know people, places, times."

Kara finished her beer with a contented sigh, and daintily wiped her lips. The bartender kept watching her, no doubt curious what someone like that was doing with someone like me. He probably assumed I had a lot of money and was stepping out on my wife.

We ordered hamburgers and took them out to the deck overlooking the ocean. It was a beautiful night; the just-past-full moon loomed over the surf breaking gently on the beach. Here and there bodies huddled together in the shadows. Some of the lucky winners in the dance floor mating game, no doubt.

I was too tired to be good company, so we ate in silence. Finally, Kara went inside to listen to the band. I just watched the waves come closer and closer to the huddled bodies on the beach.

CHAPTER
5

The next morning, my mental alarm clock woke me up and drove me to my to-do list. I toiled over assignments and schedules for all the interviews and research that we needed to accomplish in the next several days until I had an ambitious but achievable schedule, then joined Kara and Ted for a run on the beach. Showered and refreshed, ready to attack the day, I charged into the new war room that the hotel manager had laid out according to Kara's specifications.

Sherwood blew my plans out of the water. "Good list, Clifford," he said, chewing on a Danish. He paused, gave me a little grin, and shrugged. "Sorry, but I have to leave tonight for Galveston." Galveston was a Blue Team case involving two savings and loan executives who allegedly were a little free and easy with their depositors' money. It was set for trial in a couple of weeks. "I want Keith's story before I leave," Sherwood said, "and I want as much of this other information as we can get first."

I stared at my legal pad. This was not unusual: Sherwood often forgot to let the rest of us know what he was doing. I sighed and began to redeploy.

• • •

A couple of hours later, I opened the door to the war room to find boxes stacked in every available open space. The equipment had arrived from the firm. Before Sherwood had changed everything, Kara was to set it up. Now she was at the hospital, trying to find out what she could from the medical staff. I sighed, flipped on the television to monitor the hearing, and started to work with my little Swiss Army knife.

The manager of the Mariner had not been at all helpful. Oh, he was cooperative enough, but he did not know anything. He hoped this terrible matter would be resolved soon. What he really hoped, I surmised, was that the hotel corporation would not hold him responsible for hiring a killer. Travis Keith had come highly recommended by one of the manager's classmates from the hotel school at Cornell University, who ran another establishment in the same chain at a Utah ski resort called Mount Passarell. Keith had rented equipment there last winter.

Victim 13, Allison Bolder, had disappeared at Mount Passarell last winter.

Edgar came in and groaned when he saw the boxes. "Whatever happened to quill pens for lawyers?" he muttered as he pitched in to help.

I found the VCR and hooked it up to tape the hearing that was about to start. "Any luck?" I asked Edgar.

"Talked to the arresting officer. Everson. The locals found him on the side of the road and took him in the woods where they had Keith tied up. The girl was unconscious. Keith was dazed himself. Seemed more confused than anything else, according to Everson. I have the arrest report and the inventory of personal effects."

I glanced at the inventory. It included a gym bag that contained a six-inch knife with a double-edged blade. The

Ripper used a knife with a double-edged blade. The rest of the bag's contents looked like a shopping list of household items: snacks, suntan lotion, condoms, trash. Keith must have lived out of the thing.

"The other big news," Edgar said, "is that two detectives are in town from that task force that coordinates the Ripper investigations. They're from Caliano, California, one of the more aggressive jurisdictions."

We had unloaded most of the boxes and were sorting out wires when the hearing started. Ed Bernsten and the FiveAlive News Team were all over it. I sat down to watch; Edgar cleared a place on the table for his laptop and began to write up his notes.

The hearing went as expected: short and to the point. The prosecutor presented Deputy Everson and a few affidavits, plenty to get the case bound over, but nothing particularly informative. Judge Whoten denied bail, despite Sherwood's impassioned and well-reasoned plea. The television people were all excited when the judge set a trial date three months off, but that was just to comply with the state's Speedy Trial Act. Everyone else knew that it would never happen that fast.

I dived into my major function as Team Leader: juggling resources to accomplish what could not be accomplished in the time allotted. I was on one phone talking to several associates about legal research when Pete called in on another line to say that he had arranged an interview with the rescuers. As I hung up with him, Kara returned from the hospital.

She stood at the door, staring in shock at her war room, then gingerly picked her way through the spaghetti tangle of wires draped over shipping boxes and pieces of computer equipment. "What in the world have you all been doing here?" she said.

"Oh, we got involved with some projects and didn't have a chance to finish. Sorry." I tried to sound contrite. Edgar buried himself in his memo, pretending to be an innocent bystander.

"Well, you all get out of here and go investigate something while I put this together." She rummaged through the piles, fussing the whole time. "You all haven't lost any of the parts, have you? I swear, they shouldn't let lawyers open boxes. You all never put anything away."

"It's all there somewhere. How did you make out at the hospital?"

She moved a pile of diskettes from one of the chairs and sat down, looking around in dismay as she talked. "Well, I met Dr. Lawson, Dorothy Catterman's attending physician. He's the nicest little man, just talked and talked and talked."

After learning all about Dr. Lawson's life history and current marital problems, Kara actually found out some information about the Catterman woman. She was heavily sedated, suffering from miscellaneous internal damage and bleeding that had required surgical repair. Brain damage remained a possibility. But she would live. The doctor saw no specific signs of strangulation. She had rope burns on her wrists and ankles.

"Dr. Lawson asked me if I wanted to see her"—Kara shuddered slightly—"but I thought I better not. The police have some men sitting there in the Intensive Care Unit with a tape recorder, but she hasn't said anything coherent, so they spend their time flirting with the nurses." She glanced at Edgar. "What's in the envelopes?"

I wouldn't let her look at the pictures. Instead, I sent her over to Clippers to see what else she could find out about the victim.

• • •

"This next place will be a kind of change of pace for you all," Pete Bannister told Edgar and me. "I recommend you take off your ties. They don't see too many ties at the Red Horse Tavern." We were in Pete's car, driving down a back road on the mainland side of the sound.

"Now these two boys are not exactly your upstanding citizens," Pete explained. "The Swiltons are a sort of clan down here. There's a bunch of them and they do have a tendency to marry each other, if you know what I mean.

"I don't know Eddie and Bobby, the Swiltons we're going to see. They have a roadside shrimp stand for the tourists. I don't recommend buying from them; the local joke is that Swilton shrimp glows in the dark."

He turned onto a dirt road. "The Red Horse Tavern is a Swilton hangout. The place is kind of rough, but I've done a little work for Joey, he's the owner, so I don't think we'll have a problem."

Calling the Red Horse kind of rough was like calling the Bombardiers kind of loud. It was a clapboard shack with a rotten pier leaning out into the inlet. The building once might have been white with a green roof, but now it was a blend of gray and sand and wood rot. The neon sign buzzed loudly. As Pete pushed open the unpainted wooden door, I noticed the Health Department rejection notice clearly displayed as required by law.

We squinted while our eyes adjusted to the darkness. The place fell silent. Even the jukebox went off. Inconspicuous we were not.

"Mr. Pete, how you doing?" A very large man with a scraggly beard and an apron the approximate color of the building came up to us.

"How's by you, Joey?" Pete said. "These're some friends of mine. Looking for Eddie and Bobby. They here?"

The patrons decided it was not a raid or a fight and

returned to their discussions. The jukebox came back on. Joey pointed to a far corner. It looked like our boys had been there awhile. An impressive collection of dead long necks filled the table.

"Pete," I said as we pulled back on the main road, "I've interviewed folks in small towns all over the South, and I thought I'd heard about every accent there is. But I swear I couldn't understand a word those guys said."

"Well," he answered sympathetically, "they were pretty drunk. You get a Swilton slurring his words and it's kind of tough to make out."

"I was never clear on which one was Eddie and which one was Bobby," said Edgar. That made me feel better. He was a trained professional.

By comparing notes, we managed to piece together their story. On the night in question, they took a short cut through the woods at the south end of the island, across from Clippers, to check on some crab pots they kept in the sound. They heard screams. They found Keith beating Dorothy Catterman and ripping off her clothes. They yelled and tried to grab him. He fought back ("like in them kay-rat-tee movies"), but one of them managed to club him with a rifle. They freed Dorothy, used the rope to tie up Keith, then ran back to their truck to go for some help. As it happened, Deputy Everson had spotted their truck on the side of the road and stopped to investigate. He radioed for assistance, and the rest was history. Bobby and Eddie were heroes.

We only asked a few questions, like why they carried a rifle. "Bears," Bobby (or Eddie) giggled.

Pete took them through the story three times. Best we could tell, it was almost word for word each time. Set in stone by now.

"They're impeachable." I was confident. "The prosecution can't be happy with them as the principal witnesses. They just recited the damn thing by rote."

Pete did not share my enthusiasm. "Swiltons aren't exactly known for their imaginations, Cliff, and that's a pretty big story for those boys to make up all by themselves. Keep in mind they've been holding court in there for three days now, telling that story to anyone who came in. But it still could be basically true. That's the way local folks might see it, anyway."

"What were they really doing in those woods?" Edgar asked.

"Probably poaching. Looking for deer to shine. And I expect they do have some crab pots over there. Most likely, they planned to park by the road, check the pots, then do some hunting. If anyone came by, they'd have the crabs as an excuse. No cop or game warden is crazy enough to poke around alone in those woods at night anyway. Too easy to get shot. The most he'd do is what Everson did, wait by the truck and call for help if he hears shots."

Pete probably was right about a local jury, but despite what he said, I felt a little better about this case. The Ripper cases were a different story.

Sherwood had Ted handle the initial part of Keith's interview; he wanted the client to have confidence in the handholder. Ted tried his best to tone down his usual academic vocabulary. He was nervous: this was almost an audition for Red Team Leader.

Ted started by reassuring Keith that the hearing had gone splendidly, then covered the background information we had gathered. Keith mostly listened. I had thought he was in shock yesterday; now I began to believe he was always like that: remote, unresponsive, as if observing a not particularly interesting lecture. Sometimes he was present, other times he was gone.

Per standard operating procedure, Ted went through the charges, which now included sexual assault and attempted murder, covered more background, then repeated the charges, with particular emphasis on what exactly the State had to prove. He even made Keith repeat the elements of the crimes. A nice touch.

Sherwood took over after a break to let Keith collect his thoughts and refine his story. He was Uncle Lew again. "Tell us what happened, Travis," he said softly.

Keith shrugged. "It was nothing like they said, Lew. We were getting it on pretty good in the woods, and then something smashed me in the head, and that's all I remember. Next thing I knew, I was all tied up and this cop and these two big rednecks was looking at me."

The only time Sherwood displayed patience was with clients. "Let's go back to the start, Travis. How did you meet Dorothy Catterman?"

Keith shrugged. "At the Mariner. The Shag Shack. We just talked, danced."

"Why did you go to the Shack?"

"Just to have some fun."

"Did you talk to anyone else?"

Keith suddenly smiled, a big broad smile. "Oh, yeah," he said. The smile gave him a charming, boyish look. "Talked to some of the guys that work there, the bartender, I forget his name. And danced with a few other young ladies."

"Do you remember any of their names?"

He shook his head; the smile was still in place. "No, sir. Hard to get names there. It's real loud, you know. Fact is, I didn't know Dorothy Catterman's name until Pete told me. I thought it was Dora or something." The smile was frozen there, no longer appropriate.

Sherwood nodded and wrote something on his legal pad. Keith's smile gradually disappeared as he waited. He glanced up at the bars on the window.

"What happened after you met Dorothy?" Sherwood asked, putting a slight emphasis on the name.

Keith kept his eyes on the bars. "Oh, we danced some. Talked some. After a while, went out on the beach and made out. She was pretty hot." The smile came back. His eye fell on Kara and he suddenly looked nervous. "Sorry," he said. She gave him a neutral little smile.

Sherwood brought him back. "How long were you at the beach?"

"I don't know. Awhile. Then"—he took a deep breath—"I asked her did she want to go somewhere more private. There were too many people lying around on the beach. She said yes, so we got in my car."

Sherwood just waited this time. Keith looked back at the bars on the window. "We drove around for a while. Stopped in somewhere to get some beer and some, uh, rubbers. Then I pulled off on a side road and we took a blanket and the beer and stuff and went back in the woods."

"Where was the store? And how did you pay? Cash? Credit card?"

"Cash. A Quik-Stop or something. On the beach road."

Sherwood nodded, encouraging. "Then what?"

"Like I said. We started to get it on pretty good and something happened and I don't remember anything till the cop was there."

"That's it?"

"That's it."

Sherwood rose and walked around the table once, stretching. "Ted?" he said as he moved to the corner and stood watching. He was taking the measure of the man as a witness.

Ted cleared his throat. "Did you tie her up?"

"No, sir."

"Why did you have a clothesline with you?"

"I keep it in my gym bag. To tie my surfboard on the car."

"Where is the surfboard?"

"Back in my trailer. I take it with me when I open the stand in the morning."

"Why did you have a knife in your bag?"

Keith glanced at the head of the table and seemed to notice for the first time that Sherwood's chair was empty. He looked around in alarm and found Sherwood in the corner. "Look," he said, with the first sign of energy we had seen, "I didn't do any of this, man. I'm telling you."

Sherwood walked over and patted him on the shoulder. "We have to ask the questions, Travis. These are questions the prosecutors will ask. Don't worry, we're on your side."

Keith slumped in his chair and stared at Ted. "What?" he said.

"Why did you have a knife in your bag?"

The man sighed. "I got all sorts of shit in my bag." He looked at Kara again. "Sorry." He leaned forward, intent now, like he wanted to be believed. "See, I just throw stuff in there and carry it around. Clean it out once in a while. That knife"—he paused—"that knife's from the Army. I always carry it around. Lots of times you need a knife. Nothing wrong with that, is there?"

That night in the war room Sherwood slowly read Edgar's memorandum, making an occasional note in the margin. He had sent Pete home, and Edgar was having dinner with Sheriff Sanderson. Ted and Kara, who had already finished the memo, eyed the manila envelopes in front of me on the conference table. "I don't want to look at those," Kara said softly. Ted was silent.

Sherwood put down the memo. He looked around the table at us and sighed. "Let me see them," he said.

I pushed the envelopes across to him, curious to see his reaction. Normally, he would look at the worst evidence with no change in expression. It was a skill that came from years of sitting in courtrooms. You never react, even when the prosecution's witness has just surprised you with some damning testimony, because the jury may be watching. I could do it in court, but it was not automatic every place else. I couldn't do it with something like this.

Sherwood gazed at me with those piercing blue eyes for a moment, then slid the top picture out of the envelope. He looked down, winced visibly, gasped, and looked back up. He took a deep breath and looked down again. "Horrible," he said in a very soft voice. "Just horrible." Then he set his face in a mask and reviewed all of them, one at a time, taking care to replace each in its envelope. Kara looked away to avoid seeing them.

Sherwood stared at the last picture. "Horrible," he said again. Then he cocked his head to one side and brought the photograph closer, studying something. He frowned, put the picture back in the envelope, and looked up at me. "They're right. This Ripper's a vet."

"Stevens said you'd recognize that," I said.

"Yeah. They talked about it in Nam. Never saw the real thing, but I saw something close in SERE."

"What's SERE?" Kara asked.

"It's an acronym for something like Survival, Evasion, Resistance, and Escape. POW training. They ran some of the troops through it before they went to Nam. Simulated being separated from your unit and captured as a POW. They'd strand you on this island to live off the land. After a couple of days, some instructors playing the role of enemies captured you and treated you like the NV treated POWs." He stood and demonstrated. "Did you see how that rope runs behind the back and around the neck, then down to the ankles? That's the way the NV used to tie up prisoners."

That brought back a memory from my Navy days. "You know," I said, "I remember some of the pilots on the carrier talking about SERE. They said it was terrifying, even though you knew the so-called enemy was on your side and wouldn't kill you."

Sherwood shook his head. "When I went through SERE, they had things like that scattered around." He pointed to the manila envelopes. "Called them 'warnings.' The idea was to condition you to running into them in the jungle. They used dummies, but realistic as hell. Sprayed them with something to attract flies, just like real life. Scared hell out of you when you came across one."

Sherwood didn't talk about his war experiences, but the Navy Cross hanging on the wall of his office added to the legend. The framed commendation described some kind of ambush. In interviews, he always said that experience had led him to attend law school and then specialize in criminal defense. It made him want to help the underdog.

Sherwood stared at the envelopes for a minute. "This may not be so bad. They still must have that training for pilots, and special operations types. Maybe even Army Rangers. Clifford, have Edgar check it out. Find out the status of the training and whether they still display the 'warnings.' And find out who's been through it. Probably thousands and thousands of people. Maybe training films; find out if they made any."

He free-associated. "Movies. Kara, see if any war movies have scenes like this in them. Or descriptions in books. Or magazines. Check out survivalists and those paramilitary clowns that run around playing soldier. They might have their own SEREs. We want to show that so many people know about this 'warning' that Keith's military training doesn't prove anything."

It was classic Sherwood, changing bad facts into good facts. Before long, he would develop some theory that Keith's military training precluded him from being the Ripper. A secret hypnotic suggestion or something.

Kara looked at her watch. "Lewis, don't you need to leave?" she said.

Sherwood checked the time. "In a minute." When you fly your own plane, you can be flexible. "What's our defense in the Catterman case, people?"

I piped up. Pete was not here, so I could brainstorm freely. "I'll tell you, I think Keith's story can fly. What about this? It's just as he says. Keith picks up the girl—that all unfolds the way he told us. They're in the woods, and here come Eddie and Bobby on their little poaching expedition. They see a chance to get some action, so they slug Keith and attack the girl. She puts up a fight; they beat her, tie her up, and get ready to rape her. That explains her rope burns."

I was pacing the floor now, liking this theory better and better. "Then they hear that cop, Everson. It's a warm night, he has his window down. Maybe they spot his light, maybe they hear his radio. Anyway, they panic. They untie the girl, tie up Keith, and run out and tell the cop their rescue story. Our man's an innocent victim. And so is Dorothy Catterman."

"I swear that sounds a little like *Deliverance,*" said Kara. She was an English major. Maybe my theory was not as original as I thought.

"These Swiltons are real lowlife," I said. "Pete seems to think people will believe them for some reason, but you can eat them alive on cross, Lew."

Sherwood cautioned, "Pete has a pretty good feel for local sentiment."

"Yeah, I know, but we're only talking reasonable doubt here." I plunged on. "Obviously this all depends on what the Catterman woman says. If she comes out with a contradictory story, then we fall back on a kinky sex scenario. The locals probably think Clippers is Sodom and Gomorrah anyway. We suggest that she screamed rape because she was embarrassed when the Swiltons came across them. Dig up some dirt on her background, turn her into the one on trial. The usual sex crime defense." Kara wrinkled her nose at that. She had never worked on a rape case.

"I suppose it's possible," said Sherwood, without conviction. "At least it's a working theory. Ted, don't let Keith get too locked into his story yet." Ted nodded.

"I think it depends on what Dorothy Catterman says," Kara offered. She was right.

Sherwood dismissed Kara and Ted to go have dinner. She made him promise that he would indeed leave for the airport shortly, then offered to bring me something back. When they left, we began to plan for the long haul.

Sherwood drummed his fingers on the table. "I'll have your hide if you tell the others this, but this Catterman case doesn't worry me. Pete easily could handle it alone. It's the Ripper claims that are key here. This is too important to fool around. I want you and Edgar personally to investigate each one of these."

He had just sentenced me to an endless string of hotel rooms and airport lobbies. But I couldn't disagree with him because he was right.

Sherwood drove the point home. "Ted can cover things here, and you can use Edgar's investigators or some of our people to dig into Catterman's background, but I don't trust them at the murder sites. I want you and Edgar there. Kara if you need her. No one else." He tapped one finger on the table for emphasis. "I want detailed reports of everything you find out. We need to hit this fast and hard, Clifford. I have a feeling it's going to break wide open any minute. You get what you can out of Keith tomorrow, then hit the road."

"Do we have a budget here?" I asked. The $5,000 was long gone. "All this travel will be expensive."

Sherwood thought for a minute. "Don't worry about it. Don't be extravagant, but spend whatever you have to. We need to make sure Pete gets paid. I talked to the sister; she can afford to cover him. For us, well, there's a book or movie at the end of something like this. We can get our fee out of that. If I have to, I'll write it myself." Sherwood had written three books about his most publicized cases, all of which had sold well and brought business to the firm.

We covered more issues, and Sherwood doled out another month or two worth of work for someone, most likely associates, to complete in a week or two. "We can't let a jury see those pictures," he said at the end. "Find a way to keep them out." I made a note.

"What do you think, Lew?" I asked when he finished.

Sherwood was piling his papers in his open briefcase. He stopped and looked at me. "Right now, Clifford, I'd rather have the prosecution's case than ours. We need to change that."

I wanted him to read some of the articles I had pulled off the computer, so I went to retrieve them from my room. When I came back in, Sherwood sat at the head of the table. The victim photographs were spread out before him. He glanced at me, then turned back to stare at them. "Just horrible," he said. "We have to keep them out."

CHAPTER
6

The next morning, we asked Travis Keith about the Resort Ripper.

"Travis?" I said gently. "Try to remember. I know it's hard."

Keith stared at the bars on the window of the interview room. He had been staring at them for a good three minutes, silent, unmoving. A bird looking out from its cage, I thought. His fists clenched and unclenched. Maybe he was a tiger waiting for an opening to escape. Finally, he sighed and gave me a look like my son did when he was trying to tell a story and could not think of the words.

"I'm trying, Mr. Nielson," he said, "but I just don't know when I was there."

Pcte broke in. "Let's take a little break." Keith resumed his study of the window. I stretched, then moved behind Edgar and looked over his shoulder to study the list on the table. It showed the dates and places of the Ripper murders. Edgar was keeping score with his own system. A little "W" meant Keith had worked at that resort. A check mark meant he had been there. An "N" meant he had never been there. A question mark meant he didn't remember.

So far, they were all W's and check marks. Even Santa Catalina and Stowe.

I started over. "All right, Travis. First, please call me Cliff. Now, let's recap some of this.

"You were discharged from the Army about ten years ago because you refused to follow an illegal order. Right?" He nodded.

"You decided to 'live to have fun,' and started working at different resorts in season, right? Once in a while you take some odd jobs here and there?"

"Yeah," he said. "Once in a while."

"And you almost never go back to the same resort the next year?"

"I want to see new places."

"But you can't give us the dates you were at any of these places where the murders happened?"

"Man, I told you. I don't worry about dates. It's like winter and summer, you know?" He looked worried and upset. "I forget. I been a lot of places."

"That's okay." I tried to be reassuring. "We'll figure it out some other way. Let's finish the list first. What's next, Edgar?"

Edgar ran his pen down the side of his Ripper list. "Just a couple more. Caliano, California."

Keith's brow furrowed. "Where's that?"

Kara pushed the Rand McNally across the table to him. "It's right here, Travis. On the Monterey Peninsula."

Keith studied the map, his lips moving slightly as he read names to himself. "I think I been through it. Been to Carmel. Worked once at this place: Poloma Beach." He pointed to a dot on the coast that looked to be about an hour's drive from Caliano. That rated a "W" from Edgar.

"Summer or winter?"

He gave me a surprised look. "Summer, man. No snow there in the winter."

"Sorry. That was a dumb question. You remember anything about it?"

He was back to the window again. I turned so he couldn't see me give Kara an exasperated glance. This had been going on for hours.

"Yeah," he finally said. "I tended bar at that place. A hotel. Can't remember the name. Surfing sucked, so I quit and went on down to San Diego."

We finished the list with about the same results, and I asked Edgar to pass it to me. Keith had been to all of them; worked at most.

I gave the next question some thought. "Travis, you remember hearing about any murders while you were at these places?"

"Yeah, some. Mount Passarell, for sure. Maybe some others. Sometimes guys would talk about them. I don't pay much attention to the news though."

"How do we explain that you have been to almost all of these murder sites?"

He winced, then spoke urgently. "Listen, man, there's lots of guys like me." He gestured at the list. "Those aren't little road stops, you know. Lots of people go there. A bunch of us move around and work these places."

Ted piped up. "Sort of a subculture of migrant resort workers?" Keith looked at him blankly.

Edgar said quietly, "Do you have any names?"

Keith thought some more. "Yeah. There's a guy named Tommy. He's worked a lot of these places. Others too. Boots. Skip. There's guests. I'd run into guests that I'd seen somewhere else all the time. A guy named John—I was thinking about him last night for some reason." He paused and shook his head. "Only met him once, I guess, but there's others. Girls too, you care about them?"

"Any last names?" Edgar was taking notes.

"Tommy is Tommy Parsons."

"How about the others? Boots, Skip, John?"

"Dunno."

"Do you know where any of them are now?"

"Tommy's from like Kansas or Nebraska or someplace like that. John was from the South. Boots, Minnesota or Michigan maybe. Don't know about Skip."

This was getting us nowhere. "Travis," I said, "I want you to make a list of everyone you can think of that might have been around these places when you were. Give it to Ted, then you all can go over it. Work on it for the next few days, okay?"

"Sure."

"Let's think about how we can get some dates when you were at these locations. You have any credit cards? Checking accounts? Tax records? That sort of thing?"

"Sure."

"Where are they?" This was like pulling teeth. I heaved a mental sigh of relief that Ted was the handholder and not me. I would not have the patience.

"Around. I got safe deposit boxes a couple of places. My sister's got some. I use her address."

"This is your sister in Iowa?"

"Yeah. Call her."

Ted made a note. "I'll talk to her," he said.

I checked my list of information I wanted before Edgar and I set out. "Travis, I need to know something. Have you ever been arrested before?"

He hesitated for a long moment. "In the Army. I told you about that."

"Any other times?"

"Once or twice for things like peeing in a parking lot, joyriding. When I was a kid. Kid stuff, you know. Some fights later on. I've been a bouncer. It goes with the job."

"And?"

"There was this one time." His voice was tentative. "Girl said I raped her. Wasn't true though, I swear. She was a guest at a resort, a rich kid, you know, and her mother caught us getting it on, so she hollered rape. They dropped the charges."

I tried not to react. "All right, give Ted the details on that. Any others?"

"Maybe some speeding tickets, if you need to know about them."

"Yeah, give Ted everything you can remember." I started to wrap it up. "We'll get all the records and use them to put together some dates with these places. You work on those lists and give Ted the details over the next couple of days. Edgar and I are hitting the road tonight to check out these murder spots. So we won't be around for a while, but we'll check in with Ted. He and Pete will be here."

"Where's Mr. Sherwood?" Keith asked with a note of doubt.

"He's in Galveston with another case. But don't worry. He'll stay right on top of this too. We keep him posted, and he knows everything that's going on."

Always leave your client on a positive note. That was a Sherwood's Rule. I patted Keith on the shoulder. "This has been a big help, Travis. You take it easy and work on remembering those names and all you can, and pass it on to Ted and Pete. We'll take care of the rest."

Back at the war room, Edgar and I went over our notes, scratched our heads over how to find the people Keith had mentioned, then considered the next step. "Why don't you go home?" I said finally. "I'll catch the last flight tonight or the early flight in the morning, and meet you at the firm tomorrow. We'll lay out an itinerary then and take off tomorrow night or the next day."

He looked dubious. "You sure?"

"I'm sure. We'll be on the road for most of the next month. Go see Elise and Bobby."

I had ulterior motives, several of them. I wanted to call my son Preston out in Kansas. I also had promised to provide Stevens with some background; I felt uneasy leaving that to Ted. Most important, this road trip could last several weeks, so I wanted another night with Kara; she would be setting up our war room at the firm. An extra night in Johnston Beach would be a nice reward, I thought. I deserved one.

Edgar left to catch his plane. I called Preston; he gave me a play-by-play of his soccer game and filled me in on all the big news from the third grade, then we talked some about his upcoming visit. After about twenty minutes, we said goodbye, I love you, and I hung up feeling lonely and depressed. I missed him a lot.

Around the time I started to come out of my funk, Ted and Kara called in to invite me to dinner with Pete. I declined and called Stevens, who said he would come right over. Then, in an abundance of caution, I called Tom Collins, my big-time Washington newspaper contact who covered the Pentagon for the *Post*. He was the brother of my best friend at the firm, Francine Collins.

"Sure, I know Tim Stevens," Tom said. "Is he trying to pry something out of you?"

"No, I just want to find out his background. Is he reputable? Can he keep a secret?"

Tom laughed. "Can a reporter keep a secret? That's like asking, 'Can I trust a lawyer?' "

"Depends on the situation," I said.

"Same thing," he answered. "Really, the question is whether he follows the rules. Stevens is a first-rate journalist, and he follows the rules. If he promises to keep something quiet, he will. You know his history?"

"Just that he was a war correspondent in Nam, and now he covers the Resort Ripper for one of the Miami papers."

Tom gave me the lowdown. "Stevens won a pile of awards back in the sixties for his Nam stories, then went to New York on a fast track with the *Times*. Left there after about a year. The story I heard was his wife hated New York: she wanted to raise their kids somewhere else. So he went with the *Miami Observer*.

"He's a straight arrow, hell of a reporter. Make sure you agree on the ground rules first."

When Stevens showed up, I found a couple of beers in the refrigerator, and we went out to the balcony. Per Sherwood's instructions, I fed him our version of the Catterman incident and my Swilton theory. He rolled his eyes. "Any evidence to support any of this, counselor? Or are you dreaming?"

"We are pursuing the investigation," I said pompously.

"Uh-huh." He said the words aloud as he wrote: "No Evidence," and underlined it twice. Then he took a swallow of beer. "Where's Sherwood?"

"Galveston, I guess. He has a trial there."

Stevens had put his pen down. "How do you keep in touch with him?" he asked. "Those beepers?"

"The computer network helps."

"What's he like to work for?"

Most lawyers in the firm, especially those who worked in other departments, would say Sherwood was one of the worst bosses in the world. Incredibly demanding. Unreasonable in his assignments. Intolerant of anything less than total sacrifice to the job.

I considered those characteristics part of a commitment to excellence and to his clients that made Sherwood such a great trial lawyer. If you wanted to be a great trial lawyer, he was a superb role model. You learned more working for him than you could anywhere else, and after he trusted you, he gave you enormous responsibility.

None of that was for public consumption. I looked at Stevens with a deadpan expression and said, "Working for Lew Sherwood is inspirational."

"He's not married anymore, right? Ditched wife number two a few years ago?" I didn't answer. "How does he meet those women he squires around to the celebrity parties?"

I handed Stevens a copy of Sherwood's official firm biography. "This is all I know about Lew's personal life, Tim."

He scanned it, muttering. "All-State football player, blah, blah; Navy, blah, blah; Medals, blah, blah; Murder trials, blah, blah; Ramwell and Bosely, blah, blah." Then he tossed it to one side. "That's a pretty press testimonial, but it's pure bullshit. Hell, I've written that story three times already. More vividly, I might add. Give me some real stuff, will you?"

I shrugged. "That's all we put out on Lew. We feel very strongly that press attention should focus on the facts of the case, not on the lawyers."

Stevens gave me an exaggerated wide-eyed stare. "That was very good, Cliff. And with a perfectly straight face." Sarcasm dripped from his voice. "And of course I know that Lewis Sherwood doesn't like attention. That's why we see him on TV talk shows and in magazines every day. Shit, give me a break."

Stevens was not the first reporter to pump me for scandal or inside information. I decided to nip this in the bud. "Tim, I'll talk about the case, like we agreed. If you want to know something about Lew, ask him." I stood. "Another beer?"

Stevens accepted my beer. I must not have offended him too badly.

Kara appeared with a pizza shortly after Stevens left. Mushroom, sausage, and pepperoni. I shoved papers aside to make room on the table, and we talked about organizing ourselves as I ate.

More accurately, she told me how she planned to organize us. "I made up sets of investigation folders, one for 'Resort Ripper—General' and a separate one for each murder. The memos you all write go there. Then a 'Keith, Travis—Personal' folder for memos about him. The Legal Research files I divided into 'Johnston Beach' and 'Resort Ripper.' Won't those have different legal issues?"

My mouth was full, so I simply nodded. She described the rest of her plans. A case like this would be the death of many trees, and one of a paralegal's tasks was to organize the paper for the lawyers, who were incapable of doing it themselves.

"Now, on the computer," she said, "we'll keep the indices to the files, and I'll put the memos in full text so you can search them online." That would allow us to enter words and phrases and find everything that had to do with the topic. It could save hours of rummaging around in files, trying to find a memo you vaguely remembered from months before. It also freed us from lugging huge piles of paper around the country. If we wanted something, we could call in on our laptop computers and get it.

"Do you want the evidentiary documents on CD-ROM?" Kara asked. She was way ahead of me now. Ordinarily I would have told her to go ahead, but here I needed to watch the cost. Taking pictures of every scrap of paper and converting them to computer disks gets very expensive very quickly.

"Hold off on that," I said. "For now, we can scan in selected documents and keep them on the firm system."

Ted appeared and Kara started describing her organization to him, so I took a post-pizza swim, showered, then stretched out on my bed to watch the late news and wait for her. She frowned as she entered through the adjoining door. "Bad news, Shug."

"What?"

"Anna Sorrells sent me a message. Lewis is pulling me off to help him in Galveston." Anna was Kara's counterpart on the Blue Team.

"Aw, shit. Why?"

"Anna's pregnant, you know. Her doctor told her not to travel. And her husband told her a long time ago she had to quit working for Lewis because of the pressure. So she's transferring to civil litigation. Lewis wants me to take over and get things organized."

This was serious. It left me with no one to put our case together in an orderly fashion. Not to mention what it did to my social life. "What are we supposed to do?" I whined.

Kara shrugged. "I'll brief Belinda. Al and Sheri can help too."

"None of them has any experience."

"They have to learn sometime, Cliff."

I started pacing the room, and then I lost it. "Jesus." The Ripper stories were on the credenza; I threw them at the TV. "He fucking makes me go out myself and investigate these damn things, then he takes you away. And says he wants everything done in a fucking month. How the hell does he expect me to do it with no fucking help? All because those other assholes can't run their own case?" I stared at the wall, breathing heavily. "Shit."

Kara stood out of range, watching, until my tantrum ended. Throwing those papers helped. Her voice was soothing. "He has confidence in you, Cliff. He knows you can handle it." When I did not react violently, she moved close to me with a sly grin. "It's nice to know you think I'm so wonderful."

Things were just getting interesting when the damn beepers went off. Sure enough, Sherwood demanded Kara's presence immediately. That ruined the mood. She gave me a quick hug and a wistful smile. "I have to pack and catch that plane. You be sure to miss me, hear? Enjoy the resort tour."

"Yeah," I said. "It'll be great."

CHAPTER
7

I had worked up a major case of self-pity by the next morning when I walked through the heavy cherry doors at the firm. Lisa, the pretty young receptionist, smiled at me. As usual, a couple of the younger bachelor lawyers hung around her desk, pretending to read messages. They would strike out: Lisa's taste ran to bikers and men who could two-step. Very few of our lawyers could two-step.

I studied the Big Three on the wall behind Lisa while I waited my turn. The Founders, Mr. Ramwell on the left and Judge Bosely on the right, looked down benignly from their gilt frames. Senator Braxton, in the middle, gazed with determination at some distant vision.

The Founders were a remarkable pair, if you believed the published histories of Queenston. Back around World War I, Mr. Ramwell represented the largest bank in the state, and Mr. Bosely had the railroads and textile manufacturers. According to legend, they dined together one evening at the Queenston Club, then retired to share brandy, cigars, their client lists, and their vision of the future. The partnership they formed soon had its pick of any of the legal business in town.

By then, Atlanta, to the west, had emerged from the ashes of Sherman's March, and Charlotte, to the east, was becoming a major financial center. Despite a prime location near the intersection of three states, with access to navigable rivers, Queenston had barely grown from the sleepy town that Sherman had not bothered to torch.

The Founders responded by forming the legendary "Group of Nine," a benevolent oligarchy of civic and business leaders who ran Queenston, regardless of what the mayor and city council may have thought. They did their job well: Queenston and Atlanta now jockeyed for position as the unofficial capital of the South, having left pretenders like Birmingham and Charlotte far behind.

The Founders would have liked the place now, with 300 lawyers, a national reputation, and a lobby that exuded the subtle aroma of money and power, but I felt sure they would disapprove of our group. Much of the firm still did. Messrs. Ramwell and Bosely had refused to do criminal defense work. Not enough money in it and not the sort of clientele with whom they cared to associate.

Lisa's admirers had moved on. "You still don't have a secretary, do you?" she asked with that blinding smile.

"Shoot," I said. "I forgot." One more disaster. Ted and I shared a secretary, but she had quit last week, and neither of us had been in town long enough to think about hiring a replacement.

Lisa was used to secretarial turnover in our group. "Mr. Sherwood has a secretary today, and he's out of town." She glanced at a list next to her phone. "Her name is Alice. Are you here for a few days?"

I wanted to grunt and stomp my feet, but Lisa was too sweet, so I just muttered "Till tomorrow," took the messages she handed me, and headed toward our side of the building. I would have to call Joanne, the office manager, to arrange for a temp. The temp would not be able to type and would ask annoying questions. This was not a positive start to the day.

The Senator nodded to me as he strolled past, deep in conversation with a man I vaguely recognized from the news. They stopped before turning into his office on the north side of the building. It was the Senator's firm now and had been for nearly three decades, except for the two-year stretch when the Group of Nine persuaded him to serve out the unexpired term of one of the state's senators who resigned under a cloud of scandal. Many thought he was the most powerful man in the state.

The Senator's guest probably was a prospective client, because the Senator gestured toward Sherwood's Forest, as a firm wag had dubbed our set of offices years before. That, of course, made us the Band of Merry Men or, especially in the presence of the women on our team, simply the Band. The Senator had located Sherwood's Forest here on the 30th floor because he wanted Sherwood nearby to display for visiting dignitaries.

I wound my way through the Forest, listening to the computer keyboards click in secretarial cubicles scattered among the maze of interior halls and paralegal offices and conference rooms. When I passed Sherwood's suite, his secretary of the week smiled at me. She was an older lady, about fifty. Joanne must have hired her. Sherwood generally picked young, attractive secretaries to drive insane.

The lawyers had the windowed offices. I opened the door of mine and sighed at the stack of unopened mail on my desk chair. Lawyers with secretaries did not have that problem. I glanced through the mail to make sure nothing was from a court and tossed it on one of the visitor's chairs. Then I cleared a pile of pleadings off my keyboard, pulled

the sticky notes from my computer screen, and checked my
electronic mail.

Nothing terribly urgent. Several orders from Sherwood,
a few reports by other team members, routine updates on
some older matters. Fortunately, most of my other cases
sat in litigation limbo at the moment, waiting for a court
date. Kara had sent two messages. One provided complete and detailed instructions to Belinda, the paralegal
who would fill in for her. The entire Red Team received
a copy.

The other message could get both of us fired if anyone
in authority read it. Our E-mail system had a feature that
Kara and I used too much and for illicit functions: the
private and confidential message. The official purpose was
to allow a sender to transmit sensitive material guarded by
a prearranged password known only to the recipient. Kara
used it to send me personal, often ribald, notes when we
were in different towns.

This one was pretty tame by her usual standards: "Hi,
Shug. Miss you. Galveston's hot and sticky. I'd
rather get hot and sticky with you. :-) The trial starts
in a couple of weeks and the files are a mess.
:-(Looks like no weekends home for a while. :-<
Have fun on your trip. Don't forget to call Preston.
xxxx & :-)->8(-:"

The little collections of colons and parentheses drove
me nuts. They were symbols that computer bulletin board
junkies use in their electronic mail messages. The idea is to
look at them sideways, as if the left-hand side of the screen
is on top. That way, ":-)" becomes a little smiley face and
":-(" is a frown. Kara had made up the grouping after the
xxxx's herself. It was obscene.

Kara thought the little figures and faces were cute. They
made me want to throw up.

A knock came at the door, and I hastily deleted the message. It was the secretary from Sherwood's office. I struggled to remember her name. Alice? "Mr. Nielson?" she said. "I'm on my way for coffee. Would you like some?"

"Please," I said, afraid to call her the wrong name. "And I'm Cliff." Alice, if that was her name, looked cheerful. Obviously her first or second day on the job. Joanne once showed me the file drawer where she kept resumes and resignations for Sherwood's secretaries. They came in all excited about working for the great man and left babbling within a few days. The record for briefest tenure was four hours and twelve minutes, held by a lady who appeared bright and early one morning, then never returned from lunch. Sherwood never met her; he was out of town at the time. It took him two days of unanswered E-mail messages to realize she was missing.

Of course, he was the one who had a secretary today.

Alice came back with the coffee. "I told Joanne that I'm not too busy right now, and I can give you some help if you need it." She looked around the office with a slightly raised eyebrow. File folders sat in one of my visitor's chairs, overflowing onto the end table and a good portion of the floor. Another batch seemed to be breeding on my coffee table. The credenza still held the "read when you get time" collection of papers, memos, junk mail, and advance court decisions. It was nearly a foot high by now. My new mail had slid to the floor, unopened. "Maybe some filing?" she said.

"Thank you." I almost hugged her. We talked for a while about files and time sheets and other banes of a lawyer's existence. When she left, I immediately sent Joanne a discreet message, asking to hire Alice when she quit Sherwood. If the usual pattern held true, I might have a new secretary in a week or so.

• • •

A little later, I sent out for sandwiches and assembled my support staff in the newly designated war room that we would use as a headquarters. The staff was a problem. Kara was so efficient that we routinely assigned new paralegals to the Red Team for training. That worked fine as long as Kara was there, but now I had three paralegals—Belinda, Sheri, and Al—with a cumulative total of a year and a half of experience, most of it belonging to Belinda. The other two were fresh from school. Sam, the firm's computer guru, joined us.

Edgar gave them a concise overview of the murders, then I talked about the importance of numbering and filing every piece of paper. "I want all this on the computer," I told them. "We need to correlate Keith's whereabouts with the Ripper murders: Find out if he was in the area for each one, see if he has an alibi."

Belinda looked sideways at the others. She was a mousy little woman in her mid-twenties who had been competent on specific assignments but had shown little initiative. We hoped it would develop with experience. "How can we do that?" she said.

Sam wore his problem-solving face: wrinkled brow and pursed lips. "What kind of documents will you have?"

Edgar answered. "Credit-card receipts. Sales slips. Tax or employment records. We're not sure yet. Could be most anything."

Sam leaned back and stared at the ceiling through his glasses. In many ways, he looked like a typical computer guy, down to the short-sleeve white shirt and the little screwdriver he carried in his shirt pocket like a pen. In other ways, he didn't: he was black and had started at defensive tackle for three years at State. "What about the expense report system?" he said finally.

The expense report software was the result of another secretarial crisis. Like every other lawyer in the place, neither Ted nor I ever turned in expense reports until someone in the Accounting Department threatened to hold our pay checks. Then we would pile receipts and airline boarding passes on our secretary's desk and pace in front of her while she tried to make sense of them and complete the expense form. She finally vowed to quit if we did it again.

In response, Sam and I worked out a computer program that let my secretary start at the top of the pile and work her way to the bottom, typing in the information from each receipt. The computer then would calculate and print out our expense reports. The word spread, and our program soon became Standard Firm Procedure.

"That gives us itinerary, dates, locations, and sources," I said. "But I also need a way to find alibis."

"No problem," Sam said. "We can add some data elements, plug in what you know about the murders, then run a comparison. You can take it down to a minute-by-minute layout if your data's good enough." He launched into details that I understood only vaguely. The others looked totally bewildered.

I raised my hand to stop him. "When can you have it ready?"

"Three months."

I stared at him. He shrugged in apology. "Exams coming up. My sabbatical starts next week."

The fool wanted to be a lawyer, so he went to school at night during the year, with concentrated summer sessions. I thought he was crazy. Many days I would rather have had his job. I shook my head.

"I can get it started," Sam offered. "Leave you the data layouts, and you can write the reports."

Belinda saw me glance at her, and shrank in terror, afraid I was about to tell her to do it. But I bit my tongue. It wasn't their fault that I was now chief lawyer, chief paralegal, and chief computer grunt. With no secretary.

By mid-afternoon, I had developed an overwhelming urge to talk to a real person, one who did not deal in either computers or murder. So I rode down to the 27th floor to see if Francine was in.

"Hi, how about dinner tonight?" I asked.

Francine Collins lifted her light gray eyes from the papers on her desk and peered at me through the horn-rim glasses she wore in the office instead of contacts. She thought clients wanted their tax lawyers to look scholarly. I thought the deep tan and the expensive silk blouse and the tumble of auburn hair hanging to her shoulders defeated that purpose, but old habits die hard. When we first joined the firm, she always wore tailored suits with her hair up in a bun. Her husband Dennis complained that she looked like a spinster librarian.

"Clients don't trust attractive tax lawyers," Francine would say.

"Advertising agency presidents want sexy wives," Dennis would counter. She stopped wearing the bun, but she did not modernize her office wardrobe until after the divorce.

Francine smiled at me. "Well, if it isn't the Ripper Ranger," she said. "Kara out of town?"

"Yeah," I admitted. Francine was the only one at the firm who knew about Kara and me. "Is that what we're called now? Ripper Rangers?"

"That's probably the most polite thing. The Senator briefed us on your case at the partners' meeting. David Halloway pitched a fit."

David Halloway was her boss: the head of the Tax Department. "What's his problem?" I asked.

"He thinks it's unseemly. Bad for the firm's image. He's worried the clients will get nervous."

"Aw, he's just jealous because Sherwood gets all the publicity and glory."

Francine shook her head, then walked over to shut her door. "He's not the only one. Most of the other departments feel the same way." She sat back in her chair with a serious expression. "You better mend some fences, Hotshot. David controls a lot of votes when it's time to consider equity partners." Francine and I were junior partners: glorified employees with profit-sharing participation. The equity partners had more clout. The senior partners like Halloway held the real power.

"What did the Senator say to Halloway?"

She smiled despite herself. "He was very polite, as always. He listened carefully to everything David said and agreed that those were valid concerns."

"And?"

"And then he very diplomatically told him to shut up and mind his own business."

I chuckled. "Wish I'd been there. The Senator gives Lew anything he wants. That's why I don't give a shit about Halloway's votes. As long as Lew's on my side . . . " I shrugged.

Francine was about to say more, then decided against it. I knew she thought I was too cavalier, but I wasn't worried, because Sherwood was the Senator's personal project. About eight years ago, the president of one of the firm's major clients had been indicted for tax evasion, and the firm had to associate a criminal lawyer. The Senator saw the bills and concluded there is money to be made in criminal law if you represent the right kind of criminal. He conducted a quiet search for the best criminal defense lawyer in the country, then began to woo Lewis Sherwood.

It was a successful marriage. Sherwood's prominence brought in a flood of profitable legal matters for the firm's other departments. That pleased the Senator. Sherwood became rich and more famous, and he could hang out with celebrities and engage in as much (tasteful) self-promotion as he wanted, so long as he kept winning cases. That pleased him.

Most of the other departments thought we were a bunch of crude elitists, and we could not expect much support from them at voting time, but the Senator wanted to keep Sherwood happy, which was all that mattered. The Senator was the most senior partner. What he said, went. Sherwood took very good care of his people at the partners' meetings. Of course, if you screwed up, you were no longer one of his people. I didn't plan to screw up.

Francine did not bother to tell me again that I put too much faith in Sherwood. She changed the subject. "When did you get back?"

"This morning." I leafed through a tax book on her desk. It was incomprehensible to a dumb litigator like me. "I leave tomorrow for a quick tour of a dozen or so murder sites. Seriously, how about dinner? We can try Tony's."

"Sorry," she said, sounding like she really meant it. "Tonight's the reception and benefit concert for Children's Hospital. Want to buy a ticket? Only seventy-five dollars. It's for a good cause."

I had no desire to put on black tie and eat bad hors d'oeuvres. "Do I actually have to go?"

Francine laughed. "No, you don't have to go. I wouldn't put either of us through that. It's Chopin, not the Beach Boys." She had abandoned her efforts to get me culture after I snored audibly at "Swan Lake" several years ago.

• • •

We settled on drinks at the Bench and Bar, a lawyers' hangout across the street. It was early—most big firm lawyers downtown worked until at least seven—and after our eyes adjusted to the perpetual semidarkness of the dim candles and dark wood fixtures, we found a free corner booth. That was the best place to talk; before long the tables in the center would be full of deal-makers bragging about how hard they worked and litigators lying about their victories.

After the waitress brought Francine's chardonnay and my Coors Light, I told her about the Swiltons. "So I think we can lay it off on them," I finished, then waited for some appreciation of my brilliance.

"Did he do it?" Francine asked, toying with her wine glass.

"Who, Keith?"

"Yes. Did he attack that girl?"

I shrugged. "That's up to the jury."

She looked up at me now. "You once said a jury is twelve people who don't know anything and can't even get out of jury duty. Then you said your job is to keep them from learning what everyone else in the courtroom knows."

That had been a joke. I searched her face for any sign of humor. None there. "It's the system," I said. "Juries usually get it right."

"And they absolve you from making your own judgments."

I was not looking for a fight. "I met a friend of Tom's," I said. "A reporter named Tim Stevens. He pumped me for information about Lew."

Francine decided to let me escape with the change in subject. "Like what?" she asked.

"Like what's he like to work for."

"That's easy. It's like working for Stalin."

This was another old topic of conversation, so I ignored it in hopes of finding something lighter. "Stevens also wants to know about Lew's social life."

Francine laughed aloud. "Who doesn't? Where does he get those women? I don't think that one at last year's summer clerk party spoke English. Someone said she was a grand duchess of someplace."

"I liked the *Vogue* cover girl at the Christmas party, myself," I said.

"I guess I missed that one," Francine said. Francine had not attended a Christmas party since she caused a stir at one back in the days when she still wore her librarian costume to work. At the party, she came with contacts in place and a low-cut, backless gown that Dennis talked her into buying. By the end of the evening, all the men had lined up to dance with her, even the Senator, while the Firm Wives huddled in the corner, shooting dirty looks at their husbands.

The next summer, Dennis took off with a model he met through his agency, and Francine said the hell with firm politics. She dressed as she liked, quit working so hard, skipped firm functions if she wanted, and developed outside interests, like the symphony. She was a lock for equity partner as the firm's rising star in international taxation. The clients didn't care what she looked like or if she went to the Christmas party.

She took a sip of her wine, still thinking about Sherwood's social life. "Has he talked to Tricia?" she said. Tricia was Sherwood's last wife. They had divorced about four years ago.

I shook my head. "Didn't sound like it. Where did she end up, do you know?"

"D.C., I heard from somewhere," she answered. "You ever find out what happened?"

"No. Lew never talked about it, not even when she left. I just heard she was gone one day. Right after we finished that bribery case in Michigan." I thought back. "I only met her once or twice, at his annual party for the Band."

"I don't think I ever talked to her." Francine finished her wine and looked at her watch. "Tell me about this Ripper case," she said.

"No," I said. "It's bad. I'm tired of it, and you'd ask me hard questions about morality. I can't deal with morality right now."

This time she didn't laugh. Instead, she leaned over and put her hand on mine. "All right then," she said in a serious voice. "How are you, Cliff?"

"Have another," I said, pointing at her empty wine glass.

She hesitated, then flagged the waitress for another round. "I guess it's all right," she said. "Liz is picking me up tonight."

"Who's Liz?"

She gave me a disgusted look. "You had a date with her once."

After Anita left, Dennis and Francine took me on as a reclamation project; they even fixed me up a few times with acquaintances. Liz apparently was one of them. "Oh, yeah," I said, trying to cover. "How is she?"

Francine just snorted.

"I have a serious question," I said after the drinks came. She raised her eyebrows. "Don't let anyone know about this, but I'm worried about Ted Brookstone. He has family problems. I feel like I should give him some advice, but, you know . . . "

She knew. We were a small mutual support group, Francine and I, and hardly the models of successful family relationships. "The usual thing?" she asked. "Everything is wonderful for a few years, then the babies come and the husband's never home because he spends all his time on the road or at the office?"

I nodded. It was easy to recognize the pattern in someone else.

"My sympathy's with the wife, you know that." Francine pointed an accusatory finger at me. "Every Monday you all fly first class to somewhere glamorous, and she's stuck at home with the ear infections and driving the station wagon to the pediatrician." Francine had no children, but she and Dennis and Anita and I had been a very tight foursome. When Preston was born, they considered him part of the family. She still had a crib in her attic from the days when we brought him over and put him down to sleep while we sat by their pool.

"So what do I tell Ted?" I was no good at this kind of thing.

She shrugged. "What the Senator keeps saying. Balance your life."

"That's easy for him to say. He doesn't have to bill twenty-five hundred or three thousand hours a year."

Francine sipped her wine. "Has Martha given Ted the ultimatum yet?" she asked.

"Don't know," I said. "Anita gave me mine just before we made junior partner." I thought back and sighed. "I told her to give me a year more and everything would change."

"I remember that." Anita had cried on Francine's shoulder. She gave me the year, and nothing changed. I made junior partner, the workload increased, and my goal became equity partner. I tried hard for a few months to be a devoted family man, but cutting back on work was like cutting back on smoking. Somewhere along the way, in high school or college or law school, the habit of striving for the next goal had become too ingrained. Sherwood took on more cases, and sometimes I didn't even make it home on weekends. When Anita finally did leave, I was not very surprised.

Francine leaned over and spoke softly. "Cliff, do you remember when Dennis told you that you were about to lose your wife to your career?"

That had been about a week before Anita left for good. I had brushed him off. Francine kept on. "And you said you only needed a little more time?" I nodded.

"That's what Ted will tell you, Cliff." Her eyes were half closed, distant. Dennis had not given her an ultimatum. "Don't bother." She sighed. "People will do what they'll do, and it doesn't matter what anyone tells them. You and Anita taught me that. And Dennis." Her voice trailed off.

Dennis had been a nice guy. But he had hurt her badly.

CHAPTER
8

We started where the Ripper started: Lake Wachita, in upstate New York. The town lay at the south end of its namesake finger lake, southeast of Syracuse, southwest of the Adirondacks, and a lot further from New York City than I expected until I studied the Rand McNally. This was the smallest resort area on our list: the primary attractions were cross-country skiing in the winter, lake activities in the summer, and the Lake Wachita Inn, a hotel/convention center with three championship golf courses.

The chief of police, Thomas K. Prescott, was about forty, slender, with rimless glasses and an earnest air. According to Tim Stevens, he was a former New York City detective who ultimately chose lifestyle over money. We sat in his sparsely furnished office in the nondescript one-story brick police station a block from the lake.

"Tim Stevens tells me I should talk to you," Prescott said. "I don't know why I should."

"I think Tim told you who we are and why we're here," I said. In fact, Stevens had made the call from our Johnston Beach war room. The chief nodded slightly.

"To be honest," I said, "we are just starting. By the time

we're done, we will know more about these Ripper cases than any other organization, up to and including the FBI. That's the way we work."

He nodded again, waiting for the end of my spiel. I bragged some about our methods, stressed Edgar's experience and integrity, then ended on the high ground: "We have a common interest here. Just like you, we want this killer caught. A dozen young women have been terrorized and slaughtered, and that has to stop."

Prescott did not move. "They tell me the killer is sitting in jail in Johnston Beach," he said.

"Maybe he is," I said. "If so, that's the end of the problem. But what if he isn't? We need to know that. You need to know that. That's our common interest."

Prescott leaned back in his chair and put one foot on the desk, keeping his eyes on mine the whole time. He held out one palm, as if weighing my argument. "Isn't your interest to get your client out of jail?" he asked. His tone was not argumentative. "I don't see any reason to help you do that."

I felt like I was arguing a motion to a judge. Sometimes they ask questions even when they have already decided how they will rule, either to be polite or out of a sense of malicious fun. But other times they really want to know. Either way, you answer their questions.

"Our job is to present a defense," I said. "We don't invent the facts and we don't decide the case. If the State can prove its charge, so be it. If it can't, then maybe there's nothing to it."

He kept his face neutral. I decided he was the analytical type. "I would hate to think everyone has stopped looking for the Ripper," I said. "It's cost versus benefits, Chief. You have nothing to lose, and we may find something useful to you."

Prescott gave me a final look, then turned to Edgar: "You know about the task force?"

"Yes."

"Tim Stevens has been calling around. Lewis Sherwood is a hot topic of conversation. You know the FBI liaison man, fellow named Henders?" Edgar nodded.

"Henders thinks very highly of you, Browning, but he says the Bureau opposes any cooperation with Lewis Sherwood or his people. Why is that?"

Edgar gave me a dirty look. "Lewis sued the Bureau a while back. They weren't happy about it."

"That Greater East Coast Securities case?" Edgar nodded again. "I read about it," Prescott said with a knowing look. "I suppose they weren't happy." Greater East Coast was a securities fraud case where Sherwood convinced the court to suppress some illegally seized evidence. We got the criminal case dismissed, then turned around and sued the Bureau and the individual agents who had done the seizing. Our clients now enjoyed the fruits of their allegedly ill-gotten gains in the Caribbean, supplemented by a comfortable cash settlement from the government. Edgar had refused to work on the case.

"Politics," Prescott muttered. He suddenly sat upright in his chair and gazed at Edgar. "They tell me your client is the man," he said. "Is he?"

"Don't know yet," Edgar said before I could answer.

I winced inside, but that must have been the right answer. Prescott picked up his phone and dialed an extension. "Come on in," he said, then hung up. He leaned back, relaxed now, with a more open expression.

"I've only been here two years," he said. "Our mayor and town council were . . . unhappy with the progress my predecessor made. This was the first one, you know. No one knew it was a serial killer. They thought he should have solved it in a week."

He shook his head and looked at Edgar. "Sometimes civilians don't quite understand the problem." Edgar smiled in agreement. The chief snapped back upright. "Anyway, I've studied the files, and it's still an open case, but we can't do much with it. Four years is a long time."

The door opened, and a huge woman in a police uniform looked us over. She was easily six feet and well over two hundred pounds, with short gray hair and a stern expression. "This is my deputy chief, Erica," Prescott told us. "She's been here forever. She can tell you about the case."

Erica found a chair while the chief laid out the ground rules. "You can have everything from our files, unless"—he looked at Erica—"you know of something they shouldn't get." Erica shook her head. "Erica sits on the task force, so she can talk to you about that, but some of the jurisdictions want to keep their information confidential." He shrugged. "They have good reasons, and it's part of the agreement, so we won't show you any of their material."

"Fair enough," Edgar said. Then he turned to Erica. "Who runs that group?"

Her voice was soft and high, with a friendly warmth. She spoke in a flat Midwestern accent. "Mr. Henders from the FBI chairs the meetings. Some of the members are very active: Caliano, Mt. Passarell. Most of us just listen. Not much any of us can do."

"Tell them about our case," the chief said.

Her eyes grew distant, sad. "It was horrible," she began. That had been Sherwood's word. I had a feeling I would hear it often on this trip.

Stevens had already told us most of it. The victim was an attractive young marketing representative named Brenda

Petrillo, who was at the Lake Wachita Inn for a regional sales meeting. She was last seen in the hotel lounge on a busy night, listening to the band. A day later, some hikers found her remains on one of the resort's trails.

"I was the first officer on the scene," Erica said in a low voice. "Horrible." Her lower lip quivered slightly.

"Was she seen with anyone in the bar?" Edgar asked.

Prescott looked at Erica. She was biting her lower lip. He answered for her. "Not really. This was in the fall. When the foliage turns, the tourists come out in force. 'Leaf-lookers,' the natives call them. And they had a convention of optometrists, I think it was, and a couple of sales meetings, so the Inn and the other hotels were full. So were most of the bed-and-breakfasts. The lounge at the Inn is the only place around with a band during the week; it was jammed."

"Brenda had a roommate from her company," Erica said, "but that woman had a late meeting, then went back to the room for the night. A few other people from the company saw Brenda at the lounge, but they didn't remember anyone else."

They showed us the files and the physical evidence, such as it was. The pictures were like the one Stevens had given us, from many more angles. Edgar looked at them closely while the rest of us pretended to think about other aspects of the case.

"What's this?" Edgar said. He pointed to something on the victim's breast. It looked like a bloody wound to me.

"One of his trademarks," Erica said in a low, bitter whisper. "He always does it. The task force thinks it's an animal of some kind."

"What animal?"

Erica shrugged. "On some of the other victims, they say it looks like an elephant or a pig. This one, I think it looks more like an elephant." She backed away. "I haven't looked at the pictures from the other jurisdictions."

Edgar made some notes. "What about interviews, leads, that sort of thing?" he said.

The chief sighed. "We don't have a very big force here," he said. "And my predecessor had never had a case quite like this. Remember, this was the first one. He handled it like most murders: started with family, friends, acquaintances. He did get registration cards from the Inn—that box over there. They talked to the others at the sales meeting, then asked most of the guests if they heard or saw anything. Nobody had." He paused, unwilling to offer direct criticism. "Unfortunately, they did not have the resources to check all the other motels up and down the lake. And to be fair, we have four major cities within a three-hour drive."

"The State people came down to help a little later," Erica said. The chief snorted. That was the end of the discussion about them.

"No leads, I assume?" Edgar asked.

"No. She was married, but separated," Prescott said. "They focused on that angle. The husband had an airtight alibi, passed a polygraph. Nothing there."

"He was badly shaken," Erica said. "I talked to him two or three times."

I thought I better get the bad news out too. "Have you done anything to find out if our client was in the area?" Keith had remembered "passing through" Lake Wachita, but had no idea when.

Prescott studied me again. "I am hoping, counselor, that you will tell us that, eventually." I kept my face blank. He sighed. "We plan to go around with his picture when we get it. And go back through all of that." He gestured to the files. Then he grinned. "Let me know if you find his name, will you? It can save us a lot of time."

Cooperation only goes so far. "We'll share what we can," I said. We arranged to meet again the next day for a tour of the area, and Erica led us off to the copy machine.

• • •

Alice had reserved us three rooms at the Lake Wachita Inn—one each for sleeping and one in between as a sort of conference room. I munched a room service sandwich as I read my E-mail, sent Kara a slightly lewd response, then started fooling with the modifications to the computer program that Sam had suggested. Edgar dived into the police files.

We each muttered to ourselves as we worked. I quickly discovered that Sam's "No Problem" would not be easy. I could print out perfect expense reports for Keith, but making the program sort and search and match up dates and locations would be tricky. After a couple of hours, I made a definite decision to get back to it later.

The papers from the Lake Wachita Inn sat in a box next to Edgar's elbow. I started to leaf through its contents: a combination of printouts and copies of registration cards and bills. The printouts were a daily list of registered guests by room number. The registration cards looked like standard hotel forms, with credit-card imprints on the back. The bills had the actual credit-card receipts attached. Brenda Petrillo's name was on the printout, but there was no receipt for her. The room had been prepaid by her company.

I glanced through the lists and noticed little check marks next to most of the names. "What are those?" I asked Edgar.

"The guests they interviewed," he said. "The report summaries are over here. Basically, no one saw anything."

I flipped through the registration cards. Most of the addresses were from New York or Pennsylvania. The optometrists convention was a regional gathering. The sales meetings drew from a wider area throughout the northeast and part of the midwest. A few other guests were from more distant spots: one from Virginia, one from Alabama, couples from Illinois and Kansas. Out of curiosity, I searched for the corresponding bills. Edward P. Tarleton of Birmingham, Alabama, had rented a movie and had two room-service breakfast charges. Mr. and Mrs. Harrison Clay from Moline, Illinois, charged dinners at the Inn's restaurant and lunches at the golf club snack bar. I felt like a voyeur.

"What can we do with this?" I asked Edgar.

"Not much," he said. "Read through the interviews and see if anything stands out."

I had software on the brain after playing with the expense report program. "What about putting these in the computer and looking for matches? See if these names turn up anywhere else?"

Edgar stood up and stretched. He flipped through my pile with a frown. "A lot of work, Cliff," he said. "And not likely to produce anything. Nothing says the killer stayed here, much less used his real name. You heard the chief. They didn't even canvass other motels in the area." He shrugged. "I think it's a waste of time."

The great paranoia of a litigator is that the key to the case is hidden in a box of papers somewhere and no one knows about it. "Maybe I'll set up a data base for Belinda," I said. "She can have someone enter parts of this, at least. Names, dates, locations, addresses, that sort of thing."

"Whatever you think," Edgar said in a voice that told me he didn't care.

I looked at the computer, and he looked at the police files, and we simultaneously decided to quit for the night. I dug a couple of beers out of the hospitality bar, and we moved to the balcony overlooking the lake.

"Have you done many of these before?" I asked him.

"Serial killers?" he said. I nodded.

"A few. None very much like this. The ones I worked, the victims were mostly hookers. Easy targets. You don't see a hooker around for a few days, the chances are she's just moved on. This is different. These victims have families and friends who'll look for them."

"What kind of guy does it take to do this?"

"You've seen the articles the firm librarians found. The Bureau has a section that develops profiles. The usual profile shows a single male, no satisfactory personal relationships, a loner, often sexually inadequate. History of early sexual abuse. Above-average intelligence. Paranoid. Seeks control. Most of them don't last in the same job very long, and they move around a lot."

Edgar waved his beer for emphasis. "Most of that's true, I suppose, but the damned profiles aren't very useful. For every characteristic, there are enough exceptions that you can't rely on them to exclude a suspect. And other factors are there sometimes and not there sometimes." He put the beer down. "Then they throw in a probability factor to cover their butts. Like the weatherman. If you say 50 percent chance of rain, then you're right whether it rains or not."

"What else?" I asked.

He took a slow drink of beer while he thought. "He's a psychopath. And he must be a smooth operator to get these girls to go with him, particularly after all the publicity."

A boat went by on the lake. We watched it pass, then Edgar sighed. "All this publicity. Our perpetrator probably gets his rocks off reading about it. I bet he likes the challenge too; no easy targets like hookers for him."

"Why do the police release so much information?"

He shrugged. "There's a fine line. You can get leads from people reading the stories in the paper, and maybe some readers will be more careful and you can save a few lives."

"Any chance it's a woman?" I asked.

"Very, very unlikely. The victims have had intercourse, and serial killers are almost always men."

"How about more than one man? Two working together?"

"Not unheard of, but also very unlikely."

"Does Keith meet the profile you described?"

"Enough of it."

"Couldn't you at least hesitate a little?"

"I've already thought about it, Cliff. We're not dealing with a huge amount of data here, you know. Fortunately for the rest of us, the population of serial killers is pretty small. So about all you can say is that most of them have most of those characteristics.

"Keith has most of them. Single. No attachments. Moves around. But he doesn't have them all. From the way he talked, he's more than adequate sexually. We'll need to look into that more. But there's something strange about him—a tension, like he's ready to explode. That rape charge bothers me."

It bothered me, too.

Erica took us to the scene where Brenda Petrillo was discovered—just a trailside clearing in the woods—then joined us for dinner that night. Next to the body, Erica said, the hardest part was the family. The look on their faces as they searched for a reason. "I couldn't give them one," she said with a catch in her voice. "How can you?"

Every three months, on the first day of the quarter, Erica wrote the Petrillos a note. "Never anything to say, really," she said. "I just want them to know we haven't forgotten. People feel like you forget them, sometimes." She shook her head. "Then Mr. Petrillo died a few months ago. Heart attack. I went to the funeral. Poor Mrs. Petrillo. She was so broken up."

The next morning, we talked to the Inn manager, who was not at all excited to see us. He knew nothing, he could tell us nothing. Frustrated, we drove to the police station, where Erica tracked down the chief for a final meeting. "Why do they think our client is involved in this?" Edgar asked.

Prescott looked at Erica, then shrugged. "As I understand it, he was caught in the act with a similar MO. And he has the right background. I suppose that's the main thing."

"And the picture," Erica added.

We all stared at her. Edgar finally broke the silence. "What picture?" he said.

She looked at the chief defiantly. He looked back at her for a long moment, then sighed. "An artist's rendering, from one of the murder locations. They sent it to the task force members and asked us to keep it confidential. We have, until now." He glared at Erica.

She glared back. "We showed it to people around here. No reason they shouldn't know about it."

I interrupted. "May we see it?" The chief finally nodded to Erica, who left to retrieve the picture.

"I'm not playing games with you," Prescott said in a somewhat apologetic tone. "But I won't tell you where it came from. They have a good reason to keep it quiet." His voice stiffened. "Don't let anyone know that you have it, understand?" We agreed.

Erica returned and handed a paper to Edgar. He looked at it, stonefaced, made a note in his pad, then passed it to me. I put on my sitting-in-the-courtroom face.

I have a limited imagination, because I never can recognize a person in real life based on an artist's conception. But when I saw this one, I immediately resolved to have

Keith shave his mustache and get a haircut. As he was now, he was the spitting image of the picture. Even the written description was bad, if not worse: "Approximately 5'9", 170 pounds, brown hair, brown eyes. Tattoo on left arm."

"Aw, shit," I thought. Then I hoped I hadn't said it aloud.

CHAPTER
9

Three weeks after we visited Lake Wachita, the judge in the Galveston trial caught the flu and recessed for a couple of days, so Sherwood called us back to Queenston for a status conference. When the team gathered in the new war room, Sherwood, who had not seen any of us since he left Johnston Beach the day of the hearing, sat down at the head of the conference table and got right to it: "Okay, people, sorry to rush you, but I'm leaving in about an hour, so we need to move this along."

He looked at his notes. "Where's this picture?" he asked me.

Edgar handed him the artist's rendering and provided copies to the others. Ted looked at it and groaned.

The Red Team now included three associates and three paralegals. Kara, detached to the Blue Team, had stayed in Galveston. Her message this morning was curt: "Lewis won't let me come home. :-< We have some real problems down here. I hope you enjoyed your travels. See you sometime, Shug. xxxx & :-)-›8(:" I detected exhaustion. She needed a break.

Everyone needed a break. Edgar and I had journeyed to

nine murder sites, with two in California left to go. Touring the country's most popular resorts sounded much better than it was. We logged more time in airports and rental cars than in the Great Outdoors, and the results were mixed, at best. The resort managers did not want to revive their own local tragedies, and most of the police and prosecutors were far less helpful than our friends in Lake Wachita. By the third or fourth site, the horror passed, and I became a sponge, absorbing but not reacting to an endless litany of atrocities.

Sherwood stared at the picture for a long minute, then looked at me. "This is not good," he said in a low voice. He tapped it against his hand. "Who was the eyewitness and what did he see?"

"We don't know yet, Lew," I said. "Every place we've been denies having an eyewitness, so it must come from one of the two California sites. Tim Stevens didn't even know it existed. Yesterday he said he heard a rumor of an eyewitness in Caliano. That's where we go in a couple of days."

"No alibis yet, I assume?" That was directed to me. I shook my head. "We need a defense here," he muttered. "Clifford, give me something to work with. I have this damn Galveston trial, and after that San Francisco; I can't focus on this case right now. We need an angle here or this boy's in big trouble."

"We're trying, Lew," I said.

He sighed and looked at his watch. "Everyone's read all the memos, right?" Everyone nodded. "Let's go around the room and hit the highlights or fill in the gaps. Ted, what's new in Johnston Beach?"

"I've become quite concerned about our client," Ted said. "The last few days, Travis has been fading. Yesterday, for example, we were reviewing his charge accounts, and he just stopped and stared at the window for about ten minutes. He wouldn't respond to questions, even when I touched his arm. It was eerie.

"Personally, I believe we should bring in a psychologist or psychiatrist to talk to him. I'm afraid he may be developing severe mental problems."

Sherwood shook his head. "No. It's too early." He glared at Ted. "Never involve a shrink until you know what you need him to say. Sherwood's Rule. We haven't settled on a defense yet. What if he says Keith is competent and we need to go with insanity?

"Keith's probably a little depressed. Stay upbeat with him. I'll come down and give him a pep talk after this trial's over." Sherwood nodded to himself at that thought. "Anything new on the victim?" he said. We still had not interviewed Dorothy Catterman, mainly because Sherwood had been busy but also to give her time to regain her memory.

Ted, duly chastened, shook his head. "No. Catterman should be released in a week or two. Dr. Lawson says her story agrees with what Keith told us to the point where they left the Mariner; she still draws a total blank after that. Hypnosis is a possibility, but it could render her testimony inadmissible. Pete doesn't think the prosecution will take the chance unless we agree. I assume we do not want her memory refreshed?"

"I don't," Sherwood said. "Anyone feel differently?" No one spoke.

"Okay. Good job. I want to argue any hypnosis motions myself if it comes to that. And I still want to interview her as soon as possible. Clifford?"

"You've seen Edgar's reports on our trips to the Ripper crime scenes. We're in the process of getting Keith's records. Some of the credit-card bureaus have not responded yet, but none have objected. We filed requests for his military record and other federal government items; we'll send requests to the various states in the next week or two.

"Belinda"—I pointed to her—"has entered most of the information that we have so far into the computer so we can match Keith's movements with the Ripper crimes. We're looking for any evidence that he was somewhere else. The problem's the geography. For example, one of the murders was in Vail, and Keith was working in Snowmass at the time, so he would have been close enough, but the mailing addresses don't reflect it in a way that the computer can recognize. Different town names. I'm thinking truncated ZIP codes may be the way to go."

Sherwood's foot started to jiggle. He couldn't care less about these kinds of details, so I quit. "Fine," he said. "Keep me posted. I want a summary out of the computer, you know the type of thing I like."

Edgar reported on the investigation into Dorothy Catterman's personal background. "Unmarried female, age twenty-four, junior executive trainee. Several previous love affairs, no indications of unusual promiscuity or deviant sexual behavior. Nothing remarkable." Belinda and Sheri looked uncomfortable. They were both about twenty-four.

Sherwood looked at his watch again, and the meeting rapidly wound up with some miscellaneous information. Edgar was developing a summary of physical evidence; he had sent our pet pathologist copies of the Ripper victims' autopsy reports. One of the associates was surveying other serial murder cases to identify successful and unsuccessful defense strategies. She had complained to me earlier that she could not find any successful defense strategies: all the defendants were convicted or locked up forever as part of a deal to avoid the death penalty. I suggested she lower her standard of what constitutes success.

When we finished, Sherwood tossed the picture across the table at Ted. "See what our man has to say about this." Then he surveyed the assembled team. "We need a defense here, people. Let's go out and find one." He passed out a few months' worth of assignments to be completed in the next week, then left for the airport.

The associates and paralegals scattered to various corners of Sherwood's Forest. "How are we really doing on records?" I asked Ted.

"Not good," he said. He had flown to Iowa to visit Keith's sister, and he and Pete had searched Keith's mobile home in Johnston Beach. "What Travis keeps or what he throws away is hit and miss. We have some credit-card receipts. He has safe deposit boxes around the country. We found some keys, but there could be others. For taxes, Travis just hands a preparer a bunch of receipts. We'll have to go to the IRS for copies."

"How's the sister?"

"She can't believe he would do such a thing."

Edgar grunted. "I'll go over the record requests with Belinda. Maybe we can expedite some of them. Although I'm not having much luck with the Defense Department." He turned to me. "Old bank card records may be hard and expensive to dig out. That could throw a loop in your computer program."

All we can do is try, I thought.

I paddled my raft over to the edge of the pool, and Francine traded my empty beer can for a full one. In the background, the traffic noise filtered through the privacy fence, muffled by the shrubs. Francine's house was in an old, established neighborhood, one of the few oases of suburbia left near downtown Queenston.

Francine wore a string bikini that would have shocked the Firm Wives. I was probably the only one at the firm ever to see her that way. In fact, I had seen her in less. A couple of times back in the old days, after a few too many drinks, Anita and I had skinny-dipped in this very pool with Francine and Dennis.

There had been times after Anita, too. When Dennis left, Francine was badly shaken, and we gravitated to each other more or less by default. It lasted about a year, until, without any particular event or dramatic confrontation, we both realized we had nowhere to go as a couple. We became best friends and now had a strictly platonic relationship.

I floated on the raft while Francine dangled her feet in the water, occasionally getting up to baste the chicken that cooked slowly on the grill. "Did anything *good* happen on your trip?" she asked.

"I did see Preston," I said. "We had a layover in Kansas City, so I shuffled the schedule and drove out to Anita's place. That was nice. He's grown, Francine. He's a big boy now. He'll be chasing girls before long."

"Like his daddy?"

I laughed. "I hope he does better than that. Anita said to tell you 'hi,' by the way."

"How is she?"

"Doing well, I think. She's working again, at a bank Seems happy, I don't think she's going with anyone." Anita and I managed to maintain a friendly relationship, probably for Preston's sake. Francine had no child to provide a link to the past. As far as I knew, she had not seen Dennis since the divorce.

Francine took a proprietary interest in Preston. "His visit is in two weeks?" I nodded. "What should we do with him?"

"Probably the zoo and the movies. I might take him over

to Atlanta to a Braves game. Edgar said he could work out with his son's soccer team. He'll enjoy that. He'll want to see you, I know." She was Aunt Francine to Preston. He genuinely liked her, and she came through with some pretty good Christmas presents, too.

We ate at the poolside table, still in our swimsuits. The chicken was good, the beer was cold, and I had seconds on both. Then I told her about the Ripper case. She winced when I circumspectly described the victims' photos. "How can you look at something like that?" she asked.

"It wasn't easy," I admitted. "You know, most of the time you worry about the legal case and don't think much about the crime itself. You even tend to forget that your client actually may have hurt or killed someone. It's more of an intellectual exercise: who has what evidence, what are the elements of the crime, that sort of thing. Like a jigsaw puzzle." I sighed. "But those pictures make it too real. I don't feel good about this case."

"Did this Keith do it? Is he the Ripper?"

Francine had a habit of asking questions I avoided. That one was a severe breach of etiquette among criminal lawyers: the proper question is whether the State can prove it. But Francine was a tax lawyer, and she did not follow the same code.

I thought about it now. That artist's rendering. Finally I admitted the truth to myself. But I would not admit it to her. "He's the prime candidate right now," was all I said.

Francine frowned at me. "So what do you do?"

"We keep digging and hope something comes up that changes everything." Her eyes stayed fixed on mine. This was becoming uncomfortable; I tried to change the subject. "Why do your eyes look so green?"

"New contacts," she smiled. "They're colored. Like them?" I nodded approval and rose to fetch another beer.

My gambit didn't work. "If he really is the Ripper, you'll lose, won't you?"

I popped the top and shrugged. "Not necessarily. Really, they don't have very much evidence in any of these cases, except for this potential eyewitness in California. But Lew is good with eyewitnesses, and if he can impeach that testimony, there's not much else to support a murder conviction."

Now Francine wore a look I couldn't read. I kept on. "So if you look at each case by itself, it's not too bad. The real problem is the pattern and practice evidence, if they can show he was around for every Ripper murder, which we can't disprove right now. If that gets to a jury, the prosecution says, 'Look. He was here and so was the Ripper. He was there and so was the Ripper.' And on and on eleven times. Then it's a different story."

"That's a compelling argument," she said, with the same expression on her face. It might have been disbelief. Or disapproval.

"Yeah. One of the associates researched typical prosecution tactics in serial murder cases. Usually they bring formal charges in their strongest case or two, then introduce evidence of the others to show a pattern or practice. That would hit us hard. But if we can keep it out, we probably have a pretty good chance in any individual situation. So the associates are researching how to keep it out."

Francine almost spoke, then held whatever she had to say. I cleared the table and washed the dishes while she lay on the pool deck and listened to music. Finally, when I came and sat next to her at the edge of the pool, she asked, "What would you do if you were sure he did it, but you thought of a way to get him off?"

The truth was that I usually did not think about a case in those terms. You take your client's story, if he has one, and you do the best you can to convince yourself the story is true. We evaluated a case on the chances of winning an acquittal, not on whether the client was in fact guilty. This one was different, though. I had seen those pictures.

Fortunately, I had a personal safety valve. Sherwood would handle that kind of moral judgment, not me. If he were convinced of Keith's guilt, he would negotiate some sort of plea at the appropriate time.

If I explained that to Francine, she would take off on Sherwood again, so instead I gave her the party line: "Our job is to give the man the best defense we can. The burden of proof is on the State. It's not our fault if the prosecution can't make its case. Anything less than an all-out, vigorous defense is a disservice to our system of justice."

It sounded pompous as hell, and it was. She shoved me in the pool.

I managed to grab her leg and pull her in after me, and we started wrestling in the water. Her wiggling, nearly-naked body aroused some lusty urges, and I almost made a grab to untie her strings. I knew she would let me. But I stopped myself. I needed a friend more than I needed to get laid.

Through the mist, I heard the persistent signal of my damn beeper. As I reached to quiet it, I scraped my knuckle on the pool cement and nearly fell off the lounge chair. That woke me up. I had a light blanket over me, and Francine was not there. She apparently tucked me in and went to bed. My watch said 2 A.M.

The damn beeper was in my pile of gear near the grill. It didn't say "Special Priority," so it was not from Sherwood. But it did say "Urgent Message," which usually meant someone else on the team. I hunched the blanket over my shoulders, got my laptop out of the car, and plugged it in to Francine's poolside phone jack.

The message was from Ted: "Cliff. Sorry about the hour. Called your apartment, but no answer. Martha's mother has been rushed to the hospital. Quite serious. I am driving Martha and children to Chattanooga. Can you cover for me in Johnston Beach until I get there? Hope to fly down tomorrow, but it depends on her condition. Thanks. I owe you one. Ted."

Hell, I thought, this sure messes up my schedule. Then I realized what a jerk I was to have that thought. It was too late to bother Alice or reach the firm's travel agency, so I dialed up the computerized ticket service. While my computer went through the log-on procedure, I saw my reflection in Francine's sliding glass door. I was sitting by a pool, nearly naked, with a laptop computer at two in the morning. I had to get a life.

CHAPTER
10

No actual people greeted me when I arrived bright and early at our Johnston Beach hotel, but the computers sat ready for action in the war room. I checked in with Pete Bannister and confirmed that he would visit Keith; all I had to do was hang out in case of emergency. I loaded up one of the computers and tried to get my Ripper-tracker program working.

After a few hours, I thought I had it. Through much trial and error, I figured out how to make the computer compare Keith's records with the dates and locations of the Ripper murders and come up with one of three classifications for each crime: Possible, Incomplete, or Alibi. It was an Alibi when an entry like a sales receipt or a restaurant charge showed that Keith was somewhere else at or about the time of the murder. It was a Possible when all the records were consistent with Keith's being in the vicinity. Incomplete meant not enough information one way or the other.

I tried it out. It was way too slow; Sam could make the code more efficient later. But eventually the printer spit out a report for Keith's data.

Not good. Of the thirteen murders on the official Resort

Ripper list, two were in the Alibi category: Santa Catalina and Stowe, the ones that did not belong as Ripper cases. Only one was Possible: Mount Passarell. The other ten were Incomplete. From our interviews with Keith, I knew we should have more Possibles, but I had no way to tell whether the problem was my program or that Belinda had not entered the information.

I had some other options for testing. As co-developer of the expense report program, I still had the master password, so I dialed up the firm's computer network and located the expense report files for me, Ted, and Kara. Each of our data bases was much larger than Keith's, and for some reason Ted's was about fifty percent bigger than the other two. They would provide a good test.

Ted called from the Chattanooga airport while I waited for the computer to finish. They had paged him as he boarded a flight for Johnston Beach; his mother-in-law had died. The funeral was Saturday, the day after tomorrow. Could I cover until then?

I said the standard sympathetic things and told him to take as long as necessary. I could not believe he had been ready to leave with the lady on her deathbed. Martha would be hopping mad.

"The only thing I have pending," Ted said, "is to talk with Travis about that artist's sketch. I don't know how soon Lew wants it. Maybe I can get there day after tomorrow . . ."

I interrupted him. "Look, Ted, I'll take care of it. You get back to Martha. Please tell her how sorry I am. Is there some place to send flowers?"

"They haven't made the arrangements yet. I'll keep in touch on E-Mail." His voice dropped slightly. "Thanks, Cliff. You're great to do this. See you in a couple of days." He hung up. Poor guy.

The printer started to spit out reports. Mine was first. I had two Alibis, ten Incompletes, and one Possible: Santa Catalina. Shit, I thought, it didn't work. Then I remembered my Los Angeles trip a couple of years ago: that could have triggered the Possible. The two Alibis and ten Incompletes bothered me too. I expected a few times when I had no expense reports for a period around a murder, but having the same number as Keith was too much of a coincidence. Maybe the program was not looping properly.

Kara's report came off next. She had six Alibis and no Possibles. The rest were Incomplete. Seven of them. At least it wasn't stuck on two and ten.

Ted's report was total gibberish. The damn thing listed all the locations three times: once it gave him all Alibis, the second time it gave him all Incompletes, and the last time all Possibles. So much for a quick fix. The program must have a bug in it somewhere that kicked it back up to the start at the wrong time. Now I was back at square one, because I couldn't count on it being right for anyone else, either.

I cursed computers, turned on the TV, and ordered room service.

The next morning, I tried to organize everyone's life, including mine. Ted called to ask me to stay through the weekend. He was trying to make peace in the family. That was fine with me. Today was Thursday, and I could use the catch-up time because the following Thursday I was to pick up Preston in Kansas for his two-week visit. That prompted me to retransmit my "going-on-vacation" memo to remind everyone that I would be unavailable.

I called Edgar at the firm and dispatched him to investigate the California cases, promising to join him as soon as possible. Pete Bannister agreed to meet later at the jail to show Keith the artist's conception.

Just when I was about to take another shot at the computers, Kara beeped me with an urgent E-mail message: "Big news, Shug. WE HAVE A DEAL!! :-) :-) Lewis worked out a plea. :-) This young 'un is headed to Virginia for Mamma's home cooking. :-> See you soon. xxxx & :-)->8(-:"

That was big news. I called Charlie Hancock in Galveston to offer congratulations and get the lowdown. Charlie was my Blue Team counterpart, and Ted's leading competition to succeed me as Red Team Leader.

Charlie was ecstatic. Sherwood had negotiated a hell of a deal—relatively small fines and no jail time—and the judge had sent the jury home until further notice; he was expected to approve the bargain shortly. Sherwood had immediately headed off to San Francisco for another trial, a White Team case where the State alleged our client was a major drug distributor. No one liked drug cases, but the defendants often had amassed enough money to pay handsomely, so we took them.

Well, that was all very exciting. I sat in Johnston Beach, bored to death.

Most of my next two days were spent hunched over the computer. I took a few breaks: jogged in the morning, shopped for a few beach things for Preston, and went with Pete Bannister to see Keith.

The Keith visit disturbed me. Keith's face lit up when he saw me, then fell when only Pete accompanied me into the room. "I thought Mr. Sherwood might be coming," he said, then turned and stared at the small barred window in the interview room.

Pete worked for a half hour to bring him back—talking, cajoling, even challenging. Eventually we had his attention, and I showed him the artist's rendering.

Keith stared at it, gently rubbing his right hand across his mustache. He tilted his head and studied it at an angle, then lifted his eyes, first to Pete, then to me. "It looks like me," he said in a soft voice.

"How long have you had that mustache?" I asked him.

"Since the Army." He sounded distracted. I thought we had lost him again, but he came back to the picture. "It looks like me," he repeated.

I tried to reassure him. "Travis, it's not necessarily so bad. That looks like a lot of people. Put a mustache on Pete and it resembles him a little." Pete forced a smile.

Keith looked at Pete, nodded, and went back to the picture. "Yeah, I guess," he said softly. Another minute or two passed.

"You know?" he said. Then, "No. Guess not."

"What?"

"I don't know why, but I keep thinking about this guy John. You know Pete and Ted always ask me who I saw at some of these places. Ever since that first time you all were here, I keep thinking about John." He shook his head. "But it don't mean nothing."

"Tell us about John," I said.

"He's a guy I met somewheres. I was, let's see"—Keith lifted his head to look at the ceiling—"tending bar, seems like. At a ski place, so it would have been the winter. Anyways"—he looked back at the picture—"this looks a little like John. But his hair was shorter. And it says here brown hair; his was blond. His mustache was different."

At least he showed some interest. "His looks could change," I said. "Hair dye, you know. And he could have trimmed his mustache. Did he have a tattoo?"

"Dunno."

"Why do you mention him?"

" 'Cause he looked a little like this. And 'cause, like I said, I been thinking about him for some reason."

Pete took over. "What else do you remember about John?"

Keith shrugged. "Not much. He was in the bar or something, we got to talking. Sat around talking and drinking." He gave a small smile. "Told him what I did—move around, you know—and he said he'd like to live like that. Turned out he was a vet too, so we told some war stories. Hell, he even had someone take a Polaroid picture of us. Good guy."

Pete leaned forward. "You ever see him again?" Keith shook his head.

"Where was this, Travis?" Pete asked.

"Out in Colorado, somewheres. Aspen, maybe. I don't know."

"Was there a murder around that time?"

Keith pursed his lips and furrowed his eyebrows. "Seems like maybe there was." Then he shook his head in frustration. "I don't know. That place, the manager was an asshole. So I quit. Could have been a murder, I don't know. I never paid much attention."

Pete looked at me. My turn. "Is this the same John you mentioned before? The one from the South?"

"Yeah. He had an accent: that's what got us started talking. He said, 'Too many Yankees around here,' and I said, 'You got that right.' "

"Any idea where in the South he's from?"

Keith shook his head again. "Alabama, Mississippi. One of those places." He cocked his head to one side, concentrating. "It was Alabama. 'Cause there was a football game on and he kept hollering 'Roll, Tide.' Said he was from there."

"He was a big Bama fan?" I tried to keep my voice neutral.

Keith studied my face. "Yeah." He spoke slowly, watching me. "Wore a sweatshirt with the mascot on it."

"The elephant?" He nodded. "Can you tell me any more about John?" I asked.

He thought again. "I think he was from Birmingham. Isn't that where Alabama is?"

"The University of Alabama is in Tuscaloosa," I said.

"Maybe that's it." Suddenly he stopped talking and stared at the wall. We waited for him to continue, but he was done.

"Why are you thinking of John?" Pete asked finally.

Keith shrugged. "Don't know. He just keeps coming into my head. Only saw him that once." Then he was gone, back to wherever he went when he dropped contact with us.

"Pitiful, isn't he?" Pete said as we walked over to his office. "He's like that more and more. Al Sanderson's worried about him: has him on a suicide watch. We need to get him some psychiatric help. Ted said he'd talk to Lew."

"Lew wants to wait a little bit," I said. "He's afraid of an opinion that would hurt us."

"I guess." Pete had a note of doubt in his voice. "The sister told Ted there's a history of mental illness in the family. I don't guess that helps in your Ripper cases."

It sure didn't. I shook my head.

"What about this John thing?" Pete asked. "You sounded interested in it."

"A real long shot," I said. "Some cops think the Ripper carves a little elephant on his victims. Probably doesn't mean anything." I must have sounded discouraged.

Pete slapped me on the back. "Cheer up. You got to go through the valley before you get to the mountaintop. It'll turn around for you."

He paused. "I think Travis sees Lew as his only chance to get out of here. I know Lew's busy, but Travis needs a little encouragement or something."

"I'll try to get him down here," I promised. "He's been tied up with these trials, but I see what you mean."

We stopped at Pete's front door. "If it helps," he said, "I am cautiously optimistic on this part of it here. I've done more checking, and Eddie and Bobby definitely are bad actors, even by Swilton standards. Word on the street is the Swilton clan knows more than they're letting on. I'm starting to like your idea that they attacked Dorothy Catterman. Dorothy goes home next week; unless she remembers something that hurts us, I'd say we have a shot at it. Still up to the jury, of course."

That was at least a small ray of sunshine through the clouds. I drove back to the war room, dispatched a summary of our interview with Keith to the team, then turned back to my computer program.

By Friday afternoon, I was ready to give up. Four or five times I had found some errors, made changes, recompiled the program, and run the reports. By now, Kara and I had Alibis for several other cases, and Keith was Possible for four, probably because Belinda had updated the information. But Ted still bombed out.

Finally, I looked at the raw data itself in his file with a binary viewer, and spent forty-five minutes searching through unintelligible computer garbage before I realized the problem. Ted had a different data layout. Somewhere along the line, Sam apparently did some special programming for him, because his data base contained both personal and firm items, charged to several different credit cards.

That made me mad. The expense report system was my baby, and Sam had changed it without telling me. Worse, the change blew my computer's little mind. I had told it to expect certain kinds of data, but it found a different layout when it looked at Ted's expenses. With a substantial effort, I could change my program to work on his files, but then it wouldn't work with anyone else's.

I threw the piles of useless reports on the floor, stood up, and glared at the computer screen. My neck was killing me, my back ached, and I had wasted all this time testing with a data base that could not possibly work. "Screw you," I snarled at the computer. It took my hostility in stride. I left to take a swim.

Later, as the shower pounded on my back, I had the kind of brilliant idea that only comes with water running over your head. When I had looked at Ted's raw data files, I noticed several place names that were Resort Ripper murder sites. It took me aback for a moment, but once I thought about it, it made sense. Ted took a family vacation at least twice a year. Martha liked to go to resorts where the jet set hung out, and, unfortunately, so did the Ripper.

That gave me a theory for excluding the pattern and practice evidence that we were so worried about. Thousands of people visited these resorts every year; conceivably, a few of them also might have been in the vicinity at the time of the murders. A jet-setter, perhaps, or another member of Keith's subculture of migrant resort workers. If we could identify some, we might discredit any attempt to use Keith's movements as evidence. So what if he was there, we would argue. Here are half a dozen other people who were too.

The computer could help us find those people. We already had some hotel registers and employee rosters, and I already had a data base for Belinda to enter the Lake Wachita Inn information. I could easily write a program to analyze it. Maybe it could find some alternative suspects for me, or at least give us some ammunition to create reasonable doubt.

Humming happily, I dried off and went to get dressed. Suddenly, without a knock, the door opened. I grabbed for the towel I had dropped.

It was Kara. "Hi, Sugar," she said. "Don't bother with that towel. I've been real lonesome."

Kara was a Southern belle, but she slept like a log and snored like a longshoreman. The noise woke me up about two. I looked at her, wondering again how such a beautiful person could produce such an awful sound. Usually I prodded her or rolled her over, but after the stories she told me about Galveston, I didn't have the heart to disturb her sleep.

Apparently, Galveston had been pretty grim. Sherwood was so frustrated with the trial preparation that he blew up one night and fired two paralegals outright. He even shipped an associate back to the firm. She soon would be seeking other employment. Kara had worked her ass off to pull things together for him.

Then the trial started. Any trial is a tense time— it's like giving a single performance of a new play, with no rehearsal. If the critics on the jury like it, your client goes free. If they don't like it, he goes to jail. The pressure is enormous.

Sherwood in the courtroom was an incredible experience, but being part of his trial team could be a nightmare. You spent the day in court, then worked all night to get ready for the next day. On trial, Sherwood was so on edge and so insistent on being prepared for any possibility that he drove everyone nuts with his demands. He could become almost vicious when things were not done to his liking. My theory was that sitting in the courtroom day after day as the ole country lawyer without a care in the world built up tension that he had to blow off at night. If you expected it and understood why, you could live with it.

In Galveston, they had gone through all the trial preparation and most of the trial itself when Sherwood negotiated a plea bargain, much to the surprise of his trial team. The abrupt ending to the case was something of a letdown, but on the bright side, Kara unexpectedly found herself free. She had gone home to Richmond, then came down to keep me company for the weekend.

I pulled on my gym shorts and went onto the balcony. My new theory of finding other suspects rolled around in my mind. I still liked it. It offered a possible path to acquittal for Keith. Locating people who had been at these resorts might be a massive job, but it was doable. There had to be many people like Keith who worked at beaches in the summer and ski lodges in the winter. Some of them were bound to fit the pattern. With real luck, we could find a commando or two.

It is very easy to get carried away at two in the morning.

The waves pounded softly, and I tried to fall asleep in the lounge chair, but uninvited thoughts kept floating through. Like Stevens' daughter. Like the victim pictures. Like Francine's question: What if Keith really is the Ripper?

Forget about it, I finally told myself. Even if we find absolute proof of Keith's guilt, we can't tell anybody. It would be privileged information. We still would have to present his best case, or withdraw and help him get other lawyers. So no point in thinking about it.

Think about something else. Kara, for example.

To the casual observer, Kara looked like she belonged in Hollywood or New York. I knew she had considered acting or modeling—she had appeared in some local ads in Virginia—but it never panned out. She became a paralegal because a sorority sister at her exclusive Virginia women's college said it was a good job for an English major and a law firm had an abundance of single men. She was right about that. Unfortunately, most of them were lawyers.

Kara was a great paralegal. On a case, she ran our lives, kept us on schedule, and handled all the details that were too important to trust to the lawyers, who could think lofty thoughts but sometimes had trouble tying their own shoes. At work, she was efficient, imaginative, and totally unscrupulous in getting what she wanted.

Our personal relationship had started the winter before last, when we were stuck for weeks in a godforsaken corner of Montana on a tough, high-profile case. Our client had allegedly hired his own private army and started a range war, leading to charges of kidnapping and murder. We got him off, but it took some fancy legal maneuvering and a super job by Sherwood.

Neither Kara nor I had much in common with the local Mormons, and the town closed up about eight every evening, so we begun having a nightly drink in one of our rooms after dinner. One night it turned into a couple of drinks and bed. It was very good, so we kept it up. We managed to keep our personal and professional lives separate; the firm would not tolerate a lawyer sleeping with his paralegal.

Francine thought Kara was using me until a rich lawyer came on the market, but she was wrong. I was the one who backed away from any commitment, and Kara sensed it. My divorce still hurt, and I had no intention of becoming emotionally involved again until I graduated from Sherwood's team. We did not talk about love, or even the future. We just carried our spare clothes in a tote bag and took them away with us every night.

Kara was young and in no hurry, but I could not expect

her to wait forever while I got my act together. Our relationship was another decision I would have to make sometime. One of many decisions. Like what if Keith really is the Ripper?

I looked at my watch. That was enough deep thinking for four in the morning. I went in and woke up Kara and found a much more pleasant way to get to sleep.

CHAPTER
11

Saturday, we lay on the beach. Sunday, we drove down the coast to a historic seaport to visit the aquarium.

Monday, everything went to hell.

Ted showed up on the early flight, Pete Bannister came over, and we began to review the gaps in Keith's records so they could try to pin him down some more. Kara's friend Dr. Lawson informed her that Dorothy Catterman would be released Friday to go home to Connecticut. Still no improvement in her memory. We decided to bring Sherwood in on Thursday to interview her. Some associates and paralegals appeared to go through records from Clippers and finish factual research for various potential motions. The place was hopping.

About eleven, every phone started to ring, every computer tied to the firm system started to toot, and every damn beeper in the room went off simultaneously. Scared Pete to death. As senior man, I went first.

It was Sherwood, forwarding a message from Edgar Browning. The grand jury in Caliano was about to hand down an indictment formally charging Keith with a Resort Ripper murder. Sherwood wanted us all there. Now.

• • •

Between a midnight visit to the firm, an early bird flight to the Coast and time zone changes, I lost track of the precise hour, but I thought it was still Tuesday morning when I looked around our new West Coast war room and wondered again who would pay for all this. Kara, working very fast, had arranged basically the same setup in Caliano as we had back in Johnston Beach.

The Caliano suite had more of a Spanish flavor, and the ocean was on the opposite side of the building, but other than that we could pick up right where we had left off yesterday. The big differences were the view out the window—a craggy rock cliff looming out of the sea instead of a sandy beach—and Sherwood and Edgar rather than Ted and Pete at the conference table. Ted had stayed behind in case the authorities tried to sneak in an extradition request.

Edgar briefed us. "The chief of police here and I go way back. He was in my class at the FBI Academy. I believe he's been very straight with me, and now that the indictment's locked up, he doesn't mind filling me in. He says, Lewis, they have made a tactical decision not to play games with you. They may hold back a few things, but not much."

He flipped through his notebook. "Okay. The prosecution. The chief deputy DA handled the grand jury and she'll take the lead at the trial. She's young, but she trained in Los Angeles and had experience with serial cases there. The DA's a smart politician: he'll leave everything to the experts. My friend is solid, and he has good detectives. The Bureau's helping out in the background.

"The indictment has been drawn up, signed, and will be handed down in"—he glanced at his watch—"about fifteen minutes."

"Get over there," Sherwood directed one of the associates. "Mix in with the crowd if there's a press conference."

The associate scurried out. Someone in the lobby would give him directions.

Edgar began on the case itself. "Keith is charged with the kidnap and murder approximately two years ago of one Maria Theresa Perez. This is definitely a Ripper case. Her body was found on Wednesday, June 18, at a local beach, posed on some rocks. We have pictures.

"Perez was a legal assistant at a large firm in Los Angeles." That drew a few winces around the table. "Age twenty-three, never married. Excellent reputation. She was here with a friend, Melissa Elizabeth Kimble. The victim was last seen at a bar late on the evening of June 17 in the company of a man introduced to Kimble as 'John.' Kimble claims to have had a very good look at 'John.' She is the source of the artist's conception that we have seen. They did not circulate it publicly because they were concerned about Kimble's safety. Remember, she had been introduced to this man."

Edgar laid his notebook on the table. "That's the kicker," he said. "The Kimble woman claims she recognized Keith when the national news covered his arrest. And she has picked his picture from a mug book. Twice."

The room was still except for a slight squeak from Sherwood's chair as he leaned back and listened. He was in his absorption pose. "Do they have any corroboration?" I asked after a moment.

Edgar frowned. "Unfortunately, yes. You recall Keith told us he worked as a bartender in Poloma Beach, about an hour and a half from here. The Caliano people had obtained records from virtually every hotel within two hundred miles; after Keith's arrest, they found his name on their computer list and pulled his employment information. The time sheets show that on June 17, Keith was on the day shift until four. The murder was that night. The next day, he had a scheduled day off. On June 19, he was back for the night shift. So he's not covered, at least on the employment records. A couple of weeks after the murder, he quit. He told us earlier he went to San Diego. I don't know if the police here know that yet or not."

Edgar paused for a reaction, then flipped open his book. "The rest is what we would expect. They are particularly impressed by the military connection; they're making good progress tracing Keith's presence in the vicinity of other Ripper murders. They seem very well organized."

Ted, who was listening through a speaker phone, piped up across the wires: "We discussed this time frame with Travis. He denies any involvement with the murder, of course. He said he quit the Poloma Beach job because, as he puts it, the surfing was crummy and the tips weren't great. He thought both would be better in San Diego. He does not recall what he was doing the night of the murder or the next day. Probably surfing, he says."

Sherwood sat up straight, ready for action now. "How is he holding up?" he asked.

"The indictment has hit him very hard," Ted answered. "We had a great deal of trouble getting even that limited information from him. I think the confinement itself adds to the problem. They have him on a twenty-four-hour watch, you know."

"Ted, I want to meet with Sheriff Sanderson and the prosecution when I'm there Thursday," Sherwood said. "Let's see if we can get him more exercise and better conditions. We have to keep that boy in shape to have a prayer of winning this thing. I don't want him moping at the defense table, looking guilty."

He looked back to Edgar. "Anything else?"

"Two items. First, do you want to talk to the Caliano police or prosecutor yourself?"

"Not yet. You keep working them until they clam up on you. Then if we need to, I'll come pound on the table and be an asshole about everything."

Edgar nodded agreement. "Next, I have an appointment to interview the eyewitness, Kimble, on Thursday. I better change it since you won't be available. When's a good day for you?"

Sherwood drummed his fingers on the table, then shook his head. "There aren't any; I have to go back to San Francisco and ride herd on that case." He paused, then shook his head again. "Leave it the way it is," he said. "Clifford can cover it. Don't you all spook her." That surprised me. Usually Sherwood wanted to do initial interviews with key witnesses. Either he was not worried about her or he had become overwhelmed. Or both.

I had another problem. "Lew, I'm not available for that interview. My two weeks with my son start Thursday; I'm flying to Kansas to pick him up. Remember? I sent a memo around about it?"

A look of irritation flashed across Sherwood's face, quickly replaced by one of apology. "Aw, Clifford, I'm sorry. But I need you to do this. I can't be everywhere, and I can't trust anyone else to cover this interview. Can you move the visit back a couple of days? We'll make it up to you on the other end." Kara gave me a sympathetic look across the table.

Well, it was an important interview, and I wouldn't trust anyone else either. Maybe Anita would understand. Or at least go along with it. "Sure, Lew. I'll just change my schedule a bit."

"Thank you, Clifford. I really appreciate it." That taken care of, Sherwood started issuing orders. Research the extradition questions. Prepare motions and briefs. Visit the scenes. Interview everyone in California. Kara, be in Johnston Beach Thursday for the Dorothy Catterman interview. Everyone scribbled madly on their legal pads.

When he was about to wrap it up, I interrupted. Sherwood would jump in his plane and fly to San Francisco, and I would not see him again for three weeks. I didn't want to wait that long before implementing my hot new idea to exclude pattern and practice evidence.

I tossed my theory out on the table. "The Kimble woman's testimony is the only substantial evidence here. Chances are you can shake her identification on cross, Lew, but even if she holds firm, apparently all she can say is Keith and Perez talked. That's not enough to support a conviction. They have to introduce the other murders and the pattern and practice evidence."

"Okay," Sherwood said, impatient that I was belaboring the obvious.

"So here's my idea on how we keep that out," I went on. "We show that Keith's movement pattern is not unique. We use the computer and find maybe half a dozen more people who also were near most of the murder sites. That shows that simply being in the vicinity is not probative of anything, so it's not relevant and introducing it would be highly prejudicial. With luck, the judge keeps it out, and they have an extremely weak case on Perez. Even if he lets it in, we have a good issue on appeal."

Sherwood looked dubious, but I plunged on. "This is the place to do it, Lew. They indicted here because they think this is their best case, and if we beat it here, the others will cave in. Particularly if we win in Johnston Beach, too. I'd like to get some more help and start looking for these other pattern matchers. Maybe this John character that Travis mentioned the other day."

When I quit, there were no cheers from the crowd. They watched Sherwood for his reaction.

He stared at me for a long minute, then shook his head slowly, a look of disgust forming on his face. "Sherwood's Rule, Clifford." His blue eyes pierced mine; his tone grew sharp. "Wishing the facts were different ain't gonna make it so. If such people exist, which I doubt, you have a snowball's chance in hell of finding them, and we can't waste the time for you to learn that. We have too much to do already without chasing after some fantasy."

I just sat while the others turned their heads, embarrassed. Sherwood had disagreed with my theories before, but he never shot them down in such a summary fashion, particularly in front of the rest of the team. He must have sensed my surprise. The glare softened; he rubbed his hand across his eyes. "Clifford," he said in a normal tone, "I'm sorry. This has been a tough few days. You keep brainstorming. That's the only way we'll come up with new ideas."

He encompassed the room with a sweep of his arm. "You all keep it up too. Maybe somebody can think of something. God knows we need it." Then he packed up his briefcase and gestured for me to follow.

We walked down the hall to a lounge area near the elevator. He set his briefcase on one chair and waved me into another, then looked out the window at the rock-lined coast.

Sherwood lowered his head reflectively, rounded his shoulders a bit, stuck his hands in his pockets: the ole country lawyer. He slowly paced back and forth.

I started to say something, but he held up his hand. "Clifford," he said, "I am very sorry to have been so abrupt in there. I guess it's Galveston, and San Francisco, and now this indictment . . . " A sheepish smile spread across his face. "I haven't spent enough time on this case. You've carried the load, done a hell of a job. Now this delay in visiting your son . . . I want you to know I appreciate it."

I felt better. "Thanks, Lew," I said. "It's just that we can't get a break on this thing."

He nodded slowly. "There's a reason for that," he muttered. Then he took a deep breath.

"Look, Clifford, we have to face facts here." He spoke slowly, reasonably. "Our client was caught red-handed attacking a girl at a resort. We have an eyewitness who saw him at a different resort with another girl who turned up dead the next day. Best we can tell, he could have been on the scene at just about every one of the Ripper murders. The victims are bound and mutilated with a method that's almost a signature, and Keith probably was trained in precisely that method. He has no alibis."

I could not tell whether this was a speech or a discussion, but I assumed I should be a sounding board. "Not necessarily, Lew," I said. "We don't have all the information yet."

Sherwood smiled patiently. "I know. But this isn't Perry Mason. This is real life. In real life, when two people are together and one of them is murdered, the other one is usually the one who did it."

I rose and faced him. "My instinct says we can do something with this 'John' thing. Remember, Keith described a man named John and said he looked like that picture. Then the witness says it was John. That could mean something."

He rolled his head like his neck hurt. "Keith watched you like a hawk when he told you about that, didn't he? Especially the part about the elephant, I bet."

I thought back. "I guess he did."

Sherwood sighed. "Don't fall in the trap of putting too much faith in your client, Clifford. It's an old story in a criminal case: a client says whatever you want to hear. I'll talk to Keith about it Thursday, but don't get your hopes up. And don't waste your time looking for a 'John from the South somewhere.' "

He turned back to the window and studied the shore again. "Juries don't like clever legal theories, Clifford. Sherwood's Rule: Juries are simpleminded. If it looks like a duck, walks like a duck, quacks like a duck, it's a duck. I can present all the evidence in the world that it could be a platypus, but that jury will just go back to the jury room and say, 'Sherwood is a heck of a lawyer, but I know a duck when I see one.' "

The deep drawl of the ole country lawyer started to fade. "I don't care what they say on voir dire, and I don't care what evidence we manage to keep out, in this case every person on the jury will know that Keith is supposed to be the Resort Ripper. We can't dodge that issue."

He turned back to me. "And I'll tell you one other thing. Your idea is to exclude the pattern and practice evidence, right? By saying this fellow John or somebody else could have been there?" I nodded.

His shoulders were back now; he stood ramrod straight. "You really think we can talk some judge into keeping out evidence that the prime suspect in the Ripper case was present at other murder sites?" Now his tone was one of pity for my foolishness. "Guess what? Judges read the papers just like you do. And they don't like men who carve up women like Christmas turkeys. No judge will let a serial killer walk because of some clever legal argument. That goes for appeals judges too. I don't care what the Constitution says; there's not a judge in this land that would take the chance of letting the Resort Ripper out on the streets."

I felt like a juror in his spell. In a low voice, almost inaudible, Sherwood said, "And I'm not so sure I want to be responsible for letting the Resort Ripper out on the streets. Do you?"

I had nothing to say. He picked up his briefcase. "We owe our client the best legal representation we can give him," he said. "If we can, we find solid evidence that he didn't do it. Real evidence, not some hocus-pocus with mirrors. Because make no mistake about it, in real life we have the burden of proof in this one. We go to trial without that evidence, Keith goes to death row. It's that simple.

"Maybe that proof doesn't exist. If so, then the best legal representation we can give him is to keep him off of death row. That will take some pretty tough negotiating, and we need to start soon, because once a prosecutor locks himself in on a case like this, he can't afford to plea-bargain. He'd take too much flak."

Sherwood pushed the elevator button. When the door opened, he blocked it and shrugged, with an almost apologetic smile. "So you see, Clifford, I don't need what-ifs and maybes. I need facts and I need bargaining chips, and I need them now." The elevator doors closed.

I passed Kara on the way back to the war room. She looked to make sure no one else was around, then gave me a soft kiss on the cheek. "Lewis was just tired," she whispered in my ear. I shrugged and went into the room. Everyone but Edgar had left.

Edgar looked at me quizzically. "What was that all about?"

"He apologized," I answered. "I think it's the pressure. We kissed and made up in the hall."

Edgar could read Sherwood almost as well as I. In this situation, maybe better. "It sounds to me like Lewis is getting ready to cut bait on this case. He thinks it's a loser."

"What do you think?" I asked.

"I think Keith did it. I think he's the Ripper." Edgar had been a cop too long to be circumspect. "Your idea's a nice theory, but I have to agree with Lewis. I doubt you'll find anyone with the same travel pattern, and you may not realize how hard it would be to look. We'd have to sub-poena every hotel and employer for miles; they won't give us that information voluntarily, you know. You're talking about thousands and thousands of people. And what if your man used false names?"

"Well," I sighed, "I guess it's a moot point anyway."

"I'm sorry about your visit with your son," Edgar said softly. "I sure didn't mean to screw you up with this inter-view. I thought Lewis would handle it himself. Can you change your schedule?"

"Yeah, I think so," I said, with more confidence than I felt. "This has happened before. Anita's pretty understand-ing. I'll call her tonight."

"I know I'd be lost without Bobby around." Bobby was Edgar's son, the soccer player.

"Thanks." I did not care to talk about it anymore. "Why didn't they pick up on Keith when they originally investi-gated the murder?"

"Actually, he's been on the police list of potential inter-views, but that list is enormous. Remember, this is within driving range of the Bay Area, and it's a vacation spot to boot. They had to sort through a huge, mobile resident population, plus people from everywhere flooding in and out during the summer. And tips and calls from all over the country. These days, any time a girl spends the night out, her roommate calls the police. Young love isn't what it was in my time."

"What did they do?"

"The only thing they could do: start in the immediate vicinity and work their way out. In fact, they did what you're talking about: interviewed hotels and businesses and got lists of guests and employees. It took the detectives three or four weeks to get to Poloma Beach. By that time, Keith had quit, his only forwarding address was in Iowa, and they had no reason to focus on him. He didn't disappear the day of the murder, and guys in those kinds of jobs quit all the time. Nothing triggered any special interest."

"So his name just sat there?" I asked.

Edgar nodded. "A matter of limited resources."

"Can we get that data base?"

Edgar shook his head. "If it has investigative information and conclusions, they'll never give it to us." He looked at me curiously. "Why?"

I shrugged. "Maybe I want to chase after a fantasy in my spare time."

Anita was not very understanding. Or, more accurately, she understood entirely too well.

She listened in silence as I explained how we had to change the schedule for Preston's visit a little bit. When I finished, she was near tears.

In a faltering voice, she told me, "No."

"What do you mean no?"

"No. I won't let you do this to Preston again."

"It's just a couple of days."

"Right, Cliff," she answered bitterly. "It's just a couple of days. And in a couple of days it'll be just a couple more days. He's so excited now. I won't do that to him over and over. If I have to, I can make up one excuse, and let him cry once and get it over with. But I will not let you string him out again."

"It won't string out. I promise."

"You've promised before. It's happened before. It happened last summer. It happened at Christmas. And your special birthday trip turned into you flying in for a few hours."

She was right. "Look," I said, "he'll understand."

Now she started to get mad. "Of course he'll understand. He's not a baby anymore. He already understands that his daddy's job is a whole lot more important to his daddy than he is. And you know what? He's right."

I started to object, but she kept on. "I'm sick of it, Cliff. I've done my best to build you up in his eyes. You're his hero. But I can't keep making excuses." Anita was crying now. "Any more lies to cover for you, and Preston will stop believing me. I won't lose my son's trust because of your precious Lewis Sherwood."

"It's not Sherwood's fault. He needs me to do this for him."

"Wake up, Cliff. I used to think you were blinded by ambition. Now I'm beginning to think you're blinded by love for the damn guy. He doesn't care about you."

"Come on, now." This was too much.

She kept on. "Oh, if you get hit by a truck tomorrow, he'll be charming and do the right thing. Send beautiful flowers. Deliver a moving eulogy. But really he'll be pissed off because he has to train someone else. He's using you. You and all the rest of them are disposable assets for the greater glory of Lewis Sherwood."

This was a new version of an old discussion from various times and places. Anita hated Sherwood. She blamed him for the failure of our marriage.

"So what's the bottom line here?" I got back to the reason I called.

"If you're not coming Thursday, don't bother to come at all. I'll make up one more reason for Preston. But I swear to God, Cliff, it's the last time."

I searched for some way to salvage this. "Anita, I only have one more year to go with Sherwood. After that, I'm pretty much my own boss. Can't we work something out for just one more year?"

She blew up. "It's always one more year with you, isn't it?" That was what I had told her the first time she announced she was leaving me. She had waited that year.

I heard her taking deep breaths to calm down. When she spoke again, her voice was soft and sad. "Cliff, I want you to see him. I want him to love you. You know that."

"So what do we do?"

"You think it will change in a year. I doubt it, but maybe it will. Let me break it to Preston tonight. You call tomorrow. Don't promise him anything. Then, show up whenever you can. If we have plans already, tough. Call me in advance if you want, but I'm not changing schedules for you anymore, and I'm not telling him you're coming until you're at the front door."

I had no rebuttal, so I agreed. We exchanged a few conciliatory little words, then hung up. Most divorced couples that I knew had gone from love to dislike, if not to outright hatred, but I never could work up even a good anger toward Anita. We just had different priorities in life.

I sat in my room, staring at the wall, feeling sorry for myself and missing Preston. Kara came in a little later; she understood as soon as she saw me. She stroked my head while I tried to be a big boy. Big boys don't cry, my father had told me a long time ago.

CHAPTER
12

Melissa Kimble was a surprise. I expected a California Valley Girl type, and here was this petite, demure brunette with a soft, little voice, telling us about the last night of her best friend's life. We sat at a round table in the conference room of her lawyer—a small, twitchy, sharp-faced man. Actually, he was the lawyer of a Mr. Elbertson, Melissa's boyfriend, who had decided that she needed help dealing with the likes of Edgar and me. Elbertson hovered protectively behind Melissa. Everyone was nervous, except the court reporter that Elbertson's lawyer had insisted transcribe the interview.

"So on Tuesday the 17th you and Maria spent the day shopping in Carmel?" I asked.

"Yes."

"Did anything unusual happen during the day?"

"No."

"Why don't you tell me what happened later?"

"Well, we got back to our hotel, the Crown Bay, late in the afternoon. We'd heard about a restaurant in Caliano called the Seal's Rock; it was supposed to have good seafood, so we changed clothes and went there for dinner."

"How did you get there?"

"I drove my car. We had dinner, and Maria said why don't we go see what the Taproot's like? It was just a couple of blocks away. Somebody at the pool told us they had a good band. I thought that would be fun, so we walked over. Left my car at the Seal's Rock; a parking place is kind of hard to find around there sometimes."

"What happened at the Taproot?" I asked.

"We sat at one of the tables and had a beer and listened to the band. Once in a while a guy would ask one of us to dance. Talked to some guys who stopped at the table. You know."

"Did you notice Maria talking to any men in particular?"

"Not then. Just some guys. You know."

"What time is this?"

"We probably got there about ten. And we were at that table about an hour, so eleven, maybe. Then Carl asked me to dance." Carl was Mr. Elbertson.

She looked adoringly at Elbertson. "I danced with Carl, then we talked some, then we moved back to a table on the other side of the bar because it was hard to hear next to the band. I didn't see much of Maria after that. You know. Once in a while I noticed her out dancing."

"Then what happened?"

"Well, Carl and I talked for at least an hour, and we sort of hit it off right away, I guess you could say. We're still dating, as a matter of fact. Anyway, Carl suggested we go to a different bar where it was a little quieter. I wanted to do that, but I didn't want to strand Maria, so I went looking for her."

"Did you find her?"

"Yes. She was at another table back behind the bar, in a different corner. I hadn't seen her go up there. She was talking to the man I told the police about."

"The man you described to the artist?"

"Uh-huh. So I went over to Maria and asked her if I could talk to her a minute off to the side. I mean, I didn't want to talk in front of this guy she was with."

"Did you say anything to him?"

"Just hi. Maria said, 'This is John.' He said, 'Hello, nice to meet you.' "

"Did he say anything else?"

"No."

"Anything in particular about his voice or accent?"

"Not really. He might have sounded kind of Southern, you know, but he didn't say much. Maria and I moved off a ways and I told her about Carl and asked would she mind if I left with him?"

"What did she say?"

"She laughed and said go ahead. I gave her my car keys. Then she said, 'Congratulations. Maybe I'll get lucky too.' And she pointed to John. John saw her do that and he sort of waved at us. Then I left with Carl." She started crying softly. "That's the last time I saw her. Alive. I shouldn't have left her there."

We took a break. Elbertson comforted her while the twitchy lawyer brought in some water and tissues. The court reporter frowned at me. Melissa wiped her eyes. "I'm ready."

This job really sucks sometimes, I thought. "Melissa," I said as gently as I could, "I know this is hard, and I'm sorry we have to ask you to go through it. Can you tell us what happened after that?"

She blushed, glanced at the lawyer and the court reporter, then sighed. "I spent the night at Carl's house." She gave Edgar and me a defiant look, waiting for a reaction. Elbertson and the lawyer glared at us. We both sat impassively, so she went on. "I didn't go back to the hotel until Wednesday afternoon. About one or two."

"That's the 18th?" I asked.

"Yes. Carl drove me to the Crown Bay. We'd made a date for that night, and I wanted to see if Maria wanted to go with us. But she wasn't in the room."

"Did it look like she'd been there at all?"

"I couldn't tell. The housekeepers had been there, so the beds were made. Everything else pretty much looked the same as when we'd left."

"Where was your car?"

"The police found it later at the Seal's Rock, where we'd left it. They never did find the keys."

"What did you do then?"

"Well, I wasn't worried then. I mean, I thought maybe she'd gone shopping again. Or maybe she was with John. You know. We didn't have any sort of schedule or anything. So I put on a swimsuit, left a note to tell her where I was, and went down to the pool.

"I stayed at the pool until it was time to get ready to meet Carl. I think we were supposed to go out about six?" She looked at Elbertson for confirmation; he nodded. "So it would have been about four-thirty or five when I went back up to the room.

"Maria hadn't been back: my note was still there. I checked the front desk; she hadn't left any messages or anything. So I started to get worried, but I didn't know what to do. I mean, if I called the police or something, and it turned out she was with John or somebody, then she'd be really embarrassed. So I decided to wait and see what Carl thought we should do, maybe go look for her or something. I took a shower and got dressed. Then I heard on TV they found a woman's body. As soon as I heard that, I called the police. I just knew it was her." She started to sob again.

"You're the one that identified the body?" I asked. She nodded, crying. Then she tossed her head back and stared at me through bleary red eyes, waiting to go on.

"I understand that you think this 'John' is Travis Keith," I said.

"I don't know Travis Keith, Mr. Nielson. I just know what John looks like. The police showed me a lot of pictures. I told them which one was John. And I saw on the news that they'd arrested someone. They showed a picture of him, and it was John. That's all I know."

"You're sure?"

"I'm positive. That's the man who killed Maria."

After she took another break to compose herself, I gingerly asked a few follow-up questions.

"Did you and Maria go out together regularly?" I asked.

"Yes, usually to plays or church functions." Great. "But this time we'd decided to sort of let loose." She looked at me a little defensively. "We had a bit to drink at dinner, and we thought it might be fun to go to a singles bar. We were on vacation, you know."

"After you met Mr. Elbertson, you didn't talk to Maria again except when you left?"

"That's right."

"Can you identify any of the other men you saw with Maria that night?"

"No. Carl and I were back in the corner, so I really only caught a glimpse of her now and then."

"From the time you left the Taproot until the time you identified the body, you don't know where Maria was or who she was with, is that right?" I was cross-examining her. A bad habit.

"That's right."

"You have no way to know for certain whether she left with 'John,' or met someone else, or indeed walked out alone, do you?"

"No, I guess not."

"It was dark in the Taproot, wasn't it?" That was clumsy. My purpose was too obvious.

Melissa answered slowly. "They have candles on the table. I could see John's face clearly. I even saw that he had a tattoo on his left arm."

"Can you describe the tattoo?"

"No, his sleeve covered most of it."

After a few more questions, I decided we would not get anything helpful by being friendly, so, feeling like a jerk, I ventured onto some sensitive territory.

"Please don't take this wrong," I started, "but I need to ask. You said you weren't worried about Maria at first because you thought she might have spent the night somewhere else, like you did. Did Maria have a habit of going off with men she picked up at a bar?"

That brought yelps of outrage from both Elbertson and his lawyer, but Melissa silenced them with a wave of her hand. "Listen," she said angrily, a steel core under that demure exterior, "Maria was no virgin, if that's what you're driving at, but she was no slut, either. She was a perfectly normal young adult single woman. We were on vacation and went to a bar, just like you probably did when you were my age." That made me feel old.

She challenged me with a look. "That upsets me, Mr. Nielson. Think about it. Maria and I, all we did was go to a bar. And your client chopped her up like so much hamburger." Her voice quavered, but her jaw was set. "Now you show up and ask me if she partied a lot? Does that make it okay for him to kill her? Does it?"

I felt like a butterfly pinned to someone's bulletin board. Everyone stared at me, waiting for my answer. "I had to ask, Melissa," I finally muttered. Then we thanked her kindly and left. No help. No proof for Sherwood.

• • •

At the war room, I had a message to call Ted in Johnston Beach. He answered on the first ring. It was mid-evening back east, and I could tell he had sipped a few drinks.

"What's up?" I asked.

"I think I should brief you on our day here." His tone was ominous.

I sat down and pulled over a legal pad, feeling like a blocking dummy ready to absorb another blow. "What did Dorothy Catterman say?" I asked, dreading the answer.

The meeting with the Johnston Beach victim had gone fairly well, Ted reported. Sherwood, the reassuring father, quickly put her at ease. From Ted's description, she sounded entirely too much like Maria Perez and Melissa Kimble.

To my great relief, he told me that Dorothy actually backed up Keith's story, as far as it went. They met in the Shag Shack, danced and talked, liked each other. They necked some on the beach and headed off for somewhere more private. What the hell, she'd thought. I'm on vacation. Who cares?

On the way, they stopped at a convenience store for Keith to get some beer and condoms. She had felt a little funny about asking him, but she wanted to make sure he had one. Can't be too careful these days, you know. AIDS and all. The last thing she remembered was driving into some woods. She woke up in the hospital in great pain.

"That doesn't sound too bad," I said. "It matches pretty well with what Keith told us."

Ted laughed, a bitter bark. "One big problem," he said.

"What?"

"Dorothy didn't know his name was Travis Keith. He told her his name was John."

I felt the case start to slide all the way down the tubes. "He didn't really?"

"He did really. John. No last name. Just John."

"Shit," I groaned. "That's the name the Ripper suspect gave the eyewitness out here."

"I know."

"I just interviewed the witness. She swears it was Keith, and that he told the victim his name was John."

Ted did not answer. We both were silent for a minute. "What did Lew say about it?" I asked finally.

"Nothing, then," Ted responded. "He was very gentle with her. Quizzed her a little more, left his card, asked her to call if she remembers anything later. Her mother's taking her back to Connecticut tomorrow. Lew sent her some flowers later, with a nice little note."

As they left, Ted continued, they talked to Kara's friend Dr. Lawson, who said Dorothy's memory could come back any time or might never return. He could hardly miss with that prediction.

"It was all downhill from there," Ted muttered.

"Downhill?" I said. "You mean there's more?"

Ted either didn't hear me or ignored the question. I heard the ice click as he sipped his drink. Suddenly he became positively chatty. He rambled on about his family. Martha was still in Chattanooga, and it was touch and go whether she would ever come back to Queenston. He had tried to talk her into joining him at the beach this weekend but no luck. She had hung up on him earlier in the evening.

I offered condolences and gently steered him back to the case. "What happened after the hospital?"

"Everything went to shit." I looked at the phone in amazement. Ted never talked that way.

"How exactly did it go to shit?"

"Lew got a message that Galveston's back on. The judge refused to approve the deal. Charlie thinks somebody applied political pressure. So now they go back on trial, and on top of that, the judge announced they start again tomorrow. Lew was furious. I thought he'd smash the phone against the wall."

That was downhill. Especially for Sherwood. I didn't blame him for being upset. Nothing could be worse than coming off a trial high and having to do it all over again. What's more, between Galveston and San Francisco, he had been on trial for about three straight weeks now, with a crisis in the Ripper case thrown in. That was a lot of pressure for anyone, even Sherwood. I thought I had detected some unraveling two days ago. He must be a walking time bomb by now.

Ted went on with his tale. As ordered, he had set up a meeting with the prosecutors and sheriff to seek modifications to Keith's confinement conditions. Instead, Sherwood and prosecutor Ledbetter got into a knock-down drag-out over the anticipated extradition request from California. The argument had to do with some technical details that were not worth fighting over, according to Ted. Pete tried to referee, but to no avail.

After riling up the prosecutors, Sherwood presented his demands for more exercise and less direct surveillance of Keith, which were summarily denied. In fact, the authorities informed him, they would step up the security because of the California indictment. Sherwood argued a bit, but Ted said he did not have his heart in it.

All pumped up by that excitement, Sherwood marched his little retinue across the street to see Travis Keith. "This is a pep talk, right?" Ted said. "Keep your chin up and all that? To keep Travis from becoming more depressed?"

He gulped his drink. "So Lew starts off with 'Hi, John'

and proceeds to call him a stupid bastard for giving a fake name to Dorothy Catterman."

"Christ," I breathed.

"Yes," Ted went on, drawing out the "s." His words slurred even more. "Travis never says a word. He just sits there while Lew paints for him, in great detail, a totally bleak picture of the case, including how you have an unshakable eyewitness out there.

"Lew closes with, and I quote, 'If you're holding back on us, mister, you'd better goddamn well spill it. And if you've got something that'll help, you better goddamn well let us know, 'cause you're about three-quarters of the way up the creek without a paddle, and I sure as hell can't find one.' End quote. Then he gets right up in Keith's face and nearly screams, 'You got that, John?' He spit it out just like that. 'John!' "

"What did Keith do?"

"His eyes got real big, and he stared at Lew, then at me, with a terrified look, and he sort of muttered 'John?' Then he shrank. I swear to God, Cliff, he shriveled up. Lew stormed out. He must have said something to Sheriff Sanderson on the way, because Sanderson came in and started yelling at Pete. Travis just sat there. He hadn't moved when we left. He might be sitting there still for all I know."

I tried to picture it. Sherwood had been known to explode on occasion, usually during a trial, when the pressure built to the point of eruption. Each time was the stuff of instant legend. About all you could do was hunker down and let it blow over, like a hurricane. And, like a hurricane, he usually was calm and even apologetic the next day. But the storm was fierce while it lasted.

Pete Bannister was pretty upset, Ted went on. "When we got to the car, Lew was perfectly calm, making some calls on his cellular phone. Pete lit into him; you should have seen it. Pete told Lew he'd gone way over the line, that his conduct was outrageous."

"That doesn't sound like Pete," I said.

"Well, he was mad. Lew just listened to him. Then he said, 'I know guys like that, Pete. You have to break them down before you can build them back up. He'll be fine.' "

Pete didn't buy it. He told Sherwood the kid needed a shrink. Pete thought he might go over the edge. Thought he might already be over the edge. When they dropped Pete off at his office, Sherwood told him he would think about it.

"Then, as soon as Pete's gone, Lew starts chewing on me," Ted groaned. " 'No shrinks,' he says, 'it's not time yet.' I guess he thought I'd put Pete up to it. He spent the whole rest of the way to the hotel yelling at me about nothing and everything, then he stuck his head in the war room and yelled at Kara to pack, and the two of them headed off to fly to Galveston. I haven't seen him lose it like that in a long time."

"Sorry I missed it." I really wasn't, of course.

"What do you suggest I do?"

I didn't know. Lie low and give Sherwood a chance to cool down. Maybe mend some fences, starting with Pete. We could ill afford to lose him. Maybe stroke Sanderson so he did not take it out on Keith.

Ted took a couple more gulps of whatever he was drinking. "What am I going to do, Cliff? Martha's leaving. I know it. And I love her."

Based on my track record, you're asking the wrong guy, I thought. But I knew the answer, and I knew he would not like it. "What you should do is get a job as a corporate counsel in Chattanooga," I told him.

"I can't do that. I'm too close to making it for good in

the firm. All I need is one more year. You know that."

"I know," I said softly.

After Ted hung up, I went out to sit on my hotel room balcony and look at the ocean, which was how I spent much of my time these days. Edgar was with his Caliano police buddy, and the rest of the crew worked like little beavers in the war room. I did not care to talk with them.

I pictured the courtroom during Keith's trial. The prosecution would put on Melissa Kimble, who would tell her story and make a positive identification of Keith as John. Then Dorothy Catterman also would identify him as John and tell the story of her attack. Add Everson's account of the Johnston Beach arrest, throw in the evidence that Keith could have been in Caliano that night, then show the jury the pictures of Maria Perez. Hell, they might not even need other pattern and practice evidence.

I thought about bagging it and moving to Johnston Beach. Hang out a shingle, maybe team up with Pete Bannister. Get a boat, go out in the ocean every day. That sounded like a pretty good life. Better than working your butt off with no family, no outside friends, and a client whose hobby was chopping up young girls.

Face facts, Sherwood had said. So I did. One of the facts I faced was that I had spent far too much time lately whining to myself about what a tough life I had. Some tough life: an annual income that most people would consider obscene, a partnership at one of the best law firms in the country, the best trial lawyer in the world as a mentor, and some of the most interesting cases around.

Maybe Keith was guilty. That wasn't my fault. Like Sherwood said, all we owed him was the best defense possible. He was getting that. It was probably more than he deserved. Not worth getting all depressed over.

Maybe things weren't that dark after all. Every case has a low point. This couldn't get much lower. From here, we either would get a break or have a guilty client who would benefit from a Sherwood-negotiated plea bargain. That wasn't so bad.

I sucked in some deep breaths of that shore air and resolved to play tennis tomorrow. Rejoin the human race. Find an outside interest back in Queenston. At least I was alive. That was better than Maria Perez.

I went back inside as the other team members drifted off to dinner. I was expecting a call from Tim Stevens, who was in Caliano covering the indictment, so I decided to play with the computer for a while. I dialed up the firm and transferred the latest version of Keith's records, then ran my analysis program.

Edgar appeared, lugging a pile of paper, while the computer crunched the data. "You asked for it," he told me. "The Caliano data base printout. You have no idea how much talking I had to do to get this out of them."

I looked at the pile in dismay. "That's the whole thing, I hope."

"Nope. It's only the list of interviews and potential interviews. Names and cities. They wouldn't give me any more details. My friend laughed when I tried to get a disk file copy."

I picked up the top couple of pages. It was names, in alphabetical order by last name, with the city and state. One per line, beginning with "Aaron, Benjamin P., Seattle, Washington." About thirty a page. The pages weren't numbered, but the pile had to be two or three hundred sheets.

"Who are these people?" I asked, leafing through the pile. There was "Keith, Travis J., Davenport, Iowa," in the middle.

"Everybody they talked to, might want to talk to, might want to think about talking to. The only reason my friend gave it to me was he can't use it—they printed it one time to show the prosecutor what kind of volume they have to deal with. The data base itself has categories like 'resident,' 'guest,' that sort of thing, with all the details that they know. But he wouldn't give me any of that. It'll take a subpoena."

"I doubt we can get one, but I'll have someone look into it." I leafed through, looking for a "John" from the South. There was "Adamason, John F., Birmingham, Alabama."

"Hey," I said. "Look at this."

Edgar walked to look over my shoulder. "Look at what?" he grunted.

"A John. From Birmingham. Remember that resort guest Keith told me about? He was from Birmingham."

Edgar flipped through the pages. "I thought he said Tuscaloosa or somewhere else in the South," he muttered. "Here's a John from Atlanta. And one from New Orleans. And Lord knows how many others. Plus a few without cities." He looked at me suspiciously. "What are you thinking now?"

"He said Birmingham. The guy was an Alabama football fan. 'Roll, Tide.' " I stared at him. "With an elephant on his sweatshirt."

Edgar groaned and shook his head. "You're really straining now, Cliff."

I shrugged. "It's a lead. Isn't that what you law enforcement people do? Check out every lead?"

Edgar scowled at me. Then he walked over to the telephone and dialed a number. "Birmingham," he said into the receiver. "A listing for John F. Adamason." A pause. "Thank you."

He hung up. "No listing."

"Can you check it out?"

He sighed and made a note in his book. "I thought Lewis said to forget about that."

"Sometimes Lew says things and changes his mind later," I said. "But don't write up a memo about it, okay? Just let me know if you find this guy. Then"—I looked through the list—"maybe we can scan this into the computer and massage it to go into our data base. Look for other names. Belinda already entered that information from Lake Wachita."

Edgar looked skeptical. "Maybe," he said, looking over at the printer that had stopped humming. "This yours?"

He handed me my report on Keith. Hot damn. It said "Alibi!" And it said it for Caliano! A turning point.

It wasn't quite as good as my computer report made it sound. Maria's murder was late June 17 or early June 18. The computer had found a credit-card receipt for a gas purchase on June 18 in San Rafino, California. Edgar pulled out our Rand McNally, and we found San Rafino. It was on the coast, about 200 miles south of Caliano.

"Not exactly airtight, I guess," I said.

"But much better than nothing." Edgar closed his eyes and thought. "Let's see. Presumably he was in Poloma Beach until four on the 17th, and he was back for the night shift on the 19th. San Rafino must be at least four, maybe five hours from Poloma Beach. So it depends on what time on the 18th he was there."

He looked back at the report. "This name sounds like a convenience store. Could have been open all night. But two years ago." He shook his head. "We'll never find out what time he made the purchase. Maybe Ted can ask Keith; this might jog his memory."

"I don't think we can count on that." I told him about Sherwood's visit.

Edgar shook his head when I told him that Keith had introduced himself as "John" to Dorothy Catterman. "That could just about seal it," he said.

"Maybe," I said. "But I still want to follow up on Adamason. Particularly now that we have a glimmer of a possible alibi. I wish Lew hadn't been so tough on Keith. We need to ask him about that receipt."

"Well, Lewis usually knows what he's doing." Edgar shoved his chair back. "Maybe that computer of yours will pay off after all. Does Belinda have all the data in?"

"No, not by a long shot. I think she's making good progress on the receipts Keith had in his safe deposit boxes and trailer, but we're still waiting for the credit-card companies, the phone companies and some others, as far as I know. It'll be coming in for some time, if it still exists."

"Yeah, I know how it is. I still don't have Keith's military record. Those bureaucrats take forever." Edgar stood to leave. "I'm meeting my friend for dinner. Tomorrow, I'll see what we can find out about this gas purchase. It's a start, Cliff. If nothing else, maybe it's one of those bargaining chips Lewis wants."

My alibi did not impress Stevens. "Forgive me if I don't make this a headline," he said.

"It's confidential, anyway. But I promised to let you know if we had anything."

"What's Sherwood think about it?"

"That's out of bounds, Tim. You know I can't give you trial strategy." Sherwood had called from Galveston; I spoke carefully as I filled him in on the Melissa Kimble interview, for fear of setting him off again, but he was fine. The storm had blown over. He had nothing to say about his visit to Johnston Beach once I told him I had talked to Ted.

Sherwood did not think much of the potential alibi either, but he did want me to let Stevens know. "We need Stevens to think we have at least some chance of getting Keith off so the word filters out to the prosecution. Keep them off balance. This isn't a client confidence, and it's in Keith's interest to leak it."

For what it was worth, I had now leaked it. Stevens pulled out his notebook. "You guys have Keith's service record yet?"

"No. We have a request in for it, but it's 'under review' or something."

He nodded, a disgusted look on his face. "It's you damn lawyers and your damn privacy laws. Can't get military records, can't get college or law school records, hell, I can't even get high school records."

I stared at him. "What are you talking about? Keith didn't go to college or law school."

Stevens moved closer to me and put his hand on my arm. "You owe me, right? I've helped you."

"You've been a big help."

"Then maybe you can help me," he said. "I have in mind a piece—either a feature article or a book—on Sherwood. He's a great story: war hero, those early murder trials, all those other high-profile cases, hobnobbing with all those celebrities."

"It's been done."

"Not like I want to do it. I want to get behind him. Find out what he's really like. I have a hunch there's a lot more story there than anyone's told. Your boss is a very intriguing guy, you know?"

"I know."

Stevens had an excited look that I had not seen before. "Here's the fascinating part to me." He pulled out the bio I had given him and pointed to the paragraph about

Sherwood's early years. "You have a high school football hero, great player but without the physical tools for the big time. Usually those small-town jocks go to the local college or into the service, then end up selling insurance back in the old home town. But every once in a while, a guy comes from a background like that and becomes rich, or President, or a famous lawyer like Sherwood. What makes them different? That's the real story. What turned him into what he is now?"

Now he had me curious. "What exactly are you looking for?" I asked.

"From you, Cliff, I want some background. Some leads on possible sources. Strictly confidential: no quotes, no attributions. Unless of course you want them."

I shook my head. I was surprised Stevens had even asked. Helping on an exposé of a member of the firm simply was not done. "I don't think so."

"Suppose we get Sherwood to authorize it? He might, you know. He's a real publicity hound."

"I don't think he would. And to be honest, I'd rather you didn't ask. Even if he clears it, I don't want to be in that position."

"What are you afraid of, Cliff?"

"I'm not afraid. Just not interested. And please don't push any of the others. We'll talk about the case, but that's it."

He didn't take it personally. Reporters must be used to rejection.

CHAPTER
13

Ten days later, Belinda finished the Ripper Wall. It stretched across the long side of the war room, a time line of all the Ripper murders, with each victim's name and picture, key dates, evidence notes, and other comments. We planned to plot Keith's movements on an overlay.

I sat at the conference table studying the scrubbed young faces on the Wall. Most of the pictures were college year-book or early job application portraits. They looked eager and full of life. It was depressing as hell.

After leaving Caliano a week and a half ago, I had become a real office lawyer, as opposed to a travel agent's dream, catching up on work at the firm during the days and spending off-duty time with Francine. Kara was still on trial in Galveston; Sherwood apparently kept her so busy that she did not send me E-mail messages every day. The case had gone to the jury, and the Blue Team expected a verdict any moment

All was quiet on the Ripper front. I could have taken my vacation, but Sherwood was on trial, and as Red Team Leader, I thought I should wait until he was done. I did some actual legal work—reviewing draft briefs—and spent much of my time fooling with the computer, devising a technique for inserting the names and addresses from the Caliano printout into our data base with very little human intervention.

Those were intellectual problems. The Ripper Wall reminded me that this was about real people. Real dead girls: Maria and LouAnne and Brenda and all the others. We had acquired a huge pile of paper, but we had made no progress proving Keith had nothing to do with the dead girls.

A sudden commotion in the hall broke my reverie. The Blue Team was back: the jury had come through with an acquittal after midnight. The overjoyed clients furnished unlimited champagne and a plane to fly the team to Queenston, and the celebration had begun in mid-air.

As tradition demanded, the entire Band poured into the hall to offer congratulations and listen to the warriors lie about their battles. The way the Blue Team told it, the case ranked among Sherwood's greatest triumphs. He somehow convinced the jury that our clients' somewhat indiscreet handling of depositors' funds was standard business practice.

To add to the excitement, the White Team reported that their San Francisco case was over too. By phone, Sherwood had worked a deal to reduce the drug charges from major dealing to simple possession. The White Team would be back tomorrow. Their victory party would not be as boisterous; the case was too disreputable. I felt sorry for them.

That shot the morning. I had lunch with Charlie Hancock, the Blue Team Leader. "Taking some time with the family?" I asked.

"Yeah," he said. "We're heading to the beach tonight. Man, this has been some long haul. All those financial records, then three weeks on trial with Sherwood . . . Well, you know."

I did. "Where is Lew?"

"No idea. He slipped out sometime last night. You know how he is after a trial like that. Maybe he flew to Hollywood to see that actress." He slurped his soup. A recent *People* magazine had pictured Sherwood squiring this year's major temptress to an awards dinner. We hoped he would bring her to the summer clerk barbecue.

"By the way," Charlie said, wiping his mouth, "thanks for loaning us Kara. She was a godsend. You need to give her some comp time if you can; she worked her tail off."

"I'll try. Did she come back with you guys?"

"No, she left last night too. I assumed she had something to do for you."

"Maybe Lew sent her somewhere. I'll try to get her some time off." She probably was asleep in her apartment. I would call later.

Charlie gave me a blow-by-blow of the Galveston trial. Sherwood had demolished the two major prosecution witnesses on cross-examination, then delivered a closing argument that left some of the spectators in tears. Not easy when your clients are rich savings and loan executives. It must have been a brilliant performance.

"But I'll tell you what," Charlie said, "it was touch and go there for a while. We had that one explosion where Lew started firing everybody. Then when the judge rejected the plea bargain—whew." He shuddered at the memory. "I don't know what you all did to him in Johnston Beach, but he came in that day loaded for bear. Chewed everyone up one side and down the other. I had to lay in a gross of Kleenex for the paralegals."

"He ate Ted alive that day too," I said.

"It was awesome. Ready to go?" I picked up the check.

Another tradition; Charlie would buy when we got Keith off. As we sauntered back to the firm, he told me about the Blue Team's next big matter: an alleged pornography ring in Newark. I strongly encouraged him to bring the evidence back to the firm; I even offered to set up the computer system for him.

Charlie promised to think it over and disappeared into his office. The excitement had died down, and most of the other Blue Teamers had taken off. On my way back to the war room, I stopped to send Kara a congratulatory E-mail. No message from her, but I did receive a love note from the Accounting Department. My expense reports were two months overdue; if not submitted within twenty-four hours, they would notify the Senator.

That was serious business. The Senator had been known to freeze a partner's draw until time sheets and expense reports were submitted. No draw meant no money. It was an effective remedy.

I cursed bean-counters and rummaged through my desk and briefcase for every receipt I could find, then walked over to beg Alice for help. Alice was fast approaching the longevity record for a Sherwood secretary. Her smile was warm, but she eyed the pile of papers in my arms without enthusiasm.

"Help," I said. "The Fifth Floor's after me." That's where the Accounting Department resided. It was out of the lawyers' immediate reach by design.

"Expense reports?" she sighed. I nodded. "Put them over there," she said. "They're mad at Ted too. I told Louise she better not bother Mr. Sherwood. I swear, you lawyers are so busy, and they worry you about something like this. Poor Ted, that's the last thing he needs right now."

"What do you mean?"

"You don't know about his father?" I shook my head.

"His father's ill. Ted flew to Alabama last night."

"I didn't know that," I said. Who was covering in Johnston Beach?

"It was sudden. I found these receipts here this morning; he must have dropped them off on his way."

"Thank you for taking care of this, Alice. You're a great lady." I turned to leave.

"It's a shame," she said. "Poor Ted. Now, you use the old expense report program, is that right?"

I had forgotten about that. "Yeah. What's the story on the other one?"

"It's something Sam did for Mr. Sherwood," she said. "Ted uses it too. So do some of the other lawyers. Why don't you? It's more work for the secretaries, but the lawyers like it."

No one ever told me about it, that's why I didn't use it. "What's the difference?"

"It lets you put in all kinds of receipts—billable, nonbillable, other business, personal—then sorts them out into the different accounts. I don't know how Mr. Sherwood could live without it, the way his files are." She gestured toward the file cabinets that lined her office. "Lord, he has records from all his companies, receipts for lamps for his house, records on his plane. Everything's in there, in no order. I'm organizing them; it isn't easy."

"I'm not surprised," I said. "He's gone through a lot of secretaries, you know."

"He's not going through this one."

"How does this new expense program help keep him organized?" I asked.

"It divides everything up. Firm expenses come out on one report, the SFL Company expenses on another, Imperial Operations on another, and so on."

"What are those?"

Alice dropped her voice. "You know how rich people put things in corporations? I think Mr. Sherwood set them up when he went through his divorce. One of the girls told me the rumor was he hid assets so the wife couldn't find them. He has one company called Imperial Operations for his plane, another called SFL Company for his book royalties. There are others."

I reached over to her credenza and picked up one of Sherwood's books. Sure enough, the copyright was in the name of the SFL Company, Inc. We established corporations like that all the time for our own clients.

"I still don't see what that has to do with the expense reports," I said.

Alice shook her head. "It gets complicated. When he uses the plane for firm business, the expenses go to Imperial Operations, then Imperial Operations bills the firm. So you need to decide which expense goes with what. Sam's program does all that."

Alice launched into something about accountants and tax records. I began to wonder whether I should try to find someone else to do my expense reports. Then I realized she was waiting for an answer. "I'm sorry, what?"

"I said, why don't you use it? The new system."

"I don't have any other companies."

"Neither does Ted, but he likes it. He gives me receipts from all his credit cards, the firm's and his own, and it sorts them out for him. When they go on vacations, or when part of his travel is personal and part of it is firm business, the program takes care of it. He finds it very useful."

"I'll think about it," I said, deciding to kill Sam when he returned from his sabbatical. My program, and he had made all these improvements without telling me. It hurt my feelings.

Alice swore that she would get me back in the good

graces of the Fifth Floor, so I went back to my office and checked my E-mail. Nothing from Kara. Nothing from Ted, either. I called our Johnston Beach war room. No answer. I called Pete Bannister.

"Where's Ted?" I asked him.

Pete hesitated for a beat. "You haven't talked to him?" he asked. "His father is very ill. Heart problems."

"That's what I heard. I'm surprised he didn't let me know. Is anyone from the firm down there?"

Pete sighed into the phone. "Now, Cliff, Ted was worried about that. He was going to stay. I told him not to be foolish." He seemed a little testy. "I think I am capable of informing you if anything develops with Travis."

I sensed ruffled feathers. "Pete, that never entered my mind. Honest. I'm concerned about Ted."

He sounded mollified. "That boy's been tight as a drum since Lewis was here. You heard about that?"

"Yes."

"Ted was right upset." He paused, then spoke tentatively. "I think someone up there needs to know. Confidentially, he has some personal problems. His wife?"

"I know about it."

"Good. I'm glad to hear that." Pete's voice contained a note of relief. "He had that pressure already, and now his father. All that piles up, makes it hard to keep your head on straight. I'm worried about him snapping." He gave a rueful chuckle. "Between Ted and Travis, I'm feeling like a psychologist down here."

"Travis the same?"

"No change. Talk to Lew about a psychiatrist, will you? And do what you should about Ted. I get the sense telling Lew about it may not be such a good idea."

He was right about that. After we finished, I called Ted's home. No answer. Martha must be in Chattanooga or

Alabama. I didn't know numbers or names for either place, so I sent Ted an E-mail message, saying not to worry and to call me when he had a chance.

The combination of the Blue Team victory and the Fifth Floor broadside had wiped out my day, so I tried to plan my night. I called Kara's apartment; the answering machine picked up. We never left messages for fear someone else might hear when the machine played. Francine had left that morning for a tax conference in Washington and a weekend with her brother Tom. Charlie, my regular tennis partner, was on the way to the beach.

I checked my E-mail one last time. Finally, a message from Kara: "Hi,Shug. Guess you heard the big news. :-It's back to Mamma for a few days,then see you."
That was terse. She must be exhausted.

I called a law school classmate whom I had not seen in months and suggested a tennis game. He was at another large firm in town. He was divorced too. He accepted in a heartbeat.

Friday afternoon, in the war room, I compared my printout of Keith's itinerary to the Ripper Wall, seeking inspiration. Edgar knocked on the jamb of the open door. "You looking for me?"

"Hi. Just want to compare notes."

He pulled up a chair next to me. "I have accomplished my mission," he said with approval as he surveyed the time line. "You all finally are doing it the right way. Just like a police task force."

"Next week we'll wear brown shoes and white socks," I said. "What's the word from the Coast?"

"Nothing useful in Perez's background. Good family, father a judge, well respected at work. We learned about a couple of past relationships; the men checked out clean. At this point, I have to say she was a girl who talked to the wrong guy one night." He pointed to the Wall. "Like them."

"Anything new on that credit-card slip?"

"It was a convenience store, like I thought. We dug out the receipt itself. It's one of the manual forms, not computer-generated, so we can't tell what time of day it was. No way anyone would remember a single customer from two years ago, even if somehow we could track down the sales clerk. We need a few more receipts to build up a pattern."

"But it's consistent with him heading south to go surfing on his day off," I said. "At least there's that." He nodded, and we looked at the Wall again, then I remembered something from a while back. "How'd you ever make out on the SERE business, you know, the military training where they supposedly teach them about 'warnings'?"

"Lewis was right, they still have the training. Keith told Ted he went through SERE, but he denied seeing any 'warnings.' Admitted he heard about them." Edgar frowned. "The damn military's worse than the Bureau. The office I talked to claims no list of attendees exists. They must have records somewhere, but we may need a subpoena to get them. I sent a memo around about it," he ended with an accusatory look.

"I remember the memo, just forgot when we were supposed to hear something. Sorry." Edgar became upset when we did not read his memos.

He shook his head. "They won't even tell us whether they still use those 'warnings.' They say it's 'Classified Information.' " Edgar grunted in disgust. "On top of that, they haven't provided Keith's military record yet. 'It's in review,' they say. Damn bureaucrats."

"I know a guy," I said. Francine's brother Tom, the Pentagon correspondent. I leafed through my address book and found his number. "He always brags about his contacts," I told Edgar as I dialed the phone.

Tom answered immediately. We exchanged a few pleasantries, then I said, "I want to ask a favor."

"Sure, what?"

"You still cover the Pentagon, right?"

"Right."

"You told me one time you could get anything out of that building in a day."

"Not everything. Not the codes to launch nuclear weapons." A pause for effect. "That might take a week. But damn near anything else. What do you want?"

"You know we represent Travis Keith, the guy accused of being the Resort Ripper?" He did. "Can you get his service record for us?"

Tom laughed. "What's going on? You're the third person this week who wants me to get Keith's service record."

"Who else wants it?"

"Tim Stevens. He wants that and he wants Sherwood's. Said you guys won't give him anything. I mentioned it to our national desk, and now they want Keith's record too."

Stevens must have struck out on his own sources. "I told Tim we don't have Keith's yet; I guess he doesn't believe me. And he's writing a book about Sherwood. You going to help him?"

"I told him I couldn't. The *Miami Observer* is the competition; we have people on the Ripper cases too. You can give it to Tim if you want to. Sherwood should have a copy of his own service record."

"Sherwood doesn't talk about the war," I said.

Tom grunted. "A lot of vets are that way."

"Will you help us?"

"Sure. Give me Keith's social security number and full name and dates of service if you have it." Edgar found them in his book. I heard Tom's pen scratch as I read the information to him.

"I assume you know you can get this through channels," he said when I finished.

"We requested it when we took the case, but they say it's 'in review.' What's that mean?"

"Maybe they can't find it. Or, it could mean they don't want you to see something."

I thought about it. "Keith was involved in some sort of special operations, and he was discharged for refusing to obey orders. Claims the order was illegal."

Tom sounded more interested now. "Can you ask him for more details?"

Right now I couldn't ask him for anything. "I need to hold off on that for a while."

"Then I'll find out for you. Anything else? How about something hard?"

He was a cocky guy, so I called his bluff. "I need a list of every person who received SERE training since about 1968." Edgar pointed his thumb over his shoulder. "Make it 1960. Or ever. I don't know when it started."

"You're kidding, right?" Tom said.

"No."

"Let me think about that. I doubt they have such a thing on hand; maybe a computer run. Maybe. The nuclear codes would be easier. Anything else?"

"Yeah." I had a hunch. "Can you see if a John F. Adamson has a military record?" Edgar stared at me, then shrugged.

"Spell it," Tom said. I did. "Do you want to give me any more clues?" he asked. "Dates? Branch of service? Social security number? Century? Anything?"

"Probably some time since World War II. And he may be from the South. Possibly Birmingham, Alabama, but that's not certain."

"Oh, that narrows it down. What is this, a test? A bar bet? Francine put you up to it, didn't she? And here I am feeding her dinner tonight."

"I really need this," I said. "Thanks."

"I won't ask if you want anything else," he grumbled. "Only three wishes to a customer."

"That's it," I said. "And we don't need it in a day."

I heard his pencil tap. "I can get you Keith's service record and something on Adamason next week sometime. Don't hold your breath on the SERE item."

Edgar was appropriately impressed when I summarized the conversation for him. We looked at the Ripper Wall in silence for a minute.

"What else?" I asked.

"I need more information from Keith," he said, "but he hasn't spoken since last time Lewis was there. I asked Ted to get something on that credit-card slip as soon as Keith snaps out of it. That, and anything more about this John." He frowned. "Where is Ted, anyway?"

"Family medical problem." I assumed that was true. I still had not heard from him. "Anything on Adamason?"

Edgar shook his head. "You can pick them, I'll give you that. No current record of any such person in Birmingham, Alabama, that I can find long-distance. No phone number, no address. I talked to a private directory service and persuaded them to check prior listings for several years, but still no luck. If I had a social security number, or even a credit card, we could do something."

That didn't sound right. "Is that usual?"

"Well, the easy explanation is he's moved. Or he's like Keith: uses a relative or friend's address."

"Someone who moves around a lot?" I asked.

Edgar immediately caught my reference to the serial killer profile. He shook his head and sighed. "To find the guy, I need someone there to do a records check. You didn't want Lewis to know about it. If I hire an investigator, or if I fly to Birmingham myself, I'll have to tell Lewis."

It might be time to bring it up again with Sherwood. "I'll talk to him when he gets back," I said. "We need to watch expenses; they're out of sight already. I backed off hiring temps to enter information in the computer because it costs too much."

Both of us turned to the piles of papers that we had collected from the various Ripper murder sites. "How are Al and Sheri coming with entering names?" Edgar asked.

"Slow but sure," I said. "I tried to estimate how long it should take. I assumed they can enter two names and addresses a minute, maybe four hundred names per hotel for the week before and after each murder, maybe twenty hotels per site. Eleven locations. Anyway, it came out to at least five months for full-time, experienced operators. For Al and Sheri—longer." I threw my hands in the air. "Those are all guesses anyway. We only have what the police would give us; we know it's not complete."

Edgar walked over and picked up some copies from the pile. "If this Adamason really means anything, then he could turn up in here."

"I want to compare cities too," I said. "Someone might use a false name but put their real city. Or even state." Edgar looked skeptical. "It's a chance," I said in my own defense. "If it's in there, maybe we can pull it out."

Edgar waved at the pile of boxes in the corner of the war room. "I'd rather find more tangible alibi evidence. And have Dorothy Catterman decide Keith did not tell her his name was John."

We talked for another hour, then Edgar looked at his watch. "Got to go. Soccer."

"Still undefeated?"

He looked surprised at the question. "We play for the fun of it." Then he grinned. "What's defeat? No one's scored on us yet."

Edgar was the John Wooden of the Queenston Junior Soccer Association. He started coaching his son's team in the five-year-old league. Bobby Browning was seven now and had yet to play in a losing soccer game.

After Edgar left, I stayed in the war room, staring at the Ripper Wall. Eleven murders over nearly five years. The closest together were about a month and a half apart, the longest stretch without one was six months. Something had to trigger them.

Edgar and I had talked about it, and he agreed, but pointed out that it was the Ripper's trigger, not ours. It could be fights with a boss, or getting turned down for a date. Who knew?

Both we and the cops (according to Edgar) had looked at all the external factors anyone could think of. Moon phases. Weather. Foreign affairs. Nothing turned up that remotely correlated.

So I sat, hoping something would seep out by osmosis.

My damn beeper beeped. It was an "Urgent" message, personal and confidential from Kara. Very short: "Hi, Shug. Come home to your apartment. I bet you find a surprise."

I opened my apartment door and found Kara's surprise. It was—Kara. Nude.

CHAPTER

14

The front of the Lake Wachita Inn, the view in the promotional postcards, faced the lake. The main floor of the sprawling brick building opened onto a wide semicircular porch. On both sides of the porch, curved staircases wound down to the lawn, an immaculately tailored grouping of croquet courts and bowling greens divided by a well-lighted crushed gravel footpath that led to the lakeside boardwalk.

He sat on a bench on the north side of the lawn where he could see both the porch and the expansive deck at the head of the pier jutting into Lake Wachita. He was comfortable there: out in the open, but the ground-level lights that marked the walkway did not directly illuminate his face. Hard rock came from inside the building to his right, while a jazz combo played more quietly on the deck.

By now most of the patrons had settled on one kind of music or the other. Occasionally couples strolled between the building and the deck. When they passed, he pretended to drink from the plastic beer cup he had fished out of a trash can. Most who walked by ignored him; a few nodded *to a fellow guest enjoying the cool summer night.*

The crowd on the deck, mostly older folks or romantic couples, sat and listened to the jazz combo or walked hand-in-hand along the boardwalk. A few small power boats and canoes floated offshore, drawn by the music. The horde in the main building was more fluid, moving in waves back and forth between the porch and the interior. Summer Friday nights at the Lake Wachita Inn were a regional tradition.

A girl at the porch railing peered toward the deck like she was looking for someone. He had noticed her before. Short blond hair, swept back on the sides, and bangs. The knit tank top showed a nice figure, but the baggy shorts did nothing for her. A little plump, maybe, but wholesome and the right age.

The girl looked over her shoulder into the lobby of the main building, then gazed at the deck again. She shifted her weight and lightly tapped both hands on the railing, a look of frustration on her face. He casually scanned the rest of the lawn. No one around. "Come on, sweetheart," he muttered.

Still studying the deck, she slowly walked to the north stairs. He felt a sudden rush of adrenaline. Not bad. She paused for a last look, then started to descend without more hesitation. She had made up her mind.

He rose and moved to the path, the empty beer cup in his left hand. A guy coming in for a refill, just like several he had seen. He timed his walk to arrive at the turn to the staircase just as she reached the bottom.

Each of them moved to the right as they approached one another: the instinctive way-clearing. Her eyes were straight ahead; he waited for the glance. It came when they were about five feet apart. "Hi," he said with the neutral smile that passing strangers give one another.

She returned his smile with a nod. As they passed, he turned and let her move a step farther. She neared the turn toward the lake, out of view from the porch. "Excuse me," he called in a conversational tone.

She stopped and turned, a question on her face. He stepped toward her. "Sandy?"

She looked confused. He moved into position a yard away and looked at her face. "Oh, I'm sorry," he said with a laugh, touching his forehead with his right hand. "This is embarrassing. I thought you were someone I knew."

She smiled and shrugged. "No, sorry," she said. Her look lingered for a fleeting second. He knew what she thought: that was a pretty feeble pick-up attempt. She hesitated, ready to turn away as soon as he ended the exchange.

"I feel so stupid," he said.

He drove his right hand hard into her, fingers rigid, just below the sternum. Not a killing stroke, but disabling. As she doubled over, he caught her: his left arm across her back, elbow cradling her left armpit, forearm across her chest, and his right hand at the pressure points in the neck. He maneuvered her right arm around his back and held it in place.

He carried her that way, staggering a bit when her feet dragged, other times weaving. Any watcher would see a solicitous and slightly high date taking care of his drunken lady friend. But, as he had calculated, no one saw them.

A few feet into the woods, he found his gym bag and slung it over his shoulder. Then he chopped her neck with the side of his hand and hoisted the body across his back in a fireman's carry.

He stood in the waist-deep water and studied his work, idly scratching a mosquito bite on his arm as he compared her to the checklist he had written and memorized. The tattoo decal on his left biceps slid under his finger: the damn thing was not as waterproof as claimed. He carefully balled it up and slid it inside the surgeon's glove on his left hand: can't let them find that.

He was sorry now that he had returned to Lake Wachita. This would spoil his memory of Brenda Petrillo. Over the years, he had refined his methods and developed variations, but Brenda still ranked up there near the top. This one might not even make the list.

That night in the lounge years ago, Brenda had talked and talked: about her job, about her soon-to-be ex-husband, about her mother's inheritance. And she had been a sexy little thing. But all he knew about Susan Cranford Bond was what he found in a quick look through her purse. A driver's license that said she was age twenty-three and lived in Lake Wachita, a student ID card from SUNY-Albany, a letter from a boyfriend talking about their life together as Christians. The sex—forget it. How could you form memories from that? At least she was not like the others. He had accomplished that much.

He had braced Susan against the exposed portion of some submerged tree limbs while he tried to work with his knife. Water had seeped into the plastic bags wrapped around his feet and legs as makeshift waders, and he slipped on the rocks and mud underfoot. Even though it was a cool night, the mosquitoes were out, attracted to his bare skin and the lake muck and sweat that covered him.

Only Susan's upper body rested above the surface, and he had floundered through the water to finish his handiwork below according to plan. The need to confuse them and destroy potential evidence hampered his creative freedom. The water probably would wash away fibers and hairs and other traces he might have missed, but he hated sloppy *work, so he had exercised his customary care in the genitals, difficult as it was under the circumstances. The neck was easier.*

He nodded. Almost done. Then he froze as a gentle, rumbling sound carried across the water. A boat motor. Too early for a search party. But she was a native. Damn. He moved in slow increments to avoid splashes or action that might catch an eye. He had covered himself in mud—they would not see him—but the white of Susan's skin against the dark shoreline might attract attention.

Quietly, gently, he slid her under the water, then crouched, ready to duck down himself if necessary. There. Around the bend. A red running light. Two fishermen trolling. He waited, judging his distance, feeling for footing. If they came too close, he would have to kill them, too. Sloppy, very sloppy.

The fishermen's voices became distinct; they talked about baseball and the Bills' prospects for the fall. He fingered his knife. Then the engine roared into life, and the boat took off across the lake. He watched the red light turn white, then green as they drove from sight.

All right. Just finish. This was the best he could do under the circumstances. He wedged Susan back on the tree limbs, upper body exposed, legs drifting out toward the lake center. Litter lined the shore, so people came here. Someone would see her: more boaters, or hikers. If not, he would call in a few days with an anonymous tip.

Some random slashes to bewilder them more. Then he carved the elephant. A different elephant, this time, to add to the confusion; he had practiced on an orange. But he had to leave an elephant. "Roll, Tide," he muttered with a smile when he finished. One of his few smiles of the night.

• • •

He waded farther into the lake to wash himself, stripped off his sodden briefs, then made his way through the woods to his gym bag. Not worth recording in the book, he decided as he dressed. He replaced the wig on his head and reglued the mustache that he had feared would come off in the water. The nose putty was a total loss; he would have to stop on the way to redo that.

This late, hours after the bands quit, cars no longer overflowed the lot at the Inn, but he had parked in an area reserved for overnight guests so the rental car would not stand out. No signs of unusual activity, no signs of a search, no one in the lot. Another dissatisfaction. He preferred to stay around for the excitement of the body's discovery. Local news always had more coverage than the national media. After finishing with Brenda, he had enjoyed a good night's sleep here at the Inn. Tonight, after all this work, he still had a long trip ahead of him.

He tossed his bag in the trunk and set off to the north. Definitely not worth recording, he thought as he drove through the night. Then he smiled. This was business. The next time would be just for pleasure again.

CHAPTER
15

Kara was incredible that night. Sex with her was always fantastic, but this was the best ever, with the possible exception of our first time in Montana. That had been discovery. By now, we knew each other's needs and wants, and tonight we met them all, one after the other, on and on. Then we tried some new things.

Finally, in the early hours of the morning, I fell back on my bed, exhausted. "Time out," I gasped. Kara giggled and lay still, rubbing my chest with her fingertips.

After a few minutes, she slid out of the bed and went into the bathroom. When she came out, she slipped on her panties and started to pick up her other clothes.

"Where are you going?" I asked in bewilderment.

She dressed slowly. "Cliff, I need to tell you something."

I pulled myself groggily to a sitting position. I was never very good at talking afterward, and this had a bad sound to it. "What's the matter?" I muttered.

Kara sat on the edge of the bed, took my hand, and gazed deep into my eyes. "This has been wonderful. And you're the nicest guy I've ever met."

She patted my hand tenderly. "But we're not going any-where, Cliff. You know that and I know that. You don't love me. You can't love anyone right now. You have your career, and you're not over Anita yet.

"I love you and always will love you in a special way, but I have to get on with my life." She sighed. "I've thought and thought about it. You're not my life, Cliff, and I'm not your life."

The words were too smooth, the delivery too polished. She had rehearsed this. I felt like I was in a bad movie. I should say something, or make some sort of gesture, but I was foggy from sex and beer. So I just stared at her.

She continued with the script, her voice sweet and gentle. "Cliff, you're a wonderful guy. Someday you'll meet the right woman and be very happy. But you won't meet the right woman this way. We have to break it off, for both our sakes."

Kara paused and searched my face for a reaction. I still didn't know my part. "I don't understand," I said.

She probably had prepared for anger, or pleading, or tears, but she didn't expect imbecility. She stood up, a little frustrated, then bent over and tried again.

"We need to stop seeing each other," she said, sounding each word as if talking to a slow child. Ad-libs now. "Not at work, of course. We'll still see each other at work. But we need to stop"—she couldn't think of the appropriate phrase—"dating."

"Dating?" A light began to shine back in the dim recesses of my mind. She was dumping me. "Why?"

Kara sighed in exasperation. She had just told me why. I stared at her. My mental gears suddenly meshed; my brain lurched into what passed for action. I thought of the last few hours, of anticipating her E-mail notes, of looking forward to seeing her when we were apart. I thought about being alone. I wanted to keep "dating."

None of this made it to my face: I sat there with the same stupid expression. Now she thought I was acting. "Stop it, Cliff," she said with a hint of anger. "You know what I'm talking about. You planning to propose any time soon?"

"No," I admitted. "I'm not ready for that."

Her face softened, and she raised her eyebrows. "See?" she said gently.

Words suddenly gushed out of my mouth. "Kara, I don't know what's going to happen tomorrow. Or the next day. I just have to get through it, a day at a time. In another year, maybe, who knows? You can't wait a year?"

She shook her head slowly, not a negative answer but to say that I didn't understand. "I've waited more than a year already, Cliff. It's been a great time. I meant what I said. But everything's changed now, and I can't screw it up, Shug." She bent down and kissed my cheek. "We have to stop it, Cliff. This is the best way. Goodbye. Thank you."

She turned to walk to the door. "Wait a minute," I said. "What changed everything?"

She paused, deciding whether to tell. Then she came over to the bed, put her hands on my shoulders, and looked deep into my eyes. "You have to promise not to tell anyone," she whispered. "But you have a right to know."

Her eyes danced with excitement. "It's Lewis. We're dating secretly. I think he's going to ask me to marry him. And I'm going to tell him yes."

After I found some gym shorts in the corner, we moved out to the kitchenette and made coffee. Kara had no girlfriends. Women often disliked her because of her looks, and she spent no time cultivating friends. That left me her only possible confidant, and she was ready to unload the happy story on someone. As she chatted away, I began to feel like we were at some bizarre teenagers' slumber party.

They had started in Galveston, shortly after the trial resumed. One of those things that happen when you are thrown together. "A little like us in Montana," she giggled and blushed. Late one night, working in Sherwood's room, their eyes met across the room-service table and sparks flew. The bed was nearby. That was handy, I thought bitterly. I remembered how the tone of her E-mail messages had changed. Hell, I probably could pinpoint the day it started if I hadn't deleted them.

A whirlwind romance. They left Galveston after the trial, went to a small lake resort in Wisconsin, and spent two days in bed. "I wanted to tell you in person," she said, "so I made up that fib about going to see Mamma." They left Wisconsin because Lewis had a meeting with his publishers. "I made up a story that I had something to do here in Queenston," she said, "so he dropped me off. I wanted to see you and talk to you." Then she smiled that big lusty smile. "And mess around one last time. That's terrible and immoral, isn't it?" She giggled again. "But it was fun."

Apparently it wasn't enough fun to keep her with me. I hoped I would not hear a comparison of my bedroom skills with Sherwood's.

"And you know what?" Her eyes were wide, her voice excited. "He's such a considerate, wonderful man. Look at this ring." As usual, I had failed to notice a new piece of jewelry. It was a huge emerald.

"He talks about what we'll do in the future. Lots of hints; a woman knows. He's building up to a proposal, Cliff. I just know it."

I listened, occasionally pouring more coffee and murmuring periodic oohs and ahhs, while I tried to sort out my feelings. At this point I was numb, disbelieving. I wondered what I would do. I had no idea.

On the intellectual level, I told myself that I expected this someday. I never thought Kara would drift along with me forever. But I didn't really expect her to two-time me. Especially with Sherwood.

It hurt. That was a surprise too.

Then I got mad. Not at Kara. At Sherwood. The son of a bitch screwed up my marriage, screwed up my visit with my son, and now he was screwing my girl. Was it a vendetta? "Did you tell Sherwood about us?" I asked.

She smiled. "No. Of course not. I won't let anyone know about us, Cliff. Ever. Don't worry."

I thought of him flying her to all his jet-set hangouts. It wasn't fair. I cared about her. Sherwood had gone through two wives and Lord knows how many other women as beautiful as Kara. She would be just another bauble to discard when he was through. Kara was only twenty-five. I didn't want him to hurt her.

Of course, my cold selfish side said, that meant she would come crawling back to me after he tired of her. Then I could decide if I wanted one of Sherwood's cast-offs.

I didn't like my cold selfish side.

Kara finally finished her tale. "I have to go, Cliff. I'm meeting Lewis at the airport; we're flying to Florida. Thanks for understanding."

"I hope it works out for you," I said, "I really do." I really did. That made me feel a little better about myself.

She smiled gratefully and gave me a hug and a peck on the cheek, then squeezed my hand. "I hope we can be friends, Cliff. Can we?"

"Of course we can." Why the hell not? Francine used to be a lover, now she was a friend. Anita was still a friend, sort of. No reason I couldn't do it with Kara. Maybe that was my role in life. Cliff Nielson: every woman's friend.

A last hug and kiss, and she was gone. I went to my front window to make sure she made it safely to her car. The sun peeked over the trees next to the pool. I stared at the parking lot for a long time after she pulled away.

I went back to bed and lay there, waiting for the stages of loss to wash over me, but all that came were the same thoughts I had before. I read for a while, watched TV for a while, and eventually dropped off to sleep.

About noon, I walked out to the living room and tried to decide how to get on with my life. Francine was still in Washington. I shouldn't go to her anyway. I crawled to Francine every time anything went wrong in my life. Eventually she would tire of the surrogate mother role.

I started down my short list of current potential playmates, trying to rustle up a tennis game. No one answered at Ted's house. He probably was still in Alabama, or in Chattanooga by now. Charlie Hancock was back from his vacation, but he had three boys, and therefore three baseball games to attend. We made a date to play on Sunday. Edgar was not much of a tennis player, and he had soccer. Maybe I should coach youth sports. It seemed to occupy a lot of time.

Finally I found my law school buddy. It was 90 degrees; we had no trouble getting a court. After volleying for five minutes, he made the most sensible suggestion I had heard in a long time. We called the airlines, discovered that all the schedules worked, and flew to Atlanta for a Braves game. Why be a rich lawyer if you don't blow some of it once in a while?

Charlie and I played tennis late Sunday morning. He beat me soundly, which I attributed to all the beer I had the previous night at the ball park and on the airplane. My buddy and I had taken cabs everywhere: no DWIs for us.

Charlie's Saturday night had been a rented Disney video and soft drinks. He sipped on his beer in the tennis club snack bar and listened with envy as I bragged about my glamorous bachelor baseball trip. I ordered iced tea. No sugar. The waitress walked away muttering about Yankees.

Later that afternoon, I swam at my apartment pool and flirted mildly with an attractive phone company marketing representative who, I learned, lived in the very next building and had no plans for the evening. Then I came in and took stock. A whole day and a half, and I had not missed Kara too badly. I suddenly had grand visions of enjoying life. Keep moving, that was the trick. Don't dwell on Kara.

I called Francine to go to dinner. No answer, so I left a message on her machine and took a shower, then sat in front of the TV. Give it another hour, I thought, and call the phone lady. CNN brought me up to date on the day's sports, then the day's latest news.

A couple of tornadoes in the midwest had overturned some mobile homes, but no one was hurt. That was good. Famine in some place I never heard of. That was bad. A typical Sunday report, padded with feature stories.

After an update on medical research, the anchor reached off-screen for a note. "This just in. The Associated Press reports that police in the upstate New York resort community of Lake Wachita have discovered the body of a young woman who was reported missing yesterday. Sources indicate that the woman may have been the victim of the serial killer known as 'The Resort Ripper.' This would be a stunning development, because a suspect in those cases, Travis Jeffrey Keith, is being held in a Johnston Beach jail, awaiting trial on a number of charges. Police caution that the possibility of a so-called copycat killer cannot be excluded.

"A CNN crew is on the way to Lake Wachita, and we will update this story as events unfold. To repeat . . . "

My damn beeper went off.

The location had changed, but the scene was too familiar: newspeople jostled for position on the steps of the Jordan County courthouse while onlookers stood behind the yellow crime scene ribbon that served as a crowd control device. It was lunchtime; the townspeople decked out in their business attire mingled with the tourists wearing shorts and knit shirts. Tim Stevens, next to me, muttered as he was elbowed by a television cameraman. "Those TV clowns always get the best view," he groused.

This time I actually was incognito. With a T-shirt, jeans, and a small note pad, I thought I blended in well with the press corps. Stevens had laughed when he spotted me, but he did not blow my cover; he even introduced me to one of his colleagues as a former intern for the *Observer.* Edgar stood on the other side of the crowd, next to Erica, the deputy chief.

When the mayor emerged, flanked by Chief Prescott and the district attorney, the TV lights came on and the photographers' cameras flashed. His Honor was a small, plump, fiftyish man who had spent more time on his necktie knot than on his hairpiece, which tilted slightly to one side. After posing nervously for a few moments, the mayor approached the mound of microphones.

"Ladies and gentlemen," His Honor began, "we have some information for you, after which we will take your questions. I have a brief statement." He and the Town Council jointly pledged to support the law enforcement agencies in all respects. This incident was a terrible aberration that cast a somber shadow on this great recreational center, but prospective visitors should rest assured that the chamber of commerce was working with the managers of the surrounding resorts, who had voluntarily increased security so that the Lakes Area was now among the safest in the country, and so on, and so on. Some of the TV crews switched off their cameras to save their batteries.

The only news came at the end of his little re-election speech: "Because of possible similarities, early yesterday I directed the chief of police to initiate immediate communication with the interstate task force coordinating investigation of certain murders throughout the country." He neglected to mention they were members of that task force by virtue of the earlier Ripper murder in his town.

"Representatives of the Caliano, California, police department arrived yesterday to provide assistance." He gestured to an indistinguishable pair of tanned, sharp-looking professionals standing to his left. "After investigation, they have agreed with the conclusion reached by our own police department: this tragic event does not fall within the unique parameters of the Resort Ripper cases, and it was not committed by the same individual."

The camera shutters exploded, and a murmur swept the crowd. Some of the reporters spoke softly into their portable cellular phones. That would be the lead sound bite for the evening news. Chief Prescott shifted his weight and looked off into the distance.

The mayor concluded: "I and the Town Council are confident that an arrest will be made within a very few days." Prescott looked even more uncomfortable at that one.

When the press conference finally broke up, the reporters without cellular phones raced off to file reports, while the TV people staked out locations for their standups. Stevens and I strolled off together. "Where's your boss?" he asked.

"Johnston Beach. He plans to announce that this exonerates Keith. He'll hold a press conference at 5:35 to get live feeds into the evening news and maybe preempt some of what these guys said. He sent us to cover things up here."

"Who's us?"

"Me and Edgar," I answered. "Sorry, Kara's in Johnston Beach with Lew."

We waited for Edgar at the corner of the block. He had an envelope with him. "We meet with Chief Prescott tonight, at Erica's farm. I have directions. Prescott's unhappy about what they made him say today, but he's under a lot of pressure from the mayor. They don't want anyone to know they're talking to us. He wants you to come too, Tim. But only off the record."

Stevens shrugged. "What's that?" I asked, pointing to the envelope.

"Medical Examiner's report, some other memos. He wants us to review them before tonight and tell him what we think." He smiled. "Erica says Prescott calls those guys from Caliano 'the Beach Boys.' He wants an objective third-party opinion from us."

Stevens grunted. "Probably the first time anyone's called you objective, isn't it, counselor?"

We talked over lunch at a small coffee shop. "What's your reading on this, Tim?" I asked. "Is it the Ripper or not?"

"Who the shit knows, pardon my French," he said. "It could be. He would know Keith is on the hook for the other murders, so he could have changed his style to buy some time. The MO is definitely different on this one, like those Caliano guys said."

"How so?"

"For one thing, maybe the main thing, this one didn't go with him voluntarily."

"How do you know that?" Edgar asked.

"I talked to some people who knew her. Susan wasn't that kind of girl. All the other victims were looking for action, or at least were susceptible to persuasion, because they were away from home, ready for a good time. This girl was spending the summer with her parents. She got her MBA last spring and had a job in Syracuse starting in the fall. Hell, she even had a house guest: her undergraduate roommate. She couldn't go off and spend the night somewhere else like the others could."

"Maybe she ducked out for a quickie." I meant to play devil's advocate, but I remembered Melissa Kimble and immediately regretted my choice of words.

Stevens frowned. "No. She and the roommate went to the Inn to meet some friends. They split up to look for them. I'm telling you, she wasn't the type. Her boyfriend's a divinity student. Everyone thought they'd become engaged this summer. Hell, her roommate thinks Susan was still a virgin."

"Why didn't they look for her, then?"

"They did. The roommate began to worry when she couldn't find her, but the concierge brushed her off. Finally, when the place began to clear out after the bands quit, she found the night manager, who knew Susan. The two of them searched the property, then got the late-shift staff to help look. The manager called the police early Saturday morning. Someone on a boat found her late that afternoon. Prescott tried to keep it quiet to get a jump on the investigation, but word leaked Sunday. That's when I heard about it."

Edgar made notes in his little book. "What are the other MO differences?"

Stevens grunted. "They've been pretty closemouthed about it. She was in the water, not tied up. And that"— he pointed to the envelope with the Medical Examiner's report—"will tell you the mutilations are different."

It began to sound like a false alarm from our perspective. "With all that, why is there any question?" I asked Stevens.

"The victim was nude, chopped up. The killer got out of there without a trace, and that takes skill in a muddy area like the edge of the lake. He didn't try real hard to conceal the body, either. All those point to the Ripper."

Stevens shook his head. "We'll see what happens tonight. I don't trust those detectives either; they want this one to be different so it won't screw up their case against Keith. I'll tell you one thing. If Keith weren't in jail down there, they'd put it on the Ripper list, at least for now."

I looked at my watch. Sherwood would be expecting my call. I was surprised he hadn't beeped me by now. "Okay, I have to report in. Anyone see any reason Lew shouldn't claim this shows the Ripper's still on the loose?"

No one did.

I drove back to my hotel and called the Johnston Beach war room. Ted answered.

"How's your father?" I asked him.

He spoke in a near whisper: obviously not alone. "He'll be fine. Only a close call, thank God." I could barely hear him. "I'm sorry I didn't call you or answer your message. I was in such a hurry I forgot my computer."

"No problem." I tried to reassure him. "Did you go on to Chattanooga?"

"No," he said. "I needed some time to myself to think things out."

Ted sounded uncomfortable. I would have to catch him later in a more private setting. "Lew there?" I asked.

"Let me put you on the speaker phone," Ted said with a note of relief.

Sherwood, Kara, and Pete were with Ted. After some discussion, we decided Sherwood should say that the killing in Lake Wachita "casts even greater doubt on the credibility of the prosecution's claim that Travis Keith is the Resort Ripper." In addition, Sherwood would manifest "alarm that the police seem to be abandoning their efforts to catch the real killer." This created "a dangerous and misleading sense of security, when in fact the murderer could be free and active, as shown by this tragic event in New York State, hundreds of miles from here."

That sounded pretty good. He would close by expressing, on Keith's behalf, "sorrow for the families of all the victims, both for their loss and for the inability of the law enforcement officials to find the responsible party or parties." His client would "join the country in praying that this reign of terror will soon come to an end."

His client, of course, had said no such thing. In fact, his client may not have said anything at all for over two weeks. I asked.

"No," said Pete, "he's still pulled in tight as a hermit crab."

Sherwood was anxious to get to his press conference, so we only briefly discussed assignments. Edgar and I would stay in Lake Wachita and investigate. Ted and Pete would begin to soften up the Johnston Beach prosecutor. Sherwood wanted to spend his time working in the firm war room; he felt a bit out of touch after concentrating on the Galveston case. Kara would help him in Queenston.

Before, he would have sent Kara to help me. I pictured them at Johnston Beach and remembered the last time she and I had been there together. Then I shook it off. "You plan to come up here at all, Lew?" I asked.

"Not unless you tell me I need to. If I show up, the press will make it look like we're interfering. I don't want jurors to think that. You cover it. Let me know if you need help." He was about to sign off.

Might as well be a sport about it. "Congratulations on Galveston," I said.

"Thanks," he said. "Keep us posted."

I knew neither Edgar nor Stevens would want me tagging along to hamper their work, so I called the firm on my computer and downloaded the latest updates. By now it took some significant phone time: the data base of Keith's receipts kept growing and the hotel records were coming on line too. While my analysis report on Keith ran in the background, I checked my mail.

Kara had sent me a message earlier in the morning. "Hi," it started. "It's terrible about that poor girl in Lake Wachita. :-(I prayed for her last night. I hope we can help find the guy that did it. Cliff, thanks again for being so wonderful. I hope you had a nice weekend. I'll see you soon, FRIEND. :-) Love, Me."

I took a deep breath, reminded myself of my new, positive outlook on life, then pulled the analysis report off the printer. It was looking better. Three more entries had appeared as potential alibis for Keith. None of them were any more solid than that credit-card slip in Caliano, but if I reviewed them through rose-colored glasses, I could convince myself that we had a hope of building a defense. At least I knew now that the computer would alert us if something were in there; a key piece of evidence would not fall through the cracks because no one noticed it.

Next, I printed out an alphabetical list of the names in the other data base. The list was twice as long as last time: Belinda's crew was churning and burning to get the data in. As it printed, I pulled off the first few pages.

On the first page, "Adamason, John F., Birmingham, Alabama," appeared twice. Could be an entry error, I told myself. Don't overreact.

I pulled up the corresponding full records from the data base. One entry was for Caliano: we had no backup information. The other was a different location. Adamason had stayed at a hotel near a resort called Tandy. He checked in three days before the murder of LouAnne Robinson and left two days after. My mystery "John" had been at two of the murder sites.

CHAPTER
16

Edgar studied my printouts, then pursed his lips and looked at me with a puzzled expression. He started to speak but instead reviewed the lists again, then took off his glasses and stared at the hotel room wall.

"Well?" I said finally.

He sighed. "I don't know. It could be something. But then again . . . " He turned back in my direction. "I don't have anything to say, except we should check it out. What are the documents from Tandy that support this?"

"I called Belinda, and she doesn't know." I tried to keep the frustration from my voice. Belinda should have cross-referenced the data base entries to copies of the source documents, but she had skipped that step to save time. Another item for Kara to correct.

Stevens called from the lobby. Edgar made a note in his pad. "All we can do is try to find this guy," he said. "Don't get your hopes too high. Most of the time, leads like this turn out to be nothing."

"That's it. What do we have here?" Chief Prescott finished his summary of the case and looked at Edgar. He obviously thought Edgar would provide him with the most help. Stevens was his second choice. He ignored me.

Edgar pushed his chair back from the table and picked up the Medical Examiner's report. He walked around the pleasant country kitchen, studying it again, while the rest of us watched silently. Erica, dressed in jeans and a sweater, offered us refills on the decaf coffee. Prescott looked like a young lawyer on vacation in his rimless glasses, knit shirt, jeans, and deck shoes worn without socks.

Edgar returned to his seat and laid his glasses on the table. "It's different from the others," he said. "Are your friends from the Coast still here?"

"They leave tomorrow," the chief answered.

"I suggest you ask them for their investigation files. You might say you need them to cover your bases for political reasons. They'll bitch about how long that will take, but I think you want to see that information."

"The task force has copies," Erica said. "We can get them there if we need to."

Edgar nodded. "Anyway, let's run through it." He started ticking items off on his fingers. I took notes on my legal pad.

"First, differences. One, this probably was an abduction of some sort. The working theory in the other cases is the perpetrator met the victim in a social setting, and they went off together. Here, the going-off-together part seems unlikely, although he could have lured her away from the crowd under some pretext."

The chief took notes too. "We have those drag marks near the woods," he said.

"And this was not the kind of girl that would go off with anybody," Stevens added. Erica nodded agreement. She had said earlier that she knew the Bond family well.

Edgar held up his second finger. "Two, the body was

submerged in a lake, not laid out like the others. No evidence of a rope or any binding. And the mutilations are different." His third and fourth fingers sprang out.

"They've been identical in the others?" Prescott asked.

"Not completely," Edgar said. "He made them more elaborate over time. But even the one you had here four years ago had the basic characteristics that he's followed all along.

"Finally," Edgar waggled his thumb, "he's never repeated a location before."

"Lucky us," Prescott muttered. He looked at Edgar. "So, bottom line, the MO is different. That means a different killer. That's what the Caliano people said."

Edgar rose and began to pace behind the table. "True, it's a different MO. But there are similarities too."

He started ticking his fingers again. "One, this victim matches the profile of the Ripper victims: same age, attractive, single woman at a resort, and so on.

"Two. Our pathologist theorizes the victims are subdued by interrupting blood flow to the brain, probably by pressure on the neck's arterial system. That would cause bruises in the neck area, but the mutilations up there make them impossible to detect. As I read your ME's report, his findings are consistent with that theory, including mutilations in the neck. I'd like our pathologist to review this.

"Three. The killer wanted the body found."

He stopped and thought, then slid several photographs across the table and peered at them. "You have the pictures from your first victim?" he asked Erica.

She reached into one of the cardboard boxes on her floor and pulled out an envelope with the pictures of Brenda Petrillo. Edgar shuffled through them, selected two, and laid them next to two of the Susan Bond photographs. He bent down to study them again. The rest of us watched him in silence.

Finally, he said, "Yeah. Look here." He had his left forefinger on a Petrillo picture, his right on one of Bond.

Prescott, Erica, and Stevens leaned over to examine where he pointed. They did not leave me any room, and I had no desire to push my way in. "See that?" Edgar said. "There on the breast?"

They all nodded. Prescott was confused. "They're different, aren't they?" he said.

Stevens bent closer. "Maybe." His voice was solemn.

"What?" I asked over Erica's shoulder.

Edgar did not lift his head. "It's not the same. But it could be an elephant."

I blew a soundless whistle through my lips. "Roll, Tide," I muttered.

We took a break and wandered out to Erica's back porch for some air. The chief stood off to one side, staring out at a dilapidated tractor barely visible in the light from the kitchen window. Off in the distance, the fireflies danced over a pasture.

"I have some questions," he finally announced. We followed him back in. It was two o'clock.

The chief peppered Edgar with technical questions. He wanted to know about the two "Ripper" cases that did not match the pattern. Did they have similar mutilations? No, Edgar explained, and the cause of death was stabbing. No elephant. He went through the other differences in graphic detail. Erica supported him with her information from the task force.

"This elephant carving is on all the others?" the chief asked.

"I believe so," Edgar answered. Erica nodded.

"So it's him?" Stevens asked.

"If that's an elephant," Edgar said, "it's either him or a

copycat. If it's a copycat, it's one who knows a lot about the Ripper. That detail hasn't been published anywhere, has it, Tim?"

"No, it hasn't," Stevens confirmed.

Edgar turned back to Prescott. "Three possibilities, then. It's the Ripper, or your killer has inside information, which implies a cop or someone with access to cops, or it's a strong coincidence."

Prescott fixed him with an unblinking stare. "What's your gut tell you?"

Edgar hated questions like that; I expected him to tap-dance and give an equivocal answer. But he looked at the chief with some sympathy, then moved his head slightly from side to side, balancing the scales. Finally, he shrugged. "I think it's the Ripper," he said.

A chill ran down my spine. Now that we might have what we were after, I wasn't so sure that I really wanted it. The Ripper actually could be out there.

The chief grilled Edgar on other points until he was satisfied. "You folks have a client down in Johnston Beach. As I understand it, they have an awfully good case against him. What's his story?"

Edgar shook his head slowly. "I wish to God I knew," he said. "To tell you the truth, and Cliff will confirm this, I thought Keith probably was the perpetrator." That made me nervous—it bordered on disclosing confidential work product—but Edgar went on before I could interrupt. "You asked me for a gut reaction. I gave it to you."

"You positive your client's still in jail? No brief escape?" The chief was grasping at straws and knew it.

"Positive," Edgar confirmed.

"Well, shit," Prescott muttered. He got up and paced around the kitchen restlessly. "I don't like the choices you give me, but they sound right. Erica, you know anyone local with commando training?"

Erica shook her head. "No one from here, Chief. You never can tell about the summer people, though."

"My California friends suggested the killer's probably a local boy, maybe a jealous ex-boyfriend. They're a big help." The chief's voice dripped acid. "And your friends at the Bureau," glaring at Edgar, "say to call them if we need technical advice or if we find a federal offense. Look for drugs, they said. At least the state cops gave us some manpower, but they're better at catching speeders than murderers."

We waited for him to finish. He stopped pacing and looked at his watch.

"All right. Let's knock off. I'm not sure I buy the Ripper theory. And I can't drop the local angle. But in my experience, if you don't have a suspect in the first forty eight hours, then you're in for the long haul." Edgar nodded agreement. "And my instincts tell me this isn't a local boy. Chances are our killer came in, made his hit, and left. So I have to cover all the bases. Any ideas or suggestions?"

Edgar had a few, but the chief's problem was not in knowing what to do; it was having enough people to do it. The Lake Wachita force was swamped locating and interviewing potential witnesses.

I piped up for the first time in a while. I had toyed with the idea of telling him about my John Adamason but decided it was too tenuous at this point. We did not want to look like a bunch of flakes who had not gotten their act together. But I wanted to follow up. "You said you have hotel registrations, rental car contracts, employee lists, that sort of thing. It's a long shot, but we can look through those to see if anything pops out. Familiar names or whatever."

"Erica, you and Edgar work out a way to get them copies tomorrow," the chief said. "It'll be sometime after the press conference. The mayor wants me to tell the world we should have an arrest any minute now. Four years they've been looking for the Ripper, and he expects me to solve it in three days." He surveyed us slowly. "And Erica, tomorrow you and I will call every detective on that task force. I want to talk to them."

We rode back to our hotel in silence. It was late, and no one had much more to say.

Most of the media had moved on to the next disaster du jour; the daily press conference in the Town Council chambers drew only a sparse crowd. Stevens gave me an *Observer* identification card, and I went because I had little useful to do. Edgar was the investigator, and Stevens the investigative reporter. My job was to hang around and listen to what they uncovered.

Afterward, Edgar met me back at my hotel with a sheaf of handwritten lists, hotel registration records, and computer printouts. He announced that, although he would be delighted to help, Erica was driving him to her farm to review some of the photographic evidence. Besides, everything he knew was in my computer, wasn't it? He would be back around dinnertime.

The pillow I threw at him smashed against the door frame as he ducked and left. Turkey.

At least these cases were in resorts, where the hotel rooms had good views. This one overlooked the lake. I piled the papers on the little balcony table and started plowing through the hotel registrations.

After a couple of hours, the names began to dance on the paper and blur into one another. A few of them sounded familiar, but when I cross-checked against my other lists, they did not match.

Lake Wachita was smaller than the other resorts. The area had fifteen or twenty hotels but not many separate nightclubs and bars, so the employment lists were relatively short. Judging from the records, most of the employees were local and full-time.

Chief Prescott's thoroughness impressed me. He had enlisted the state police to obtain passenger manifests from all the airports within a couple hours' drive. I recognized several well-known newspaper columnists departing from Syracuse, but no other names that I recalled.

I moved on to the rental cars. On lists from the Syracuse airport, I found Stevens' Black Camaro and my Buick. And on a list from another location, there was Edward P. Tarleton of Birmingham, Alabama.

The city caught my eye first. The name rang a bell too, but Tarleton was not on the Caliano list, and I couldn't find any reference to him in my personal memo files. Finally, I dialed up the firm's computer system and searched our data base. The entry reminded me where I had seen the name before.

Edward P. Tarleton, of Birmingham, Alabama, had been a guest at the Lake Wachita Inn four years ago, around the time of the first Ripper murder. He had checked in three days before, and left two days later. Just like John F. Adamason, of the same city, in Tandy.

General aviation facilities always confused me: I was accustomed to airports with terminals and one-way roads. This was more a collection of buildings that looked like warehouses, with planes scattered at random over the pavement. The little single-engine aircraft parked close in; several private jets were off to one side. In the background, a

Piper Cub ambled down the runway and lurched into the air. At least I assumed it was a Piper Cub. They all looked the same to me.

I finally spotted what appeared to be a headquarters and aimed my car in that direction. On the hour and a half drive from Lake Wachita, I had tried to decide what exactly I was looking for. I still was not sure.

I passed the rental car lot on the way. It had a dozen slots, but only three contained cars. I did not see the black Toyota that Tarleton had rented.

The building must have been a converted hangar: it had a cavernous, and mostly empty, lobby with a few vending machines, some deserted counters, and offices built from prefab walls. According to the sign over the rental car counter, customers with reserved cars should see the General Manager. Those returning cars were to leave the keys in the lock box. Receipts would be mailed. To rent a car without a reservation, pick up the white wall phone. Apparently it was a long-distance operation. Amazing what you can do with technology.

One office door said "General Manager" and the other said "Flight Operations. Authorized personnel only." As an unauthorized person, I picked "General Manager."

A head topped with a khaki ball cap popped up from behind the papers and folders piled on the desk in the middle of the room. "Help you?" it said.

I launched into the only story that had occurred to me on the drive. "Hi," I said. "My name is Clifford Nielson. I write feature stories for the *Miami Observer.*" I flashed Stevens' card at him. "I'm working on a series about general aviation facilities, and I need some background on how they operate. I happened to drive by and noticed your place here. Do you think you could spare a few minutes for some questions?"

• • •

He was a nice fellow; I hoped he wouldn't waste too much time searching for his name in the *Miami Observer*. I eased my conscience by warning him that the story might never appear and promising to send a copy if it did. As we toured, I feigned interest while he showed off various state-of-the-art gadgets. After about an hour, I started on my real questions.

"Do these planes just show up and leave whenever they want to?"

Pretty much, the manager said. FAA flight plans are mandatory for flights above a certain altitude, optional for others. The FBO, that was Fixed Base Operator, did not receive those. "If they refuel, we have a record of that. Or if they rent a car or something. But in VFR conditions, that's good visibility, it's up to the pilots. They land and take off when they want."

"This is a dumb question, but how do you pay for gas for an airplane?"

"Just like for your car. Credit card. We'll take cash in small amounts, but everyone uses a credit card."

"Do you keep any records of that?"

"When they refuel, the truck calls in this information." He pointed to a log sheet. "We keep track of the amount, the type, the truck so we can trace it back if we need to, and the plane's N-number. That's the registration number on the tail."

I leafed through some of the logs. "How many planes do you refuel in a day?"

"Depends," he said. "On weekends, we're pretty busy with hobbyists. During the week, it's more business travelers going to meetings at the Lake or in Syracuse. We can handle the larger aircraft," he added proudly, "so we get a fair bit of business traffic. It's cheaper for them to come in here than

into the city, and much less hassle for the pilot, so a lot of
the corporate jets land here and rent a car. Sometimes they
have limos meet them. Those big-cheese corporate types
go first class, you know."

I pretended to pick a day at random. "Here, for example.
You had a lot of activity this day. Was it unusual?"

The manager took the paper. "Oh, I remember that day.
That's the day before they found that girl who got killed
down at Lake Wachita. Yeah, that was a real busy couple
of days. There was some sort of symposium in Syracuse.
Business, law, media. I'm not sure what it was about."

"Can I get a copy of this for reference?" We walked to
the copy machine; I tried to think of a way to justify looking
at credit-card receipts, but nothing came to mind.

"How do you run the rental car business?" I asked.

He shrugged. "It's really out of Syracuse, but we offer
it as a service. A pilot can call in ahead of time and make
a reservation, and we'll make sure a car's here for him.
Drop-off too. We keep a small fleet, then coordinate with
Syracuse to cover the reservations."

"Do you keep records of that, too?"

"Not really. We send the contracts to Syracuse. I keep
a book here showing the car and the customer and the
driver's license number." He pointed to a bound notebook
on a counter. I picked it up and thumbed through it. I
found the page and tried to look like I was taking notes as
I jotted Tarleton's license number on my pad. An Alabama
license.

"Anything else?" the manager asked me.

I wanted to show him the artist's conception of John
from Caliano, but I had not brought it with me. Some
detective.

CHAPTER
17

"What's the matter with you, Clifford?" Sherwood bellowed. I snapped to attention. I had been staring at Kara's ring, thinking about her and Sherwood. This morning, they seemed to have the same professional relationship as always. Just like she and I did at work. I knew from her E-mail messages that the romance was still in full bloom.

"Sorry," I muttered. "Headache. It's killing me."

The Red Team was gathered around the conference table in the firm war room. When I returned from the small airport at the other end of Lake Wachita, I found a message from Sherwood, summoning us to a major team meeting. Edgar and I took the next available flight. Today, the whole team was there, even the second-stringers, who sat in chairs along the wall, pens and legal pads at the ready.

"You need a break, Clifford," Sherwood told me solicitously. "This case has been a bitch for you. Take the rest of the week off." He paused. "Hell, this is Wednesday already. Take next week, too. Don't let me catch you in here. Same for you, Edgar." Sherwood was in a buoyant mood. He was fresh from his customary time off after winning a big case, his bargaining chips were falling into place, and we finally had an angle on the case. His love life was in fine shape too, but most of the others didn't know about that.

Sherwood resumed his introduction. "All right, people. Edgar thinks the Ripper's still out there." Edgar looked uncomfortable. "So it can't be Keith." Sherwood smiled, then his face grew solemn. "Of course, that girl's death is a tragedy. We have to do anything we can to help stop this maniac. For those of you who may not be aware of it, we are cooperating with the police in Lake Wachita. That's what gave Clifford his headache."

He went around the table for updates. Edgar had already briefed the Lake Wachita situation. I simply added a few words about Chief Prescott's view of the "help" provided by the Caliano police and the FBI. I considered mentioning Adamason and Tarleton, but decided to wait until we could discuss it privately. It was still insubstantial: Edgar and I only had time to determine that Birmingham information had no listing for an Edward P. Tarleton.

Ted reported on Johnston Beach. The official prosecution position was that the Lake Wachita murder had nothing to do with their case. Travis Keith was charged with an assault against Dorothy Catterman, they said. The Ripper allegations were someone else's problem. No formal extradition motion yet from California; the Caliano prosecutors probably were evaluating the Lake Wachita murder's impact.

Keith had drifted farther out. Yesterday the jailers found him banging his head against the wall; it left blood all over the cell and a nasty cut on his forehead.

Sherwood shook his head slowly when Ted finished his report. "I misjudged that boy," he said. "I really thought he'd come around. Now, I don't know." He rubbed his chin thoughtfully, then nodded to himself. "Ted, we need to get Travis some help. Find a psychiatrist to evaluate him. Let me know which doctor you recommend before you engage him."

He paused a minute and smiled broadly. "You need some time off too, Ted. Brad"—pointing to one of the associates—"you cover in Johnston Beach until the end of next week. Ted, you line up a shrink, then go home. Say hello to Martha for me." Ted shot me an astonished glance.

The rest of the group, Kara excepted, clamored to make their reports. They wanted the rest of the week off too. No such luck. The benevolence was over; it was time to get down to work.

Sherwood handed out assignments like the Easter Bunny passes out chocolate eggs. Research this, check that, contact him, call her. The younger team members began to look a little dazed. We veterans had seen it before, and, besides, we had the week off.

The assignments showed his thought process. Several had to do with psychological evaluations and a defendant's capacity to stand trial. Others involved dismissing indictments based on newly discovered evidence. Bargaining chips. Sherwood finally had something to sink his teeth into.

"Okay, people," he ended. "I intend to spend the next few days right here, studying this material. You all"—he waved his arm to encompass the backbenchers—"stay available. I may need some help." Their faces fell in horror. "Let's get trucking, people."

Sherwood left, and the troops scurried off to carry out their assigned missions. We front line warriors sat and contemplated our surprise shore leave. Then Edgar, who knew better than to linger, left to pack up.

"Who should we call for a psychiatric evaluation?" Ted asked.

"Wilfried Banzinger's always good," I said. "He usually comes out with what we want, if you prep him in advance."

"I'd prefer someone who can help Travis," Ted said. "He's in pretty sad shape. I'm afraid he'll hurt himself badly."

"I guess Banzinger actually treats patients. I've only seen him as a witness. Could Keith be acting?"

"I suppose." Ted sounded doubtful. "If he's faking, it's an exceptional performance. The head-banging incident was real."

"Professional wrestlers do that all the time. They cut their heads with razor blades, I've read."

"I don't think this is an act." He sighed. "Well, that's what the psychiatrist is for. I'm not sure exactly what result Lew wants."

"Lew said to give him a name first. When you do that, ask him what kind of briefing to provide the shrink. That's what we did in Montana, remember, Kara?" She nodded. "If he's true to form, Lew will say we only want the truth, but then he'll let you know which version of the truth he prefers. You can repeat it the same way to the shrink."

I picked up my address book and flipped through it. "I had Banzinger's number somewhere . . . "

"I have it in my office," Kara volunteered. "And three or four others Lewis has used before. Let me get it for you, Ted." Ted and I watched the movements under her skirt as she went through the door. We both sighed and exchanged a glance of mutual recognition.

"How's your life?" I asked after a brief pause.

"Not great." Ted pursed his lips and stared blankly. "Dad's out of the hospital; he'll be okay in a few months. But Martha says she might stay in Chattanooga. As soon as I arrange for this psychiatrist, I'll drive up there. I hope a few days together will help."

"Hope so."

"Thank you, Cliff." His shoulders slumped forward as he stared at the table. "This has been a strain."

"Use the time off to recharge," I said. "Take care of the family."

He peered through his glasses with a worried look. "You, uh, haven't heard any rumors around the firm about Martha and me?"

"No," I told him. "I'm not plugged into the rumor mill anymore." It didn't matter anyway. The firm paid lip service to family, but the decision-makers really cared more about your billable hours than your home life.

"It's really too bad," he sighed. "Travis is like this, and Pete has that lead."

"What lead?"

Ted looked at me in surprise. "You don't know about it?" He leaned forward. "Oh, that's right. You've been in Lake Wachita. I thought Lew told you."

"Told me what?"

"You remember Pete has good contacts in the Swilton clan? Well, he received an anonymous phone call the other day. Someone claimed they heard Bobby Swilton in that bar where they hang out—The Red something—bragging about how they set up Keith and here he turned out to be the Resort Ripper. Thought it was hilarious. Sounds like your theory could be right. That was your theory, wasn't it?"

"What did Lew say?"

"He likes it. Told Pete to check it out. Said it's another bargaining chip. I'm surprised he didn't let you know about it."

Me too. "We've both been busy," I said. "I guess he forgot."

Kara came back with the psychiatrists' information, and Ted left to find Sherwood. Kara gave me a sly wink.

"How are you?" I asked. Womankind's best friend, that was me.

A wide grin spread across her face. "Wonderful," she purred. "Life is great." Then she glanced at the Ripper Wall and frowned. "Except I finally looked at those other pictures. I don't know, Cliff. The idea of anyone doing that . . . " She shook her head. "Those poor girls."

"Yeah." Nothing more to say.

Kara shook her head again, then sat up straight. "Don't tell Lewis, and don't take it out on Belinda, but we need better organization here. I'll have it in shape by the time you get back."

I thanked my lucky stars. "They can't find anything when I ask for it," I said.

"I know, Shug. Remember, they're new. But I can fix it. Anything you need?"

"Yeah. There's a guy named Edward P. Tarleton who stayed at the Lake Wachita Inn around the time of the first murder. He's in the data base. I need all the backup documents on him: the bill, anything else you can find. Same for John F. Adamason. He was at Tandy and in the Caliano printout. Also, I want everything on anyone else from Birmingham, Alabama, who shows up in the data base anywhere."

She wrote on her legal pad. Without looking up, she said, "I'll find the documents and scan them so you can call in to see them. Anything else?"

I gave her a few more items that had been irritating me. When I finished, she asked me, "What are you doing for this vacation?"

I had no idea. "I just found out about it."

"Go see Preston."

That was the best idea I had heard in a long time. I left to call Anita.

Alice groaned when I appeared at her door with my expenses. "Put them on top of Ted's. I'll do Mr. Sherwood's first, then yours."

"No rush," I said. "I'm leaving tonight for Kansas. Personal, for once." She smiled with approval. "He there?" I asked, gesturing toward Sherwood's door.

Sherwood waved me in when I knocked. "Thought I told you to get out of here," he growled from behind his desk. "I mean it, Clifford. You'll burn out."

"I'm leaving tonight to visit my son," I said, slipping into his visitor's chair. He nodded. "I want to let you know about a possible lead."

Sherwood leaned back, feet on his desk, in his absorption mode, while I told him about Adamason and Tarleton. "I think we should put some resources on this, Lew," I ended. "I admit it's a long shot, but we have to pursue it."

He rocked slowly, rubbing his lower lip while he considered it. His head ticked slightly left, then right, as if he were weighing options. "This all comes from Keith's story about a 'John' from Birmingham?" he asked.

I nodded. He half shook his head. "I'll lay you twenty-to-one there's nothing to it then. You haven't dealt with as many of these people as I have. They say something, anything, and watch to see what you react to. Then they embellish." He paused again, then spoke almost to himself. "I hate to waste the time and money. The Senator's already on my ass about the expenses."

I was ready to press the argument when he shrugged. "What does Edgar say?"

"Edgar thinks we should follow up."

Sherwood chuckled. "Typical cop." He spread his arms wide in defeat. "All right. But it can wait. Don't bother Edgar with it until he gets back. That will give me a chance to dig into the files. After you all come back, the three of us can come up with a reasonable approach."

He let his feet fall to the floor and pointed dramatically at me over his desk. "As for you, Clifford, get your butt out of here. If I see you or find out you're even thinking about the Resort Ripper for the next week and a half, your ass is grass. You hear me?"

"Yes, sir." I saluted. "Give me another hour or two to wrap things up, and I'm gone."

"You better be," he growled as I left.

I sat alone in the war room and stared at the pictures on the Ripper Wall. Someone had added a wire-service photo of Susan Bond: her SUNY-Albany yearbook picture. She looked young, and hopeful, and happy. Just like the others.

Edgar entered, briefcase in hand, suit coat on, ready to leave. "Never look a gift vacation in the mouth," he said. "You need to get out of here."

Everyone wanted me to leave. "I am." Then I looked at the Ripper Wall again. "What are we missing here?" I asked, as much to them as to him.

He collapsed into one of the chairs. "The pattern," he muttered, staring at the picture of Susan Bond. "That's why I don't know about this last one."

"I thought your gut told you it was the Ripper up in Lake Wachita," I said. "You backing off now?"

He shrugged. "Gut is gut. Gut is hunch. Gut is not fact. It was a different MO, and I don't know if that patch of skin is an elephant or not." He tapped his fist on the table lightly. "If we knew what he was up to, we'd know about Lake Wachita."

Edgar cupped his hands over his mouth as he surveyed the time line. I could barely hear him. "Most serial killers start slow and build to a frenzy," he said. "But this guy's steady. You have one, then a few months later you have another one. That makes me think some sort of event or emotional buildup triggers it."

"I can't see anything to set Keith off," I said. "The murders happened at all different times of the year, no special time of the month, no correlation with any events in his life that we know about."

"You can't tell," Edgar murmured.

"Keith's had plenty of women. That rules out sexual frustration. Isn't that one of your profile keys?"

"I told you there are exceptions to every characteristic. Maybe he gets hyper when a girl turns him down. Or it could be something we simply don't understand." Edgar gazed at me over one shoulder. "I think it usually is a waste of time to try to put yourself in the killer's mind. You can't think like they do. You have to find some objective sign when you look for a pattern."

"What kind of objective sign?"

He shrugged. "If he murders someone every time he has indigestion, that doesn't help us. What helps us is if he murders someone every time he has a big bowl of chili. Then at least we might get a tip from someone at a chili joint. Look for objective correlations." His eyes were back on the Wall now. "I can't find one for Keith."

"Then he's not the Ripper," I said. "Isn't that the conclusion?"

"Or," Edgar answered, "we just haven't found it yet."

We both picked up our belongings. Edgar left while I took a final sweep around the room for anything important. As I started to turn off the light, I took one last glance at the victims on the Ripper Wall.

They all gazed back at me from their pictures. Waiting for me to identify their killer.

"What do you want me to do, girls?" I muttered.

The girls didn't answer. They trusted me to take care of them.

I made it to the airport with a full six minutes to spare before my flight, and I raced through the terminal with briefcase, overnight bag, and computer all flapping in different directions.

"Hey, counselor," I heard someone call. Tim Stevens waved from a waiting area at one of the gates. I glanced at the departures screen. A five-minute delay. Plenty of time to be sociable.

He sauntered over. "What are you doing here?" I asked.

"Heading for Johnston Beach to interview Ledbetter. I swear, that shitass puddle jumper to Johnston Beach is the only airline in the world that doesn't change planes in Atlanta. Had to make a stop in Queenston. Where you bound?"

I explained and glanced at my watch. Three minutes. Stevens looked glum. "What's your problem?" I asked.

He shook his head. "Bad trip. Sometimes in this business, you find out things you didn't want to know."

Two minutes. "I don't get it."

"It's the classic debate. The public's right to know versus the individual's right to privacy. Don't you lawyers argue cases like that all the time?"

He was too abstruse for me. "I have to run. I wish we had time to talk."

He held up his finger as if he had a sudden thought. "You can help me." He pulled a folder out of his briefcase. "This is a draft of a story. Read it when you get a chance and let me know what you think. Tell me if I should print it or forget the whole damn thing. I need someone with a sense of moral balance to take a look. None of those in our business." They called his flight; I shoved the folder in my own briefcase, and raced down to my gate.

My flight was delayed two hours because of bad weather in New York and Boston. The gate agent did not appreciate my helpful reminder that neither New York nor Boston lay on the route between Queenston and Kansas. He muttered something about equipment and crew hours.

I piled my luggage in the waiting area and wandered down to the souvenir stand. Preston had grown into small men's T-shirts now, so I bought him one featuring our Triple-A baseball team. I found a regional decorating magazine for Anita and picked up a sports magazine and a thick paperback spy thriller for my in-flight reading. Anything that did not feature murders or lawyers.

CHAPTER
18

Preston had grown at least a foot in the month since I had seen him last. My blond-haired little boy had become a tow-headed kid, complete with Kansas City Royals ball cap and shoes that required an instruction manual. He was cool with his greeting: "Hey, Dad. Let's play HORSE." That's the way a nine-year-old boy says I'm glad to see you.

He beat me two out of three in the driveway, then we took the bag Anita had packed for him, threw every kind of ball we could find in the trunk of the rental car, and drove off for Kansas City, where the Royals had a weekend home stand. "Don't forget camp Monday morning," Anita called out as we left. It was the local university's annual basketball camp, featuring three starters from one of last year's Final Four teams. I would have signed up for it myself, but you had to be under nineteen.

When we carried our gear into the suite hotel in Kansas City, I left my computer and briefcase in the trunk. After a moment's hesitation, in an ultimate gesture of defiance, I even tucked the damn beeper in there. To hell with it, I thought. I'll blame the beeper company.

We spent the next three days at the ball park, swimming

pool, or basketball court. Halfway through our first one-on-one game, Preston discovered I couldn't go left without my knee brace, so he ruthlessly used his cross-over dribble to drive past me for layup after layup. Finally, I parked myself under the basket and slammed them back in his face. I still had a foot-and-a-half height advantage. "That's cheating," he said. Then he picked me apart from the perimeter.

Nothing like your son beating you at basketball to bring on middle age.

The Royals swept three from the Angels, and Sunday night we headed home to a suite motel not far from Anita's house. Preston watched the flat terrain pass until dark, then leaned against the door. I thought he was asleep. "Dad," he said after a while, "did that man in Johnston Beach kill those women?"

"You know about that case?" I asked.

"It's been on the news. Mr. Sherwood was on a couple of times. And Mom said that's why you couldn't come before. Did that man kill them?"

"I don't know yet," I said.

"Aren't you his lawyer?"

"Yes."

"Then how come you don't know?"

I didn't have a good answer to that question.

Monday, Preston insisted I go to his camp with him. I came away a big fan of that university's basketball program. The coach himself took extra time with the young ones, and the players horsed around with the kids as if they were teammates. Preston was in awe as a seven-footer gave him tips on playing the low post.

"Dad," he said from the other bed in our room that night. "Why don't you move to Kansas?"

I knew he had a reconciliation in mind, but it was too late for that. "I have to stay in Queenston," I said. "But after next year, we can spend more time together." I hoped it was true.

I went back with him Tuesday. That night, I dreamed about the Ripper Wall. Wednesday morning, I dropped Preston off at camp, then opened my trunk and pulled out my computer and briefcase. I had a promise to keep to those girls. "Hi," Kara's E-mail message from Monday started. "Lewis is ready to 'hit the road.' We might leave tonight. He said to pack for a couple of weeks. Do you think he has Las Vegas in mind? :-) It wouldn't surprise me. Give Preston a hug for me and wish me luck. Love, Me."

Alice must have put out the word to leave me alone, because the only other E-mail of significance was a note that Dr. Banzinger would interview Keith tomorrow. I downloaded the latest data bases—Kara had the team in gear, because now they were so large I worried about having enough available disk space on my hard drive—and started to work on my slim leads.

I called Birmingham information again on the off chance that something had changed. No change. No listing for Edward P. Tarleton or John F. Adamason.

One of the data bases was new: Kara had created an index to the documents that she had scanned into the system. The scanning was like a fax: it let me see an image of the actual document on my computer screen. Among the records was Tarleton's hotel registration card from the time of the first Lake Wachita murder. I downloaded the image and dialed the number shown as his business phone. It was in the Birmingham area code. The recording told me I had dialed a number that was not in service: check my listing and try again.

The registration form had a credit-card imprint. I called Francine. "Hi, how was Washington?"

"Good. Tom sends his regards. Said to tell you he is hot on the trail, whatever that means. I heard you're on vacation. How are Preston and Anita?"

We chatted for a few minutes, then I said, "Listen, I need a favor. An easy one. I need one of your bank contacts to check out a credit-card account for me." Francine did international tax work for one of the major banks in the Southeast and had gotten me information before. It is scary how much banks know. "This is legitimate, I promise. You can even bill the time."

"Okay," she sighed. "Give me the number. I'll call you back."

I thanked her profusely and hit the computer again. A fair bit of connect time on an online telephone directory convinced me that both Adamason and Tarleton had either moved or did not have phones anymore.

The Birmingham city government transferred me to four departments before announcing they would not provide tax-record information over the phone. Jefferson County yielded the same results after only three transfers. I knew the people at the courthouse would laugh at me if I called about land records.

Alabama vital records would not respond to requests for birth-certificate information over the phone. Neither would the archives. The state motor vehicles department would not give out information on driver's licenses over the phone. I did not bother to call the post office.

I considered finding an Alabama detective and paying for him out of my own pocket, but Edgar would be incensed.

Finally Francine called. "Okay, I have the credit-card account info for you." She read slowly so I could take notes.

"This number is for a corporate account. BSE Enterprises, Inc., Birmingham, Alabama. Address is a post office box." She gave it to me, complete with ZIP and phone number. "Solid credit history, payments current, payments historically kept current. Actually, they have about ten cards on the account, with different names and numbers. You want them all?"

"Sure."

"I thought you might." She listed them. One, of course, was Edward P. Tarleton. Another was John F. Adamason.

I signed onto the data base of hotel guests and searched it for the names on the BSE credit card list. Three more matched. Five names on that list, so far, had been near Ripper murder sites.

Back on the phone to Birmingham information. No listing for BSE Enterprises, Inc. I tried the phone number Francine gave me. "Law Offices," a woman's voice answered. I hung up.

Since it was a Birmingham address, I located and dialed up an electronic service for Alabama corporation records. Bingo. BSE Enterprises was incorporated in Alabama five years ago. The record gave three names for officers and directors; one of them also was registered agent. None of the names were on the list of charge card holders. I guessed from the addresses they were Alabama lawyers. The sole shareholder was RTV Corporation of Birmingham, Alabama, at the same address.

The RTV record was almost identical to the BSE record. Same officers, same directors. The only difference was the sole shareholder. It was SFL Corporation of Birmingham, Alabama, also at the same address.

I checked SFL's listing. The information was the same with one glaring exception. Two of the individuals' names were the same as the others. The President and sole share-holder was Lewis F. Sherwood, of Queenston.

● ● ●

Now I remembered. SFL was one of Sherwood's companies, the one that held the book copyright. That had to be a mistake. Maybe there were two SFL Corporations. Not supposed to be, but computers were no smarter than the people working them. I did the search again. Same answer.

The street address listed for SFL and BSE and RTV was the same as that of the registered agent. I looked him up in the electronic version of Martindale-Hubbell and could tell by the listing that he was a solo practitioner specializing in small corporations. He probably was listed as the business address for many of his clients: a common method to satisfy legal requirements for folks who chose not to list their home address or for out-of-state residents.

I called up the image of Tarleton's receipt from Lake Wachita and studied the signature. It was illegible, just like Sherwood's. Just like mine for that matter.

The only other thing I could think of to do from Kansas was call into the firm's system and download Sherwood's expense report file. Alice said he mixed business and personal expenses in there. Maybe something would turn up.

It was password-protected. I banged on the table in frustration. I had insisted on that damn feature to prevent what I was trying to do now: a hacker poking around in a private file. No one ever used the capability, not even me. I checked my own expense file. Now it was password-protected too. So was Ted's. Alice must have done it. I couldn't very well call her and ask her for the password to Sherwood's files.

The phone rang. It was Francine.

"I just received this very strange call from Tom," she said. "What in the world are you up to?"

"What do you mean?"

"He wants to come down to talk to us. You and me. Tonight if possible. Have you two done something illegal?"

I heard the disapproval in her voice under the light tone. She was half serious about the question.

"No, I swear."

"He wouldn't tell me what it's about. Just that it's very important. I told him you were out for the rest of the week, and he said you should fly back for this."

I doubted that Tom's information could be that important, but I knew I would not be able to relax until I found some explanation for Adamason and Tarleton and the BSE charge account. I couldn't do that in Kansas. "I'll come back," I said.

I booked a flight that would give me enough time to bring Preston home from camp, then called the firm system again and tried to get into my own expense file. Three tries was all it took: "Cliff" and "Nielson" didn't work, but "CWN" did. People tend to use passwords that are easy to remember; that makes them easy to figure out.

"LFS" worked for Sherwood's electronic expense files. I searched the raw data for the names of Ripper murder sites. Lots of hits.

I ran the computer program I wrote to analyze Keith's movements on Sherwood's file. It took an hour and produced three reports full of gibberish. Just like it had for Ted.

My program files from the time in Johnston Beach when I worked with Ted's records provided a starting point; I could salvage some of that effort. I started to modify the program to work on the new expense account data base. It took all of my time until I had to leave to pick up Preston.

I dreaded telling Preston that I had to leave, but Anita, bless her heart, had prepared him before I arrived. She had told him not to expect more than a couple of days, so nearly a week was a bonus. And, in truth, he was ready to go home and sleep in his own bed and resume his routine. He was exhausted, but not willing to admit it.

I was the one near tears when we hugged goodbye. "I'll be back as soon as I can," I said.

"See you, Dad." He stood on the front porch and waved at me until I rounded the corner.

On the plane, I finished compiling the modified analysis program and started it on Sherwood's expenses, with the report going to a disk file rather than to a printer. While it ran, I took Stevens' article out of my briefcase and began to read.

He had an interesting way of drafting stories. He would write some text and insert notes enclosed in brackets. Later, I assumed, he would go back and remove the notes or complete the research.

The first part was standard stuff from Sherwood's bio:

[TITLE—KING OF THE COURT?]
by Timothy J. Stevens

[Open with anecdote—maybe quote from the SLDF guy: "It actually got to be kind of funny. Lew was so well known that no one would go up against him. It was like walking Babe Ruth intentionally every time he came up to the plate. All Lew had to do was show up, and the prosecutor would offer a plea."]
[OR] [Something about piercing blue eyes fixed the witness and ask question???] [OR] [Montana???]
[Find a lead, dammit]

Lewis Sherwood, viewed by many as America's greatest criminal lawyer [whom XXX has called "America's greatest trial lawyer"] also is one of America's great success stories. Born in poverty in a small Alabama town, Sherwood now moves easily in the most powerful circles of the nation's movers and shakers. But he has never abandoned those less fortunate.

I skimmed through the article. Most of it I already knew: Sherwood's success at defending accused murderers, how Senator Braxton lured him to the firm. Then I came to a part that was new to me:

[Put in childhood]

Sherwood rarely talks about his youth, probably because it holds few fond memories. Perhaps he should. Sherwood's story is one of achievement despite obstacles that most would find insuperable.

Sherwood had no father. His mother was a waitress who fought a continuing, losing battle with alcohol [and a part-time hooker—can we say this? She's dead. See notes.]. Long-time residents of Andis remember the boy to this day. [Quote Barker, the "childhood friend?"] Sherwood grew up as the toughest kid in the toughest neighborhood in Andis. [Barker: "Everyone was scared shitless of Lew."] He was smart, ruthless, and feared. [Barker: "He had a hell of a temper, and when he lost it, people got hurt."]

Most kids from that environment end up in jail, or worse. A few channel their aggressions. For Sherwood, the saving grace was sports.

Football in the South is a religion, and Sherwood became a Knight Templar. [Too hokey] Although not large, even by the standards of his day, Sherwood led his team in scoring for three straight years and excelled on defense. All-State his senior year, local residents foresaw a brilliant college career, but he was too light and a step slow for major college football. [Barker: "Bear Bryant nearly gave him a scholarship to Alabama, but he found a boy from Mississippi who weighed twenty pounds more and could run like a damn deer. Lew was pissed."]

Every small Southern town has a high school football moment that defines its character. For Andis, that moment came in the fourth quarter of the state championship game, as the outmanned Bulldogs struggled to preserve their one-point lead over perennial power Washington. The Washington team marched down the field behind the rushing of Number 24, its star player, Eddie Tarleton. On a key third and goal, Sherwood flew over tackle and hit Tarleton in the backfield, causing a fumble that Andis recovered.

Tarleton lay motionless, back broken, paralyzed for life. [Barker: "Before that play, Lew said, 'I'm getting that Number 24.' Then afterward, while the paramedics were out there working on 24, he's back in the huddle grinning. 'Got that son-of-a-bitch,' he kept saying. Man, he was pumped."]

[Note—follow on Tarleton. Barker thinks he died in Birmingham a few years ago.]

[Note—put a break here and decide whether to use this or not.]

I read and reread that article until the computer finished its work on Sherwood's expenses. When it beeped, I called up the report and read it on the screen, line by line. One Alibi, for the Stowe case that didn't belong on the list. Two Incompletes. And ten Possibles.

That night, I drove straight to Francine's house from the airport, but I no longer had any interest in whatever Tom

Collins wanted to talk about. I needed to find an explanation.

Sherwood couldn't possibly be the Resort Ripper. Most likely, something was wrong with my computer program. But those corporations . . .

I couldn't just ask Sherwood. "Excuse me, Lew, this question came up when I broke into your electronic expense report files." The only alternative was to get the original documents to verify what the computer had told me. That was unsavory, but possible: I knew where Alice kept the key to her file cabinets, and Kara had told me she and Sherwood were out of town.

I decided not to say anything to Francine or Tom. Tom was an outsider, and a reporter to boot. I couldn't let him know I was poking around in Sherwood's files. Not to mention how stupid I would look when the explanation became apparent. There had to be an explanation.

Tom Collins was a tall, thin, bespectacled male clone of Francine, except not nearly as neatly dressed. He affected the longish hair and rumpled look of a reporter who was close to power and knew a great deal more than the powerful themselves.

We sat in Francine's sunporch. "Preliminaries first," Tom said. "Keith's record." He tossed a pile of papers on the table. I started to pick it up and look through it.

Tom stopped me. "Look at it later. No surprises for you there. He did have SERE training; he was in the jungle. That was the holdup: they were reviewing it for classified operations. I pulled and shredded the items that really are secrets. No need for you to have them. That order he claims was illegal—the one that got him his discharge—probably was valid. Looks to me like Keith was a guy that couldn't take the discipline."

Tom took a swallow of Coors and pointed to the pile of papers. "Got you a description of the SERE training. That's all I could find. They don't have a list of attendees. Now, Adamason."

Francine rolled her eyes to show her lack of interest in the proceedings. Tom ignored her. "I don't know what you're looking for, but the only John F. Adamason from Alabama I could locate was a kid from Jasper. Navy. You want to find him, go look on the wall at the Vietnam Memorial. He was killed in action."

I shook my head. "Must be the wrong guy. The one I'm looking for was at a hotel within the past year."

Tom shrugged. "Whatever. Anyway, it's a small world. That led me to the part I think you need to know," he said. "It could be important."

"I believe I shall retire to the ladies' parlor," Francine said in a mocking tone.

"No. Stay here. I want you to hear this." Tom had a serious expression.

I had other matters to worry about too. "So what is it?" I asked. "You found the Lost Squadron or something?"

"This kid Adamason. I tried to get his service record in case you needed it, but it was very touchy for some reason. Something to do with his outfit: SWU 71.3.2. That ring a bell?"

Francine and I looked at each other. "No," she said, letting her exasperation show.

"That's Sherwood's old unit. Tim Stevens gave me the designation when he asked me to help him." Tom pulled out some notes and shifted into his pundit tone of voice. He had spent years pitching story and book ideas to editors and also was an on-call expert analyst for television news; he could and would deliver a dissertation on any subject at the drop of a hat.

"I decided, hey, while I'm here, might as well find out about Sherwood's record. I ran into road blocks everywhere, just like Stevens did. They're pretty free in the Pentagon with the 'Secret' stamp. That made me curious. So I went a different route.

"I called a couple of friends and managed to locate some people. At first, they wouldn't talk to me, and they never talked at all on the record, so I won't tell you who they are. But I believe them. This is about Sherwood. You want me to go on?" I did.

"Sherwood was not a nice person," Tom continued. "He was one of the nastiest people in one of the nastiest units in a nasty war. You've heard of SEALs, I imagine." Francine and I both nodded. "Sea, Air, Land. Their mission is to sneak ashore under cover of darkness and wreak havoc and clear the way for naval operations. Sherwood was a SEAL."

I had not known that, but it did not surprise me because I could not picture Sherwood as a typical sailor. SEALs were far from typical sailors. I had run into a few SEALs at the Officer's Club in Little Creek, Virginia, during my Navy days. After a few beers, they told some hair-raising stories. SEALs were known to be crazy. Even crazier than the fighter pilots, who by definition were crazy because they landed airplanes on aircraft carriers at night. But fighter pilots usually were not dangerous. No one wanted to piss off a SEAL.

Tom went on with his story. "In Nam, some of the SEALs had a different mission. The buzzword was POST: Psychological Operations and Selective Targeting. English translation: terrorism and assassination. They operated in the North, trying to scare hell out of the populace and wipe out the leadership.

"My sources say Sherwood was good at it. Maybe the best. He became something of a legend among the small group who knew about those operations.

"Let me back up. After we committed ground troops at a heavy level, the Vietcong started a terrorist technique they called 'warnings.' The idea was to capture an enemy, bind him up, torture him until he died, then mutilate the body in a ritualistic fashion and leave it to warn others not to mess with you.

"Like I said, the Vietcong started it on our troops. But our guys turned it into an art form.

"Sherwood's unit specialized in 'warnings.' But they weren't after soldiers; their mission was North Vietnamese morale. They grabbed civilians and left them as 'warnings' to the other villagers. Snatched them out of their beds in the middle of the night. The people would get up the next morning and find one of their neighbors posted as a 'warning,' right in the middle of the village. Probably a pretty effective little morale squelcher. The North Vietnamese called these Panther attacks. The special units found out about that and started carving little panther symbols somewhere on the bodies to heighten the mystique.

"Your boy was a Panther who went after head honchos. That's even worse for morale, presumably, to see your leaders cut up like roast pigs. Sherwood's biggest hit was a district chief in Hanoi itself. Left him in a major intersection.

"The North Vietnamese hated these guys, of course. They couldn't catch them. They almost never found signs of them, except for the 'warnings.' The Panther units were trained to move and operate silently, to cover their trails, and to leave no evidence of their presence.

"Now, I'm not talking about a lot of people here. There were only two active Panther units, and they only had five to ten men each. That made them hard to find. But one day they slipped up: a company of North Vietnamese regulars cornered both units together.

"The Panthers were surrounded and badly outmanned. Only three made it out alive. Sherwood, of course, and a guy who's one of my sources, and a kid named Thomas. But the rest bought it. Including your Adamason.

"The three that got away vowed revenge. They tracked that NV company and picked off pickets and guards and anyone else they could lay their hands on and left them as 'warnings.' It's an amazing story. Those three drove that company south the way trained sheepdogs drive their herds by nipping at the heels of the ewes.

"They drove them right into an Army cavalry position. A firefight broke out. The NV got the worse of it and tried to surrender, but the Army guys kept firing. The Panthers stopped any retreat. It was a massacre.

"When it was over, the Panthers approached the Army unit. A jumpy private shot and killed Thomas. Sherwood walked right up to the kid that did the shooting, looked him in the eye, and cut his throat. Then he started chopping him up. He smiled the whole time. Took half a dozen soldiers to subdue him.

"This all put the brass in a tough spot. They couldn't decide whether to court-martial Sherwood or decorate him or just ignore him and wish he wasn't there. The Army wanted to nail him for murder, of course, so they locked him up. But he got a smart Navy Reserve lawyer who allowed as how the brass probably didn't want to have word of the massacre on the record, and how they probably didn't want word of the Panthers on the record, and how he couldn't defend his client without making all that public.

"So they held their noses and gave him that Navy Cross and discharged him. They also canceled the Panther program. But they had another couple of units in training, and the techniques and tactics of 'warnings' were part of their education. My source swears they still teach it to certain special operations units."

Tom stopped abruptly, finished with his story. Francine and I stared at him in horror. Bells clanged in my head; I tried to keep my voice calm and level. "That's a hell of a story," I said. "What do you plan to do with it?"

"Nothing. I don't intend to tell Stevens. Unless something else comes up that makes it fair game or really newsworthy, I'll tuck it away in my files with all the other horror stories I've picked up about Nam. That was a long time ago."

"What do you want us to do?" Francine asked softly.

"Nothing. Or whatever you think. I thought you should know about it. A guy like this doesn't change, not down deep. Be careful of him."

CHAPTER
19

The 30th floor was deserted when I arrived at the firm after dropping Tom at the airport. It was after midnight; all the lights were off. I spread some papers out on the desk in my office, then went to Sherwood's suite. Alice's keys were in her top drawer.

After making certain I was still alone, I unlocked the drawer labeled "Sherwood, L.F., Personal Files, D-F." That would include "E" for expenses. His expense files were in chronological order. Referring to my list of Ripper murders, I pulled out piles of paper for the dates surrounding each, locked everything back up, turned out the lights, and headed to the copy machine.

I considered keeping the originals, but Alice might have noticed and asked Sherwood. Instead, I sweated it out over the copy machine, hoping desperately no one would come by.

I took the copies back to my office and slipped them into a plain manila envelope, then, after checking again for any sounds, raced back to Sherwood's suite. The same routine as before, in reverse this time. Once the originals were back in their files and safely locked up, I opened Alice's drawer to return the keys.

"Clifford?" The voice came from behind me. I whirled to face Sherwood. He stood there in the entrance door with a pensive look, holding a briefcase.

"Jesus, Lew, you scared me," I said, hoping he could not hear my racing heart. Had he seen me in the files?

"What are you doing?"

I gambled that he had just walked in. "Expenses. The Fifth Floor is after me again. Then I needed a stapler. You know, you never can find one; the damn secretaries lock them up at night. Alice showed me where she keeps her keys so I could get hers if I need to. But she made me promise to put it back." I felt like I was babbling.

"Oh, yeah," he grunted and turned on the light in his office. My heart started to descend from my throat back to its normal location. He sat and picked up the phone, then called to me before he dialed. "I thought you were in Kansas, Clifford."

"Just got back. I came in to finish these, then I'm taking off again." I paused. "Didn't I hear you were out of town?"

"Leaving in a few minutes." Sherwood looked up and smiled. "Go on, beat it. I don't care what those bean-counters want, don't you come in here when you're on vacation. You need a hobby, Clifford."

"Yeah, you're right. Night, Lew."

"Night." He hit a speed dial button on his phone. As I walked out, I heard him say, "Ready to go?" I wondered if he were calling Kara.

It took me the better part of a day—actually pieces of night and day—to verify the data base entries with the paper receipts from Sherwood's files. I plugged away, occasionally taking a nap or eating whatever I could find. The phone rang from time to time; I let my answering machine handle it. Charlie called looking for a tennis game. My law school buddy suggested a trip to Toronto for the Blue Jays and Yankees. I did not return either call.

I did pick up when Francine called. "Are you all right?" She sounded worried.

"Yeah," I said. "Fine. Just playing with my computer."

"You seemed so upset when you took Tom to the airport. I mean, that's terrible what Sherwood did in the war, but . . . " She let her voice trail off. She was about to say it did not surprise her.

I did not want to involve Francine. "That was a long time ago," I said. "I'll call you later, okay?"

"Do you want to go out for dinner tonight?"

"No, I'm in the middle of this computer thing." I forced a laugh. "It's driving me nuts." She would not hang up until I promised to call her the next day.

I deliberately turned my brain off and simply checked one piece of paper after another against the corresponding computer entry. Occasionally I found differences and made the corrections. When I finally finished, I called up my modified program and ran it.

While the computer worked, I leafed through the papers I had copied from Sherwood's files. I had entered them as they appeared in the pile, without regard to dates and locations. Finally I found the one I was looking for: the charge-card receipt for the refueling near Lake Wachita. It was signed by E. P. Tarleton.

With the receipt, I could trace back to the entry in the fueling log the FBO general manager had given me. I wrote down the N-number of the plane, then called the local FAA office. The lady was very pleasant, but I had to do some serious sweet-talking before she agreed to look up the registered owner of that airplane.

It was Imperial Operations, of Birmingham, Alabama. Alice had mentioned it. To be certain, I went to the Alabama data base again. The same familiar names, the same post office box, the same street address. SFL Corporation was the sole shareholder of Imperial Operations. No one else flew Sherwood's plane: he was there the night Susan Bond was murdered at Lake Wachita. That was my last night with Kara. Sherwood told her he was at a meeting with his publishers.

I stared at the refueling log and thought about Susan Bond until the printer finally stopped. It was the same as before: Ten Possibles, two Incompletes. Not counting Susan Bond.

The computer printout went out of focus. My stomach knotted, my heart pounded, a cold sweat broke out on my forehead, and no matter how deeply I inhaled, the air wouldn't reach my lungs. I thought I would pass out. It's my heart, I thought wildly. Just fucking great. I'm dying here of a heart attack, and no one will find me for three days because I'm on vacation.

I took deep breaths, and in a few minutes my equilibrium returned, but when I surveyed the piles of paper around on the floor, I did not want to look at them anymore. I did not want to be in this apartment anymore. The sun was out, so it was daytime. I had lost track of which day.

"Look, Clifford, we have to face facts here," Sherwood had told me in Caliano. I took my laptop computer down to the pool at my apartment complex, found a table, and moved it so I was in the sun but the umbrella shielded my computer's screen. All right. What are the facts?

"Suspect X," I typed. Keep personalities out of it.

Suspect X was a prosperous, prominent person. He had

commando training. He was intimately familiar with "warnings" used in Vietnam.

Suspect X had a history of physical violence in high school and in the military.

Suspect X had access to various credit cards in various names. Two of the names were dead men he had known in the past. The others? Unknown. With at most one exception, those credit cards had been used near the time and place of each Ripper murder.

Suspect X was at Lake Wachita when Susan Bond was murdered.

Suspect X was intimately familiar with the details of the murders, at least from the time of Keith's arrest.

Suspect X traveled constantly in his own plane. His movements were not questioned by, and often not known to, employers, coworkers, or acquaintances.

Suspect X's height and weight generally corresponded with the only descriptions available of the Ripper. His hair and eyes did not. He had no tattoos.

Suspect X came from an abusive home environment. He might hold a grudge against the University of Alabama. He clearly knew "Roll, Tide" and the elephant mascot.

After adding a few more points, I studied my short memo on the computer's flat gray screen. Then I took the computer to my apartment, printed two copies, and erased the disk file.

Give it a minute, I thought. I took one copy back down to the pool.

Leave personalities out of it. This is Suspect X we're talking about. Analyze him. I started asking myself the questions that I would have asked an associate.

First, is everything in it true?

It is. If Collins' and Stevens' sources are accurate.

Next, is it proof?

Some is, some isn't. A lot of hearsay there. And it's all circumstantial.

Anything wrong with circumstantial evidence?

No.

Could you get an indictment with this?

Yes.

Could you get a conviction with this?

Maybe. Less certain.

If you had to defend Suspect X, could you get him off?

On this evidence alone, perhaps. But if the prosecution develops it correctly . . .

Is the case against Suspect X better than the case against Travis Keith?

Yes.

Does this make Suspect X the prime suspect in the Resort Ripper cases?

Yes.

Chief Prescott's question: What does your gut tell you?

Suspect X is the Resort Ripper.

What do you do now, Clifford?

I wish I knew.

What I did then was catch a plane for Johnston Beach.

"Well, a surprise visitor," said Pete Bannister when I walked into his office. He shook my hand warmly. "It's been a long time. What brings you here?"

I had coached myself to behave normally. "I want to visit Keith," I said. "I've never been involved in a case where I've had so little contact with the client."

Pete grimaced. "You'll be disappointed, I'm afraid. It's a sad thing."

"He's no better?"

"No, worse if anything. The psychiatrist saw him this week; you should get his report soon. I sure hope he can help Travis. Come on back, let's visit for a minute."

We went into Pete's office, and I settled into his guest chair while he cleared papers from his desk. "Sorry about the mess," he said. "I have a hearing in a half hour. DWI."

"Don't let me interrupt you."

"No, I'm all set. But I can't go with you to see Travis until later today. Judge Whoten has a calendar call after this hearing."

"That's all right. Don't bother. I'll go over by myself. By the way, please don't tell Lew or the others that I came down here." Pete raised a questioning eyebrow.

"Nothing sinister," I explained. "Lew sent me and Ted and Edgar off for a few days vacation with explicit instructions to forget about the case for a while. I've had Keith on my mind, but I don't want Lew to know about it."

"Lew's right. You all should take more breaks from this. I know Ted needs it. And even Lew looked right tired when he was here for that press conference after Lake Wachita."

"Well, I'll go see Keith and satisfy my conscience, then head back home." Act normal. "I hear you developed a big lead on the Swiltons."

Pete shook his head slowly. "Yeah, that's another thing that makes it so sad about Travis right now. I have become convinced he's innocent in the Catterman case. Lot of reasons to think Bobby and Eddie are the bad guys here, not Travis."

"Tell me about it."

"Well, it's still kind of soft. Ted or Lew may have told you, I got this anonymous phone call?" I nodded. "Anyway, it turns out this is fairly common knowledge among the Swilton clan. See, it's like—what is the word they say the Mafia uses? *Omertà?*"

"The code of silence?" I asked.

Pete nodded. "That's it. Around here, sometimes everyone in town—police, newspaper, community folks, everyone— thinks something happened one way, but the Swiltons know it happened some way else. They don't tell, they don't let on. They just keep their mouths shut and sort of laugh at the establishment."

"What are you, an honorary Swilton?"

He chuckled. "Almost. You remember I told you I'd represented a few Swiltons? Well, I started quietly asking around. Turns out the word among the Swiltons is it happened the way you guessed back at the beginning. Bobby and Eddie were out poaching, came across Travis and the girl, slugged Travis, and were about to rape the girl when they heard Deputy Everson. So they beat up both Keith and the girl and made up the story about saving her. Can't prove it yet, but that's the word that's out there."

"You're kidding."

"Nope. There's a few decent Swiltons, the ones I talk to, but most of the clan thinks it's funny, both because these thugs got away with something, which is disgusting to me, but also because Keith turned out to be the Ripper. See, that makes Bobby and Eddie heroes. Kind of tough on Dorothy Catterman the way they did it, but what the heck, they saved her life really, because the Ripper would have killed her. That's the twisted logic Swiltons use." Pete shuddered at the idea.

Sound normal. Act like you're interested. "Does Sheriff Sanderson know?" I asked.

Pete shrugged. "Al's been around a long time; I can't believe he won't hear about it, but I haven't told him. Lew said to keep it low-key for a while, so I'm casually lining up some of these folks for when we decide how to turn it into evidence. You all haven't talked about it?"

"No, I've been up in Lake Wachita. The day I came back,

Lew sent us on this vacation. I haven't had a chance to meet with him."

"Was that the Ripper up in Lake Wachita?"

"Edgar's instinct says yes, but we can't tell for sure at this point."

"Well, maybe we can save ole Travis on this thing after all. I had my doubts at first, but it sure is looking better. I hope he comes around. Right now, isn't much to save." Pete looked at his watch. "I have to run. You want to get together later?"

"No, I really am heading back. Good luck on your hearing."

"Thanks. Sorry to run out on you." Pete gathered up his papers and hurried off. I walked over to the jail.

I waited for Keith in the same room where we'd had the first interview. The authorities had repainted it. It was still the same institutional green, but the water spot that looked like the United States was gone now.

The guard brought Keith in. I thought of the way Preston looked when he fell asleep on the floor and I walked him to bed: he would move and take directions, but he was sound asleep. Keith acted the same way. The guard steered him into a chair, then turned to me. His name tag read "Harkin." "I'll leave if you want, Mr. Nielson, but I suggest I stay over in the corner. Can't be sure what he'll do. Mostly he sits like that, but you know about that head-banging, I reckon."

"That's all right, Harkin. I need to be alone with him. Lawyer-client, you know."

Harkin looked dubious. "Up to you. I'll be right outside the door; holler if you need me."

Keith sat in the chair, immobile, staring blankly at the barred window high up on the wall. He was shaven, hair neatly combed. They had kept him cleaned up; that was one benefit from our regular visits.

"Travis?" I said softly. "It's Cliff. You remember me?" No response. No indication that he had heard me. I moved around to intersect his line of sight, but not so close that he would feel threatened.

"Travis?" I repeated. "I know you didn't do it. Can you hear me? I know you didn't do it. Not here, not anywhere. We'll get you out, Travis." Still nothing.

"It was John, wasn't it?" I went on. "And you know who John really is, don't you?" His head lowered, and he focused on my face. But he said nothing.

"That's right, isn't it? I need to know, Travis. I need to know so I can help you. It was John, wasn't it?" There was a slight movement that might have been a nod.

"Travis," I said, moving closer to him, and lowering my voice to just above a whisper. "You're not alone anymore. I know who John is." Those dead eyes showed a flash of life. "It's Sherwood, isn't it? John is really Sherwood."

Keith snapped upright, his eyes suddenly bright and darting. He moved his head left and right. And screamed.

Harkin and two other guards poured in and hustled Keith away. The screams echoed and faded as they went down the hall. Sheriff Sanderson appeared in the doorway, his bulk filling the frame, his face flushed with fury. "What the hell happened?" he roared.

"I was just talking to him."

Sanderson was disgusted. "Sherwood comes down here and just talks to him and he turns into a tree stump. You come down here and just talk to him and he turns into a screaming banshee. You all sure got a curious way of helping your client."

He glared at me. "Ain't for me to say if he's guilty or

not; all I know's he started out like a pretty nice guy. Now look at him." He stormed out, slamming the door so hard the frame shook.

I sat in the chair Keith had left and stared at the window. In my mind, I heard that scream over and over. When I was a kid in Virginia, I had a golden retriever that I took out in the fields to chase rabbits. The rabbits always got away. Except once. I never forgot the sound of the rabbit's scream when my dog got it; it turned me off forever on hunting and killing things. Keith sounded just like that rabbit.

Back in Queenston, I understood why Keith was the way he was: sheer overload. Instead of dealing with the problem, I found myself watching old movies, or beach volleyball and championship body building. I picked up the phone several times to call Francine, then hung up. She called twice, but I put her off with contrived excuses. I did not touch my computer.

The pile of frozen dinner trays in the kitchen and the mound of newspapers next to the couch finally got me out of my apartment after a few days. I drove to one of the city parks, jogged for a while, then found a bench in a clearing next to a wading pool. Mothers and nannies sat around the fountain with their charges.

Eventually, the splashing and delighted screams faded to background noise as I clicked through my options.

Talking to Sherwood was out of the question. You do not walk up to a serial killer and say you want to chat.

Francine? At some point I would tell her all about it. But what could she do now? She could give me good advice, that's what she could do. But I hated to involve her.

Kara? No.

Anita? No.

The police? What police? Chief Prescott up in Lake

Wachita seemed like a pretty good type, but his jurisdiction was strictly local. Sheriff Sanderson was the same. The Queenston police? This was Lewis Sherwood we were talking about.

Edgar? Possibly. Anyone else at the firm? Doubtful. Stevens? Not the press.

The real problem was whether I had guts enough to believe what I knew from the facts. The facts told me that Lewis Sherwood was the Resort Ripper. I had a better case against him than the Caliano people had against our client. And Keith's reaction confirmed it for me.

But what if I made the charge, and I was wrong? I would be history at the firm and a pariah in the legal profession. "He's the one who accused Lewis Sherwood of murder. What an idiot."

On top of that, I was not sure what I was allowed to do anyway. Normal people can tell the authorities what they know. Lawyers often cannot. We have ethical considerations. We hold privileged information. In some situations we are sworn not to reveal secrets. On the other hand, we have some obligations to prevent future criminal activity.

Even the American Bar Association would not require a lawyer to protect a serial killer.

I could not let him kill another girl.

I needed advice, from an older and wiser head. I wished my father were still alive. Or my mother. My brother was flying jets in the Far East, and he was even less reliable and trustworthy than I. A minister? A counselor? A shrink? Get serious.

Then I thought about the Senator.

CHAPTER
20

Ellen, the Senator's secretary, smiled at me when I entered her anteroom. She glanced at the lighted buttons on her phone: "He's talking to someone, but he said for you to go right in."

I knocked softly and poked my head through the door. The Senator waved me in as he continued his conversation: "That's true, Governor, but think of the impact on the economy . . ." He gave me a little head shake and mock grimace; that meant he and I could understand, but these politicians were not as quick. He pointed to a chair and waggled his finger. That meant sit down.

While he talked, I sank into the armchair next to the small coffee table and gazed at the artwork. He had surprisingly modern taste in art for a refined Southern gentleman nearing seventy. Behind his desk, a bookcase filled the wall; it was stuffed with assorted law books and autographed first editions, interspersed with a sampling of his plaques and awards. The other end of the office was homier, with a couch, armchairs, and the coffee table.

After some political chitchat, the Senator hung up and came over to sit on the couch. "Cliff, glad to see you.

We have not had a chance to visit in a long time. Lew has kept me advised about your excellent work on this Ripper matter." Lew probably had done no such thing, but the Senator was courteous to pretend that he had been following the case.

He kept up the small talk for another minute, then shifted to a let's-get-on-with-it tone. "Now, what can I do for you?"

"Senator, I need some advice on an ethical matter," I started, "and I thought you were the best person to come to about it." The Senator nodded agreement with my assessment; he had chaired several bar committees on ethics. I began the story that I had concocted the night before.

"Let me say this has nothing to do with the firm or anyone in it. Or for that matter, as far as I know, anyone in the state." That freed him from any direct responsibility.

"A law-school classmate of mine called me last night at home. He is a partner in a large firm in the Northeast. I'd rather not be any more specific than that. He has a serious problem, and he can't talk to anyone local about it."

I thought I detected a hint of skepticism in the Senator's face. Lawyers hear the "I have a friend" line a lot. He remained silent, however, and I plunged on. "My classmate believes that one of the senior partners in his firm is engaged in criminal activity." The Senator's eyebrows raised a bit, and he looked over his glasses at me. "He doesn't feel comfortable providing much detail, except to say that the activity is major, clearly criminal, and involves violence of some sort." The eyebrows arched still higher.

"To make matters worse," I continued, "my classmate discovered this in the course of representing a client who is charged with the same crime. I sensed he believes the client is innocent and the partner is the real culprit. That's all he told me. I didn't want to hear much more."

I spread my hands to show I was finishing. "He doesn't know what to do. He's concerned about discussing it with anyone in his firm or in the area, because they might figure out the partner involved. He called me because he knows of your work with the ethics committees. I told him I would talk with you on an anonymous basis."

The Senator pursed his lips and sat back for a moment, contemplating a glass and wood figure on the table. Then he looked at me with a steady gaze. "Are we really talking about a 'friend' here, Cliff?"

Those years with Sherwood had not been wasted. I feigned surprise and lied with a combination of sincerity and affront. "Yes, sir."

He seemed satisfied. "Well," he began, "this young man has a real problem, doesn't he?"

"Yes, sir."

The Senator glanced in the direction of the several ethics texts displayed in his bookcase. "Let's start with the client. Your friend has a conflict of interest in that he is unable to give his client full, complete, and zealous representation within the bounds of the law, since the senior partner's potential involvement means the firm, and therefore your friend, has interests opposed to those of his client.

"Under those circumstances, he is required by the Code of Professional Responsibility to withdraw from representing the client. And so is his law firm, of course."

That disposed of the client. He took off his glasses and tapped the earpieces against his lip. "Now, with respect to the senior partner, we have various considerations. Your friend might want to research the published opinions of the applicable Ethics Committees."

He put his glasses back on. I tried not to squirm. "I believe he is obliged to urge the senior partner to disclose the criminal activity. If the senior partner refuses, then your friend must disclose it to the authorities himself, unless the information comes from sources that are governed by attorney-client confidentiality, in which case he is obliged to remain silent. As you know, there are some exceptions that may or may not be applicable. Of course, he could not in either circumstance remain involved in the case."

He paused again, reviewing what he had just said. It was a law-school ethics lecture. I knew all that. What I wanted to know was what the hell I should do.

"From the ethical perspective, those seem to be the requirements," the Senator continued. "Your friend might want to request an opinion from his state's Ethics Committee or the American Bar Association. They allow anonymous requests, as you know."

My frustration might have shown. He looked at me, then shrugged slightly. "That's what the book says. Not much help to your friend, is it?"

"No, sir. Not really."

"You and I have our own ethical obligations, you know. We cannot advise him otherwise."

"I know."

"He may desire counsel. If so, you can inform him that we might be able to represent him, if necessary. Perhaps as a professional courtesy if cost is a problem." I knew then that I had received as much of an answer as I would get unless I broke down and told him everything. But I wasn't prepared to do that yet. I wanted to consider my options some more.

"Thank you, Senator. That's very generous." I rose to leave. "I'll pass it along to my friend."

"Cliff," he looked over his glasses, "as a practical matter, you might tell your friend that he better be damn sure he's right."

"He knows that, Senator."

• • •

On my way back to Sherwood's Forest, I cursed myself for blowing it. The Senator had given the only answer he could to the clumsy question I posed. I could not go back with another hypothetical approach: he would never believe it. It would have to be all or nothing, which meant dumping the whole thing in his lap.

The war room was a good place to think. I opened the door. And froze. Sherwood sat at one end of the conference table, surrounded by mounds of files, with my computer printouts spread out in front of him. Yellow highlighter lines and scrawled notes covered the areas not filled with print.

He looked up and smiled. "Hello, Clifford," he said, then returned to his studies, scribbling furiously on a legal pad as he looked through the papers. I just stood there. He glanced back up at me, puzzled. "Something wrong?"

I found a voice somewhere. "No. No. Surprised to see you, that's all. I thought you were out of town."

Sherwood shrugged. "The Senator summoned me back to meet some potential Japanese clients. He's on a foreign business development kick, you know." He chuckled a self-deprecating chuckle and spread his arms as though taking a bow. "Apparently," he said, "they want to meet me. The Senator thinks it will clinch the deal." He shook his head and went back to his papers.

I forced myself to walk to the file cabinets, trying to appear normal. The labels floated in and out of focus. Finally, I pulled two: "Johnston Beach—Victim" and "Travis Keith—Personal." I took them to the other end of the table and opened one, pretending to read.

The victim file contained the life, times, and current status of Dorothy Catterman. On the right-hand side, the paralegals had neatly entered and marked with tabs all our memos and reports. The left side of the folder was a table of contents. I wondered what Ms. Catterman would think to see her relatively brief life laid out in a folder like this. Then I looked at the Ripper Wall. Each of those girls had a folder too.

Urge the senior partner to disclose the criminal activity, the Senator had said. He neglected to say exactly how to go about it. I glanced over at Sherwood, who was staring at the ceiling, deep in thought. Say something, I told myself. "Looks like we're in pretty good shape down in Johnston Beach," I said.

He brought his head down slowly and looked at me for a moment. "Why do you say that?"

I waved at the files. "According to all this, the prosecution still doesn't have much except the Swiltons. We can bring out Keith's story through Dorothy, because they match as far as she remembers. Then you tear up the Swiltons on cross, suggesting they're the real villains. Cap it off with Pete's evidence on what the Swiltons have been saying. And that's it."

"As long as Dorothy's memory doesn't come back and contradict something."

"Sure, but if it hasn't by now, it probably won't."

Sherwood frowned. "I'll count on Pete's evidence when we have it in hand, not before. You can't rely on small-town rumors. And whatever happens, it still goes to the jury, Clifford. Sherwood's Rule: Never place your faith in a jury." That was a good rule for everyone but Sherwood. He could make any jury eat out of his hand, and he knew it. But he was like a football coach who always builds up the opposition.

"Don't forget the Ripper evidence," he added. "I'm not confident we can keep that out, and whether we do or not, the jury will know about it." He turned back to his papers.

What the hell, I decided. "But that's looking better too, don't you think?"

Sherwood scratched his ear. "You talking about those credit card slips?"

I took a deep mental swallow. "That and those two names from Birmingham: Adamason and Tarleton."

He acted as if he had forgotten. "Oh, yeah. Those names. You done anything more about them?" His tone was casual.

I shook my head, hoping my face was as casual as his tone. "No. You said to wait until we talked about it. I just meant those are potential leads."

Sherwood sighed. "Yeah, I forgot. I'm leaving after this dog-and-pony show, and Edgar's not around. Maybe we'll talk about it sometime next week."

He looked at me for several seconds, glanced at the shut door, and moved to the chair next to me. He put his hand on my arm and patted it lightly, then leaned over and spoke in a low, conspiratorial voice. "I'll have your hide if you tell this to any of the others," he started. I stared at him, suddenly nervous.

Sherwood waved with his free arm. "I have been through all this, Clifford," he said in the solemn tone of a doctor carrying bad news to a patient. "Every bit of it. It's clear as a goat's ass. Keith is guilty as hell." He lowered his head in sorrow. "Now, we have to decide what we can do for him." Then he looked back up at me. "But don't waste your time chasing something that isn't there. We don't make the facts, Clifford. We have to accept them."

I tried to think of something to say. "What about Lake Wachita?"

Now he had pity in his tone. "Lake Wachita is someone else. Read your own reports on the MO."

"The elephant carving?"

"I have studied those pictures. Frankly, you all are dreaming. That is not an elephant. Lake Wachita was not the Ripper."

"That's not what you said at your news conference." That did not get an answer; it did not deserve one. I pressed on, plunging into unknown territory. My voice rose a little. "All they really have on Keith are his movements and a shaky identification."

Sherwood acted surprised that I raised objections. He took his hand off my arm and sat back with a look of frustration. Those icy blue eyes made me feel like a very small virus under a very powerful microscope.

"You disagree?" he asked.

"I think it's too early," I said.

"Sherwood's Rule, Clifford. Never let your advocacy blind you to reality." The tone of condolence disappeared. "You bring me another military commando who was present at each of those locations, who had the opportunity to commit each of those murders, who was caught red-handed attacking another victim, and maybe I'll rethink my opinion."

He leaned close; I wanted to pull back. "Such a person does not exist, Clifford."

We stared at each other. Sherwood remained absolutely still, waiting, either curious or wary. "Well . . . " I finally started, not sure what I would say. A knock sounded on the door before I could go on.

It was the Senator, prospective Japanese clients in tow, showing off Sherwood's Forest. Sherwood rose to greet them and, incidentally, block them from coming in. He transformed to the sophisticated business lawyer personality. "Let's go down to my office and I can brief you on our operations," he said, gently herding them in that direction. The door closed behind him.

"I think we'll be more comfortable there," I heard as his voice became indistinct.

My forehead and underarms were soaked, even though we kept the air conditioning so high in the war room that most of the paralegals wore sweaters. What was he doing? What was I doing? I had been sitting in a room with a serial killer. People do not sit in rooms with serial killers and have conversations with them.

He knew he matched the profile he so carefully set out. He knew he was a military commando who had been in each of these locations. Why had he summarized it so neatly?

A test? Trying to find out what I knew? Or if I knew?

Was I next on his list?

I had not considered the possibility of personal danger before. A shudder traced its way up my spine. The son of a bitch was a murderer. He could kill me as easily as he killed those girls on the wall.

That was an ethical consideration the Senator had not mentioned. If you confront a killer and urge him to turn himself in, you stand a better-than-average chance of getting killed yourself. My dilemma suddenly took a new perspective. I might be loyal to the firm and the Code, but I sure as hell was not willing to die for them.

Calm down. Think. Sherwood won't murder you here in the war room. He won't murder you at all unless you do something incredibly stupid. Like talking to him one-on-one. But take a few precautions. Tell somebody.

Think it through. This can't go on much longer or you'll end up in a padded cell next to Keith. Or worse.

What was he doing?

Don't try to think like them, Edgar said. But I could think enough like Sherwood to know he never did anything on impulse. Even his explosions, spontaneous as they seemed, were calculated. He planned these murders, too. It takes time to scout a location, it takes time to spot a victim, it takes time to convince her to go off with a stranger. These were not spur-of-the-moment events.

Lake Wachita? A bargaining chip. He changed his methods to cause confusion. If he had done it the usual way, Keith would be off the hook, and he did not want that. Now the prosecutors were uncertain, so they might be willing to bargain. He created the opportunity he wanted.

The "Travis Keith—Personal" file was next to my arm. I opened it to the last entry: Dr. Banzinger's report. The summary of conclusions: "In my professional opinion, at this time Mr. Keith lacks capacity to understand the nature of the proceedings against him and is unable to provide information or otherwise assist his defense counsel."

Those were the magic words to establish legal incompetence to stand trial. Another bargaining chip. Sherwood had driven Keith over the edge. Deliberately.

It fell into place. He had managed to involve himself in the Ripper case; who knew why? Maybe a joke. Or a challenge. Or to control the outcome. The eyewitness out in Caliano probably worried him, and when I discovered John Adamason and Edward Tarleton, he decided to end the game.

Sherwood needed Keith to be the Ripper for his own protection, but his ego demanded a "victory" as defense counsel. That meant a plea bargain of some sort. So he set out to create a scenario to make it happen. A man of action, I thought bitterly. He had finished his Galveston case and turned his attention to this one. Too bad for Susan Dond and Travis Keith.

As I leaned back, gazing at the Ripper Wall, my eyes fell on a victim whose story I found particularly poignant. A beautiful blond girl from Minnesota: Inga Tillitson. The yearbook picture was from her college, where she had been homecoming queen and Phi Beta Kappa. She apparently was a talented artist and a genuinely charming person. Everyone expected great things from Inga. They found her near a cross-country ski trail.

I walked over to the time line. Inga was last seen on a January 25th. That was a Super Bowl weekend. I remembered that weekend. The Montana case had just ended, and Kara and I spent that Sunday naked in her bedroom, eating popcorn and watching the game.

We had just finished the Montana case. And Lake Wachita was right after Sherwood finished the Galveston case. And Mount Passarell was right after we finished a case in Cleveland.

I tried not to run down the hall to my office.

I rummaged around my files and found my daybooks for the past four years: one of the advantages of being a pack rat. Then I pulled my small copy of the time line on the Ripper Wall and started comparing. Best I could tell, almost every murder occurred within a few days after Sherwood completed a big case. The two copycats did not match, of course, and I could not tell about several others because I had been involved in different matters. But for the rest, it fit. Caliano, for example, came after the Greater East Coast trial that had made the FBI so mad.

I had the pattern. And I thought I had the trigger, or at least part of it. I pulled out Sherwood's bio file and found the article I remembered. It was a profile for one of the major women's magazines a couple of years ago.

"What is it like to try a major criminal case?" the interviewer had asked, lobbing softballs.

Sherwood hit it over the fence: "It's incredibly hard work, but it's exhilarating, a natural high. In fact, when the trial is over, and you've won, there's a tremendous desire to celebrate, of course, but also a tremendous let-down and need to release the pent-up tension that builds when you sit in court day after day.

"That's why I always take time off after a major case, to get all that out. And that's why I like to stay so busy, to keep that excitement going."

He was releasing pent-up tensions. Seeking excitement. A hell of a way to go about it.

Someone knocked lightly on my office door. I shoved the article back into the bio folder and covered it with some loose papers. "Come in," I said, pretending to look through one of the memos on my desk.

It was Sherwood. From my seated perspective he seemed to fill the doorway. "I wasn't sure if we finished what we were talking about in the war room," he said softly. "You started to say something else, and we were interrupted."

I wrinkled my brow and frowned, then shook my head and shrugged. "I can't remember what I was going to say, Lew. It must not have been important."

He studied me thoughtfully. Then he nodded. "Let me know if you think of it."

"Thanks."

He turned to leave, then stopped and came back into the office. He was the ole country lawyer. "You know, Clifford, I was thinking this afternoon. I've run your ass ragged for about five years now, isn't it?"

"About that."

"That's long enough for anyone to put up with me. I'm selfish: I'd like to keep you on my team. You're one of the best I've seen. But that's not fair to you. You're ready to head up your own group. Hell, you've been ready. I plan to talk to the Senator about that and about an equity partnership. You deserve it."

"Thank you, Lew."

"It won't be any problem. I'll start things in motion, and as soon as this case is over, we'll announce it. That'll be pretty soon, I think."

He moved out the door with a jocular parting thought: "You've made it through a lot. Just hang on a little bit more without screwing up and you'll be all set."

CHAPTER
21

Francine eyed the manila envelope on her coffee table as if it were a letter bomb, set to explode at the slightest movement. She was not about to touch it.

"What am I supposed to do with this?" she asked.

"Nothing. Nothing at all." I tried to sound reassuring. "I just want someone to have it. In case something happens. If it does, make two more copies and mail them anonymously: send that one to the Director of the FBI, a copy to Edgar, and the third copy to Tim Stevens at the *Miami Observer*." I thought for a moment. "And maybe make one for the Senator."

The envelope contained my case against Sherwood. It had taken me two days, working mostly at home, late into the night. A long memorandum detailed all the evidence, with copies of the supporting documents attached. The original was in my safe deposit box. My brother the airline pilot had the other key. Years could pass before he opened it, so I wanted someone responsible involved.

Francine gazed steadily at me. "You sound like someone in a paperback novel who just discovered that Hitler is alive and well and living in Utah, but some evil secret organization is after him." She moved to the back window of her sunporch and looked out at the pool, arms folded.

She still wore her work clothes: a silky white blouse with a yellow pattern, and a beige skirt. She had kicked off her shoes when we came through the door. My coat and tie lay across the back of her couch. That afternoon, I had exploded into her office and dragged her home to spill out my story.

Without turning, she spoke softly, almost musing. "Cliff, this is crazy." Her fingers played with the jade pendant that hung from a gold chain around her throat. "I should throw you out of here, I really should."

"I'm sorry," I said miserably, and truly. "I don't have anyone else to go to." I moved closer to stand behind her. "He's a killer, Francine. I can worry about ethics and politics forever, but if he finds out that I know about this, I could be history."

She turned and looked up at me with doubting eyes. I kept talking: "I honestly don't feel like I'm in any danger. But it's possible, and the thought made me realize if I walk out of here and get hit by a car, no one in the world will know about Sherwood, and he'll keep killing. So someone, somewhere, has to know. Not do anything. Just know."

"Why not go to someone more qualified? Like Ted?"

"Ted has too much else on his mind."

"And I don't?" Her neck stiffened. "I have a comfortable life, and you come in here with your murder mystery and screw it all up. You've made me privy to something I don't want to be privy to. I don't want to know about this, Cliff, I really don't." She turned back to stare at the pool.

After a few moments, her shoulders heaved from a deep sigh. She turned, then sat back on the couch. "All right," Francine said in a brisk voice, "let's decide what to do."

She was a lawyer counseling a client. Thank God.

"You believe me, right?"

"Intellectually, I believe you. Emotionally, I'm not sure. But we've had enough emotion."

I sat in the wicker chair across from her, elbows on my knees, and told her the options I had already considered and rejected: Sherwood, the Senator, Stevens. Francine listened without comment as I rambled on. "Leaving aside ethical questions," I ended, "another option is to go to the authorities. I'm serious, by the way, about mailing it anonymously. I'm thinking about that myself."

"What's wrong with it?"

I shook my head. "A couple of things. In the first place, I'm not sure where to send it. Maybe someone at the FBI. The other problem is I think someone eventually would figure out where it came from. So it's the worst of all worlds. I might as well go in person. Then the Senator would be pissed off that I went to the cops first."

Francine leaned forward and looked me in the eye, speaking very softly. "Cliff, do you realize this finishes you at the firm?"

"I see that's possible. What do you mean?"

"I mean there's no way you can stay. Look at it. It's like the Senator told you. You're a witness for Keith's defense. You can clear him. And you'll have to testify against Sherwood." She held out her hands, palms up, to show the manifest truth of her statement.

I digested that. I must have had a disbelieving expression on my face, because she drove the point home. "I'm telling you a fact of life. Think of what David Halloway will say when it goes public. Even if they manage to sweep it under the table somehow, they'll sweep you under with it. The only possible way you stay is to keep quiet. But I know you won't consider that. I won't let you."

I had not thought it through. That son of a bitch Sherwood, I thought bitterly. Even if he doesn't kill me physically, he's already killed me professionally. Shit.

She was right: without Sherwood as a champion, I had no future at the firm. Where would I go? Over the years, I received occasional nibbles from other law firms but never pursued them. Maybe I could think of a way to keep it from being traced to me. Stevens was a possibility; he would protect his sources. Or maybe some chain of letter transfers. Francine to her brother and then on somewhere.

I suddenly felt a hard knot in my stomach. This was about murder, and I was worrying about my job and looking for a way to hide behind Francine. What a sorry excuse for a human being.

Then another sudden thought struck. I reached for the envelope, and said, "Forget this conversation. I'm not taking you down with me."

Francine had been watching with a guarded expression. Now she shook her head in frustration. "Sit down. Don't be foolish. It's not the same thing. I'm not a witness, remember?"

We waited for inspiration; it did not come. Francine read my memo. When she finished, she slid the material back in, refolded the metal clips at the top, and stared at the envelope. "If you send it anywhere," I said, "wipe your fingerprints off."

She ignored the comment. "How much time do you have?"

"If he sticks with the pattern, then it's after a big case ends. His only active big case is this one."

Francine bit her lip and asked the question I had been asking myself. "What about Kara?" she said. I had told her about Kara leaving me for Sherwood.

I tried to convince her as I had tried to convince myself. "She's with Sherwood. If I talk to her, or send her a message, he may find out. I've thought and thought—she should be safe. He's never gone after someone he knows, and these murders started right after his divorce from Tricia. Maybe if he's involved with Kara . . . "

"Remember Lake Wachita," Francine said.

"I think Lake Wachita was a maneuver to put the case in the posture he wants. Hell, it was business, not pleasure: it doesn't count. And it was after a big case." The rationale sounded less compelling out loud than it had when I thought of it.

Francine frowned. "That is not very solid. You can't sit and do nothing this time, Cliff."

"I only need a couple more days."

"No." Her tone left no room for discussion. "Not this time. This isn't some personal problem. You can't delude yourself that everything will be better if you just wait." Francine knew me too well. "If I have to, I'll do something."

She glared at me with mixed anger and determination, then the lines in her face softened. She took my hand and pulled me to my feet. "Look," she said, "I'll make dinner. You go to your apartment and pack some clothes. I want you to stay here for a while."

I started a mild protest. "No argument," she said. "If I can keep an eye on you, it's less for me to worry about. Shut up and do it."

"I'll be back in a few minutes," I said gratefully.

We talked into the night, and again in the morning, and the conclusion became so clear that we agreed without stating it. The Senator was the only answer. By the time Francine left for the firm, we both knew what I would do.

"I'll go with you," she said.

"No, you stay out of it." No reason to tarnish her career.

By now, I had reconciled myself to finding a new place to practice law, and my only concern was how fast the Senator would act. If he believed me, then he would understand the need to avoid alerting Sherwood. If he dismissed me as crazy, I would reach the right authorities through Edgar or Stevens or Tom.

When she left, I began to rehearse what I would say, as if I were preparing for an appellate argument. I practiced and modified my opening statement over and over, then did the same for my closing argument. I reviewed the memo again and reworked it to make the most convincing case.

That took the rest of the morning. Francine called several times to check on me, and she came home at lunch to approve my redraft. With a mutual deep breath, we left for the firm. At least I did not have to worry about running into Sherwood. He and Kara were out of town again.

Francine patted my hand when she exited the elevator on the 27th floor. I rode on to 30 and went directly into Sherwood's Forest to print my revised memo on my laser. The sounds of a party in the main conference room echoed across the lobby. Probably a birthday or new baby.

I sent my memo to the printer and went to the lobby to ask Lisa if the Senator was in. As I passed the conference room door, Ted lurched out, waving a half-full bottle of champagne. "Cliff, ole buddy," he cried, thrusting the bottle at me. "Where the hell you been? Drink up. It's over."

I stared at him. "What are you talking about?"

"It's over. Kaput. Finished. We won. Come on, lemme get you a glass." He started back into the conference room.

I grabbed his arm and spun him around. "What the hell are you talking about?"

"Calm down, Cliffie. The case is over. Now come on in and get a glass, and I'll tell you about it."

Stunned, I allowed him to lead me into the conference room. The Johnston Beach gang was all there; they must have come in together. I did not see Sherwood or Kara, but they could have been in the crowd somewhere. Red Team victory parties were legendary, and as a practical matter the firm shut down when we won a case. Even the Senator would make a token appearance, then shut his door and pretend not to hear.

The conference table was laden with pizza, munchies, and champagne, and someone had draped a computer-generated banner over the eighteenth-century landscape on the far wall. "Congratulations," it read, with the scales of justice on either end. Ted thrust a bottle of champagne in my hand, took a swig from his own, and pulled me back out through the lobby and partway into the hall leading to Sherwood's Forest. Unanswered phones rang in the distance, and the noise level grew in the conference room. I saw Francine hurry in, a worried look on her face.

"Lemme tell you about it." Ted's normally precise speech was a bit slurred.

"Go through it slowly," I said.

"Lew worked a deal. No trial. No convictions. No admissions. Keith'll be committed to a nice state hospital for the criminally insane. Charges held in abeyance until such time as he is discharged, which we all know is never. The judge bought it: He's signing the order now, and it'll be announced this afternoon, in about"—he looked at his watch—"twenty minutes. Lisa," he yelled, "we need a TV in the conference room to see the press conference. Tell Stan to tape it too." Lisa smiled and picked up the phone.

"When did all this happen?"

"This morning, I guess. I mean, Lew must have been talking to the prosecution for a couple of days, but we didn't find out until this morning. He showed up in the war room, gave us the word, and sent us all home. Alice had the party ready when we got here. I went looking for you right away, but no one knew where you were." He started back to the conference room; I stopped him.

"Where's Sherwood?"

"He's still there. He kept Kara with him and sent the rest of us back. He and Pete are taking care of the paperwork. Come on, let's go back in."

"Hang on a second." It had happened too fast. I automatically took a sip out of the champagne bottle in my hand while I tried to sort it out. "What about Caliano?"

"That's in abeyance too. Lew persuaded the prosecutor there to go along with it, and he has an agreement from Johnston Beach to contest any extradition efforts. It's wrapped up tighter than a drum."

"How did Keith react?"

"Who knows? I didn't go see him; Lew and Pete did. Probably just sat there." The merriment vanished from his face. "You know, that's the part I feel bad about. But like Lew said, don't forget this is a serial killer. You get involved with these people, you tend to forget that they're really bad guys. Is that a Sherwood's Rule?"

"I guess." My mind raced. "So Kara's still down there with him?" Ted nodded. "Are they coming back later today?"

"Don't know. I assume Kara will. But you know Lew: he'll probably disappear for a few days. Come on, the press conference is due to start and my bottle's empty."

I let him drag me back into the conference room. From the other side of the table, Francine shot me a worried look. I made a helpless gesture back. The party had grown to about forty or fifty people, and Ted started hushing everyone as he turned the television to CNN. The Senator appeared at the door, converting this to an official firm event. He was ushered to a chair close to the tube.

When the camera panned the Johnston Beach courthouse steps, I spotted Stevens in the press section. Kara stood beside him. Whoops of recognition came from the party-goers as Sherwood and prosecutor Ledbetter emerged and approached the bank of microphones. Behind them on the steps, I saw the assistant DA from Caliano and Pete Bannister.

Ernie Ledbetter began. Travis Jeffrey Keith had been evaluated by several prominent psychiatrists, he stated, and the unanimous judgment of the experts was that the defendant lacked capacity to stand trial. An order to that effect had been entered. Keith would be committed to the state's facility, where he would receive treatment until he was competent to stand trial on the charges against him. The defendant's sister had been appointed guardian and had agreed to the commitment.

I glanced at Ted, surprised about the sister. "She also will sign a book deal on Keith's behalf," he whispered. "That's how we get paid."

The prosecutor went on to describe the law relating to the commitment and assured the public that this man would not be released. Finally, Ledbetter praised defense counsel for his splendid cooperation in reaching a resolution that met the ends of justice and protected the people of the State. A barrage of questions erupted, but he declined to answer any until the others had spoken.

The Caliano prosecutor made a little speech about the ends of justice and so on. Her bottom line was they would go along with the deal. She did not look happy.

Sherwood was eloquent. He talked about the majesty of the legal system, how the law protects all people, the fundamental premise that a defendant must have the capacity to assist in his own defense. He emphasized that there was no adjudication of guilt. He would work with the institution and provide all possible assistance to restore Keith to a healthy mental condition. Sure he would, I thought.

The press corps started shouting out questions. Most of them were variations on the same theme: Was this the end of the Ripper? The prosecution and police were confident that it was. Sherwood simply repeated that no adjudication had been made. Once it became apparent that most of the questions were stupid or repetitious, the noise level at our party started to rise again.

The Senator gestured for someone to turn down the TV volume, then stood, tapping a pen against a glass for attention. Hisses of "shhh" passed around the room.

He had a toast: "On behalf of the firm, I want to offer our congratulations to Lew Sherwood and his team—Cliff, Ted, the others—for their fine work and their excellent result in a very difficult matter. It is fair to say that they have achieved a resolution that is extraordinarily beneficial to the client under the circumstances, but which meets the needs of the public as well, and thereby brings great credit not only to them but to the firm as a whole. Here's to you, ladies and gentlemen."

"Hear, Hear" ran around the room, followed by "Speech, Speech." Most faces turned to me as the Red Team Leader, but I modestly deferred to Ted, on the ground that he had sacrificed the most.

Fortunately, he was not yet drunk enough to embarrass himself. While Ted made like an Oscar winner, thanking everyone from Sherwood to the janitorial staff, I eased over to the opposite corner of the room. Near the front, the Senator checked his watch and slipped out the door. A couple of minutes later, through the glass wall, I saw him say something to Lisa, then board the elevator. He carried an overnight bag.

Francine joined me, clinking her glass against mine. "Congratulations," she said loudly enough for anyone near-by to hear. Then, in a low, faltering voice: "Time's up."

It took me ten minutes to work my way through the well-wishers and sneak out of the room, with Francine behind me. I stopped by the reception desk. "Is the Senator in?" I casually asked Lisa.

She smiled at me. "He's gone for the day." Then she looked at her board. "For the week, actually. He has a meeting in Washington. Do you want to leave a message?"

"No," I muttered. I marched around to my office and picked up the phone. Francine settled into my visitor's chair on the other side of the desk.

I called Edgar. His secretary said he would not be in the rest of the week. I called his home. His wife, Elise, told me he was at the City Soccer Center. No, there was no phone there. Did I want to leave a message? She would have him call as soon as he got back, but she did not know when that would be. This was the first day of the tournament; he might stay to scout the other teams. Her son was riding with a friend.

Cursing now, I leafed through my address book for the number of the Johnston Beach hotel where Tim Stevens usually stayed. Stevens was not in, of course, so I left a message for him to call me immediately at the firm, my place, or Francine's. Then I called the *Miami Observer*, Stevens' home in Miami, and the commuter airline counter at the Johnston Beach airport and left the same message.

"Edgar and Stevens?" Francine asked when I hung up.

"Yeah," I said. "What about Tom? Can he help us?"

"I'll call him, but what do you want him to do?"

I wasn't sure. "I want a fallback in case I can't reach Stevens or Edgar. What we need is someone who can get to the right person at the FBI on short notice. Maybe you can find out if Tom will be in town up there."

"I'll call him." She hesitated. "What about the Senator?"

I shook my head. "We can't wait on him. I have to get somebody moving soon."

"What's your plan?"

"In the best case, we don't have a problem, because Kara's with him. Maybe if he has a playmate, he'll keep his cool. Or at least lie low for a while.

"In the worst case, we have a couple of days according to past patterns. I'll brief Edgar and Stevens: they'll know how to approach the right agencies. I need Tom in case something happens, and I can't get up with them today."

Relief swept over her face. At least I was putting it in someone else's hands. "Don't you need to warn Kara?" she asked.

"Dammit, Francine." I paced in front of my office window. "I don't know what to do about her. I want to get her out of there, but I can't think of a way to contact her without Sherwood finding out. E-mail? He could read over her shoulder. Answering machine? He might be there to hear the message."

"What about an innocuous message? 'Congratulations. Call and tell me all about it.' That sort of thing?"

"No. Let me talk to Edgar or Stevens first. I don't see him going after her anyway. All these victims were strangers; he won't bother anyone at the firm."

Not totally convinced, Francine called her brother while I debated whether to drive out to the soccer field and look for Edgar. It was about twenty minutes away.

Francine hung up after talking quietly into the phone. "Tom's out of the office, but his wife said he'll be in town for the next few days. She'll have him call me tonight if not before." She fanned her face with a memo from my desk. "I'm not used to this excitement. We have a much more sedate practice."

She had slumped back into the visitor's chair, high heels off and legs tucked up under her. Her skirt rode up her thighs. Absently, she took a sip of champagne. Without thinking, I had brought the bottle back with me.

There was a knock on the door, and Ted stuck his head in. "Where are you, man? Oh, excuse me." He glanced at Francine curled up in my chair with a champagne bottle. He thought he had interrupted a tryst. Not unknown during and after a victory party. That was one reason the Senator usually left.

"Come on in," I said.

He stayed where he was, swaying slightly. "Everyone's wondering where you are. Dinner at Patoots tonight. You're in, aren't you?" Patoots's waitresses received the heaviest tips in town, largely because they served dinner dressed only in G-strings. No sexism: The waiters and busboys wore similar attire. We had provided Patoots with enough business over the years that they closed the place to the public for Red Team victory parties.

"I'll meet you there," I said. "I have a couple of things to take care of. I didn't plan on a victory party today."

"Sure," Ted said with a knowing smile as he backed out and pulled the door shut. "We'll look for you there."

"This will hit the gossip mill within ten minutes," Francine sighed unhappily.

"Sorry," I said, picking up the ringing phone.

"What do you want, asshole?" Stevens bellowed in my ear. "You have a hell of a way of keeping a deal. I give you

all that help, and then I find out about this from a goddamn
AP reporter. Next time, you can shove your goddamn deals
right up . . . "

"I didn't know about it, I swear."

"Yeah, and you got some swamp land to sell me too.
Shitbird."

Francine winced: she could hear him from her chair.
"Tim," I said, trying to override his voice, "honest. I didn't
know a thing about it. I need to talk to you."

"So talk."

"No. In person, right away. Where will you be?"

"I'm on my way home. What is it?"

"I can't tell you on the phone. But it's very important.
Trust me, Tim. I need to meet you."

"Are you bullshitting me again, Nielson?" He was not as
loud now.

"I didn't know about it, Tim. This is very important. I
swear to God."

Stevens sighed. "Let me look at something." The phone
rustled as he apparently rummaged around in his pockets. "I
change planes in Queenston about six. Six-ten to be precise.
That's arrival time. Got an hour layover. I can see you at
the airport."

"I need you to stay over here. Will you do that?"

"What the hell you up to, Cliff?"

"It will take more than an hour, Tim. And it's very
important. Will you stay over?"

He paused for a minute. "What the hell. But I have to
file a story, so you pay the long-distance bill."

"Fine. I'll meet you at the curb, in front of baggage
claim."

I hung up and looked at Francine. "You hear that? I'm
going to track down Edgar and tell him to clear me some

time tonight. Then I'll pick up Stevens, get Edgar, and I'll brief them together somewhere."

"Why don't you come to my house?"

I looked at her thoughtfully. "No need for you to be involved."

"I don't want to be. But neither do you. And neither will they when they find out. But none of us has any choice. Besides, you macho clowns might need a reasonable head around."

She took a deep breath and stood. "I'm leaving. Come over whenever you're ready." She put her hand on my shoulder. "You're doing all the right things, Cliff. Don't worry. Take it one step at a time. Find Edgar. He'll know what to do."

I hoped so. But I noticed her hand shook.

CHAPTER
22

By the time I left with copies of my memo for Edgar and
Stevens, the noise from the conference room had increased
in inverse proportion to the number of people remaining. Lisa gave me an exasperated grin when I approached
the reception desk; she was desperately trying to hear her
phones over the din.

"I assume you won't be back?" Lisa put her hand over
the receiver.

"Yeah, I'm out of here."

"Congratulations." She went back to her phones.

The Soccer Center, in the western Queenston suburbs,
was jammed with cars. The place was huge: there must
have been fifty fields out there, each with its own set of
kids, parents, siblings, and coaches. I had not thought to
ask Elise what colors Edgar's team wore.

I cruised the lot for about ten minutes, looking for either
Edgar or a place to park. Sorry, God, I thought. I'm trying
to do something about this killer, but I can't find a place
to park at the children's soccer field.

Finally, a van filled with cheering soccer players in yellow shirts and blue shorts almost sideswiped me; it was

driven by a mother who must have drawn the short straw.
I pulled into her vacant spot and set out on foot in search of
Edgar. The sun beat down unmercifully. I was glad I had
stopped by my apartment to change clothes.

Six fields away I spotted Edgar, surrounded by other
coaches seeking pearls of wisdom from the lips of the master. He was in shorts and a "Coach" T-shirt, with an Ohio
State ball cap on his head and a clipboard under one arm.

"Cliff," Edgar said with surprise. "What are you doing
here?" His eyes narrowed. "Not another one?"

"Not yet," I told him. "Can I speak to you a minute?"

"Is something wrong with Elise?"

"No, nothing like that. Something's come up, but it's
confidential." I tried to be low key. I didn't want the entire
soccer league to know about this.

"Sure. Will you fellows excuse me a minute?" We walked
off toward a vacant field.

He had not heard about the Keith deal, so I started with
that. I could not read his face. "That takes care of it, I
assume," he said when I finished.

"No. I need to go over something with you. Tonight. It's
very important. Tim Stevens will be there too."

"Important?" He weighed the word. "What time? How
long? We have an early game tomorrow."

"I'm picking up Tim in an hour. Right after that. I'm not
sure how long."

Edgar worked like a Trojan when he was out of town, but
he guarded his family time at home. I sensed his debating
how serious this could be. "All right. Where?" he said after
a minute.

"At Francine Collins's house." That surprised him. I gave
him the address. "We should be there about six. Oh, one
other thing, Edgar. Please, look this over." I handed him
the manila envelope.

He shoved it under the papers on his clipboard, prompting me to caution: "I don't need to say this, but I will anyway. Please take care of it." He looked at the envelope more closely and made sure it was secure under the board's clip. "If that gets out or lost, it will be very bad for me. When you read it, you'll see what I mean."

I trudged back to my car. On the way out, I saw Edgar alone in the cab of his truck, reading.

On the way in from the airport, Stevens read my material with only a few muttered comments, mostly "damn" and "shit." Out of the corner of my eye, I saw him flip from the memo to the attached receipts, copies, and other backup documents. He went through it several times. Then he looked over at me somberly. "You want to talk about this now?" he asked.

"No, we'll be there in a few more minutes. Let's wait for Edgar, and we all can go over it together."

Edgar sat in his truck in front of Francine's. I waved for him to follow me up the driveway to the parking area in the back.

We all shook hands silently, and I led them to the table around the pool. Francine came out; I introduced Stevens. "Francine's not involved in this, guys," I warned.

"Yes, Francine is," she countered.

Edgar wasted no time. "This is . . . hard to believe," he gestured with his copy of my memo. "Just in case, does anyone know where Lewis is right now?"

Stevens answered. "I talked to Kara at the press conference in Johnston Beach this afternoon and asked her to set up an interview, but she said they were leaving right away. I assumed they were coming here. I think she and Sherwood have something going, myself." He looked at me for confirmation. I nodded agreement. I had not put anything about Kara in the memo.

Edgar looked up sharply from the material he had been studying. "You mean Kara might be with him?" he asked me with alarm. "I thought she'd be with you." He looked at me, then glanced over at Francine in bewilderment. "Uh, sorry." Francine waved it off. "You have to get her back here, Cliff. Right away." He was an even better detective than I had given him credit for. He knew all about me and Kara, but never let on. Edgar's eyes narrowed. "Give us anything else you left out."

"No," I protested, "nothing, really." I sighed and told them about Kara. For good measure, I explained why Francine was involved. I tried to justify the omission: "This memo originally was for the authorities somewhere, and I didn't see Kara as important." Their disapproval hung in the air.

"Besides," I added defensively, "if she's with him, we may be able to track him down. And he won't be likely to go out on the prowl. He's never hurt anyone he knows."

Stevens groaned. "What's the matter?" Edgar asked.

The reporter was pale. "I was in Washington when I got word about the Keith deal," he said. "I managed to find a friend of his ex-wife who would talk to me. Off the record only. Tricia was the wife. You know her?"

Francine and I nodded. "You know why she divorced him?" Stevens asked. We didn't.

Stevens sighed a deep sigh. "He beat her," he said. "Came home after a trial one day and damn near killed her."

"Get Kara away from him, Cliff," Edgar said.

There was no answer at Kara's apartment. I left a message on the machine to call me immediately at Francine's number. That would get her attention: We never left messages on each other's machines. The only other thing I could do was send an urgent E-mail. I made up some excuse for needing to talk to her right away. Then I rejoined the others by the pool.

It was a hard night. They peppered me with questions, and we reviewed everything over and over. What about the physical description? He wore a wig and a fake mustache. The tattoo was probably ink. What about his eye color? I shrugged. Francine pointed to her own eyes. Colored contacts. The resemblance to Keith? Keith claimed "John" had taken a Polaroid picture.

Francine ordered food from the Chinese place that delivered, and boxes of stir fry and rice were piled on the tables near the pool, mostly untouched. Stevens spun out elaborate alternative theories, each of which we examined seriously and rejected. Edgar took the more pragmatic approach, examining each piece of evidence, testing its validity. Francine and I mostly listened. It was their show.

By ten, the talk petered out, and we all sat staring at one another or at the stars overhead. Edgar finally broke the silence. "It all fits." He waved the memo. "This is the perpetrator."

Stevens nodded in agreement. "So what do we do?"

They looked at me. "I hoped you would know," I said.

Edgar took charge. I wanted to hug him. "If this pattern's right and if he follows it, we can count on two more days, maybe three," he said, "but Lake Wachita worries me. Maybe it was to throw us off, but an MO change also could signal a rampage. I hate to rely on that time cushion."

"He didn't sound like someone about to go on a binge when I talked to him the other day," I said. "He was in control."

"You can't tell, Cliff. We have to find him and get him under surveillance." He looked at me. "Any idea where they are?"

I had not received E-mail from Kara in two days. "Her last message said they were leaving California and heading east. She made a joke about Las Vegas. But obviously they went to Johnston Beach."

Edgar shook his head. "We can't do it ourselves." He looked at his watch. "Someone needs to find that plane, then persuade the local authorities to cooperate and establish surveillance. We need the Bureau for that."

"Can't you just have him arrested?" Francine asked.

"Not on this." He pointed to my memo. "The Bureau will insist on checking it out themselves. This is mostly hearsay, and it's only copies. They won't move against Lewis Sherwood without a solid case. Unless they catch him in the act."

He was pacing back and forth now. "We need him under surveillance. Otherwise we'll have ourselves another victim. Probably loose, covert surveillance so he doesn't get spooked and go underground. That will be up to the on-scene commander."

He paused and looked around. "Anyone have any comments or other ideas so far?" We did not.

He stared at the pool. Finally he looked at his watch again. "If I call my Bureau contact and tell him all about this over the phone, he'll think I'm crazy. We need someone to go up there. I can go, I guess . . . "

"I will," Stevens said.

Edgar looked at him and nodded. "Good." He paused, thinking. "Yeah, that works. You have all the background on the Ripper, and that leaves me free to work the phones. Tim, I'll call him tonight, arrange a meeting for first thing in the morning." He moved his hand back and forth, as if lining up a target. "At this point, I'll tell him enough to arouse his curiosity and say we need to keep it hush-hush to avoid spooking the perp. Then it's up to you."

He waved his copy of my memo in Stevens's face. "Give them this. They'll fall out of their seats when they find out we're talking about Lewis Sherwood. You'll have some serious convincing to do. Then once you do that, you have to keep them calmed down." Stevens nodded.

Edgar began to pace again. "After that," he said, "I'll call an investigator I use sometimes who has good FAA connections. Maybe he can help us on that plane." He saw my look of alarm. "Don't worry. No names or reasons. We'll give him the tail number and tell him to find it."

He reviewed his plan in his head. "Okay, that makes sense. Maybe my man can find it tonight." Edgar looked at me. "Or maybe we'll get lucky and get some help from Kara. Once we have him located, I'll go out and work on the local authorities, at least until the Bureau gets in gear."

He thought some more. "I have a man in Alabama; I'll have him chase some of these loose ends. I'll call him tonight too." Edgar nodded his head in satisfaction and looked at each of us in turn. "Any questions or problems? Any other ideas, let's hear them now."

"What about me?" I asked.

Edgar looked at me thoughtfully. "You hang loose here. Serve as a clearinghouse. With any luck, we won't have to bring you in directly. No point wrecking your career unless we have to."

"It's too late to worry about that," I said.

He shrugged. "Let's wait and see."

Francine spoke up for the first time in a long time. "Who tells the Senator?"

Everyone looked at her. "What does he have to do with anything?" Stevens finally asked.

I understood. "It's his firm. We have to let him know about it." Stevens shook his head in disgust.

Edgar said, "Cliff, I suppose."

Francine looked at me. "No," she said. "You may need Cliff here to help you. I'll talk to him."

She stopped my protest before I got it out. "If you tell me one more time I'm not involved, I'm throwing your asses out on the street," she announced to the group at large. "The Senator's in Washington the rest of the week. I'll fly up with Tim and find him, then stay to help. Or enlist my brother if we need to."

She glared at me. "Stop looking at me like that. You"— she pointed to Stevens—"get on the phone and book us on the next flight. I like first class. Then let Edgar have the phone. Cliff, you check your E-mail and answering machine every few hours in case Kara has called in."

We all started off on our various duties.

The next flight to Washington left at six A.M. Over Stevens's halfhearted protest that he would go to a hotel, Francine assigned him the guest bedroom and made up the couch for me. While she bustled around, Stevens rolled his eyes with a "who does she think she's fooling?" look. I would have to think of some way to let him know we were not sleeping together.

Edgar made his calls and went home. Stevens went to bed. Francine and I sat by the pool for a few minutes more, silently sharing a sense of mixed relief and trepidation. After she went to bed, I went inside for a last check of my E-mail. My message to Kara remained unread, and she had not sent me anything. I stretched out on the couch and fell asleep, wondering where she was.

Edgar woke us up at five sharp. Francine and Stevens left for the airport a half hour later. Stevens gave me a thumbs-up from the window of her car as they pulled away. The Marines had landed.

Inside the house, Edgar was on the phone, talking to someone about flight plans. He sighed in exasperation when he hung up. "I had forgotten how hard it is to find a damn plane in this country. The FAA doesn't know where they are unless they're actually in the air, and then only if the pilot filed a flight plan. With a turboprop like Sherwood's, well, if he stays below a certain altitude and has good weather . . . he could be anywhere." He bit his lip, then handed me the phone. "Check on Kara."

At last. A message: "Hi. Guess you heard the big news. Surprise, huh? :-) Got your message, but no chance to call. You'll never guess where we went. Lewis said it was a secret. I thought he meant Las Vegas. :-(But we didn't go ANYWHERE. :-D ‹Ha Ha› I'll call when Lewis gives me a free minute. ‹Blush›. Love, Me."

What the hell did that mean?

I showed it to Edgar. He studied it with a wrinkled brow. "Didn't go anywhere?" he said. "Are they here?"

I called Kara's apartment again. The answering machine picked up. I left another message to call. I called Sherwood's condo. Another answering machine. I didn't leave a message this time. I sent Kara another urgent E-mail. "I give up," it said in part. "Where are you?" I thought about making it stronger, but I still was afraid Sherwood might look over her shoulder when she read it.

Edgar called the airport and all the local general aviation facilities. No plane with that tail number in Queenston. He called the Johnston Beach airport, on the chance she meant they had returned there. No luck.

The Alabama detective called. "Stevens was right," Edgar said when he hung up. "Edward P. Tarleton was that football player. He died in Birmingham. The address on the driver's license"—he tapped my memo with his forefinger—"is the street address for SFL and all the other companies. It's an office building downtown. He has a license in Adamason's name too. And some of the others."

"How did he do that?" I asked.

Edgar sighed. "Classic way to build a false identity: find a dead man, get his birth certificate, and start collecting records. Most government agencies don't check very well, unfortunately." He shrugged. "Probably he got the driver's licenses that way or had an out-of-state forgery. A smooth talker like Lewis wouldn't have much problem."

I checked the office. No messages. Alice hoped I was feeling better. She assumed that I, like the rest of the Red Team, was recuperating from Patoots. Edgar studied the Rand McNally, drumming his fingers on the table. He began calling airports in the neighboring states.

I checked my answering machine at home again. "Hi, Shug," Kara giggled. "We're in Johnston Beach, silly. We flew for a while, then landed somewhere, rented a car and drove back here. You know what? Now I know what Lewis does when he goes to relax. We're wearing wigs and makeup; you all would never recognize us. It's so much fun pretending to be someone else. We registered as Mr. and Mrs. something." She laughed. "Lewis is so excited about the case being over. It's like he's gonna bust. I've never seen him like this. He . . . " The tape ran out. I had my machine set on the short-record feature.

CHAPTER
23

Sheriff Al Sanderson no longer reminded me of Santa Claus: I had not seen a jolly look yet. When we finished our story, he leaned across his desk and growled: "I got to tell you, that's the most hare-brained damn tale I've ever heard." He looked down at the copy of my memo that lay untouched on his desk. "I ain't got time to play mystery games here."

Pete Bannister took the lead. "Al, I had the same reaction. But you read that"—he pointed to the memo—"it all makes sense." He looked at Edgar. "The FBI takes it seriously."

Sanderson rolled his eyes. "Oh, yeah. The FBI. Your buddy in Washington called me. They sure do love mysteries up there." He shook his head. "The FBI"—the phrase dripped from his tongue—"gonna send me people? The FBI gonna make an arrest? The FBI gonna pay the judgment when I haul Lewis Sherwood in and he sues my ass?"

Edgar had become close to Sanderson since Keith's arrest. He took a shot with the same ammunition we had used on Chief Prescott at Lake Wachita: "Al, you can't afford to ignore it. You could have the Resort Ripper right here in your county, looking for a victim."

"I do have the Resort Ripper right here in my county," the sheriff muttered. "He's sitting in my friggin' jail, according to what you all said two days ago."

I listened impatiently. We had wasted time: time traveling to Johnston Beach, time convincing Pete, now time with Sanderson. "He'll huff and puff and then he'll take care of it," Pete had said. I wished Sanderson would finish his huffing and puffing. It was already late afternoon.

He started to wind down. "This suspect is not charged with anything, is that right?" Sanderson was still trying to decide if we were merely lunatics with highly placed friends.

Edgar answered. "The Bureau wants to hold off on any charges. They're very cautious about Sherwood: they don't want to take any chances by spooking him. They're in the process of confirming what we brought them now. What we brought them is true, Al. We can't risk waiting until we have a warrant. We don't want another dead girl. Do you?"

Sanderson leaned back with a huge sigh. "All right," he said in a defeated voice. "What do you expect me to do?"

Pete and I were mere spectators now. "We need to find Sherwood and put a tail on him," Edgar said.

"What do you have on him?"

"We worked our way out from Johnston Beach calling airports. His plane's a couple hours' drive from here. The Bureau has arranged for someone to watch it. He rented a car; we have the license number."

"You got any reason to think he's still here?"

I responded. "All we have is the message from Kara."

Sanderson shook his head. "And you think they're in disguise. So our only description is a man about five-ten and a woman with a good figure. And a black Ford." He sounded disgusted.

Edgar pointed to one of the attachments to my memo. "We have a list of names he's used in the past."

Sanderson glared at each of us in turn. He had been painted into an uncomfortable corner. Finally he pulled his bulk up from the desk and looked down at us. "Okay. But let me tell you something. If the damn electorate finds out I been chasing after a prominent citizen who probably ain't here and probably ain't done nothing anyway, they'll chop my friggin' head off. I promise you, good buddies, when my head rolls down that hall, your heads gonna be rolling right next to it. Starting with yours, Bannister."

We looked appropriately threatened.

Edgar and Sanderson laid out plans while Pete and I sat useless. The sheriff would broadcast a watch for the car with clear instructions to report but not alert the driver. He would station deputies at strategic locations on the highway. He would send a couple of trusted men out to the hotels with the list of names to search registrations.

"That's all I can do," Sanderson concluded. "Got some other crimes to worry about too, you know."

Edgar nodded and looked at his watch. Sanderson gave him a shrewd stare. "You plan to go out on patrol?"

"Unless something comes up."

"What about them?" The sheriff pointed to Pete and me.

"If they want to, I think we can use them." Pete nodded. Edgar already knew I would be searching for Sherwood.

Sanderson nodded. "Give me an hour to get this in motion." He pulled open a file cabinet drawer and took out three small boxes. "I'll join you. I'm on salary, ain't no overtime for me. Here, sign for these. Brief the Junior G-men here on how they work." The boxes were portable two-way radio units.

The sheriff ushered us to his office door. "Meet me at The Skillet in an hour. You know where it is, Pete." He stood back and examined us from head to toe. "If you boys plan to blend in, you need to change clothes. Right now you stick out like sore thumbs." As we left, I heard him mutter: "Damn wild-goose chase."

"We'll stay in touch on the radios I gave you," Sanderson declared between bites of country fried steak. The Skillet was an old-fashioned family restaurant, the kind where you get your choice of three vegetables with the special. The sheriff wore white-belted slacks and a Hawaiian shirt that, stretched across an umbrella frame, would have provided shade for a family of four. Pete had changed at home; Edgar and I had hit the mall. All three of us wore short-sleeve shirts and khaki pants; Edgar had a sportcoat too. "Check in every time you go to a different location," the sheriff directed. We nodded, and he went on.

"Now, you all float around clubs and restaurants and bars. Me and my men will chauffeur you and keep our eyes open, but ain't much use in us just going out and looking for him. None of us seen him that much, and if he's really in disguise, we won't recognize him."

He swallowed a mound of mashed potatoes dripping with brown gravy. "Don't you boys go following potential victims; I don't want to waste my time explaining you're not a pervert. Young ladies are kind of jumpy after that murder up in New York State." He wiped his mouth and frowned at a gravy spot on his shirt.

"Now," he continued, wetting his napkin and trying to wipe away the stain, "If you spot him, call in. Do not, I repeat, do not, make contact or let him see you. Do not spook him. If you think he saw you, keep moving the way you were headed, get out of the place, and report in. We'll pick him up. He knows you and he knows me. So my men have to do the close work."

"Have you told your men who we're looking for?" Edgar asked.

"Naw. Just these names on your list; I didn't say nothing about Lewis Sherwood. Now, you boys remember these hotels have their own security staff. So do some of the bars. You start acting too weird, talking into your armpits or something, then they might pick up on you, and I don't want to have to explain that either, so be careful."

This was all for my benefit. Sanderson trusted Pete, and Edgar was a professional. I was the most likely screwup.

"Won't these radio earpieces give it away?" I might as well meet his expectations with a dumb question.

"Those earpieces are supposed to look like hearing aids," the sheriff explained patiently. "And the box looks like a hearing-aid box. Now I know you're kind of young to need one, but that's the best we can do. Just don't play around with it: People who wear hearing aids are used to them. Fact is most others ain't gonna notice, unless you fool with the thing.

"When you need to transmit, find a natural-looking way to cover what you're doing." He struck a pose like the Thinker, hunched over slightly so his mouth was near his breast pocket, the hand that held his chin incidentally covering his mouth. "These things got pretty sensitive microphones. Ain't no need to yell. I don't want a damn broken eardrum."

"We can practice a little on the way," Edgar said. "Who's on this channel besides us?"

"My dispatcher will monitor, and we'll keep a tape on it too, just in case. Use first names: Al, Pete, Cliff, Edgar. Her name's Donna. Remember anybody out there with a scanner could be listening to you. Keep it short and to the point.

"If you really get in trouble, Code Orange brings the cavalry." He gave me a threatening glare. "But you better be down on one knee with a knife at your throat before you use Code Orange. Else I'll show you personally what a true Code Orange is. It gets real expensive to send the troops with sirens blasting.

"And don't you bust my radio, either. These little things cost a bundle. Like I tell my men, I don't care if you drop it off a tall building, so long as you're holding on to it when it hits the ground."

He turned on his own radio and called in to Donna. With the earpiece unplugged, we could hear her voice over the noise of dishes in The Skillet's kitchen.

"Bingo on a hotel, Al," Donna said. "Clippers. They found one of those names on that list."

Sanderson looked at us with a surprised expression. "Who found it?"

"Bo Everson."

"Put him on here."

Some more crackling, and Everson was on. Yes, one of the names on the list had registered yesterday. Party of two. Everson had called the room, prepared to apologize for a wrong number, but no one answered.

"Anything on the car, Bo?" Sanderson asked.

"No, sir. On the hotel registration, they put a different license plate number than the one you gave us."

"Run it, Donna, and send it to the troops." He instructed Everson to put a watch on the hotel room, then signed off and looked at us thoughtfully.

I bounced to my feet. "Search the room," I said. "Maybe there's something in there that can help us find them."

Sanderson had a small smile on his face. "Got a warrant, sonny?" he asked. "Damn defense lawyers be on our ass if we ain't got a warrant."

I slapped the table in frustration and sat down again.

"We could wait until they get back," Sanderson said. "Save a lot of expense." I felt a stone drop in my stomach.

Edgar shook his head. "Can't take the chance, Al. Maybe we won't find them, but we have to look." The sheriff did not argue with him.

Pete spoke up. "They're probably out on the town. That means we stay with the plan and concentrate on restaurants and bars. What you say, Al?"

The sheriff nodded. "Ready to hit the road?"

He grandly pushed his plate back and waved at the waitress, who looked personally wounded at the sheriff's refusal of dessert.

By eleven, I had covered all my assigned spots three or four times, listening to the chatter over the radio while I searched. Sanderson's people had confirmed the room at Clippers was empty by sending up a room-service waiter, who knocked with no response. Now they watched it from a vacant room on the same hall. The police had run the license plate on the guest register and discovered it was fictitious.

Despite his admonition to me, Sanderson passed a lot of information over the radio. I hoped Sherwood didn't somehow have a police band scanner. Even Edgar was concerned. "Remember this is in the clear, Al," he broadcast at one point.

"What else can we be doing?" I asked Sanderson in frustration as he pulled into the Mariner parking lot to drop me off for my fourth visit of the night.

He shrugged. "That's police work, son. It takes time. We'll find them."

"Can there be a mistake? She said they registered as 'Mr. and Mrs.' "

He looked at me like I looked at people who told me what the law was. "Clippers don't much care whether folks are married or not," he said. "She probably didn't see the card. Quit worrying."

I got out and he pulled away. I took a breather in the Mariner's lot before braving the dance floor. The Fabulous Bombardiers were back, or they had never left, and my eardrums throbbed at the thought of diving back into the noise.

The night was clear and warm, and in the moonlight I could see the Atlantic past the corner of the Mariner. In the distance, I made out a merchant ship's anchor lights. Very peaceful, except when the door opened to the Seaside Lounge and Shag Shack. Parked cars filled the lot, but their owners were inside, except for a couple discussing life intently next to a blue van. The woman looked a little like Dorothy Catterman. I did not want to go back in there to the noise. But I did.

I bought my Coors Light and wandered around the club with the air of a slightly degenerate, moderately wealthy, overage playboy looking for female companionship. That was the look of most of the other male patrons too. I fit right in.

On my rounds of the nooks and crannies, I saw by-now familiar faces. A few couples had been together since my first visit, others had changed partners, and a fair number still prowled alone or in packs. Over in a far corner was a blonde I remembered because of the faintly obscene joke on her T-shirt. My last two times there, she had been talking to a guy with the height and build of a basketball player. He looked faintly familiar: I thought he had played in the ACC. Now the jock was dancing with a pert redhead and the blonde talked to a short, slender guy with a receding hairline.

I watched the blonde for a moment, then scanned the area near her. Two tables over, a tall brunette sat with her back to me. Her frizzy permed hair rose high above her head, then tumbled over her shoulders to touch the back of the chair. She was talking to a tablemate out of my view. Something about her seemed vaguely familiar: her posture or the way she moved. I stepped to one side and saw—Sherwood.

I didn't recognize him at first. In fact, he looked very much like Travis Keith. He had shoulder-length brown hair and a mustache, and something was different about his nose, but when I squinted, I was sure it was him. He sat with his back against the wall at a two-person table in a U-shaped corner. I ducked my head and moved farther left so I could see the brunette in profile. It was Kara. I sighed with relief.

She wore heavy dark eye makeup, long false eyelashes, and garish red nailpolish. The pile of teased and tangled hair gave her an entirely different look. Sherwood rubbed the back of her hand as she gazed into his eyes and talked. She said something with a serious look on her face; he laughed, took her hand into both of his and kissed it. She brought the clasped hands back to her own lips. They were getting along very well.

I ducked back out of the table's line of sight and hit my transmitter. "Got them," I said, loudly enough to draw a puzzled look from a girl walking by toward the bar.

Edgar and Sanderson yelled in my ear almost simultaneously. "Don't let him see you," came from Edgar.

"Back off," Sanderson shouted. "I'm on the way."

I took a quick peek to make sure Sherwood and Kara were still there—they were—and climbed the stairs to the elevated bar, pushing my way to a spot on the outside rail where I could view the opening of the U containing their nook. A seat opened up in front of me, and I grabbed it.

I could see anyone going in or out of there.

About two minutes later Kara appeared, checking inside her purse as she walked. She had on an outfit that could have come from a Swilton yard sale: tight black shorts, too-high heels, and a ruffled red blouse cut so low that she was about to fall out of it. A gaudy gold chain around her neck held a round ornament that nestled between her breasts.

I hunched my shoulders and ducked my head, covering my face with one hand and the beer bottle. She hurried up the bar stairs and passed behind me to the restroom with a smug, excited grin on her face.

Then Sherwood emerged and walked to the entrance, stopping just inside the front door. He was in tight, faded jeans, a too-small motorcycle T-shirt, and dirty tennis shoes with no socks. A portion of a tattoo showed on his left biceps. He glanced at his watch, then casually looked around the bar; I turned away. When I glanced over my shoulder, he was studying a nineteenth-century circus poster on the wall.

"Hurry up, dammit," I hissed into the radio. "They're leaving."

"On the way," said Edgar.

Sherwood reviewed several other decorations, tapping his foot impatiently. There must have been a long line in the ladies' room. He looked at his watch again. Then Kara emerged and almost ran past me down the steps. She came up to Sherwood, pulled his arm slightly so he leaned down, and whispered something. He laughed, she blushed. Then they turned and went out the door.

"Shit," I said to the radio. "They're outside."

"Tail him, Cliff," Edgar shot back.

I pushed my way through the crowd at the bar rail, drawing several shoves in return, and hurried out the door. My eyes took a second to adjust to the night. The parking lot was still quiet. They stood about twenty yards away, by a black Ford backed into its space. This was a state with only one license plate, on the rear, so I could not see the number.

Sherwood leaned against the trunk, Kara in his arms. They kissed passionately. Then they pulled apart and stared into each other's eyes.

I pictured Maria Perez in the Taproot parking lot.

I desperately scanned the highway for a sign of either Sanderson or Edgar, but no cars pulled into the parking lot. Sherwood and Kara broke their clinch, and he followed her to the passenger side, opening the door and closing it behind her. Then he moved back around to the driver's side.

The Ripper Wall flashed in front of my eyes. Then Inga Tillitson.

"Hey," I yelled. Sherwood didn't hear me. I ran across the parking lot and tapped him on the shoulder. He whirled around faster than I ever have seen anyone move outside of a Ninja movie. He faced me, arms tense, poised to strike. His teeth gleamed in the light through lips pulled back in a snarl. I had never seen a human truly snarl before.

I thought I was dead.

"Lew," I said. "We need to talk."

CHAPTER
24

For what seemed like an eternity, Sherwood remained motionless, a cobra coiled to strike. Then he relaxed slightly. But only very slightly. "What the fuck are you doing here?" he hissed.

Kara called from inside the car, "Joe, what's the matter?" Her accent had an exaggerated country twang.

He called back over his shoulder, "Nothing, honey. Just a friend of mine. Be right there." Then he looked me up and down, his face twisted in a tight, humorless smile. "Well, did we pick the same place for a vacation, Clifford?"

It was Sherwood, but it was someone else, too. Someone with long stringy hair, a mustache, an American flag tattoo—and an aura of potential danger. "We need to talk," I repeated. It was all I could think to say.

"This is not a good time, Clifford." He gestured toward the Ford sedan. "Where are you staying? I'll call you."

"I know about everything."

Sherwood cocked his head to one side and examined me again, carefully. I could no more move than a rabbit face-to-face with a rattler.

A small group of men came out of the bar and stood at the

entrance, talking and laughing loudly. One of them urinated against the tire of a car. Then Kara got out of the car and walked around to us.

Her eyes grew wide when she saw me, and she broke into a huge smile. "Cliff!" She ran and hugged me tight, kissing me on the cheek. I smelled beer and cheap perfume. Kara never wore perfume.

She stepped back and giggled. "Like it?" She pirouetted. "I'm Tammi and Lewis is Joe." She still spoke with that twang. "We're rednecks," she said, dragging "red" into three syllables. "Look." Kara moved closer and pulled the front of the red ruffled blouse to one side. Next to the dangling ornament from the gold chain around her neck, I could see almost all of her right breast. She had a butterfly tattoo just above the nipple. She giggled again. "Mamma would just die to see me like this." She was a little drunk.

Sherwood stood motionless behind her. A look I had not seen before flashed across his face as she prattled on. Contempt, maybe. Or anger. I did not know if it was for her or for me.

"I need to talk to you right now, Lew," I said.

"Who's Lew?" Kara said, moving to his side and hanging on his arm. She looked at Sherwood, then at me. Her smile faded into a frown. "What's wrong, you all?" she said in her normal voice.

Sherwood sighed, and the tension left his body. I took a few deep breaths. He removed her arm gently and gave her a quick kiss on the cheek.

"Clifford says he needs to talk to me about something important," he said, his voice soft and soothing. He looked at me. "Will this take long?"

I shrugged. Sherwood pulled the car keys from his pocket and handed them to Kara. "You go back to Clippers," he said. "I'll walk over when we're done." He walked her to the car and held the driver's side door for her. She rolled down the window, and he leaned in for a passionate kiss, then whispered in her ear. She started the car and pulled away.

We watched her drive to the highway. "This better be very, very important, Clifford." He was angry, but he was Sherwood again, not that other person who had been ready to attack. "What is it you want?"

Something indistinguishable buzzed in my ear. All of a sudden, I was alone with him and I had not thought about what I would say. I babbled: "Not out here. Back inside. There's something I need to tell you."

Sherwood looked at the entrance to the Seaside Lounge and Shag Shack. He frowned, calm now. "Not in there if you really need to talk about something. There's a bar down the street. You have a car here?" He waved his arm toward the highway. "I just gave mine away."

I would not get in a car with him, nor would I walk alone with him in the dark. "We'll go to the Lounge behind the Shack." I pointed toward the Mariner.

Sherwood shrugged and started toward the hotel. I keyed my radio transmitter, leaving the button down, and followed. "Going to the Seaside Lounge," I whispered into my pocket. He walked fast; I hurried to keep up with him.

Without a word, we passed through the hotel lobby and into the side entrance that led to the grill overlooking the ocean, the same place Kara and I had dinner our first night in Johnston Beach. It was quiet, with only a few customers scattered around various tables. Nothing had changed except the bartender. The one we met during our first visit was working in the Shag Shack tonight.

The waitress came when we sat at a secluded table in the corner. I ordered a Coors Light; Sherwood, despite his redneck character, had a Chivas and water with a twist. We sat silently until the drinks arrived. I hoped to hell Sanderson and Edgar were around somewhere, listening on the radio.

"Get on with it," Sherwood said as he sipped his drink. "What do you want?"

I took a deep breath and stared in his eyes. They were brown, not blue. "I know about everything, Lew. Leave Kara alone."

He frowned. "That's what this is about? Kara?" His voice was angry again. "Jesus Christ, Clifford." Then he smiled and nodded. "Oh. I get it. You had a thing for Kara, didn't you?" He chuckled. "Well, if you want to compete for her, feel free. May the better man win."

He started to rise. "Now, if we're done, you'll excuse me . . . "

"The Ripper, Lew. I know about the Ripper."

He sat back in his chair, alert, cautious. "What do you mean?"

"I know who the Ripper really is. And so do you."

"Keith is the Ripper, Clifford. That's what I know." He spoke as if to a very dull child. "Are you feeling all right?"

"You were there, Lew. At every murder scene."

He spread his hands, a puzzled look on his face. "Clifford, what in the hell are you talking about?"

It tumbled out. "I know about BSE Enterprises, I know about Lake Wachita. Cut the crap, Lew. I'm telling you, I know all about the whole thing. Everything. It's you."

Sherwood stared at me thoughtfully for a moment, unmoving. "I haven't the slightest idea what you're talking about, Clifford," he said in a loud, even voice.

His hand shot out and ripped the earpiece from my ear. He studied it carefully, then reeled in the cord until it pulled taut between his hand and my shirt pocket. With the other hand, he reached over and took the radio from my pocket. Silently, he turned off the power and gently placed the unit on the floor, then suddenly smashed it with his heel. "Having some hearing problems, Clifford?" he said in a soft, mocking voice. Then he gathered the pieces and deposited them in a nearby trash can. Sanderson is going to be pretty mad about that, I thought wildly.

As Sherwood came back to the table, I realized that no one was within twenty yards of us. The waitress and bartender were deep in conversation under the TV at the far end of the bar, and everyone else had left except a couple on the other side of the aquarium that served as a room divider. I could barely make them out through the bubbles and fish and plants.

Sherwood sat back down and lifted his drink. "What exactly is it you want, Clifford?"

Hell, I didn't know. "I want it to stop, Lew. And I want Keith out."

"Keith's a looney tunes." So much for our former client. "You know, I talked to the Senator about you. He plans to brief you soon on the details of your partnership." Sherwood paused. "Don't go off the deep end now, Clifford. You almost have the brass ring in your hand. You don't want to fall on your ass."

"Bullshit."

"Something's come over you, Clifford. I think you need help." He walked down to the bartender and got a refill. I wondered what to do next. Where were Sanderson and Edgar? When Sherwood returned, he stopped by the window and looked out at the ocean waves lapping against the shore. "Let's go out on the veranda, Clifford."

"No."

He put the drinks on the table and sat in the chair next

to me. "You know, Clifford, you really have a problem. A couple of problems, in fact." His face was sorrowful.

"Your first problem is you have lost your mind. I think you're saying I'm the Ripper. That's crazy. Absolutely crazy. I think we need to fix you up with Dr. Banzinger. I hope you get over it soon, because saying things like that could cause you serious trouble."

He shook his head, exuding sympathy. "I should call the funny wagon and let them take you away right now. Or walk the hell out of here. But I've always liked you, Clifford, and I want to help you. You've been under a lot of strain with this case. So I'll forget this. Go back home and sleep off whatever it is you've been drinking or smoking or ingesting to cause this delusion."

I wished I could. "That won't work, Lew. I can't let anyone else end up dead." He remained silent. "Why, Lew? Why did you do it?"

He looked past me with a faraway gaze. "I didn't do anything, Clifford. You're wrong, I tell you. Keith is the Ripper." He stirred his drink slowly, letting the ice clink.

"Keith didn't do it, Lew. You did. You're John. You took that picture of him and used it as a model for your disguise."

Sherwood stared at his drink. "You're fantasizing, Clifford. That would make Keith the unluckiest son of a bitch in the world, wouldn't it? First he meets a guy who steals his looks, then he gets himself in trouble down here."

"Seize the moment," I said. "Sherwood's Rule."

"If you want to know why Keith did it, I'll tell you." He took a slow sip of his drink. "You ever been shot at?" I shook my head. "I didn't think so. Then you'll never understand the excitement of life and death. The power. The Ripper understood that. He needed that."

"Why these girls?" I asked.

"Rich bitches." Sherwood's voice was neutral, explanatory. "The kind who won't give a poor boy the time of day. The kind who call you a baby-killer when they find out you've been in Nam. Cockteasers who flash their tits at you and laugh when you're cleaning their daddy's pool."

His voice was harsh now: deep and filled with hate. "The kind who spit in your face when you get up the nerve to ask them to dance. They keep their noses so high in the fucking air that they don't even notice when they step on you. The kind who use their daddies' money and go to a resort." He paused and chuckled.

"I'll tell you a secret, Clifford. You know my first big case? We've talked about it. My client was a black man named Thomas Badgers. They said he raped one of those rich bitches. I got him off. Acquitted. He walked out free. You know what? He did it. He raped her. And I got him off. Funniest thing I ever saw, the face on that rich bitch when the jury foreman said not guilty."

Sherwood stopped suddenly, catching himself. He looked at me steadily, unblinking, and his voice grew lower. Sharp edges creased his jaw and cheekbones. "That's why the Ripper did it, Clifford. That's why Keith did it."

His eyes were locked into mine. He took a deep breath, and shook his head again, as if he had tried his best. Then he leaned close to me. "Forget Keith. Let's talk about you, Clifford. I told you your first problem. You're crazy. And you don't realize it. That brings us to your second problem. It's a bigger problem, Clifford. What if you're right?"

He took my wrist in his right hand. "If you're right, then you have a serious personal problem, boy." The pressure grew stronger and stronger. Then he gave a twist that made me gasp in pain. "Because it might not be safe."

With his left hand, he gave my right shoulder a short,

hard shove; it threw me off-balance. When I lurched to one side, he twisted my left arm behind me and pushed it high under my shoulder blade: The combination of pressure and pain shot me to my feet. "Now let's go out on the veranda and talk about this." His left hand was on my throat. I could not catch my breath, I could not make a sound. He moved me swiftly to the door.

The voice came from behind us: "Stop it, Lewis." Sherwood released my throat and turned. I gasped for breath and watched Edgar slowly approach the table. He moved cautiously, his right hand inside his sportcoat, his left arm holding the coat front, ready to clear it. I had never seen Edgar carry a weapon; I didn't know if he was bluffing now.

"Sit down, both of you," Edgar ordered. I sank into a chair, panting to recapture my breath. Sherwood moved more slowly, never taking his eyes off Edgar, who waited until we were both seated until he took a chair himself.

Sherwood spoke first. "You're in on this too?"

"It's all over, Lewis," Edgar replied. "Why not give it up? Things will go much easier that way."

Sherwood sat like a statue; only his eyes moved as he studied Edgar, me, and the surroundings. Finally, he nodded slowly. His voice was low and menacing: "I could take you both. You'd never know what hit you."

"I don't think so," Edgar said. "But it wouldn't do you any good. We're not alone, Lewis. It's over."

They were two high-stakes poker players, raising the ante, waiting for the other to break. Neither blinked. Finally, the corners of Sherwood's lips curled in a tight, lupine grin. "Is this a citizen's arrest, Edgar?" he asked in a scornful tone.

"No."

Sherwood chuckled lightly at a joke Edgar and I did not

hear, then pushed his chair back and rose. "In that case, I bid you good evening, gentlemen." He reached into his back pocket. Edgar was on his feet in an instant, his hand back under his coat. "Just my wallet, Edgar," Sherwood laughed. He threw a twenty-dollar bill on the table. "Drinks are on me. You're both fired. Clean out your offices by tomorrow. When you get the slander suit, Clifford, remember: A lawyer who defends himself has a fool for a client. Sherwood's Rule."

He swaggered out the veranda door. Through the window, I saw him look both ways, then walk to his right, in the direction of Clippers. I rose to follow him, but Edgar stopped me. "He's on his way," he called into his pocket. Then to me: "Sanderson's men are outside. They'll tail him."

I fell back in my seat and swallowed half my beer in a gulp. As Edgar moved to another seat, his coat opened slightly. He really did have a gun in there.

Sanderson's bulk filled the lobby door and moved toward us. "They have him," he said, collapsing into the chair Sherwood had abandoned. He pulled out his radio, removed the earpiece, and turned up the volume so we could hear the messages.

"Blue-1, Blue-2. We have the suspect walking along the beach, heading toward the rocks. Following at a distance."

"Roger, Blue-2."

"Blue-1, Blue-2. Okay. He's past the rocks, on the Clippers property. Coming your way, Blue-4."

"Blue-4, Roger."

"They're leapfrogging him," Sanderson told us. "Blue-2 will pass him off, then move ahead."

"Blue-4, Blue-2. He should be in view now."

"Blue-4, Negative. We don't have him."

"4, this is 2. Look at the edge of the lawn, next to the trees."

"He didn't come out, 2."

"Shit. He must have gone into the woods."

Sanderson grabbed his radio. "2, 4. Go in there after him. Blue-3, Blue-5, cover the highway side of those woods. Get moving."

He shoved the radio in his pocket and struggled to his feet. "Come on. They've lost him."

I pulled at Sanderson's arm. "See if Kara went back to the room."

He looked at me, then brought the radio back out. "Ed. Is the woman in the room?"

"Negative, Sheriff. No one's gone in."

"Ben, you got that car in the parking lot over there?"

"Negative."

"He must have told her to pick him up somewhere," I said. We raced through the lobby into the parking lot. No sign of them.

"This'd be a hell of a lot simpler if you'd stayed the hell away like we told you," Sanderson grumbled over his shoulder. "Turn right, there," he told Edgar. Edgar drove; the sheriff directed from the passenger side. I was curled up in the back.

Sanderson didn't let up. Between barking at Donna ("You wake up everybody on the force and get their asses on the street.") and chewing out his surveillance teams, he threw potshots at me. " 'Don't spook him,' I said. 'Stay away from him,' I said. 'Don't let him see you,' I said. So what do you do? You friggin' walk up, tap him on the shoulder, and take him for a drink. Jesus, I'd hate to see you try to alert him."

I bit my tongue and took it in silence. Edgar finally

interrupted the tirade. "Ease up, Al," he said. "No one wins any awards for police work tonight. He did what he thought he had to do."

Sanderson grumbled, then shrugged. "Yeah, you're right. I just wish to hell we knew how much of a problem we got here." Neither Edgar nor I spoke. We were sure we had a huge problem.

Sanderson left two men at Clippers: One to watch the room and one to watch the parking lot. He put everyone else on the roads with succinct orders: "Find that friggin' car." At one point I could hear Pete speaking in the background to Donna. He was helping coordinate.

We cruised, looking at every car, while Sanderson steadily cursed the traffic. "No sirens," he'd ordered. I must have looked surprised. "Sirens will drive him to ground. I think he'll make a break for that plane." He had Donna notify the state police and all local jurisdictions between Johnston Beach and the airport where Edgar had found Sherwood's plane.

We worked our way north to the bridge, then turned and retraced our route. We saw many black cars, some of them Ford sedans, and startled several couples by pulling alongside and staring, but no luck. We were almost in front of the Mariner when the radio crackled.

"Al, Everson has the car." Donna's voice was excited.

"Patch us," Sanderson ordered. "Where you at, Bo?"

"Side road off the beach highway, mile 19. It's parked here. No one in it. Just about where the Swiltons were when we picked up Keith."

"That way." Sanderson pointed south. Edgar accelerated while the sheriff talked into the radio. "Be careful there, Bo," he said. "We're on the way. See anything?"

"The door's open on the passenger side, and the trunk's

open. Some scuff marks in the dust here. Let me look inside again." A pause. "Woman's shoe in the passenger compartment. Seems like . . . " There was a burst of interference.

"Bo?" Sanderson called. No answer. "Bo?" he called again. We heard clicks on the radio.

A new voice came on. Low. Menacing. It was Sherwood. "Put Nielson on," he said.

Sanderson looked at me. I reached for the microphone, but he spoke into it instead. "He's not with us. We have to find him. Hold on." He visually checked to make sure he was no longer transmitting. "We'll stall him," he said. "String him out, keep him talking until we get there." Edgar nodded agreement.

Sherwood came back. "Very good, Al." He chuckled, almost a choke. "But we're in kind of a hurry here. So you have five seconds to get Nielson on, or your deputy starts to bleed heavily from the throat. Want to find out how long it takes him to die? I'll let you know when to start counting."

"Hold it," Sanderson said into the microphone.

"Put him on," Edgar muttered.

Sanderson grunted and handed me the microphone. "Keep him talking," he said.

"I'm here, Lew," I said.

Sherwood's voice was almost cheerful. "Hello, Clifford. You know where we are, I assume."

Sanderson shook his head. I tried to sound honest. "No, Lew. The deputy didn't have time to say. Where are you?"

"Come on, Clifford. You can do better than that. Here's a clue." We heard a click, then a scream over the radio. Sanderson looked at me in horror, then reached over to turn on the flashing lights. Edgar drove faster.

"Lew?" I called into the microphone.

He came back on. "Follow the sounds and the trail,

Clifford. You said to leave Kara alone. I'll do that. I'll leave her. Alone."

"Don't hurt her, Lew," my voice cracked. "Please."

"You keep asking for more, Clifford. Tell you what. I'll leave her alone. If you want her alive, then you come alone too. Just you. Then we'll chat about it. I enjoy our chats, Clifford. But if anyone else comes, then Kara won't be able to chat with us. See you soon."

"Lew," I called, desperately trying to think of something, anything to say. "Lew!"

The only sound on the radio was interference.

CHAPTER
25

This is not real, I told myself. I'm not here, Kara's not there, we're both in bed in Queenston. It's a bad dream. Wake up now.

The ten minutes it took to reach the cars seemed like hours. Edgar and Sanderson discussed tactics on the way. "We cut off the escape routes to start," the sheriff said.

"Remember he's a SEAL," Edgar said. "Make your line too thin and he'll get through."

Sanderson picked up his radio microphone, then set it down again. Sherwood could be listening. "We should send some people around in a boat; they come in from the sound. Then another group from the highway, with perimeters on the flanks. But that's more troops than I got."

"No." They had forgotten about me. Sanderson turned to stare; Edgar looked in the rearview mirror. "I have to go in alone," I said, "or he'll kill Kara."

The two professionals looked at one another. Sanderson spoke, softly. "Son, you go in there, all that happens is he kills both of you."

A strange calm had settled over me. This wasn't real: it was a game of some sort. So I would play the game.

"If you send all those people in, he'll definitely kill her, won't he?"

Their silence was my answer. "So I have to go in. It's her only chance."

Edgar shook his head. "It's no chance."

"It's her only chance," I repeated stubbornly.

They looked at each other again. By now, we were on a dirt side road. Sanderson shook his head. "We'd just lose them both, and probably lose Sherwood too."

The police car and the Ford sedan sat on the shoulder of the dirt road, next to a slight incline up to the woods. Edgar stopped twenty yards away. They motioned for me to stay put and approached the car with drawn guns. When nothing happened, they beckoned me forward.

"Hold it down." Sanderson spoke almost in a whisper. "He could be watching from in there." He shined his flashlight toward the woods. We listened. The only sound was the wind rustling through the trees.

Edgar reached in the police car and took a flashlight from the front seat; the light danced across the car's body as he searched. "Here," he whispered. A dark stain stretched from the rain gutter over the driver's side window, down across the mirror, and over the front left fender. Edgar touched it with his hand. It smeared, on the car and on his finger. "Blood," he said, and wiped his hand with a handkerchief.

Sanderson grimaced. He reached in and turned off the police radio, then turned on the spotlight. "There," Edgar said. Sanderson stopped the spotlight on the crotch of a tree limb, where something glinted. Edgar aimed his flashlight to the ground, then pointed to something I could not see. We followed him around the car and up the incline.

The shiny object in the tree was a badge. Under it was a whitish piece of something. Edgar reached up slowly and held it for us to see. It was an ear. "Bo," Sanderson said softly.

Edgar shined his flashlight toward the ground, and followed a dark line back into the woods. As it became less visible, he raised the light slightly. We saw a khaki uniform shirt hanging from a tree limb.

The wind carried a distant sound from somewhere far behind the shirt. It reminded me of that rabbit, and Keith. Except I thought this was a woman.

Sanderson turned back to the road. "I'm calling in."

"Wait," I said. "Don't bring anyone else out here."

Sanderson grabbed my arm and half-walked, half-dragged me to the police car. He shoved me into the backseat; he and Edgar sat in front. "Roll up them windows," the sheriff growled, then waited until we were sealed in the car.

"All right, hero," Sanderson said to me. "You listen up. I'm the friggin' sheriff around here. Now here's what we're gonna do. We're gonna get us some friggin' troops, because whether I got to go in and get her or whether I got to go in and get both of you, I need some backup so the son of a bitch don't waltz out and drive off in my car. And he *knows* we ain't dumb enough to send you alone. So you quit thinking like you're cheating or some damn thing. You got it?"

I just listened. "Now," Sanderson said, "I'm calling for reinforcements, then I'm going in there after the son of a bitch. No son of a bitch can kill one of my men. You two stay here. Edgar, you take command of the rest of them when they get here. That's the way it's gonna be." He picked up the radio microphone.

I started to speak, but Edgar beat me to it. "No, it's not," he said. "I'm going no matter what you say. I suspect Cliff will too." He held up his hand to stop Sanderson from erupting. "No matter what you say. So let's figure out what makes sense for three men. None of us can take Lewis one-on-one in this environment. Maybe all of us together have a chance."

When we got out of the car, another sound that might have been a scream carried through the air. Edgar put his hand on my arm. "Ignore it," he said. "He's trying to get to you. As long as she's screaming, she's alive."

Sanderson opened his trunk and produced a handgun for me, a semiautomatic. I hadn't shot anything since the Navy, and then it was a .45. Annual officer's qualification on sidearms—even the lawyers and doctors and supply officers had to do it. The gunner's mates watched to make sure no one got hurt while we took potshots at a box floating in the ship's wake. The safest place for miles around was inside the floating box.

Sanderson showed me the safety and told me to leave it on and not point the damn thing at anything I didn't intend to kill. He even gave me instructions on the holster and how to walk in the woods without shooting myself or either of them.

They decided on a fan pattern. I would be in the middle, following the trail, using the flashlight as needed. "Don't go singing or nothing," Sanderson said, "but if you step on a twig, don't panic." Sherwood expected someone; if he heard one of us, it should be me.

Edgar and the sheriff would move on either side a little ahead of me. They would avoid using their flashlights and keep station on mine. The theory was Sherwood would focus on me and miss them.

A deputy arrived: Sanderson briefed her to act as on-scene commander when the others assembled. He wanted the escape routes covered. Another sheriff's crew would

take a bass boat on the sound: They would try to look like
fishermen unless they saw something.

Every few minutes, we heard a scream.

The moon was full, but only occasional light filtered through
the canopy of trees. Fifty feet into the woods, out of sight
of the dirt road, I knew how bait felt dangling at the end
of the hook.

I was no woodsman, and I had wondered how I could
follow the trail, but Sherwood had made it easy for me. I
went to the shirt we had seen, shined the light around, and
found another marker stuck in a tree. It was like following
a trail of bread crumbs. Only it wasn't bread crumbs. It
was equipment and clothing from Everson.

The thinking part of my mind was disabled: The sensory
inputs went directly to my limbs. If I heard anything, I
stopped. If I saw any movement, I stopped. I felt, rather
than saw, Edgar to my right and Sanderson to my left, and
somehow I filtered out noise or movement from them. Time
was a forgotten concept: We could have been in there a few
minutes, we could have been in there for days. I went from
one marker to the next, slowly, very slowly, flashlight off.
At each, I turned on the flashlight, opened my senses, then
looked for the next marker. The screams had stopped.

Everson's body lay at the foot of a tree. I observed him
without emotion and scouted for the next marker. It was the
gaudy gold chain Kara wore at the Mariner. I moved on.

I passed her other shoe, her black shorts, her panties,
then her blouse. The woods had thinned; the moon was
visible above. Through the woods, several hundred yards
away, I glimpsed another light, a different kind of light.
More yellow than the moonlight.

It was a fire in a clearing. Once I realized what it was,
I stopped, still too far away to make out the flames, but I

smelled the smoke and saw the light dance on the pinestraw and needles of the trees.

Now I moved a step at a time. I lost track of Edgar and Sanderson. The ground grew softer. An odor permeated the air, a combination of fire and something rotting. The fire came into full view. Its light reflected off water behind it. Marsh.

Before I reached the clearing, I moved off the trail and stood in the shadow of a tree, protected from the rear by a shrub that towered over my head. The heat from the fire pressed against my cheek. Its light filled the clearing and cast dancing shadows on the trees standing in the marsh. I had to let my eyes adjust.

The clearing was a semicircle, perhaps fifty feet in diameter, backed by the marsh. The fire was in the middle. To its right, a gym bag lay open in the dirt. A T-shirt and jeans—Sherwood's outfit—had been thrown next to it. On the left of the fire was what looked like a dead animal. The wigs. Everson's hat was on the ground in front of the fire, the bill aimed directly to the trail I had followed.

I pulled out the gun Sanderson had given me.

I heard a new sound, a moan or a whimper, over the crackling of the fire. I circled through the bushes to my right, not feeling the scratches the branches left on my arms and neck.

Kara was between the fire and the marsh. She was nude, on her knees, her arms behind her back. The light from the fire illuminated her face. Something was in her mouth, tied in the back. Below that, a rope looped around her neck and disappeared behind her. I saw the little butterfly tattoo on her right breast.

I brought my left hand to the side of my face to shield my eyes from the light of the fire. A shape took form in the darkness behind Kara. Sherwood squatted just behind her, staring straight ahead. He was naked, except for underpants and tennis shoes, and covered with mud from the marsh. I could not make out his features because of the mud. Had he stood and backed away from the fire, he would have been invisible.

He looked slowly around the clearing and stopped when his face was pointed directly at me. I stood motionless, not breathing. A bright white gash broke the black of his face. A smile. He reached forward with his right hand and did something under Kara. Her face creased in pain and she moaned, a moan muffled through the gag. "Hello, Clifford," Sherwood said.

My thinking mind suddenly clicked on, but no wash of horror came. This still wasn't real. I took a step forward into the clearing, then moved to my right to see Sherwood more clearly. Now I saw the rope behind Kara's back: it wrapped around her wrists and ankles and knotted together somehow to keep her motionless.

The white gash still cut across Sherwood's face. "You came alone," he said. "Good for you. I didn't think you had the balls."

Edgar and Sanderson had to be there somewhere. I avoided looking for them. "Let her go, Lew," I said. "I'll do whatever you want."

He ignored me. "Did you really come alone, Clifford?" His voice was soft, abstract. "If you did, then I broke my promise. I said I'd leave her alone for you, didn't I?" He grabbed the rope between Kara's wrists with his left hand and dragged her away from me, keeping his back to the marsh. He had a knife in his right hand. She moaned through the gag as he dragged her over roots and rocks. I saw long wounds appear on her legs.

Sherwood stopped at the edge of the clearing. The gash vanished; his face was black now except for his eyes. "Here she is, Clifford," he said. "Alone." Suddenly he was gone.

Something kept me from rushing forward. Instead, I stepped back into the woods and crouched, listening, watching. Nothing to my right. Where was Edgar? I heard quiet whimpers from Kara. The fire crackled.

Then I heard a thump across the clearing. Sanderson pitched forward into the open. He lay still. Seconds later, Sherwood appeared behind Kara. He dragged her back to her original position.

He squatted behind her again. I stepped forward.

"Clifford," he said, "that's disappointing. You didn't come alone after all." The gash reappeared across his face. "That means the deal is off." He lifted hard on Kara's ropes, jerking her arms high.

I felt for the safety on my gun and circled slowly to my left, keeping my eyes on him. Edgar should be on the right. I had to stay out of his line of fire. Sherwood watched me without a word. I stepped over Sanderson without looking at him. I thought I heard breathing.

Sherwood watched until I was about ten feet from them, to his right. Then he slowly brought his knife to Kara's throat. "It's about time you dropped that weapon, Clifford," he said in a flat voice. "Someone could get hurt."

"Don't do it, Cliff." Edgar stepped out from the other side of the clearing. He held his gun with two hands, aimed at Sherwood's head.

Sherwood showed no sign of surprise. He calmly turned his head toward Edgar. "I thought you were here somewhere," he said.

Edgar ignored him. "You cut her, we shoot you, Lewis. Now let's talk about it. What do you want?"

Now Sherwood laughed. He drew his knife gently across Kara's throat, leaving a thin line of blood. She mewled like a frightened kitten. "Hostage tactics, Edgar? Wait them out?" He gestured broadly with his left hand, keeping the knife tight against Kara's throat with his right. "You all have a SWAT team out there?"

Edgar kept his gun and his voice steady. "Let her go, Lewis. We can work it out after that."

I remembered my own gun. I brought it chest-high, but I couldn't see a clear target, even if I had confidence in my aim. He had Kara there in front of him.

The fire reflected from Edgar's face as he and Sherwood stared at each other. Kara's body gleamed with sweat. The mud absorbed any light from Sherwood. The only sound now was the crackling of the fire and labored breathing from Kara. I could not hear Sanderson.

Sherwood looked at me and back toward Edgar. "I want safe passage," he said in a quiet tone.

"Let her go, and we'll talk about it," Edgar said.

He sounded almost like the old Sherwood now, debating the logic of a proposal: "Edgar, if I let her go, I have no leverage. We're at a standstill here."

"Let her go, Lewis."

Sherwood shook his head. "No. We all walk out of here together, and you meet my demands for safe passage. Then I'll let her go." He paused. "That's my best offer."

Edgar did not respond. Sherwood kept the knife at Kara's throat and rotated around her to his right, putting her body between himself and Edgar. I raised my gun and pointed it at his head. It was a clear shot now, if I were accurate. "Stay still, Clifford," Sherwood called over his shoulder. He rested his cheek against Kara's neck.

Keeping their heads together, he reached down with his right hand and sawed the rope between her legs. Then he brought the knife back to her neck, and with his left arm, lifted her to her feet, still between himself and Edgar. Kara's legs buckled as she struggled to stand. She stared at Edgar's gun.

"All right, Edgar," Sherwood said. "We walk out of here together."

He took one step and stumbled over Kara's legs. The right hand dropped to his side as he fought to regain his balance. Suddenly, it flashed up, then down again.

I thought I saw the firelight reflect off the blade as it flew through the air and buried itself in Edgar's chest. Edgar reflexively dropped his gun and reached for the hilt. Blood flowed around his hands. He looked at Sherwood, then fell to his knees. He doubled over and pitched forward on his face. I heard his glasses crack.

Sherwood turned Kara so she faced me, with him behind. He steered her by pulling the rope around her neck as he moved toward Edgar, reached down, and pulled the knife loose. Then he kicked Edgar in the head. Edgar jerked and lay still, facedown, at Sherwood's feet.

Sherwood glanced at the gun lying on the ground. I expected him to pick it up, but instead he smiled and wiped his knife clean on Kara's thigh. I could see her eyes clearly now. The pupils were dilated, the whites prominent. The heavy eye makeup she had worn for her redneck disguise was smeared across her cheek. A false eyelash hung sideways from one lid.

"Now, Clifford," Sherwood said, "I think we finally are alone. Drop that gun, and we'll chat."

I kept the gun aimed at his head. Don't drop it, Edgar had said.

Sherwood inched toward me, keeping Kara in front of him. His voice was soft, reasonable. "Clifford, put the gun down now." I tried to keep it steady, pointed at his eye.

My hand grew heavy. Shoot, I thought. But Kara was so close.

He came too near; he was within five feet now. "Stop, Lew," I said, surprised to hear my own voice. It was a croak. "No closer."

"You think you can shoot that thing, Clifford?" His eyes never wavered from mine. Rivulets of sweat had carved canyons through the mud caked on his face. "You might hit Kara, you know."

I took a deep breath and drew a bead on his left eye. Exhale, those gunner's mates had said, then squeeze the trigger. I prayed, exhaled, and began to squeeze the trigger.

Kara came flying at me. I stepped back; she fell against my legs. As I reached down to recover, something that felt like a board hit my wrist. My hand went numb, the gun dropped. I fell to my knee, then scrambled to my feet.

Sherwood crouched in front of me. His lips curled back into a snarl. I bent low, watching his waist, like I would watch the waist of a point guard about to drive for the basket. My wrist throbbed; I could not bend my fingers. He made a sharp feint to his right; I moved to my left. He looked at my gun on the ground and contemptuously kicked it to his right, out of my reach. Then he straightened and the white gash disappeared.

He was a dark silhouette against the fire. My peripheral senses took in the background: Sanderson's labored breathing, Kara inching along the ground toward the fire, slight movement from Edgar, even something splashing in the marsh. But I could not hear anything from Sherwood. When he finally spoke, it was like an explosion.

"Sit down, Clifford."

I didn't answer. Without turning my head, I slowly moved my eyes, trying to locate the gun without looking directly at it. There it was, to my left. I judged the distance. I could lunge for it and try to grab and shoot with my left hand.

Sherwood smirked and looked at the weapon. Then he took a fast step to his left; I reacted. He came right; I reacted, shifting my weight to the left. As I moved, his foot shot out and destroyed my left knee.

The pain was immediate and immense; the scream seemed to come from somewhere else. I fell on my side. Before my hands could complete their automatic grab to my knee, he had my arms jerked up high behind me and was dragging me on my face toward the fire. He reached for the rope that he had cut from Kara's feet and wrapped it tightly around my forearms, binding them together behind me. He rose, looked down at me, and gave my knee another kick. The rope dug into my arms as I spasmed from the pain.

Kara was on her knees by the fire, trying to stand. He slowly walked over and kicked her feet out from under her. She fell heavily on her back and lay still, staring at him through wide, terrified eyes. Sherwood walked past Sanderson and around the fire to the gym bag. He pulled out a length of rope and came back to us, glancing back and forth between me and the edge of the clearing. He pushed Kara's legs together and bound her ankles, then cut the rope. He took the remaining length, walked to a tree at the edge of the clearing, and tied one end around the trunk. Then he came back and tied the other end around the binding on my forearms. When he finished, he stood and looked down at me.

"Now we can chat, Clifford," he said

In the distance, a siren wailed. Sherwood cocked his head and listened. "I'm afraid we've wasted a lot of time here," he said. I stared at him. It was the ole country lawyer voice, coming out of this mud-camouflaged, half-naked creature. "We'll just chat while I work."

He casually circled the fire, glancing down at Sanderson and Edgar as he passed them. Edgar lay still now. He paused to pick up Everson's hat. He went to the marsh, filled the hat with water, then came back and threw it in my face. The shock and the odor brought me back from the pain of my knee and my wrist.

Sherwood pulled me to a sitting position. I tried to move my left leg, but it lay useless. I brought my right leg up for balance. I could not feel my wrist any longer. He went behind me and drew the line to the tree taut. Then he dragged Kara in front of me and laid her on her back, between me and the fire, a yard beyond my feet. She whimpered again. "Hush," he said. "I need to talk to Clifford."

He took his knife and straddled Kara's legs. She stared up at him, then closed her eyes. He leaned forward, and with the edge of the blade began to scrape the tattoo on her breast. It peeled off. A decal. Her skin quivered under the knife's touch.

Sherwood talked as he scraped. "I've always liked you, Clifford. I told you to hang on for a little while and you had it made. But you really screwed up." He wiped the blade across Kara's shoulder and bent to scrape the remaining pieces of tattoo. "I'm afraid we can't have that."

It was like we were at the firm, having a quiet conversation. I heard more sirens in the distance, and I thought I heard a helicopter overhead. Keep him talking. Distract him.

My voice came from a distance, cracked and broken. "You had everyone fooled, Lew."

He smiled. "Preparation, Clifford. That's the key. Sherwood's Rule. Just like trying a lawsuit." He studied Kara's breast and nodded in satisfaction. "There," he said.

"Only a little scratch." Then he sat back on her legs and studied her. She kept her eyes closed tight.

Think of something. "Your disguises were great, Lew."

He nodded, letting the knife point play across her thigh. "Preparation again. Sherwood's Rule. Think of everything. Now let me show you how we do this."

He waved his knife. "The others were dead first. So it's not exactly the same. But you'll get the idea." He looked down at Kara. "Lie still, bitch, while I explain this to Clifford." She groaned.

"You start here"—he rested the knife point a few inches below the middle of her chest—"then you go here." Sherwood traced a line with his knife tip down to her pubic hair, then across to the top of one thigh. It left a trail of blood, like a paper cut. "Then you do it on the other side." Tears ran down Kara's cheeks, her face quivered.

Sherwood looked at me with a questioning look. "See? You go in deep and cut out the cunt. We'll save that for last, this time."

He leaned forward to look at Kara's breasts. "This is the next part, up here."

He listened to the sirens. "Have to hurry," he said. He rose to his knees and began to trace a pattern along Kara's chest, first over one breast, then over the other. With a mud-caked hand, he wiped away the blood.

I desperately tried to think of something to distract him. "Tell me how you thought of Lake Wachita, Lew," I called. Get him talking again.

He wiped his brow. "Shut up, Clifford, this is important," he said in a distracted voice. "See here? The signature." He bent over to study the trail of blood he was creating. "Roll, Tide," he muttered.

Kara grunted and brought both knees up hard, into his groin. He screamed, and doubled over, falling toward me.

She rolled away. A few feet from the fire, lying on her face and shoulder, she brought her knees up and struggled to reach the rope on her ankles with her hands. I pulled against my bindings, trying to free myself, but my right hand was useless. I began to yell, as loudly as I could, trying to attract the searchers that must be out there somewhere.

Sherwood rose, clutching his groin. He roared, an animal cry of pain and anger. He reached for the knife and clenched his fist around the handle. "Fucking cunt," he screamed, and took a step back to prepare a rush toward her.

I kicked out desperately with my right leg and caught him in the back. The blow sent him flying forward, toward Kara. She dropped to her face and rolled into his shins. He tripped over her and fell facefirst into the fire.

Sherwood lay there for what must have been a full second, roaring in pain. His hair burned. Then he rose and staggered into the marsh. Kara tried again to get to her feet; I pushed back toward the tree that held my rope, hoping to loosen it.

A deep growl came from the marsh. Sherwood lurched forward, slowly approaching Kara. One of his eyes was closed, a mass of burned tissue. The other shone as if still on fire. She pushed away from him. He caught up with her and raised the knife high. She cowered between his legs.

"Lewis!" A bubbling shout from beyond the fire. Sherwood stopped and turned. Edgar lay on his stomach, elevating his upper body with one elbow. A gun was in the other hand.

He shot. Sherwood staggered, then stepped in Edgar's direction. The gun flashed again. Sherwood stopped and clutched his stomach. He looked down, then up at Edgar. He took one step forward, wavered, and stepped back. Kara was behind him now. He fell backward, over her, and into the fire.

Edgar slumped to the ground and lay still. Kara sobbed through the gag. The fire crackled. A new smell drifted through the clearing.

CHAPTER
26

The faces floated in and out. I knew most of them: Francine, Preston, Anita, Pete, Tim Stevens. They usually talked. I never remembered what they said, but they talked. Some of the faces didn't talk. Inga Tillitson never said anything. Neither did Maria Perez or Susan Bond. They just smiled at me with the yearbook smiles.

The face in the nurse uniform talked, but I didn't know her. She would come and say something and then float away. Dr. Lawson's face: It talked.

There were firm faces: Ted, the Senator. Alice, I think. Not Edgar though, and not Sherwood. Kara's face talked. It was all bruised. She wore another disguise: a blue robe over some sort of white shirt.

Something was inside my knee. An animal. A mouse, or a squirrel, or a rabbit. It gnawed with sharp teeth, trying to escape. When it gnawed, the pain was agonizing.

Get it out, I called, but no one came. I tried to reach down and rip off the top of my knee to let it out, but something heavy bound my right wrist. I tried my left, but I couldn't reach my knee. Something was in the way. The animal chewed on the bone, uninterrupted.

Somewhere in the distance, I heard a familiar voice, but I couldn't place it with a face. It grew louder and more distinct. A New York accent. Who did I know in New York with a nasal voice like that?

I opened my eyes slowly. It was Bugs Bunny talking to a duck, on a TV that hung from the wall at the foot of my bed. I looked from side to side without moving my head. Preston was in a chair on my left, watching a cartoon. Francine sat on my right. She was watching the cartoon too. I waited for their faces to float away like before, but this time they didn't.

"There's an animal in my knee," I said, but the sides of my throat stuck together, and the words came out as noises. They both looked at me. Preston's face lit up with a wide smile. "Dad," he said, taking my left hand and squeezing it tight.

Francine lifted a cup and put some ice in my mouth. "Everything's okay," she said. The ice melted, and I could feel my throat separate. She put more ice in. "Do you need something for pain?" she asked.

That's what the nurse face always said. The animal nibbled, and I winced. Francine reached for a buzzer. "Wait," I croaked. I looked at her, then at Preston. Why were they both here? "Is this Queenston? Or Kansas?" I asked.

Francine smiled. "Johnston Beach," she said. "You've been here about three days."

There was something about Johnston Beach. Something I needed to know. A searing flash of pain in my knee brought me awake, and the memories flooded in. I tried to push myself up. "Where's Sherwood?" I said.

Preston held my left hand tighter, and Francine pushed my shoulder down on the bed gently but firmly. "He's dead, Cliff. It's over." She peered at my face to see if I was really there this time. "Everyone else is fine. Kara's fine. Edgar, he'll be all right too. And you'll be fine. They had to operate on your knee."

The nurse appeared at the door. "I see we're awake," she said. "Do we need something for pain?" She moved to the IV bottle attached to the tube in my left arm.

"No." I tried not to wince when the animal took another mouthful. It wore me out. "Not yet. A few more minutes."

She gave me a professional look of disbelief and went to the door. "I'll tell Doctor you're awake."

Francine looked at me like my mother did when I stayed home from school with the flu. She gently stroked my forehead to move the hair away. "Kara's okay?" I asked.

She smiled. "The hospital released her yesterday. I tried to talk her into going home to her mother's for a while, but she insisted on staying here while you and Edgar are still in the hospital." She sighed. "Sleeping is a problem for her, but there was no permanent physical damage." Francine laughed. "We actually went shopping this morning for a swimsuit that would cover the wounds, so I think she'll be fine. She made Dr. Lawson promise not to leave any scars."

"And Edgar too?" I asked.

Francine's face was more solemn. "It was a close call. He lost a lot of blood. But they say he'll recover completely. He's in the next room." She paused. "Sheriff Sanderson . . . they're not sure. He has a broken neck. He's regained movement in his arms, but they don't know about his legs yet. He has some feeling; they say that's a good sign. Listen, you lie back and rest. We have plenty of time to cover all this." She pointed to a pile of newspapers in the corner. "I'm saving everything for you."

I looked at Preston. "Where's your mother?"

Francine answered for him. "She and Preston flew in as

soon as they heard about it. Anita sat in here for two days, Cliff, but she had to go back to work this morning. Preston wouldn't leave. He's staying with me and Kara. Anita made me promise to call as soon as you woke up so she can come back."

I closed my eyes and drifted off while Francine stroked my forehead. When I woke up, she fed me more ice. Preston still held my hand.

"You're taking care of Preston and Kara?" I asked.

Francine chuckled. "Hell, I'm running a combination sickroom, day care, and information center in that suite you all used for a war room. You're a hero, Hotshot. Everyone and his brother wants to interview you. We brought Alice down to field the calls. The Senator was in yesterday. He offered to stay and help, but I told him to go away. And I think Tim Stevens already sold the movie rights for you. I threw him out of here twice already today."

"Thank you," I said. It was all I could think of.

She kissed me on the cheek and stroked my forehead again. Every time I woke up, she and Preston were there.

That night, a nurse came to give me my pain medicine. "Visiting time is over," she announced. "Time for bed."

Francine gathered her things to leave. Preston looked at me. "I want to stay," he said.

"You can come back tomorrow," the nurse told him.

"No," he said. "I'm staying with my dad."

Francine patted him on the shoulder. "We need to let your dad get some rest."

He set his jaw. "I'm staying."

I didn't want him to go, either. "Let him stay," I said. "He can sleep in that other bed. He'll be good."

The nurse drew herself up to her full five and a quarter

feet. "I'm sorry," she said with sympathy but firmness. "We have rules, you know."

She's only doing her job, I told myself. Don't take it out on her. Then the animal took another bite, and a little surge of adrenaline hit me. Screw the rules.

Her name tag read: "Mrs. Johnson."

I put on a big grin. The old country lawyer. "I think maybe we can make an exception, don't you, Mrs. Johnson?"

She shook her head. "I'm afraid we can't make any exceptions. We have a hospital to run, you know."

I looked at Francine. "Ms. Collins," I drawled, "you know me well, isn't that right?"

Francine tried to suppress a smile. "Yes."

"As someone who knows me well, is it your opinion that I am lucid?"

"Yes."

Mrs. Johnson's brow wrinkled. I kept the grin in place. "Mrs. Johnson," I said. "Do I seem lucid to you?"

The nurse looked at Francine, who stared back with an innocent expression. "Yes," she said cautiously.

"Then listen very carefully, Mrs. Johnson. If my son can't stay, I hereby revoke any and all consent to treatment. I shall leave with him. If you do not let me check myself out of this place, I shall sue you and this hospital and everyone in it for kidnapping and false imprisonment."

Mrs. Johnson rolled her eyes. "Of course," I continued, "if you do let me leave, I shall sue all of you for medical malpractice. I don't think a jury will have much sympathy with blind enforcement of a rule that bears no rational relationship to reasonable standards of medical care. Either way, Mrs. Johnson, I shall own this hospital. I don't think it's worth it, do you?"

I fell back on the bed and rubbed my forehead with

my left hand. "Even this brief discussion has caused me severe emotional distress," I announced to the room at large. Francine covered her mouth with her hand.

Mrs. Johnson looked like she had bitten into an exceptionally sour lemon. She stared at me, then looked to Francine for help. Francine shrugged. "I think he means it," she said with a straight face. "While I cannot give you legal advice, you may wish to consider contacting your counsel and your insurer. Tell them this sounds very much like the case of Harrison versus Memorial Hospital." She pointed to me. "Mr. Nielson represented Mrs. Harrison in that case." Now I struggled not to laugh.

Preston stayed. We watched a baseball game, then turned the TV off to go to sleep. Mrs. Johnson and I made up; she brought me my pain pills and tucked Preston in for me. When the room was dark, I listened to his prayers.

A few minutes later, he whispered, "Dad? Do you have to go back to Queenston?"

I was quiet for a moment. "No, son," I said. "I don't have to go anywhere."